My Sherlock Holmes

Also by Michael Kurland

THE PROFESSOR MORIARTY NOVELS

The Infernal Device

Death by Gaslight

The Great Game

THE ALEXANDER BRASS NOVELS

Too Soon Dead

The Girls in the High-Heeled Shoes

My Sherlock Holmes

UNTOLD STORIES OF THE GREAT DETECTIVE

Edited by Michael Kurland

ST. MARTIN'S MINOTAUR ◆ NEW YORK

www.minotaurbooks.com

Library of Congress Cataloging-in-Publication Data

   My Sherlock Holmes: untold stories of the great detective/edited by Michael Kurland.— 1st. ed.
      p. cm.
  ISBN 0-312-28093-9 (hc)
  ISBN 0-312-32595-9 (pbk)
  1. Detective and mystery stories, American. 2. Holmes, Sherlock (Fictitious character)—Fiction. 3. Private investigators—England—Fiction. I. Kurland, Michael.

  PS648.D4 M8834 2003
  813'.087208351—dc21   2002035664

D10 9 8 7 6 5 4

Contents

O for a muse of fire, that would ascend the brightest heaven of invention; a kingdom for a stage, princes to act and monarchs to behold the swelling scene! Then—well, then you'd be reading Shakespeare instead of Sherlock Holmes. *Henry V,* or Hank Cinque, as we like to call him, to be exact. What do William Shakespeare and Arthur Conan Doyle have in common? They both, without really trying, created fictional characters that have attained the literary equivalent of immortality.

Without really trying? Yes, I think it's true of both Shakespeare and Conan Doyle. Not that they weren't doing their best to create wonderful stories for their public, but neither assumed that his creations would outlive him by centuries. Look at what Shakespeare named some of his plays: *The Comedy of Errors*—hey, it's a comedy; the characters keep making these errors, that's what makes it funny. *As You Like It*—as good as saying, "I think this plot is dumb, but the groundlings like this sort of thing, so here it is." *Much Ado About Nothing*—how self-effacing can you get? *Love's Labour's Lost*—sounds like a bad sitcom. (Shakespeare apparently also wrote a play called *Love's Labour's Won,* which has been, er, misplaced. If you can find a copy, say on the back shelf of some old library, you might get a favorable mention in a couple of textbooks yourself.)

And Conan Doyle, as we well know, thought so little of his popular consulting detective that he did his best to kill him off, to leave himself more time to write his serious historical works, like *Micah Clarke* and *The White Company.*

What can one possibly say about Sherlock Holmes that hasn't been said before? His exploits have been written up by Sir Arthur Conan Doyle (we'll drop for the moment the pretense that Conan Doyle was merely the "agent" for Dr. John Watson); expanded on by Adrian Conan Doyle, John Dickson Carr, and others; pastiched by August Derleth, Robert L. Fish, Anthony Boucher, John Lennon, and scores of others; parodied by Mark Twain, Stephen Leacock, P. G. Wodehouse, and untold legions of others.

Every aspect of Holmes's fictional existence has been discussed, dissected, and the conclusions disponed and disputed by such literary luminaries as Vincent Starrett, William Baring-Gould, Ronald Knox, Rex Stout, and Dorothy Sayers, to name just the ones who come to mind most easily. (If you are a Holmes aficionado you probably have your own list of favorite Irregulars, and you're slightly miffed at me for not mentioning Poul Anderson, Isaac Asimov, John Kendrick Bangs, Martin Gardner, Michael Harrison, John Bennett Shaw, Nicholas Meyer, John Gardner, or possibly Colin Wilson. Well, sorry; they just didn't come to mind.)

It has been said, by the sort of people who say these things, that there are only five universally recognized fictional characters: Santa Claus, Romeo, Superman, Mickey Mouse, and Sherlock Holmes. Some would expand the list to add Don Quixote, Don Juan, King Kong, Dorothy (the Wizard's Dorothy, you know), Bugs Bunny, Wonder Woman, Charlie Chan, James Bond, and perhaps Peter Pan to that list, and, as my grandmother used to say, they're right, too.

Then there are the ones that have fallen by the wayside. Fifty years ago almost any literate adult whose native language was English could recognize Raffles, Nick Carter, Stella Dallas, Ephram Tutt, Bertie Wooster, and Bulldog Drummond, for example. But membership in this club for the fictional elite is transient for most; characters age and fade away from the public consciousness to be replaced by more youthful, contemporary creations.

But Sherlock Holmes lives on.

It has been estimated, by the sort of people who estimate these things, that there are over a billion people living today who could tell you, at least in some vague fashion, who Sherlock Holmes was. Many of them don't realize that he is a fictional character, or that if he were real he'd be well over a hundred years old now, as is shown by the volume of mail the London post office continues to get addressed to 221B Baker Street.

What is there about this creation of Dr. Conan Doyle's that enabled him to so quickly enter the pantheon of fictional immortals, rise to be numbered among the top five, and remain there for over a century? I'll give you my theory, but you'll have to put up with a little digression. Here goes:

The detective story took some time to come into being. Edgar Allan Poe is usually credited with being its first practitioner, with his stories involving the Chevalier C. Auguste Dupin. (Did Holmes ever meet Dupin? See "The Adventure of the Impecunious Chevalier," from the quill pen of Richard Lupoff, in this very volume.) There had been detectives in stories before Dupin; there had been stories of detection before Dupin. What, then, made Poe's *The Murders in the Rue Morgue* the first true detective story? Simply it was the first story where:

- The detective is the main character of the story.
- The matter to be detected is the principal problem of the story.
- The detective *detects*; that is, he solves the problem by the application of observation guided by intelligence.

The last Dupin story was published in 1845. Over the next four decades, until Arthur Conan Doyle decided to call the main characters in his first detective novel Sherlock Holmes and John Watson instead of Sherringford Holmes and Ormond Sacker (as indicated by a rough page of preliminary notes, still preserved, plotting out *A Study in Scarlet*), few detectives worthy of the name were introduced to the world of fiction. Charles Dickens's Inspector Bucket (*Bleak House*, 1853) and Wilkie Collins's Sergeant Cuff (*The Moonstone*, 1868) are credible police officers, and their actions advance the plots of their respective books, but they are minor characters (no less than four other characters do their share of detecting during the course of *The Moonstone*), and in each book the solving of the crime takes second place to the novelists' examination of how the situation affects the other characters.

With *L'Affair Lerouge* (English title: *The Lerouge Case*; U.S. title: *The Widow Lerouge*), first published in 1866, Emil Gaboriau introduced Lecoq, a detective who uses observation, reflection, and ratiocination (Poe's word for what Dupin did; it means thinking logically) to solve his cases. Lecoq is an amalgam of Dupin and François Eugène Vidocq, a real detective who rose from being a professional thief to head the Paris Police Department in 1811. Vidocq wrote four volumes of memoirs after his forced retirement in 1827, which gave highly fictionalized accounts of his prowess as a detective.

It seems fitting that the first English-language detective novel was written by a woman: Anna Katherine Green. It was called *The Leavenworth Case,* it was first published in 1848, and it was a bestseller. In his book *Bloody Murder,* Julian Symons recounts that *The Leavenworth Case* was the favorite reading of British prime minister Stanley Baldwin. Since Baldwin didn't first serve as prime minister until 1923, it's clear that the book, as we professionals put it, had legs.

There were also any number of inferior imitators of Poe and Gaboriau and Green. From 1870, with the publication of "The Bowery Detective" by Kenward Philp, until the 1920s the so-called dime novels published hundreds, perhaps thousands, of detective stories; strong on action, suspense, disguises, racy dialog, good men turned bad, bad men who want to be good. They were weak on characterization, plot, and anything approaching actual detection, but they moved fast and, with a combination of nonstop action and exotic locales, they provided a welcome anodyne from the dullness and drudgery of everyday life.

And then, in 1887, came *A Study in Scarlet,* and all lesser attempts were washed away as though they had never been. Sherlock Holmes was instantly recognized as the master of detection, by a public who had been waiting for just such a hero without knowing what it was they were waiting for until it appeared.

To the readers of the latter years of the nineteenth century Sherlock Holmes was the perfect Victorian; not as we today imagine Victorians: uptight, prudish, repressed, overly mannered, and ridiculously dressed prigs, but as the Victorians thought of themselves: logical, clearheaded, scientific, thoroughly modern leaders of the civilized world. Perhaps Holmes was a little too logical, a bit too cold and emotionless; but this merely permitted his readers to admire him without wishing to be him. And, like Darwin, Pasteur, Maxwell, Bell, Edison, and the other scientific geniuses of the period, he solved mysteries that baffled other men. And you could watch him do it! You could see the results as that mighty brain attacked the problem of *Thor Bridge,* or *The Second Stain,* or *The Dancing Men.*

"It is my business to know things," Holmes explains in *A Case of Identity.* "Perhaps I have trained myself to see what others overlook."

And today? We have all of that, with the added delight of visiting what is, for us, the alien wonderland, of tantalus and gasogene, of hansom cabs and four-wheelers—"Never take the first cab in the rank"—of spending an hour or a day in a London where, as Vincent Starrett put it, "it is always 1895."

It was perhaps inevitable that, when Conan Doyle gave up writing the continuing saga of Sherlock Holmes, others would take up the pen. Even before Holmes retired to take up beekeeping, the parodies and pastiches had begun. Vincent Starrett, Mark Twain, John Kendrick Bangs; all couldn't resist the impulse to pastiche or parody the creation of Dr. Doyle. In a 1973 German magazine article, Pierre Lachat notes that over 300 Holmes rip-offs appeared between 1907 and 1930. And that's only in English, and doesn't count the Spanish, or Portuguese, or the extensive German series, *Aus den Geheimakten des Weltdetektivs (From the Mystery Files of the World Detective),* which features Sherlock Holmes, but does away with Watson, replacing him with a youth named Harry Taxon.

But they were, at best, weak evocations of the Master. And most of them were not at anything approaching best. Perhaps the most successful of those authors who drew from the canon not merely their inspiration, but their mise-en-scène, were those who chose not to find another ancient notebook of Watson's in the lockbox at Cox, but who tell their stories in another voice than that of the long-suffering doctor, although the tales are set in the world of Sherlock Holmes. In some of them Holmes is still a major character, as in my own Professor Moriarty novels, and in others Holmes appears briefly, if at all.

The continued existence of a fictional character, not only in the steadily reprinted works of the author, but in new works created by other authors, is one of the signs of literary immortality. If this is so, then Holmes and Watson are more immortal (yeah, I know, being "more immortal" is like being "less dead," but it's only an expression fer crissakes) than most and we're adding to his longevity here in a big way, with some great writers.

Sherlock Holmes appears in all the stories in this collection. His "Watson" in each story is not the good doctor himself, but one of the legion of memorable secondary characters that Conan Doyle created with such ease. What reader can forget—to cite a few examples not appearing in this volume—Dr. Thorneycroft Huxtable, M.A., principal of the Priory School and author of *Huxtable's Sidelights on Horace*? Or Jabez Wilson, pawnbroker of Coburg Square, with his blazing red hair? Or Hosmer Angel, the fiancé of the myopic Mary Sutherland, who found it easy to vanish on his wedding day because he never really existed?

And so onward, for one more look at Sherlock Holmes through the eyes of some of those who knew him best, but who haven't, until now, had the chance to tell their stories.

This book is a compilation of new stories about Sherlock Holmes, told from the point of view of various people mentioned in the original stories *except* Dr. Watson or Sherlock Holmes. The authors of these stories, freed from the limitation of having to speak in Watson's voice, have taken their tales in several interesting directions. How did Mrs. Hudson, Holmes's long-suffering landlady, acquire such an illustrious tenant? And just who was Mr. Hudson and what became of him? Find out in Linda Robertson's "Mrs. Hudson Reminisces." "A Study in Orange," by Peter Tremayne, will give some idea of what Colonel Sebastian Moran thought of his adversary and nemesis. In George Alec Effinger's "The Adventure of the Celestial Snows," Reginald Musgrave witnesses Sherlock Holmes's encounter with the infamous Dr. Fu Manchu.

Cara Black shows us Irene Adler's later relationship with Sherlock Holmes, a tale that, even if Watson had known about it, would have remained locked up in his battered tin dispatch box in the vaults of Cox & Co. We will learn of the early relationship between Sherlock Holmes and his maths instructor, James Moriarty. Richard Lupoff describes an unsuspected relationship between a young Sherlock Holmes and the Chevalier C. Auguste Dupin.

I should mention that, as we know, the passage of time creates lapses of memory, and, as Ryunosuke Akutagawa pointed out in his story "Rashomon," different people will see the same event from vastly different perspectives, and may relate versions of the event that seem to have no relation to each other. So it is with some of these stories. Ask not which ones are true: they all are, and they are all lies.

My Sherlock Holmes

THE CHEVALIER C. AUGUSTE DUPIN

"It is simple enough as you explain it," I said, smiling. "You remind me of Edgar Allan Poe's Dupin. I had no idea that such individuals did exist outside of stories."

Sherlock Holmes rose and lit his pipe. "No doubt you think that you are complimenting me in comparing me to Dupin," he observed. "Now, in my opinion, Dupin was a very inferior fellow. That trick of his of breaking in on his friends' thoughts with an apropros remark after a quarter of an hour's silence is really very showy and superficial. He had some analytical genius, no doubt; but he was by no means such a phenomenon as Poe appeared to imagine."

—*A Study in Scarlet*

by RICHARD A. LUPOFF

The Incident of the Impecunious Chevalier

It was not by choice but by necessity that I continued to read by oil lamp rather than arranging for the installation of the new gas lighting. In my wanderings throughout the metropolis I had been present at demonstrations of M. Lebon's wondrous invention and especially of the improved thorium and cerium mantle devised by Herr von Welsbach, and thought at length of the pleasure of this brilliant mode of illumination, but the undernourished condition of my purse forbad me to pursue such an alteration in the condition of my lodgings.

Even so, I took comfort of an evening in crouching beside the hearth in my lodgings, a small flame of dried driftwood flickering on the stones, a lamp at my elbow, and a volume in my lap. The pleasures of old age are few and small, nor did I anticipate to experience them for many more months before departing this planet and its life of travail. What fate my Maker might plan for me, once my eyes should close for the last time, I could only wonder and await. The priests might assert that a Day of Judgment awaited. The Theosophists might maintain that the doctrine of Karma would apply to all beings. As for me, the Parisian metropolis and its varied denizens were world enough indeed.

My attention had drifted from the printed page before me and my mind had wandered in the byways of philosophical musings to such an extent that the loud rapping upon my door induced a violent start within my nervous system. My fingers relaxed their grasp upon the book which they held, my eyes opened widely and a loud moan escaped my lips.

With an effort I rose to my feet and made my way through my chill and darkened apartment to answer the summons at the door. I placed myself beside the portal, pulling at the draperies that I kept drawn by day against the inquiring gaze of strangers and by night against the moist chill of the Parisian winter. Outside my door I perceived an urchin, cap set at an uncouth angle upon his unshorn head, an object or scrap of material clutched in the hand which he was not using to set up his racket on my door.

Lifting an iron bar which I kept beside the door in case of need to defend myself from the invasion of ruffians and setting the latch chain to prevent the door from opening more than a hand's width, I turned the latch and drew the door open far enough to peer out.

The boy who stood upon my stoop could not have been more than ten years of age, ragged of clothing and filthy of visage. The meager light of the passage outside my apartment reflected from his eye, giving an impression of wary suspicion. We studied each other through the narrow opening for long seconds before either spoke. At length I demanded to know his reason for disturbing my musings. He ignored my question, responding to it by speaking my name.

"Yes," I responded, "it is indeed I. Again, I require to know the purpose of your visit."

"I've brought you a message, monsieur," the urchin stated.

"From whom?"

"I don't know the gentleman's name," he replied.

"Then what is the message?"

The boy held the object in his hand closer to the opening. I could see now that it was a letter, folded and sealed with wax, and crumpled and covered with grime. It struck me that the boy might have found the paper lying in a gutter and brought it to me as part of a devious scheme, but then I remembered that he had known my name, a feat not likely on the part of a wild street urchin.

"I can't read, monsieur," the child said. "The gentleman gave it me and directed me to your lodging. I know numbers, some, and was able to find your place, monsieur."

"Very well," I assented, "give me the paper."

"I've got to be paid first, monsieur."

The boy's demand was annoying, and yet he had performed a service and was, I suppose, entitled to his pay. Perhaps the mysterious gentleman who had dispatched him had already furnished him with payment, but this was a contingency beyond my ability to influence. Telling the child to await my return I closed the door, made my way to the place where I keep my small treasury, and extracted from it a sou coin.

At the doorway once more I exchanged the coin for the paper and sent the child on his way. Returning to the dual illumination of hearth and oil lamp, I broke the seal that held the letter closed and unfolded the sheet of foolscap. The flickering firelight revealed to me the work of a familiar hand, albeit one I had not glimpsed for many years, and a message that was characteristically terse and demanding.

Come at once. A matter of urgency.

The message was signed with a single letter, the initial *D*.

I rocked back upon my heels, sinking into the old chair which I had used as my comfort and my retreat from the world through the passing decades. I was clad in slippers and robe, nightcap perched upon my head. It has been my plan, following a small meal, to spend an hour reading and then to retire to my narrow bed. Instead, I now garbed myself for the chill of the out-of-doors. Again I raided my own poor treasury and furnished myself with a small reserve of coins. In a short time I had left my apartment and stood upon my stoop, drawing behind me the doorway and turning my key in the lock.

No address had been given in the demanding message, nor was the messenger anywhere to be seen. I could only infer from the lack of information to the contrary that my old friend was still to be located at the lodgings we once had shared, long ago.

It was too far to travel on foot, so I hailed a passing cab, not without difficulty, and instructed the driver as to my destination. He looked at me with suspicion until I repeated the address, 33 Rue Dunôt in the Faubourg St-Germain. He held out his hand and refused to whip up until I had delivered the fare into his possession.

The streets of the metropolis were deserted at this hour, and mostly silent save for an occasional shout of anger or moan of despair—the sounds of the night after even revelers have retired to their homes or elsewhere.

As the cab drew up I exited from it and stood gazing at the old stone structure where the two of us had shared quarters for so long. Behind me I heard the driver grumble, then whip up, then pull away from number 33 with the creak of the wooden axle and the clatter of horse's hooves on cobblestones.

A light appeared in a window and I tried, without success, to espy the form of the person who held it. In a moment the light moved and I knew that my erstwhile friend was making his way to the door. I presented myself in time to hear the bar withdrawn and to see the door swing open.

Before me stood my old friend, the world's first and greatest consulting detective, the Chevalier C. Auguste Dupin. Yet though it was unquestionably he, I was shocked at the ravages that the years had worked upon his once sharp-featured visage and whip-thin frame. He had grown old. The flesh did not so much cover his bones as hang from them. I saw that he still wore the smoked-glass spectacles of an earlier age; when he raised them to peer at me his once ferretlike eyes were dim and his hands, once as hard and steady as iron rods, appeared fragile and tremulous.

"Do not stand there like a goose," Dupin commanded, "surely by this time you know the way."

He retreated a pace and I entered the apartment which had meant so much to me in those days of our companionship. Characteristically, Dupin uttered not another syllable, but instead led the way through my onetime home. I shut the door behind me, then threw the heavy iron bolt, mindful of the enemies known to seek Dupin's destruction in a former epoch. That any of them still survived was doubtful, that they remained capable of working mischief upon the great mind was close to what Dupin would have deemed "a nil possibility," but still I threw the bolt.

Dupin led the way to his book closet, and within moments it was almost as if the decades had slipped away. He seemed to regain his youthful vigor, and I my former enthusiasm. Not waiting for me to assume the sofa upon which I had so often reclined to peruse musty volumes in past decades Dupin flung himself into his favorite seat. He seized a volume which he had laid face downward, its pages open, upon the arm of his chair.

"Have you seen this?" he demanded angrily, brandishing the volume.

I leaned forward, straining in the gloom to recognize the publication. "It bears no familiarity," I confessed. "It looks but newly arrived, and my reading in recent years has been entirely of an antiquarian nature."

"Of course, of course," Dupin muttered. "I will tell you what it is. I have been reading a volume translated from the English. Its title in our own tongue is *Une Étude en Écarlate*. The author has divided the work into chapters. I will read to you from a chapter which he entitles ingenuously '*La Science de Déduction.*'"

Knowing that there was no stopping Dupin once he was determined upon a course, I settled upon the sofa. The room was not uncomfortable, I was in the company of my ancient friend, I was content.

"I will omit the author's interpolations," Dupin prefaced his reading, "and present to you only the significant portions of his work. Very well, then! *'Now, in my opinion, Dupin was a very inferior fellow. That trick of his of breaking in on his friends' thoughts with an apropos remark after a quarter of an hour's silence is really very showy and superficial. He had some analytical genius, no doubt; but he was by no means such a phenomenon as Poe appeared to imagine.'*"

With a furious gesture he flung the slim volume across the room against a shelf of volumes, where it struck, its pages fluttering, and fell to the carpet. I knew that the Poe to whom the writer averred was the American journalist who had visited Dupin and myself from time to time, authoring reports of the several mysteries which Dupin had unraveled with, I took pride in recalling, my own modest but not insubstantial assistance.

"What think you of that?" Dupin demanded.

"A cruel assessment," I ventured, "and an inaccurate one. Why, on many occasions I can recall—"

"Indeed, my good friend, you can recall the occasions upon which I interrupted your words to tell you your very thoughts."

"As you have just done," I averred. I awaited further words from Dupin, but they were not at that moment forthcoming so I resumed my speech. "Who is the author of this scurrilous assessment?"

"The author's name matters not. It is the villain whom he quotes, who is of significance."

"And who, may I inquire, might that person be?"

Dupin raised his eyes to the ceiling where smoke from the fireplace, draughty as ever, swirled menacingly. "He is one whom I met some years ago, long after you had departed these quarters, *mon ami*. I had by then largely retired from my labors as a consulting detective, and of course my reputation had long since reached the islands of fools."

By this time I could see that Dupin was off on a tale, and I settled myself more thoroughly than ever upon the sofa, prepared to listen to the end:

Those were days of tumult in our nation (Dupin said) when danger lurked at every turning and the most ordinary of municipal services were not to be taken for granted. When I received a message from across the Channel I was of course intrigued.

The writer was a young man who professed admiration for my exploits and a desire to learn my methods that he might emulate them in the building of a reputation and a career for himself in his own land. I received many such communications in those days, responding to them uniformly that the entire science of detection was but a matter of observation and deduction, and that any man or even woman of ordinary intelligence could match my feats did he or she but apply those faculties with which we are all equipped to their full capacity. But the person who had written to me mentioned a particular case which he had been employed to resolve, and when he described the case my curiosity was piqued.

Your expression tells me that you, too, are aroused by the prospect of this case, and I will tell you what it concerned.

The young man's letter of application hinted only of a treasure of fabulous value, a cache of gold and gems lost some three centuries, that had become the subject of legend and of fanciful tales, but which he believed to exist in actuality and to be in France, nay, not merely in France but in the environs of Paris itself. Could he but find it he would be wealthy beyond the power of imagination, and if I would but assist him in his quest a portion of it would be mine.

As you know, while I am of good family I have long been of reduced means, and the prospect of restoring the fortunes of my forebears was an attractive one. My correspondent was reticent as to details in his letters, for I wrote back to him seeking further information but was unable to elicit useful data.

At length I permitted him to visit me—yes, in this very apartment. From the first his eccentric nature was manifest. He arrived at a late hour, as late I daresay as you have yourself arrived this night. It was the night before that of the full moon. The air was clear and the sky filled with celestial objects whose illumination, added to that of the moon, approached that of the day.

He sat upon the very sofa where you recline at this moment. No, there is no need to rise and examine the furnishing. You do make me smile, old friend. There is nothing to be learned from that old sofa.

The young man, an Englishman, was of tall and muscular build with a hawklike visage, sharp features, and a sharp, observant mien. His clothing bore the strong odor of tobacco. His hollow eyes suggested his habituation to some stronger stimulant. His movements suggested one who has trained in the boxing ring; more, one who has at least familiarized himself with the Japanese art of *baritsu*, a subtle form of combat but recently introduced in a few secretive salons in Paris and Berlin, in London, and even in the city of Baltimore in Maryland.

It took me but moments to realize that this was a person of unusual talent, potentially a practitioner of the craft of detection to approach my own level of proficiency. It was obvious to me as we conversed on this topic and that, the politics of our respective nations, the growing incidence of crime which respects neither border nor sea, the advances of science and literature among the Gallic and Anglic races, that he was watching me closely, attempting to draw my measure even as I was, his.

At length, feeling that I had seen all that he would reveal of himself, and growing impatient with his avoidance of the topic that had drawn him to my apartments, I demanded once for all that he describe that which he sought and in the recovery of which he desired my guidance, or else depart from my lodging, having provided me with an hour's diversion and no more.

"Very well, sir," he replied, "I will tell you that I am in search of a bird."

Upon his making this statement I burst into laughter, only to be shocked back to sobriety by the stern expression upon the face of my visitor. "Surely, sir," I exclaimed, "you did not brave the stormy waters of the Channel in search of a grouse or guinea hen."

"No, sir," he replied, "I have come in search of a plain black bird, a bird variously described in the literature as a raven or, more likely, a hawk."

"The feathers of hawks are not black," I replied.

"Indeed, sir, you are correct. The feathers of hawks are not black, nor has this hawk feathers of any color, but the color of this hawk is golden."

"You insult me, sir," I stated angrily.

My visitor raised his eyebrows. "Why say you so?"

"You come to me and speak only in riddles, as if you were humoring a playful child. A hawk that is black but has no feathers and yet is golden. If you do not make yourself more clear you must leave my apartments, and I wish you a speedy return to your country."

He raised a hand placatingly. "I did not wish to offend you, sir, nor to speak in conundrums. Pray, bear with me for a little longer and I will make clear the nature and history of the odd bird which I seek."

I permitted him to continue.

"This was the representation of a bird," quoth he, "the creation of a group of talented metalworkers and gemsmiths, Turkish slaves employed by the Grand Master Villiers de l'Isle d'Adam, of the Order of the Knights of Rhodes. It was crafted in the year 1530, and dispatched by galley from the Isles of Rhodes to Spain, where it was to be presented to the Emperor Charles the Fifth. Its height was as the length of your forearm. It was of solid gold, in the form of a standing hawk or raven, and it was crusted over with gems of the greatest variety and finest quality. Its value even at the time was immense. Today it would be incalculable!"

He paused, a look in his eyes as if he could envision the fantastic sight of a golden falcon, emeralds for its eyes and rubies for its claws, circling the chamber. Then he resumed his narrative.

He then did something which seemed, at the moment, very peculiar but which, I would come to realize, was in truth to have been expected of a man such as he. He leaped from his seat upon the cushion and began pacing restlessly around the chamber. At once I inquired as to what had caused such an abrupt alteration in his manner and demeanor, whereupon he turned upon me a visage transformed. The muscles of his face were drawn, his lips were pulled back to expose gleaming teeth, and his eyes, by heaven, his eyes glittered like the eyes of a wild leopard.

"I must visit an apothecary at once," he exclaimed.

In response to this demand I remonstrated with him. "Sir, there is an excellent apothecary shop upon the Rue Dunôt, an easy walk from here, but what is the urgency? A moment ago you were calmly describing a most extraordinary bird. Now you demand directions to the establishment of a chemist."

"It will pass," he responded, most puzzlingly, "it will pass."

He sank once more to his former position upon the sofa and, pressing the heels of his hands to his deep-sunken eyes, paused to draw a deep breath.

"Do you wish to continue?" I inquired.

"Yes, yes. But if you would be so kind, monsieur, as to furnish me with a glass of wine, I would be most grateful."

I rose and proceeded to the wine cupboard, from which I drew a dust-coated bottle of my second-best vintage. In those days as in these, as you are of course aware, I saw fit to maintain my own household, without benefit of servant or staff. I poured a glass for my guest and he tossed it off as one would a draught of water, extending the emptied goblet for a second portion, which I forthwith poured. This he studied, lifted to his lips and sipped, then placed carefully upon the taboret before him.

"Do you wish to continue your narration?" I inquired.

"If you please," he responded, "I beg your indulgence for my outburst. I am not, I must confess, entirely well."

"Should the need arise," I assured him, "M. Konstantinides, the chemist, is qualified to provide specifics for all known illnesses. The hour is late and he would by now have closed his establishment for the night and retired to his chamber, but I could rouse him in your behalf."

"You are gracious, sir. I trust that will prove unnecessary, but I am nonetheless grateful." Once more he paused as if to gather his thoughts, then launched upon a further exposition. "I will not trouble you with every detail of the peregrinations of the golden falcon, save to point out that within our own generation it had passed into the possession of the Carlist movement in Spain."

To this statement I nodded. "Wars of succession are tiresome, but it seems they will be with us always, does it not? I was struck by the recent surrender of Señor Maroto's Basque followers after their lengthy and strenuous resistance."

"You are well informed, sir! If you are familiar with the fate of the Basque Carlists, then you would know that Señor Ramón Cabrera has continued the struggle in Catalonia."

"He is also in dire straits, is he not?"

"Yes, it appears that Her Majesty Isabella the Second is at last about to reap the harvest of the Salic Law invoked by her royal father. But I fear I am boring you, M. Dupin."

"Not so much boring as stimulating my curiosity. Surely, sir, you did not travel here from London merely to relate the saga of a fabulous bird and then digress upon the politics of the Spanish succession. How are these things related, for surely that must be the case. If you would be so kind as to come to the point, then."

"Indeed." He bowed his head, then raised it once more. "You are aware, surely, that Don Carlos has sympathizers here in France. You were perhaps not aware that Señor Cabrera had sent an agent on a dangerous and secretive mission, to traverse the passes of the Pyrenees and make his way to the château of a French sympathizer, no less a personage than the Duc de Lagny."

"I am familiar with Lagny," I confessed. "I have had the pleasure of being introduced to His Grace and to Her Grace the Duchess. Their château is of noteworthy architecture. But of the Duke's Carlist sympathies I must confess profound ignorance."

"That is not surprising, sir. The Duke is known, if I may make a small play on words, for his reclusiveness."

He paused to sip once more at his, or perhaps I should say, my, wine. "Regarding the golden bird as an omen and token of majesty, and sensing the imminent defeat of the Carlist cause, Señor Cabrera had sent the bird to Lagny rather than have it fall into the hands of his niece's followers."

"And you wish me to assist you in retrieving the bird from the château of the Duc de Lagny?" I asked.

"That is my mission."

"You are in the employ of Her Majesty Isabella?"

"I am in the employ of one whose identity I am not at liberty to disclose." He rose to his feet. "If you will assist me—for my knowledge of the French countryside and culture is limited—you will receive, shall I say, sir, a reward of royal proportions."

"You wish me to accompany you to the château of the Duke," I objected, "there to obtain from his custody the fabled bird. What causes you to believe that he will relinquish it?"

"You have my assurance, monsieur, the Duke will be eager to part with that which he safeguards upon receiving proof of the identity of my employers."

"You have such proof with you?" I demanded.

"I have, sir," he insisted. "Upon this fact I give you my solemn assurance."

Unable to deny an interest in obtaining a share of the lucre to which he referred, and perhaps attracted to an extent by the lure of the romantic story he had spun, I agreed, at the least, to accompany him to Lagny. I have told you already that the hour of my guest's arrival was an unconventionally late one, and his disquisitive manner of speech had caused the hours to pass before our bargain, such as it might be, was struck.

At length I excused myself and proceeded to the front parlor of my apartment. The act of drawing back the draperies confirmed that which I had already suspected, namely, that dawn had broken and a new day was upon us. Feeling impelled to violate my custom and venture forth from my lodgings in the light of day, I urged my visitor to the stoop, drew shut the door behind us, and locked it. We set out on foot to the apothecary shop of M. Konstantinides. Here my guest purchased a preparation and induced it into his own system.

I was by no means unfamiliar with the effects of various stimulants and depressants upon the human organism, but even so I will own that I was startled at the strength and portion taken by this nearly skeletal Englishman. At once his air of distress left him and his visage assumed an altogether more friendly and optimistic appearance than had previously been the case. He paid M. Konstantinides his fee, adding a generous overage thereto, and then, turning to me, suggested that we set out for Lagny. Our journey was not a difficult one. We hired a hackney carriage and negotiated a fare all the way to the village of Lagny, the sum being paid from my guest's purse, and proceeded eastward from the capital. It was necessary to pause but once at an inn, where we procured a loaf, a cheese, and bottle, my English guest and I dining in democratic fashion with the hackman.

The sun drew low in the sky behind us as we approached Lagny. I was able, by drawing upon my memory of earlier days, to direct the hackman past the village to the château of the Duke. It was a tall and rambling structure of ancient Gothic construction; as we neared the château the sun's guttering rays painted its walls as if with a palette of flame. We debouched from the carriage and instructed the hackman to return to the village and to return for us in the morning.

He asked in his rude yet charmingly colorful way, "And who's to pay for me sups and me snooze, ye two toffs?"

"We shall indeed," my English guest responded, dropping a handful of coins onto the coach box, upon which the hackman whipped up and departed.

The Château de Lagny, if I may so describe it, radiated an air of age and decadence. As my guest and I stood gazing at its façade he turned to me and asked a peculiar question. "What do you hear, my dear Dupin?"

Perhaps I ought to have taken offense at this unwonted familiarity, but instead I chose to deal with his query. I cocked an ear, gave list carefully to whatever sounds there might be emanating from the château, then made my reply. "I hear nothing."

"Precisely!" the Englishman exclaimed.

"And what, sir, is the object of this schoolmasterly exchange?" I inquired.

"Sir—" He smiled. "—would one not expect to hear the bustle of life in such a setting as this? The neigh of horses from the stables, the cry of servants and workers, mayhap the sound of revelers? None of this, I repeat, none of it do we hear. Only a silence, M. Dupin, only an eerie, deathlike silence."

For once I was forced to concede that my visitor had scored a point upon me. I acknowledged as much, to which he perhaps grudgingly conceded that I was yet the master and he the eager pupil. He refrained from commenting upon the looming day when the pupil might outstrip the master in achievement, nor was I prepared to do so.

Arm in arm we approached the main entryway of the château. We carried, of course, walking sticks, and I permitted my companion to raise his and strike heavily upon the great wooden door. To my astonishment no servant appeared to grant us entry. Instead, the door swung slowly open and the two of us set foot upon the flagging on the château's foyer.

At first nothing appeared out of the way, but in moments our nostrils were assailed by the unmistakable odor of decomposition. Exchanging glances but not a word, we drew kerchiefs from our respective pockets and knotted them over our nostrils and mouths. I turned toward my companion and observed him, hatted and masked like a highwayman. Full well I knew that my own appearance was as sinister as his.

The first cadaver we encountered was that of a liveried footman. First instructing my guest to maintain careful watch lest violence appear from within the château, I knelt over the still form. Had the stench not been evidence enough of death, the condition of the footman's body would have fully convinced the veriest of laymen. He had been struck down from behind. He lay upon his face, the back of his head crushed, the pooled gore already beginning to crawl with insects.

Turning aside to draw a breath of clear air, or at any rate of air more clear than that surrounding the cadaver, I examined the clothing of the deceased in search of a clue as to the motive for his murder, but discovered nothing.

Proceeding through the house my associate and I found, in turn, the remains of maids, cooks, laundresses, and an elderly male servant whom we took to be the majordomo of the establishment. But what had happened, and where was the master of the château?

Him we found in the stables behind the château. Surrounded by stablemen lay M. le Duc. The hearty nobleman whose company I had enjoyed more than once had been treated disgustingly. It was obvious from the condition of the remains that the Duke had been tortured. His hands were bound behind his back and his face showed the discolorations caused by the application of a heated implement. Surely the intention had been to force from him the location of the fabled golden bird. Marks upon his torso were enough to sicken the viewer, while the final, fatal attack had come in the form of a sharpened blade drawn across his belly, exposing his vital organs and inducing the ultimate exsanguination.

Her Grace the Duchess had been treated in similar fashion. I will not describe the indignities which had been visited upon her. One prayed only that her more delicate frame had reached its limits and that she had been granted the mercy of a death more rapid and less agonizing that that of her husband.

Horses and dogs, like the human inhabitants of the estate, lay at random, slaughtered every one.

"Is this the work of Señor Cabrera and his men?" I asked.

"More likely of the servants of Isabella," my guest replied. "The deaths of these unfortunate persons and their beasts are to be regretted, but of immediate concern is the whereabouts of the bird." He stood over first one cadaver, then another, studying them as would a student of medicine the dissected remains of a beast.

"It appears unlikely that the secret was divulged," he suggested at length. "Obviously the Duke was tortured and dispatched first, for such a nobleman as he would not have permitted his lady to be treated as we see her to have been. Nor, I would infer, did the Duchess know the whereabouts of the bird, for once her husband was deceased, she would have had no reason to protect the secret. On the contrary, having presumably seen her attackers, she would have sought to survive in order to exact revenge for the murder of her husband."

His callous attitude toward the carnage we had only just beheld was appalling, but then the English are known to a cold-blooded race, and it may be that this Englishman felt a degree of sympathy and outrage that he did not show. Very well, then. When the hackman returned for us on the morrow, I would inform the mayor of the village of Lagny of our terrible discovery. The brutal criminals responsible would be sought and, one hoped, brought to face their fate beneath the guillotine in due course. But my guest was right, at least to the extent that our own presence at the Château de Lagny had been brought about by the report of the presence of the bird.

We would seek it, and if it was here, I knew that we would find it.

"Let us proceed to locate the golden bird," I announced to my guest. "So splendid an object should be conspicuous to the eye of anyone save a blind man."

"Perhaps not," the Englishman demurred. "I will confess, my dear Dupin, that I have withheld from you one item in the history and description of the bird."

I demanded that he enlighten me at once, and in what for him passed for a direct response, he complied. "You have doubtlessly noticed that in my descriptions of the bird I have referred to it both as golden and as black."

"I have done so, sir. You may in fact recall my bringing this discrepancy to your attention, and your pledge to reconcile the conflicting descriptions. If you please, this would seem an excellent time to do so."

"Very well, then. The bird as originally created by the captive Turkish craftsmen, of solid gold virtually encrusted with precious stones, was considered too attractive a target. At some point in its history—I confess to ignorance of the exact date—it was coated in a black substance, a thick, tarry pigment, so that it now resembles nothing more than a sculpture of ebony in the form of a standing hawk."

"What leads you to believe that the bird is still in the château? Even if the Duke and Duchess died without revealing the secret of its hiding place to their enemies, those villains might still have searched the château until they found the bird. But look about you, sir, and you will see that we are surrounded by a scene not merely of carnage, but of despoliation. It is obvious that the château has been ransacked. You did not yourself know of the bird's hiding place? Your employers did not inform you?"

"My employers did not themselves know the hiding place. It was the Duke himself who chose that, after the messengers had left."

"Then for all we know, the bird has flown."

"No, sir." The Englishman shook his head. "By the condition of the bodies, even in winter, this horror occurred at least four days ago, before I left London. I would have received word, had the villains succeeded. They have committed these horrendous crimes in vain. You may rest assured that the bird is still here. But where?"

"Let us consider," I suggested. "The interior of the château and even, to the extent that we have searched, of the outbuildings, have been torn apart. Furniture is demolished, pictures and tapestries torn from walls. The Duke's library has been despoiled, his priceless collection of ancient manuscripts and rare volumes reduced to worthless rubble. Even a suit of ancient armor has been thrown from its stand so that it lies in pieces upon the flagging. The invaders of the château may be monsters, but they are not unintelligent nor yet are they lacking in thoroughness."

I paused, awaiting further comment by the Englishman, but none was forthcoming. I observed him closely and perceived that he was perspiring freely and that he alternately clenched and loosened his fists almost as one suffering a fit.

"If the bird is still on the estate," I resumed, "yet it is not within the château or its outbuildings, logic dictates its location to us. Consider this, young man. We have eliminated the partial contents of our list of possibilities. Having done so, we are drawn irresistibly to the conclusion that the remaining possibilities must contain the solution to our puzzle. Do you follow the thread of ratiocination which I have laid before you?"

He seemed to relax, as if the fit had passed. He drew a cloth from a pocket of his costume and wiped the perspiration from his brow. He acknowledged the irrefutable nature of my argument.

"But," he continued, "I fail to see the next step in your procedure."

"You disappoint me," I uttered. "Very well. If you will please follow me."

I retreated to the main entry hall of the château, and thence to the terrace outside. I proceeded still farther, my boots leaving a trail behind me in the heavy dew that had accumulated upon the lush lawn surrounding the château. The moon had attained fullness, and the sky above Lagny was even more impressive than that above the metropolis had been.

"Do you look upon the château," I instructed my pupil, for I had so come to regard the Englishman.

He stood beside me and gazed at the structure, its stone pediments rendered in pale chiaroscuro by the light streaming from the heavens. "What see you?" I asked him.

"Why, the Château de Lagny," he replied at once.

"Indeed. What else do you see?"

The young Englishman pursed his lips with the appearance of impatience. "Only that, sir. The stable and other outbuildings are concealed by the bulk of the château."

"Indeed," I nodded. I spoke no more, awaiting further comment by the other. There ensued a lengthy silence.

Finally, in a tone of impatience, my student spoke once more. "The lawn before the château. The woods which surround us. The moon, the stars. A tiny cloud in the southwest."

I nodded. "Very good. More."

"For the love of God, Dupin, what more is there to see?"

"Only that which is vital to our mission," I replied.

As I watched, the Englishman raised his eyes once more, then froze. "I see a row of birds perched upon the parapet of the château."

"My good fellow!" I exclaimed, "it appears now possible that you may have the makings of a detective. Further, I urge you, do not satisfy yourself with merely seeing, but observe, observe, observe, and report!"

He stood silent and motionless for some time, then took an action which won my admiration. Although we stood ankle-deep in the dew-soaked grass before the château, there was nearby a driveway used by carriages approaching and departing the estate. Our own cabman had followed this path, and it was my expectation that he would utilize it once more upon his return for us in the morning.

The Englishman strode to the driveway, bent, and lifted a handful of gravel. He threw back his cape so as to free his arm and flung the gravel at the birds perched upon the parapet. I was impressed by the strength and accuracy of his arm.

With an angry outcry several of the birds flew from their perch. They were silhouetted against the night sky, their form limned in a drab black against the glittering stars and clear darkness of the heavens. One of them passed across the face of the full, brilliant moon, its widespread wings and the shining disk behind it creating the illusion that the bird was as large as the legendary Pegasus.

My student and I remained motionless, observing the behavior of the aerial creatures. They were more annoyed than frightened by the clattering pebbles, or so I inferred, for it took mere moments for the plurality of the creatures to return to their former places, midst an audible flapping of feathery wings and grumbling calls.

The Englishman bent and lifted another handful of gravel, drew back his arm and flung the stones at the birds. Once more his action evoked an angry response, most of the birds crying out in annoyance and flapping away from their perch. By now the solution to the mystery of the missing hawk was apparent.

"Good work," I congratulated my student. "It is clear that you have grasped the difference between observing and merely seeing, and have observed that which is necessary to locate your prey."

A small indication of pleasure made itself visible upon his face, the momentary upward twitching of the corners of his mouth by a few millimeters. Without uttering a word he seated himself upon the grass and proceeded to remove his boots and stockings. I watched in equal silence as he strode to the outer wall of the château.

It has been my expectation that he would return to the interior of the structure and seek access to the roof by means of interior staircases. Instead, to my amazement, after studying the wall with its closely fitted stones and creeping ivy, he proceeded to climb the exterior of the château, using his powerful fingers and almost orangutan-like toes to assure his grasp. As he advanced his cape flapped about his form like two huge wings.

As he approached the parapet he called out to the winged creatures perched there, making a peculiar sound unlike any I had previously heard. Without preliminary, the avians watching his advance extended their wings and rose from the château, disappearing into the blackness that surrounded them. All save one. A single bird remained stationary, silhouetted against the starry domain.

The strange, almost inhuman, being into which my erstwhile visitor had transformed himself, perched now beside the sole remaining avian, so high above the earth that a single slip, I could see, would plunge him to a certain doom. Yet no sound reached me from this strange personage, nor any indication of fear.

He lifted the unmoving bird from its place and in a moment it disappeared beneath his cloak. I could only infer that he had come prepared with an extra section of leather belting or rope, concealed until now by his outer garments.

Then as I stood aghast he lowered himself to lie flat upon the parapet, then reached over its edge to gain a handhold on the stone wall, then slid from his safe perch and proceeded to climb down the wall of the château, headfirst, the bird secured beneath his clothing. His appearance, for all the world, was that of a gigantic bat.

When he reached the greensward he righted himself and drew the bird from beneath his cape. "I thank you, my dear Dupin, for the lessons you have given me, equally in observation and in deduction. Our prey is recovered."

So saying he held the black bird toward me. Even through its black coating I could make out the shape of its feathers, its claws, its beak and its eyes. It was clearly a magnificent example of the sculptor's art. My student asked me to hold the figurine while he once more donned his stockings and boots. The weight of the black bird was so great that I felt even greater astonishment at his ability to descend the wall of the château with it strapped beneath his clothing.

We spent what little remained of the night exploring the interior of the château, utilizing torches which remained from that sad structure's happier era. The only clues that we uncovered were further evidence of the brutality of the invaders who had slaughter the Duke and Duchess as well as their retainers, all in a futile attempt to learn the whereabouts of the treasure which my pupil and I now possessed.

With morning our hackman arrived, somewhat the worse for wear and, one inferred, for the consumption of excessive amounts of spirit. I instructed him to take us to the village of Lagny, where we concealed the bird inside the boot of the hack, promising the hackman a generous tip in exchange for his silence. We thereupon made a full report of our gory findings at the château, making no mention of the bird. The reason we gave for our visit to the château was the truthful one that I was an old acquaintance of the Duke and Duchess and had been eager to introduce to them my visitor from England.

The mayor of the village of Lagny and the *chef des gendarmes* were duly horrified by our descriptions, but permitted us to depart for Paris upon our pledge to provide what information and assistance we could, should these be called for at a later stage of their investigation.

In due course the hack pulled up at my lodgings in the Faubourg St-Germain. A light snow had fallen in the metropolis, and I picked my way carefully to my door lest I slip and fall to the stones. Exhausted by the activities of the past day and night, I turned my key in the lock of my lodgings and pushed the door open so that my guest and I might enter. When we did so we were confronted by an unanticipated sight. My quarters had been ransacked. Furniture was overturned, drawers were pulled from their places and inverted upon the floor. The carpeting had been torn up and rolled back to permit a search for trapdoors or loosened boards.

Every picture was pulled from the wall and thrown to the floor, including that of my friend and idol the great Vidocq. Shocked and offended by the invasion of my quarters I proceeded to examine their contents, assessing the damage and grieving for the destruction of precious mementos of a long career. I clutched my head and expostulated my outrage.

Drawing myself together at length and hoping in some manner to mitigate the harm which had been done I turned to confer with my visitor, only to find that he had disappeared without a trace.

I flew to the doorway and exited my premises. The hack had of course departed long since, but a row of dark footprints showed in the fresh snow. Following without heed to the risk of falling I dashed the length of the Rue Dunôt. At length I found myself standing upon the doorstep of the establishment of M. Konstantinides. I sounded the bell repeatedly but without response, then pounded upon the door. Neither light nor movement could be seen from within the shop, nor was there response of any sort to my summons.

At once the meaning of these events burst upon my tortured brain. The Englishman was a dope fiend, the Greek apothecary the supplier of his evil chemicals. How Konstantinides has obtained knowledge of the bird was unfathomable, but it was at his behest rather than that of either the Carlists or the Bourbons that I had been recruited.

Konstantinides had ransacked my lodgings merely as a distraction, to hold my attention while the Englishman brought the bird to his shop. By now, even though mere minutes had passed, it was a certainty that both the Englishman and the Greek, along with the black bird, were gone from the Faubourg and would not be found within the environs of Paris.

What would become of the bird, of the English detective, of the Greek chemist, were mysteries for the years to come. And now at last (Dupin completed his narrative) I learn of the further career of my student, and of the scorn with which he repays my guidance.

As I sat, mortified by my friend and mentor's humiliation, I saw him clutching the small volume from which he had read the cruel words as if it were a dagger with which he planned to take his own life. All the while he had been telling his tale I had been carried away by the narrative, to another time and place, a time and place when Dupin was young and in his prime. But now I had returned to the present and saw before me a man enfeebled by the passage of the years and the exigencies of a cruel existence.

"What became of the bird?" I inquired. "Did it disappear entirely?"

Dupin shook his head. "The apothecary shop of the Greek Konstantinides was reopened by a nephew. Of the elder Konstantinides nothing was ever again heard, or if it was, it was held inviolate in the bosom of the family. I attempted to learn from the nephew the whereabouts of his uncle and of the Englishman, as well as of the bird itself, but the younger Konstantinides pled ignorance of the fate the two men, as well as that the bird. For two generations now the shop has remained in the family, and the secret, if secret there is, remains sealed in their bosom."

I nodded my understanding. "And so you never again heard of your pupil, the strange Englishman?"

Dupin waved the book at me. "You see, old friend? He has become, as it were, the new Dupin. His fame spreads across the seas and around the globe. Did he but make the meanest acknowledgment of his debt to me, I would be satisfied. My material needs are met by the small pension arranged by our old friend G— of the Metropolitan Police Force. My memories are mine, and your own writings have given me my small share of fame."

"The very least I could do, Dupin, I assure you."

There followed a melancholy silence during which I contemplated the sad state to which my friend had fallen. At length he heaved a sigh pregnant with despair. "Perhaps," he began, then lapsed, then again began, "perhaps it would be of interest to the discerning few to learn of a few of my other undertakings."

Shaking my head I responded, "Already have I recorded them, Dupin. There was the case of the murders in the Rue Morgue, that of the purloined letter, and even your brilliant solution of the mystery of Marie Roget."

"Those are not the cases to which I refer," Dupin demurred.

"I know of no others, save, of course that which you have narrated to me this night."

Upon hearing my words, Dupin permitted himself one of rare smiles which I have ever seen upon his countenance. "There have been many others, dear friend," he informed me, "many indeed."

Astonished, I begged him to enumerate a few such.

"There were the puzzle of the Tsaritsa's false emerald, the adventure of Wade the American gunrunner, the mystery of the Algerian herbs, the incident of the Bahamian fugitive and the runaway hot-air balloon, and of course the tragedy of the pharaoh's jackal."

"I shall be eager to record these, Dupin. Is the list thus complete?"

"By no means, old friend. That is merely the beginning. Such reports may in some small way assuage the pain of being aged and forgotten, replaced on the stage of detection by a newer generation of sleuths. And, I suspect, the few coins which your reports may add to your purse will not be unwelcome."

"They will not," I was forced to concede.

"But this—" Dupin waved the book once more. "—this affront strikes to my heart. As bitter as wormwood and as sharp as a two-edged sword, so sayeth the proverb."

"Dupin," I said, "you will not be forgotten. This English prig has clearly copied your methods, even to the degree of enlisting an assistant and amanuensis who bears a certain resemblance to myself. Surely justice forbids that the world forget the Chevalier C. Auguste Dupin!"

"Not forget?" my friend mumbled. "Not forget? The pupil will live in fame forever while the master becomes but a footnote to the history of detection. Ah, my friend, my dear, dear friend, but the world in which we live is unjust."

"It was ever thus, Dupin," I concurred, "it was ever thus."

THE FIRST MRS. WATSON

"Well, and there is the end of our little drama," I remarked after we had sat some time smoking in silence. "I fear that it may be the last investigation in which I shall have the chance of studying your methods. Miss Morstan has done me the honor to accept me as a husband in prospective."

He gave a most dismal groan.

"I feared as much," said he. "I really cannot congratulate you."

I was a little hurt.

"Have you any reason to be dissatisfied with my choice?" I asked.

"Not at all. I think she is one of the most charming young ladies I ever met and might have been most useful in such work as we have been doing. She had a decided genius in that way. . . . But love is an emotional thing, and whatever is emotional is opposed to that true cold reason which I place above all things. I should never marry myself, lest I bias my judgment." . . .

"The division seems rather unfair," I remarked. "You have done all the work in this business. I get a wife out of it, Jones gets the credit, pray what remains for you?"

"For me," said Sherlock Holmes, "there still remains the cocaine bottle." And he stretched his long white hand up for it.

—*The Sign of Four*

by BARBARA HAMBLY

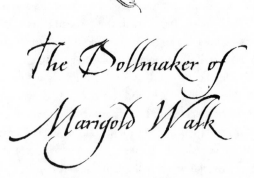

The Dollmaker of Marigold Walk

"I have seen too much not to know that the impression of a woman may be more valuable than the conclusion of an analytical reasoner."

"Folk who were in grief came to my wife like birds to a light-house."

—"THE MAN WITH THE TWISTED LIP"

My husband, Dr. John Watson, has written often that his friend Mr. Sherlock Holmes loves the solving of crimes, and the trapping of evildoers, as a huntsman loves the chase, or an artist his brush and oils.

Yet as much as the solving of crimes—and sometimes I think more so—I have observed that Mr. Holmes loves the puzzles of human behavior for their own sakes, even when they have no bearing on the breaking or keeping of the law. Cold-blooded and logical himself, the eccentricities of human conduct delight him: he takes more pleasure, I believe, in discussing with the local cats-meat-man the mathematical system by which that gentleman picks racehorses to bet on, than by bringing to justice a bank director who embezzled thousands out of mere unimaginative greed.

Thus when poor old Mrs. Wolff came into the soup kitchen at Wordsworth Settlement House in Whitechapel, weeping that she had been drugged and robbed—and left unhurt—by a well-off gentleman, I am ashamed to say that almost my first thought was to wonder what Mr. Holmes would make of such astonishing behavior.

This particular Monday night was foggy and chill, for it had rained on and off all day. I very nearly cried off from the little class I teach there, for my health has always been uncertain. But I knew the little shop girls I taught to read looked forward to it. A number of my friends come down to the Settlement House in daylight hours, to help with the washing and folding of clothing donated for the poor, or to teach the girls and boys of those horrible dockside slums—to teach also the innumerable Russians, Roumanians, Hindus, and Chinese who huddle ten and twelve to a tenement room enough English to seek employment—but I am one of very few who will work there at night. At least one night a week, and sometimes two, John spends with his friend Mr. Sherlock Holmes, either adventuring on whatever criminal case Mr. Holmes is pursuing, or dining with him and going somewhere to listen to music. On such nights I will frequently come down to the Settlement to teach, or help the regular workers there in any way that I can.

Thus I was there at ten o'clock—just finishing up that evening's chapter of *A Tale of Two Cities,* in fact—when Mrs. Wolff stumbled in from the brick-paved yard, clutching with one hand the basket of oddments she carries to sell, and with the other the dirty remains of a woolen shawl about her, sobbing like a beaten child.

"Vhy vould any do so to a poor voman, Mrs. Vatson?" she asked, when I'd brought her to the big room's tiny fire and sent one of the girls to get her soup. "Such nice gentleman he look, too, mit his beard all combed so nice, and his spectacles all rim mit gold. He buy me drink, he tell me I look like his sister—and him a goyische gentleman all in varm coat on such cold night! Look how I found my t'ings, vhen I vake up in alley behind Vish und Ring, eh?"

Certainly the contents of her big wicker basket—beautifully embroidered handkerchiefs, penwipers wrought in curious shapes, dolls of woven wicker with bright ribbons around their necks and cats wrought of folded tin with glass buttons for eyes—had been rudely treated, being now all soaked and muddy from having been dumped from the basket into the gutter and trodden on.

"I make box out of tin," she went on, as one of the girls—Rebecca was her name, and a very sweet bright child—brought her up a cup of soup. "Beautiful box, all mit buttons on it; two shilling I askin' vhor dat box. An' now it gone, an' he stole it from a poor voman, an' him mit nice hat an' his gloves an' his coat, an' bein' so nice to buy me schnapps, eh? Oy, the headache I got vhen I vake"—and indeed the woman's haggard face was the hue of ashes in the grimy glow of the gas jet and the fire. "Vhy he do a t'ing so, eh?"

"Maybe you were merely taken sick in the Fish and Ring," I suggested, "and stumbled in the alley and fell. The streets around there aren't terribly safe at this hour"—which was putting the matter mildly to say the least, the Fish and Ring being in one of the least salubrious streets of a neighborhood renowned for coshings, knifings, brawls, and hooliganism of all descriptions. "Perhaps someone happened along and stole your box?"

"Oy," she moaned, and pulled her shawl more closely about her. "Vhy vhould goyische gentleman vant poison poor voman like so, eh?"

"I don't know, Bubbe Wolff," piped up Rebecca, settling on the bench beside the woman and holding out her chapped hands to the fire. "But Zoltan Berg, he told me how that same thing happen to some woman his mama knows over Wapping."

"What?" I'd been turning over one of the wicker dollies in my hands, fascinated by the delicate workmanship; now I set it back in the basket and regarded the child in startlement. "This happened to someone else?"

"Zoltan's mama said," temporized Rebecca, an accurate witness if ever there was one. "This man came up and talked to her in the street, Mama Berg's friend, and ask her to the Blue Door Pub for mild and bitters, and next thing she know she wakes up in the alley behind the pub all cold and in the rain. She said he was a real nice gentleman, with a big brown beard and spectacles like Mama Wolff said, and said he was lonely an' she remind him of someone he knew."

The girl shrugged, skinny little shoulders in a hand-me-down pinafore and eyes too wise for a ten-year-old. Unprepossessing, the local police call them, and pert, but the more time I spend in the East End, the more I think that if ever I am granted the miracle of bearing John a living child, I would like her to have that kind of pluck and wit.

"He didn't rob her—anyway Mama Berg didn't say he did—and she got a drink out of it. And you know what sometimes happens, around Wapping and here, it could have been lots worse."

I shivered, and put a reassuring hand on the little girl's shoulder. The other reason I was the only one of my friends who would work the Settlement Hall at night was, of course, that the fiend whom the popular press had called Jack the Ripper had operated within a few streets of where we sat, only last year. Though nothing had been heard of that ghastly assassin for nearly twelve months—and though I've always believed that if one takes sensible precautions one can remain reasonably safe wherever one is—I was, when it came time for me to return home, escorted through the

Settlement's grim courtyard to my cab by at least six stalwart local gentlemen, and left to meditate, all the long rattling way back to Kensington, on the peculiarities of human conduct.

In John's stories about Mr. Holmes's cases, events follow neatly one upon another, without the intervening persiflage of day-to-day existence. This, I suppose, is the necessary difference between a painting and a photograph—the simplification of the background, that the foreground may stand in clearer relief. But in fact we live much more in photographs than in paintings, and for the next several days the Adventure of the Friendly Gentleman was crowded from my thoughts by the Adventure of the Imbecilic Maidservant, the Adventure of the Talkative Neighbor, the Adventure of the Blocked Stovepipe, and the Adventure of Mr. Stamford's Wedding Present. If I did not mention the matter to John it was only because it had become my habit to speak of the more harmless curiosities and occurrences at the Settlement House: and that, I suppose, indicates that however little harm had befallen Mrs. Wolff or Mrs. Berg's bosom friend at the Friendly Gentleman's hands, I guessed he was not quite as friendly as he seemed.

It was when I found myself in Portman Square, nearly a week later, in quest of a patent fountain pen for John's birthday, that I bethought myself of Mr. Holmes—not that he ever had the slightest idea of when John's birthday was, nor his own, I'm sure. And the thought occurred mostly because it had been some weeks since I had visited Martha Hudson.

It was only the knowledge that Sunday afternoons frequently found her at leisure in the narrow town garden behind 221 Baker Street that induced me to turn my steps along Audley Street. Ordinarily I would never have interrupted her work, which I knew—she being the landlady of two sets of rooms and two single chambers—was both physically demanding and virtually unending.

I found her, however, as I had suspected, pruning back her roses for the winter preparatory to wrapping the more delicate varieties in straw against the cold, her tall form swathed in a very atypical (for Martha) dress of blue-and-white calico and her fair hair, instead of being confined to its usual firm bun, hanging in plaits down her back like a schoolgirl's. She greeted me with a smile and a hug, and I sat on the single iron bench in the bare garden until she'd finished, when we went inside for tea. Both her widowed sister-in-law, Jenny Turner, who was living there then (though she moved out not long after), and her maid-of-all work, the egregious Alice, were away for the afternoon. The kitchen was warm and extremely pleasant with its smells of cinnamon and sugar, and we covered a wide variety of topics from John's birthday (soon) to the shape of this winter's hats (idiotic) to the progress of John's novel (frustrating, owing to the demands of making a living for himself, a household, and a dowryless wife).

"Had he not been wounded and sent home," I mused, "I think he would have remained with his regiment forever, writing tales of adventure and romance and battle in the hills out beyond Peshawar. For he has never wanted anything else, really. No wonder he drives poor Mr. Holmes to distraction with 'making romances out of logic.' "

And the two of us gently laughed. "But had he not been wounded and sent home," Martha said, "he would not have met Mr. Holmes—which would have been a shame, I think. Your husband is good for him. I know it would never have occurred to Mr. Holmes to seek out a friend, or to work at unraveling the mystery of another human soul as your husband did at unraveling his. Mr. Holmes watches people, the way he will watch the bees among the roses in the summer: fascinated but apart."

Which led us, naturally enough, to speculation about why a man of evident substance should be going about Whitechapel buying doped drinks for penniless women.

"I thought it sounded like the kind of thing that would intrigue Mr. Holmes," I said, dropping a fragment of strong-tasting brown sugar into my tea. "I would have mentioned it to Dr. Watson, only he worries about me enough going down there—not that I would ever accept the offer of a glass of mild and bitters from a total stranger. Certainly not in one of those pubs."

"No." Martha gazed thoughtfully through the many-paned glass of the pantry window out into the bare yard, her large hands cupped around the blue-and-white porcelain of the cup. "Though mind you, they're simply neighborhood pubs. If you mind your own business there you're as little likely to come to grief as you would at the Lamb down the street—unless you drink the gin, of course. Still . . . It's curious you should mention the matter. Something of the kind happened—or almost happened—two weeks ago to old Mrs. Orris, who sells flowers, and knitting, and apple dolls about the streets."

My whole face must have turned into a pair of raised eyebrows, because Martha went on, "It gave her a turn, because her niece knew Mary Kelly, one of the girls who was killed by Jack the Ripper last year. Mrs. Orris was walking home along Three Colt Street, which as you know is in a very bad part of the Limehouse, when she became aware that someone was following her. She heard the man behind her quicken his steps and she quickened hers, but was too tired to go very fast, for it was late and she'd been walking much of the day. She slowed down to go into the Ropewalk, where there were lights on and people.

"The man overtook her in front of the Ropewalk, and called out in a hoarse, husky voice, 'Madam, I should like to have a look at some of your dolls.' Now, he had been following her all the way from Commercial Road, but when she turned and stood beneath the lights in front of the pub, he came up to her, looked at her face, barely gave her dolls a glance, waved his hand impatiently and said, 'Oh, I'm afraid my daughter already has some of these,' and strode away down Ropewalk Fields at once, and disappeared into the fog. As I said, Mrs. Orris's niece knew one of the girls who was killed last year, and was very upset by this meeting, and perhaps it was that that made her more observant, but she said she did notice that, daughter notwithstanding, the gentleman was not wearing a wedding band."

At that moment the bell at the front of the house pealed. I got to my feet, thinking that it might be Mr. Holmes—Martha's story, added to the two I had earlier heard, had filled me with uneasiness. But from where I stood in the kitchen door looking down the passageway, I saw that it was a man and a woman. The man was tall and burly, extremely handsome and well-dressed in a camels' hair greatcoat and tall hat, the woman—barely a girl, I thought—elegantly turned out in copper-colored tweed that set off the striking brunette darkness of her hair. I could hear the girl apologizing, while the man snapped, "I distinctly told Holmes to keep me apprised of all and any details he might find."

The querulous outrage in the voice, coupled with my acquaintance with Mr. Holmes, struck me as absurdly amusing. After the visitors had gone Martha and I had a discreet chuckle over the thought of Mr. Holmes—who for all his protestations of logic and efficiency loved mysteriousness like a schoolboy—divulging all and any details to anyone, let alone the handsome and arrogant gentleman on the doorstep.

When I recounted the incident to John that evening he rolled his eyes and sighed, "Mr. Thorne. It has to be. Lionel Thorne has been coming into Holmes's sitting room almost daily for weeks, full of schemes as to how his missing wife might be found, and Holmes is hard put to persuade him that all his proposed courses of action will succeed in doing is driving her further into the shadows."

The first comment that sprang to my lips was that I scarcely blamed Mrs. Thorne, whoever she was, for fleeing from her husband. Though strikingly handsome, he seemed both pettish and managing, if nothing worse; but it was, in any case, not my business. Instead I remarked, "Weeks? That's unusual for Mr. Holmes, isn't it? He generally unravels his puzzles within a day or two."

"This is a rather curious case." John tamped the bowl of his after-dinner pipe with his usual meticulous concentration, as if he were cleaning a gun, while the dreamy scent of the clean tobacco mingled with that of the fire in the grate, and of the last few roses Martha had given me to bring home. We do not live richly, John and I, but after a lifetime spent one half in a dreary Edinburgh boarding establishment, and the other half in such penitential quarters as are alotted to governesses, I find a four-room mansionette in Kensington the summit of well-being and joy.

"Mrs. Julietta Thorne—according to her husband—has always been a woman of great eccentricity, whose odd ways have over the years given him great concern that one day she would have to be restrained. Six years ago she disappeared, taking with her nothing but the clothes that she wore. Since that time, though she has never applied for a penny, letters have come regularly to the family man of business—Mrs. Thorne owns considerable estates in Norfolk, her father having been the Viscount Wale, who placed all the lands in trust for his only daughter—and to the Thornes's only child, a girl named Viola, who is now twenty."

"I believe it was her that I saw," I said. "A dark girl, very pretty?"

"Indeed. The letters are posted from various European cities—several from Marseilles, one from Hamburg, and I believe from such places as Brussels and Danzig. They are invariably short, handwritten in what Holmes tells me is unmistakably Julietta Thorne's handwriting. They say that she is well and happy and occasionally give instructions about the estate, of which she has complete control by the terms of her father's will. I have read the letters—they contain nothing of a personal nature—and find them quite lucid, if a little brusque. But Mr. Thorne has been prey to mounting concern that this stubborn refusal to either return to her family or give them any means of communicating with her indicates a gradual slide into madness. A year ago he began making serious efforts to locate her; a few months ago he came to Holmes."

"And what has Miss Thorne to say to any of this?" I asked.

"It was Miss Thorne who insisted that her father come to Holmes. I understand that he was at first reluctant, but he has become a most intrusive client, calling, as I have said, two or three times a week of late and demanding to be kept apprised of every detail of the search. Miss Thorne apparently has very little to say, save that she does not believe her mother to be mad."

I tucked my feet up under me, as well as I could in the rather close confines of the chesterfield that I shared with John before the fire. We do, in fact, have two quite comfortable chairs in the parlor, but in the evening after dinner we frequently share occupancy of the enormous old green chesterfield, John with his arm about me as we read the evening paper together. I said, "It's a pity someone is not out looking for another lunatic in London," and recounted the story of the Friendly Gentleman with the beard and spectacles, as I knew it so far: "Why would anyone do such a thing?" I asked.

"I think you have the right of it, my dear." He puffed at his pipe—which had gone out—and set it aside, drawing my head down to his shoulder. On the hearth the old cat Plutarch (so named for his many Lives) blinked sleepily into the flames. In the warmth and comfort of the room I thought of women like Mrs. Wolff, and Mrs. Orris, and the little flower sellers and costers' daughters who'd come into the Settlement House, women who had not more than single unheated rooms near the river on these cold nights, and who trudged the foggy streets trying to sell their flowers or their candies or their dolls until the night grew too bitter to endure. "It sounds like the man is a lunatic, though not a dangerous one, except insofar as the women he drugs are in danger being left unconscious in alleyways."

He drew breath to say—I am sure—I really wish you would not go down to the Whitechapel Settlement, and then, God bless him, let it out. After a moment he said instead, "And the women were not harmed in any other way while they were unconscious? Other than Mrs. Wolff being robbed, which as you said might have been done by any of the street Arabs in that neighborhood."

"I am certain of it," I said.

"It's curious," John went on after a moment. "I remember how widespread the panic was in the city last winter, over the Ripper's crimes—to the extent that I had serious doubts about your safety when you started at the Settlement House in the spring. But despite all the fears he only took five victims, and they were within an understandable limit: they were fallen women, with whom a man might easily have a grievance for passing along to him some loathesome disease. The crimes were appalling, but they had a—a logic to them. But this . . . This is simply very odd."

"It's curious," I said, settling into the warm circle of his arm. "In spite of the fact that the Friendly Gentleman hasn't done anyone any harm—I thought of the Ripper, too."

In the days that followed there were, of course, many other matters demanding my attention: having the chimneys cleaned before the start of true winter, negotiating yet again with Mrs. Robertson next door on the subject of her incessantly screeching parrot, convincing Florrie—the fourth in a long line of barely adolescent maids-of-all-work—not to barter such objects as napkins and towels away to the rag-and-bone man just because he assured her that "Ladies like your missus don't got no more use for such an old thing as that."

Yet the Friendly Gentleman did not leave my mind. When I stopped to buy flowers from the girls in Piccadilly, and chatted a bit with them as they made up their bouquets and buttonholes on the steps of the Fountain, I mentioned a warning about the man. Though one woman shrugged and said, "Coo, lady, for a nice bit of gin I'd take a kip in an alley"—laughed along with her neighbors at this—others looked thoughtful, and thanked me for the alert. And at the Settlement House I put the word out among the women who walked about the city with their baskets of chrysanthemums, or feather tips, or knitting slung about their necks.

There was one woman about whom I worried in particular, who made dolls in her single room on Marigold Walk near the East India docks, and went about the city for miles selling them. Queenie, everyone called her, mostly I think because she spoke more politely than her neighbors. The dolls she made were truly exquisite, their round solemn faces bearing expressions of love, or shyness, or impishness far different from the usual vapid prettiness of a toy. Queenie would scrounge or trade bits of lace and silk from the rag-and-bone men, or beg scraps of satin from the dressmakers of Oxford Street, or beads that the dustmen found, and from these fashion angels that I would have treasured at the cost of my life in my own rather bleak and doll-less childhood. She was somewhat eccentric and absolutely fearless, and would talk to anyone about anything. Some afternoons I would see her chatting with city bankers outside the Royal Exchange as she hawked her wares, or in the early mornings with porters at the Billingsgate Fish Market. She could not be made to understand that there were folk of ill intent in the world, or that it behooved a woman alone—and she was not a girl, but a woman, I would guess, in her forties—to be careful about where and with whom she walked.

"No, but who should wish to harm me?" she asked, regarding me with mild disbelief in her large dark eyes, as the porters and costermongers and vegetable sellers of the Covent Garden market pushed and edged around us: I had encountered her in the market, deep in conversation with a tooth-less tramp and his dog, near a group of women shelling peas behind a rampart of baskets. "I mean no ill to any man, nor ever have."

I could not convince her otherwise, and in time simply bought a doll from her—a most beautiful Columbine with dark silk-floss hair elaborately braided—and went on my way with the flowers I had come there to buy. On my way through the narrow alley between baskets and hampers, stalls and barrows, I glanced back, to see one of the market women watching me closely, a hook-nosed, gimlet-eyed harridan in a virulent green plaid shawl. But when I looked again she was gone.

That evening, however, when I went to the Settlement House, all thought of her and of the feckless Queenie was driven out of my mind. I had finished my little class of shop girls, and was preparing to depart for home, when, coming out into the bare brick courtyard of the gloomy Settlement building, I was nearly bowled over by a rowdy group of the local boys, scuffling and laughing as they dashed about in the cold. Some of these ragged youngsters had been living on the street for years, variously selling newspapers, or holding the horses for gentlemen, or more dangerously darting out into the jostle and clatter of traffic to sweep the horse droppings out of the path of crossing pedestrians who would then give them a shilling. "Give them," I say, if they were decent folks, though I have been pricked to inner fury by the sight of young men—gentlemen I cannot call them—who would toss the payment out into the path of traffic, to roar with laughter at the nimble antics of the boys as they risked their lives diving for enough money to buy them a night beneath a roof.

It always astonishes me that these same boys, after twelve or fourteen hours of this, have the energy for games, but of course they do. I sprang back out of their path, but not quickly enough, and one of them collided with me, hurling me back against the brick of the wall and knocking himself sprawling through the open door and into the hall. He was at once on his feet, stammering, "Cor, I'm sorry, Mrs. W.," while his playmates jeered good-naturedly, "Argh, d'ja pick 'er pocket whilst you was at it, Ginger?" and "Hey, we gotta call 'im Ginger the Cosh!" as they crowded around me making sure that I was well.

The collision had knocked from Ginger's shoulder the satchel in which he carried his newspapers, and whatever other treasures he could find in the streets: a top, a bag of marbles (which thankfully had remained tied), and—I saw as he gathered them up again, still apologizing—a tin box that looked suspiciously like Mrs. Wolff's workmanship. I said, "Ginger," and he looked back at me, box in hand, and I beckoned him over.

"Yeah, you give it to him, Mrs. W.," affirmed the others, but I gestured them away. I think Ginger saw the direction of my gaze, and the look in my eye, because he hung back until the others had retreated.

I took the box from his hand. "I don't think even Dick Turpin," I said, keeping my voice low, "went in for stealing from old women who couldn't defend themselves."

I suspect he knew from the start that he had crossed the line of even the rough-and-ready ethics of the street, because he blushed hotly. At the same time I could see why he hadn't been able to resist temptation. The box was elaborately wrought of eight or ten different patterns of pressed-tin ceiling tiles, and was startlingly pretty. He mumbled, "Well, she was laid out drunk. I figured she'd just think as how the toff had took it."

"You saw him?" Perhaps I should have taken the opportunity to catechize him about how neither the owner's perceived unworthiness nor the unlikeliness of detection excuses theft, but the question I did ask was likelier to come to some good for someone, and not be a complete waste of breath.

"Oh, yeah. I was tryin' to sell the last of me papers, an' had gone in the alley to get outer the wind. This toff lugs ol' lady Wolff round the corner, an' dumps 'er down where the roof sticks out a bit at the back of the Fish an' Ring, 'cos it was still rainin', an' strikes a match. I saw his phiz good. Square face, beard like a holly bush, horn-rims to his goggles, an' a fair silk hat. He pulls her scarf off her head an' holds the match down near 'er face, lookin' at her close. I thought he'd light up his beard or her eyebrows. Then he blows it out an' heads up the alley, trippin' over 'er basket. I near laughed out loud, but . . ."

He hesitated, and the sharp cock-sparrow bravado wavered from his face, showing him to be, after all, a boy not much more than nine.

In a lower voice, as if fearing that his friends would hear his admission of fright, he added, "He was a bad man, Mrs. W. I couldn't see much of his face, but there was somethin' about him, about the way he moved, like he'd as soon hit you as not. . . . I seen men like that afore. The way he handled her, like as if she was a dead cat, not a woman at all. And I durstn't laugh. I don't know what he wanted with Mrs. Wolff, but for a minute I was afraid. . . ."

He shook his head, not saying what he was afraid he would see.

"I'm glad she was all right. That all he wanted was a look at her." Then, "You won't tell Mrs. Wolff it was me as pinched 'er box? It's a crackerjack box."

"It is indeed, Ginger," I said. "And you know how badly she needs the money she'll make selling it. It will make her very happy to have it returned, for she put many hours' work into it, and it may make a difference between her having a little coal to burn at night, or going cold. I'll tell her I found it by the dustbins behind the Fish and Ring."

"Narh," protested Ginger indignantly. "Wot'd you be doin' by the Fish an' Ring, Mrs. W.? Tell her I found it, an' gave it to you."

Like Mr. Sherlock Holmes, Ginger had a feeling for the likeliness of a story.

So troubled was I by this bizarre tale that when the cab came for me, I went, not to Kensington, but to Baker Street. As I gazed at the raveled blobs of yellow gaslights through the thickening fog I could not say what it was about Ginger's tale that frightened me, for no harm to anyone had actually been done, but frighten me it did. Martha must have seen it in my face when she opened the door for me—either that, or simply the fact that I seldom came calling unannounced by letter at that hour—because she asked at once, "What is it?"

I said, "Is Mr. Holmes in?"

She shook her head, and repeated, "What's happened, dear? Your hands are frozen," and led me back to the kitchen for some tea. "Mr. Holmes is out," she continued, as she sat me down in the kitchen by the stove. My hands were indeed frozen, and I had begun to cough. "He's been coming and going at odder and odder hours, slipping out through the kitchen as often as not. He startled that pea-brained Alice nearly out of her shoes the other night, creeping in dressed as the vilest old Chinese scoundrel. I told him he was lucky I hadn't set a dog on him."

But she smiled as she said it. In his tales John generally underrated Martha's intelligence, even as he was completely oblivious to her beauty, and to the fact that she was barely a year older than myself. I don't think he ever did realize that the reason Mr. Holmes never looked at other women was because Holmes and Martha had been lovers for years.

"So you have no idea when he'll be back?"

"No. He didn't come in last night. . . ." Her face clouded with the worry that she was able, most of the time, to push aside. "I suspect someone has been watching the house—watching his movements. So there is no telling." She brought the honey pot to the table to spoon some into my tea, and as she did so I moved my bag aside. It tilted over, the shift in its position causing the little Columbine doll to poke her head out over the rim. Martha startled, nearly spilling the tea, and asked, "Where had you that?"

"Columbine?" I took her out of the bag and set her against the sugar bowl, then looked up into Martha's face. "What is it?"

She signed me to remain where I was and left the kitchen; I heard her footsteps on the seventeen steps up to the floor above. In a few moments she was back, carrying Columbine's twin sister. Round-faced, enigmatically smiling, silk-floss hair braided in an elaborate chignon of the sort that had been popular about ten years ago . . .

"One of Mr. Holmes's clients brought this here this afternoon," she said. "Her mother made it, her mother who disappeared six years ago. . . ."

"Mrs. Thorne? John told me." I set the two dolls side by side on the table. The older twin's clothes were brighter, the laces new and the beads and buttons more expensive, but the same hand had beyond any shadow of doubt wrought both. We looked at each other, baffled and shaken. It was Martha who said,

"He's looking for her."

"Her husband?" Into my mind sprang the image of a big bespectacled man "with a beard like a holly bush," bending over a helpless woman in an alley, holding a candle to her face.

He was a bad man, Ginger had said. Like he'd as soon hit you as not. I was afraid. . . .

Martha jerked the bell to summon Billy from his room in the basement, and went to get her cloak.

We did not have as complete a case as Mr. Holmes might have required, to leap into a cab and take action—but both of us knew that something unwholesome and dangerous was going on.

As the cab rattled through the pitch-dark streets in choking fog, I related to Martha what Ginger had told me. "It sounds as if Mr. Thorne has been roving the streets in disguise for weeks, approaching any woman selling dolls—and goodness knows there are many—to get a close look at her. Though how he'd know his wife was selling dolls about the East End, and why she would be doing such a thing . . . Unless she really is insane, as he claims."

"Mr. Holmes guessed she was still in London," said Martha. "How, I do not know. It may be Thorne who has been following him, or trying to. His efforts to come and go in secret began soon after Mr. Thorne first came with Miss Thorne to 'help with the case.'"

"Or it could be Thorne's confederate," I said. And I told her about the hook-nosed market woman, who had watched me so closely when I spoke to Queenie at Covent Garden that afternoon. "If she saw me speaking with Queenie—and Mr. Thorne could easily have seen me here, that day I came to visit—his confederate will have told him of it."

The jarvey shook his head over leaving us in Marigold Walk, which is one of those dreary, narrow alleys leading away from the docks, where the houses lean against one another like the wounded of some endless war and the shadows seem to eat the feeble glim of the gaslights. But we could not be sure when Queenie would return. A public house on the corner spilled ochre blotches of glare on the wet pavement, and though Martha and I agreed that, at last resort, we would take refuge there, we both resolved to wait in the dark doorway of Queenie's dirty lodging for a time. Not even the usual complement of drunken sailors, ragpickers, coal heavers, and costers roved the chilly streets; only one old woman staggered along the opposite pavement, singing of Anne Boleyn's ghost in a thin, scratchy wail. It was past eleven, and only the occasional wet clop of hooves from the Dock Road, and the dim musical clank of rigging blocks in the docks themselves, carried to us through the murk.

I coughed, and drew my cloak more tightly about me. John would never let me hear the end of it, if I came down sick again from this. "Mrs. Thorne has been missing for six years now," I said after a time. "Why would her husband only begin to seek her now?"

"He made inquiries for her in Europe before this," returned Martha quietly. "But her daughter was fifteen when Julietta Thorne fled. . . ."

I shivered, remembering my one fleet glimpse of Lionel Thorne's harsh face. I remembered, too, the fear in Ginger's eyes when he spoke of the bearded man bending over the unconscious woman in the alley. "Do you think she is in fact insane, as he says?"

"When a man says a woman is insane," said Martha, her soft alto voice dry, "what he often means is that she will not do as he bids. It is fatally easy for a husband to have a wife declared insane on no other word than his own, particularly if she has any other eccentricity of manner, which, as you say, Queenie does. Then any provisions her father made for her control of her property would be voided, and her husband would become conservator. I may be wrong, and Julietta Thorne may in fact be mad as a hatter, but living apart from her husband may be the only way she could think of to preserve her liberty until her daughter comes of age. Hark!"

For we both heard now the muffled leaden click of a woman's step on the pavement. Peering hard through the gloom I saw nothing, save the blurry smear of the public-house lights. Then a shadow passed them, stooped and small, hurrying.

I sprang down the steps from the sheltering doorway, quickened my stride to meet her. I coughed again, and the little figure stopped, but I could see now that it was Queenie. I called out, "Julietta," and she turned her head sharply, startled, and started to flee—

And before her, out of the fog, loomed suddenly the dark shape that I knew was Lionel Thorne.

"Julietta, run!" I shouted, but Thorne was too quick for her. He reached her in a stride, caught her arm, spilling her basket of dolls on the pavement, and in the gaslight from the pub I saw the flash of steel in his hand. I was running, too, by this time and threw myself on the man, shoving against him with all my strength.

He staggered, stumbled off the curb. He lost his grip on the woman and grabbed me instead. I saw the flash of his knife and dodged, felt the steel tangle in my cloak and grate on my corset stays. Then the next second Martha was on him, dragging at his knife hand, and an instant after that the old woman across the street, suddenly six feet tall and shedding shawl, bonnet, and identity in a welter of old rags, landed Mr. Thorne such a blow on the chin with doubled-up fist that Mr. Thorne's feet left the pavement, and only connected with it again after the back of his head did. I heard Mr. Holmes's unmistakable light voice cry, "Martha!"

"I'm all right. . . ."

Then Holmes was on his knees beside me on the pavement—I had no recollection of falling, but I was sitting on the wet flagstones trying to get my breath, with Thorne's knife beside me, glittering evilly in the greasy light. "My dear Mrs. Watson, are you all right?"

I managed to nod—I actually felt quite dizzy—and he felt my hands and my face.

"Is she all right?" asked Queenie's voice—Mrs. Thorne's voice—and I blinked at Holmes, with the long gray wig of the evil Covent Garden market woman hanging in unraveled mare's tails about his face and the breath rolling in steam from his lips. Around us men were shouting as they came out of the pub:

"Look at this 'ere pigsticker, then!"

"By God, it's Jolly Jack at 'is tricks again, I bet!"

"You all right, mum?" (This to Holmes) "This lady all right?"

"This man tried to stab me," I said, keeping my voice steady with an effort, and pointing to Mr. Thorne, still unconscious in the muck of the road. I unfurled the side of my cloak to show the horrible rent. "Me, and this lady . . ."

But Julietta Thorne was gone.

It wasn't until after the Court of Assizes had remanded her husband to custody—upon my testimony and that of Tzivia Wolff, Gordon "Ginger" Robinson, and two or three other peripatetic hawkers of dolls—that Julietta Thorne came to the Settlement House, and asked me to take her to Baker Street to meet Mr. Holmes.

"Of course I was mad," she said, quite calmly, once we were seated in Mr. Holmes's cozy sitting room: myself, Mr. Holmes, John (who had been spending the evening with his friend while I was at the Settlement House), and Martha. "What other word would you use of a girl who insisted upon marrying a man whom everyone—including her dying father—recognized as a fortune hunter, selfish, calculating, brutal, and cold? My father begged me to wait, did everything in his power to get me to swear on the Testament that I would not marry for five years—for he knew my impulsiveness well, and knew that in a very few years my obsession would pass and I would no more consider wedding Lionel Thorne that I would consider throwing myself off London Bridge. But I would not wait."

She shook her head. She did not look so very unlike Mrs. Wolff, being roughly the same height, and like her a brunette. Not until I attended the Court of Assizes did I realize that all the women whom Lionel Thorne had accosted and drugged bore at least that superficial resemblance to one another. Six years of hardship and poverty had taken their toll on Julietta

Thorne, as they take it upon all women who must struggle to make their living. But I could see that she had once been quite a handsome girl.

"Within a few years I knew better," she continued. "My dear father, thank God, if he could not dissuade me, at least tied up the money and the property so that Lionel could not touch it, this being some years before passage of the Married Womens Property Act. This—and what he called my 'ungenerosity' to his little whims and wants concerning railroad shares and slum property—was what quickly brought out the beast in my husband. It was my money, to invest and to manage and to save as I pleased. Rather than seek out a profession of his own—he had been a member of the Life Guards when we wed, but sold his commission almost at once—he plotted ceaselessly how to gain the use of my property, after having wasted his own in quite foolish speculations that always failed, he said, through someone else's fault and malice.

"Within a few years of the marriage I better knew the man I had wed. And as the years went by, my disgust and regret turned first to suspicion, then to fear. I remained with him to protect our daughter as long as I could, but when I found in his desk correspondence with various doctors concerning an effort to have me declared mad—and Lionel made conservator of the property—I knew I must flee."

"I confess that I have not had much time to observe you, Madam," said John diffidently, from where he sat beside me on the settee. "Yet what little experience I have had with the mad inclines me to question whether such a judgment could be implemented."

"You see me now, Doctor," smiled Mrs. Thorne. "Had you seen me in the years immediately following my dear father's death, when I went from Spiritualist to Spiritualist seeking contact with him, seeking absolution and advice—when I spent hours and days locked in my room, making doll after doll as a way of removing my mind from the ruin I had wrought of my life—you might have said otherwise. Even in this country it is easy enough for a husband to have his wife declared a lunatic, particularly if she happens to believe—as I do—that the dead continue to take an active interest in those they loved in life."

"And so you fled," said Holmes. There was no trace left of the evil-looking gray-haired market woman who had stared at me so sharply in Covent Garden—no wonder he had stared, seeing me, of all people, speaking to the woman he had gone to observe as a possible candidate for the missing Mrs. Thorne. Had he been home that day when Miss Viola Thorne brought to his rooms the doll her mother had made, it would have been he and not I who first made the connection between Julietta Thorne and Queenie the Dollmaker.

But perhaps, not having heard some of the tales going around the Settlement House about the Friendly Gentleman, he would have delayed in seeking her out.

Mrs. Thorne nodded. "Among the Spiritualists I had met people who would help me, though they had no idea who I was. And after I came to dwell in Whitechapel I came to know a few seafaring men willing to carry letters abroad, to post them from Europe to make it seem that I had left the country. I could not have kept an eye on the estates through the newspapers, had I actually gone abroad. And it was absolutely necessary to let the family man of business—and my dear child—know that I was not dead. How clever it was of you to trace me, Mr. Holmes," she added, shaking a finger at the detective. "Lionel was a sly one, and he never managed that."

"Your husband—and the foreign police he contacted over the years—paid far too much attention to the country of origin of the stamps, and far too little to that of the paper," replied Holmes with a smile. "Paper and ink were definitely of British manufacture. Moreover, they were always cheap, nothing that a woman living the peripatetic life of the usual fashionable Continental traveler—which your husband supposed you to be—would use. Further, such a woman would not be sending letters from such ports as Marseilles and Hamburg. So from the first my attention was drawn to the East End. Though it was some weeks before your daughter could return to Norfolk to find one of your dolls to show me—as I had asked her to do from the first—she had mentioned at the start of my investigation that you made them. That—and your refusal to have money sent to you, by which you could be traced—immediately suggested to me a means by which a woman might make at least a bare living in hiding."

"And yet you told my husband nothing of this?"

Holmes was silent for a moment, gazing into the fire. Mrs. Thorne had only come to the Settlement House as the first shadows of evening had begun to fall, so John and Mr. Holmes had been just finishing their dinner together—preparatory to a long-promised evening of talk about certain of Mr. Holmes's early cases which John hoped to write accounts of—when Martha had shown Mrs. Thorne and me up the stairs.

"Were I the perfectly analytical reasoner Watson likes to make of me," said Holmes slowly, "I suppose there would be no reason for me not to keep Lionel Thorne absolutely apprised of the progress of my search. One can tell a seamstress by her left sleeve and a cobbler by his thumb, but the marks that evil character leaves upon a man are less easily classified—perhaps because, as Milton so brilliantly points out in the first cantos of *Paradise Lost,* wickedness takes on manifold forms, though myself I have found that goodness bears as many shapes in the world."

"Yet even a little street Arab like Ginger Robinson," I said softly, "guessed his intent was evil, without knowing how he guessed."

"I must improve my acquaintance," murmured Holmes, "with young Mr. Robinson. Had I been the perfectly cold-blooded and analytical reasoner that the Mr. Sherlock Holmes of the tales appears to be, I would not have allowed mere prejudice to influence me against the way the man looked aside when he spoke of his wife, or the too-smooth accounts of her disappearance—unblemished by the smallest hesitations of doubt as to its motives. For your husband, Mrs. Thorne, is very good at appearing to act from the best of motives."

"As I know," said Mrs. Thorne, "to my grief."

"And yet these things, like the weaver's tooth or the hostler's right shoulder, are clues too, to which my mind reacted. Very shortly after I began my researches in the East End I became aware that I was being watched when I emerged from the house. There are a number of criminals in London's underworld who might have reason to do that. But the next time Mr. Thorne came I noticed the reddening on his cheeks and lips left by spirit gum where he fastened his borrowed whiskers. As he did not mention the use of disguise to me I guessed that my pursuer was he. After that I did what I could to shake him from the scent, but I fear that he, too, was doing exactly as I was: searching for you among the thronging humanity of those wretched streets. He showed quite clearly what he meant to do with you when he found you at last, trusting—quite accurately, I regret to surmise—that your death would be put down to the return of Jack the Ripper, or to some other criminal of that ilk. Unless they are particularly heinous, or attended by some sensational circumstance, few spend much time investigating the deaths of the poor."

"He stopped me that very evening in the Commercial Road, and had I not been warned by my dear Mrs. W.—Mrs. Watson, that is," she amended hastily, "I don't know but what I might have gone with him for a drink. For in that great beard and those spectacles I did not recognize him, and he kept his voice low and husky, and his words short. He knew he had little time. Our daughter turns twenty-one this month, and he must have guessed—seeing how she spoke against him in the court today—that his chance of controlling any portion of the family money would be done when she reached her majority."

"The importance of Miss Thorne's impending birthday did not escape me," said Holmes. "What did you intend to do, when she came of age?"

"I intended to die," said Julietta Thorne, quite calmly. "Oh, not actually die," she added, when both I and John cried out in horror. "I had made my will, leaving everything to Viola absolutely and without reference to her father. I planned to stage-manage an 'accident' in Brussels or Hamburg, with some of my seafaring friends, with sufficient proof that Julietta Thorne was no more. Only in that way could I be sure of freeing myself, and my poor child, from the scoundrel I married. It broke my heart to know that I could never see my child again. . . ."

Her voice wavered, and she forced a smile. "I saw her at the Assizes today," she said. "I was in the courtroom— Did she not look beautiful, as she stood up and told her own tale of the wrongs she witnessed that he did to me, the abuses she herself had endured at his hands? There is a girl who will never know her mother's foolish belief in a man's lies."

She broke off, and pressed her hands to her lips, her dark eyes flooding with tears. "My poor Viola," she whispered. "What she must have gone through, after I fled—thinking that I would leave her, merely to save myself from unpleasantness. Now that Lionel is where he cannot get at me, I shall institute divorce proceedings, which I am sure will be granted given his attempt at murdering poor Mrs. Watson. . . ."

She held out her hand to me, and clasped my fingers in her strong, work-roughened grip. "But I fear that I shall never be able to look my daughter in the face again."

While Mrs. Thorne had been speaking, I saw Mr. Holmes turn his head, listening to sounds in the street. Listening myself, I heard a cab outside, and Martha's sister-in-law, Jenny Turner, opening the street door. Moments later the parlor door opened to reveal the tall slim dark-haired girl I had glimpsed only once on the doorstep. Mrs. Thorne gave a little cry, but her daughter only crossed the room in a stride or two, and took her mother in her arms.

As the two women held each other close John put a gentle arm around my waist, and led me from the room.

MR. JAMES PHILLIMORE

Somewhere in the vaults of the bank of Cox & Co., at Charing Cross, there is a travel-worn and battered tin dispatch box with my name, John H. Watson, M.D., Late Indian Army, painted upon the lid. It is crammed with papers, nearly all of which are records of cases to illustrate the curious problems which Mr. Sherlock Holmes had at various times to examine. Some, and not the least interesting, were complete failures, and as such will hardly bear narrating, since no final explanation is forthcoming. A problem without a solution may interest the student, but can hardly fail to annoy the casual reader. Among these unfinished tales is that of Mr. James Phillimore, who, stepping back into his own house to get his umbrella, was never more seen in this world.

—"The Problem of Thor Bridge"

by MEL GILDEN

The Adventure of the Forgotten Umbrella

In "The Problem of Thor Bridge," Dr. Watson mentions several cases which "will hardly bear narrating, since no final explanation is forthcoming." He goes on to say that "Among these unfinished tales is that of Mr. James Phillimore, who, stepping back into his own house to get his umbrella, was never more seen in this world."

I, Mr. James Phillimore, still being very much in this world, take the liberty of explaining myself what happened on that chilly April morning—believing that the true and correct details of the case should be preserved. The facts are both less mysterious and more dramatic than some of the fantastic suppositions that have been put forward in the more sensational stories of the daily press—having to do with neither black magic nor abduction by Mr. Wells's Martians, but only with human greed.

I begin:

Five years ago I met a young lady who called herself Alice Madison. She was a substantial woman with rosy cheeks and a pleasant disposition. I liked her immediately, and, it would seem, my warm feelings were reciprocated. Over a period of months our mutual respect and enjoyment of each other's company bloomed into love. She seemed unencumbered by personal affiliations, and I made a good living as a vice president at Morehouse & Co., so there was no reason we should not plan to be married.

Early in our marriage Alice took up the habit of stopping at my offices in Throgmorton Street so that we might take our midday meal together.

We both enjoyed the diversion, and we saw no harm in it so we continued to meet in this way once or twice a week. At the time it did not seem important that a large safe stood in one corner of my office. The safe contained money, as well as stocks, bonds, contracts, and other important papers that our investors might require, and having these documents near at hand saved us the trouble of sending a messenger to the bank time and again throughout the business day. Only Mr. Morehouse and I knew the combination to the safe.

My life continued without unpleasant incident until one evening when I arrived home from work to find my dear wife in serious conversation with a short round man who had a face that was florid and large-featured, if unshaven, under thick beetling brows. He was dressed as a moderately successful tradesman on holiday might be—in a suit that was slightly out of style, a little tight under the arms, and frayed at the cuffs. His hat had seen better days, and no one had thought to brush his shoes recently.

He looked at me as if appraising an animal. "'Is lordship's a likely lad, ain' 'e?" he remarked in an insulting tone.

My wife said nothing but only continued to stare at him in horror.

"Don't forget," this unpleasant man said and shook his finger at her.

"What is the meaning of this intrusion?" I cried. "Why are you pestering my wife?"

The man sneered. "Your wife, indeed," he said as he tipped his hat to me and sauntered out, closing the door behind himself. I threw it open and watched him strut along the street past a brace of waiting cabs. I closed the door and turned to my wife, intending to get to the bottom of this situation. But she paced up and down before me and wrung her hands in the most dreadful manner. Obviously, I could not interrogate her while she was in such a state. I called for water, then encouraged her to calm herself, and to sit down. After the maid had brought an ewer of water and a glass, Alice took a few sips and then buried her head in her hands, sobbing.

"Certainly," I said, "as long as I'm here you have nothing to fear from that man."

"On the contrary," she said. "I fear he can ruin our lives."

"Our lives?" I asked with astonishment. "Are we in danger? I will call the police immediately."

She lifted her head and dabbed with a handkerchief at her red-rimmed eyes. "I am afraid," she said, "that the police cannot help."

"My dear, you are not making sense." For many years, my only contact with members of the constabulary was to exchange nods if we happened to pass on the street. I had never needed their help, but had always assumed that if I requested it, it would be forthcoming.

She answered by taking a ragged breath.

"Perhaps you'd better explain," I said.

She nodded. "I must begin," she said, "by admitting something so horrible that I have been keeping it from you, fearing what you might do."

"I love you, my dear," I said, quite bewildered by her warning. "There is nothing you might have done that can be so horrible I would harm you in any way."

"I love you, too, James," she said. "And I ask only that you not think too harshly of me."

"Done!" I cried rather more loudly than I'd intended. "Only what is your admission?"

"I was married before we met."

Her words were a great shock to me, but still not so bad as I had feared. While I was still absorbing her information, she went on. "And I am afraid that I am *still* married."

Her second admission proved that I was still not impervious to surprise. And I found it difficult to keep the promise I had so recently made. Harsh thoughts filled my brain. "Go on," was all I trusted myself to say.

It was then that Alice told a story I would not have credited had I not known her so well, and seen the sincerity on her face. As it happened, my trust in her was not ill-placed because events later proved her out.

She had been (she explained) little more than a child when she met and somehow fell in love with the unpleasant man I had just met, a certain Mr. Harvey Maynard. Shortly, she and Mr. Maynard were married.

"He was kind at first, but it was not very many days later that Harvey proved to be a most disreputable and violent person," my Alice went on. "He beat me only when he drank, but he drank constantly. It soon became obvious that his love for me was just as surely an artifact of his alcoholism as was his enthusiasm for striking me with his hand. I would even have divorced him, if I could, the shame of divorce being no greater than the suffering I endured while married to the brute. When I went to visit my sister in Kent, he came and dragged me back to London.

"Then, one morning I awoke to find he had not returned from the carousing and revelry in which he nightly indulged. I cannot say that I was unhappy with the turn of events, but I admit to a certain morbid curiosity about what had happened to him. It was only some weeks later that I learned he had been arrested for a most brutal robbery and eventually taken to Dartmoor prison. Some years later I was notified that he had died crossing the moors during an escape attempt. A great weight seemed lifted from my shoulders. Shortly after that I met you, my dear, and I thought my life had turned around for good."

"Then who was that irritating little man?" I asked, bewildered. "Surely, you didn't marry him, too?"

"No, dear," she replied patiently. "I did not. That was Harvey Maynard."

"But you said—"

"That he was dead? Indeed I thought so for many years. Then, shortly before you arrived home from work today, Harvey turned up on our doorstep. He boasted with smug arrogance that while escaping prison he had met a man by chance on the moors, forced him to exchange clothing, and then murdered him. By the time the body was found it could no longer be identified properly. The clothing seemed to speak for itself."

I cannot sufficiently describe my feelings of pity for my wife and my revulsion for Mr. Harvey Maynard. I patted Alice's hand and bade her take another sip of water. When these ministrations were, for the moment, complete, I asked her to continue her story. "Certainly, there must be more," I said.

"No," she said with difficulty. "No more." She looked away from me and shuddered.

"But what did he want?"

"Only to gloat a little about his escape."

"Surely, I must call the police."

Alice sighed. "Harvey Maynard is a very bad man," she said, "but unfortunately he is not stupid. The police will certainly not find him before he boards a ship bound for South America."

For a day or two I considered the fact that Alice was, in the eyes of the law if in no other way, a bigamist. Still, that seemed a small matter next to the crimes committed by Mr. Harvey Maynard. More importantly, I could not stop loving Alice just because of the indiscretions she had committed when she was young. Now Harvey Maynard was on his way to South America, where he would most likely stay; if he returned to England he ran the risk of being recognized by the police. No, he would not disturb my beloved Alice or me ever again. Maynard's departure seemed to mark the end of the incident. What I did not know at that time was that Mr. Maynard had in fact not gone to South America, and instead had forced my wife to commit an act that was as much against her nature as it was against mine.

Not many days after the appearance of Harvey Maynard Alice came to visit me for luncheon. I thought nothing of it when she arrived somewhat earlier than usual and took her customary seat in a wing-backed leather chair opposite my desk. We spoke for a moment, and then I went about my business. She seemed to take pleasure watching me work, and I admit that I took a certain amount of pleasure watching her watch me.

"Excuse me, my dear," I said as I stood. "I must get Mr. Morehouse's signature upon these papers."

She nodded, and gave me leave to continue.

I left the room and was gone for only a few moments. When I returned Alice was still seated, but reading a book she now put back into her handbag, and smiled up at me warmly.

"That concludes the morning's work," I informed her. "Shall we dine?"

"Indeed we shall," she said and stood up.

I swung shut the safe, twirled the dial, and offered Alice my arm.

As usual, we went to Luigi's, a small restaurant on Broad Street that we both knew and liked. The beef was extraordinarily good, though the fowl was perhaps a trifle undercooked. During the course of the meal Alice attempted to tell me a hilarious story about our housemaid, Mary Anne, who had the habit of unconsciously performing little dance steps as she worked. But the story collapsed of its own weight when Alice seemed to distract herself with another thought.

"What is it, my dear?" I asked. We had not spoken of Harvey Maynard for some days, but the episode had not been forgotten.

"Nothing," Alice said with a shake of her head. Abstractedly, as if something else were still on her mind, she chewed on her beef.

That evening I found my wife in tears once again. Had some new catastrophe befallen my poor Alice?

"I have a terrible admission to make," she said as I rushed to her side.

"What?" I asked with astonishment. "Another one?"

Like light on water a smile came and went on her face.

"I did not tell you the true reason for Harvey Maynard's visit."

"Oh?" I remarked cautiously.

"He demanded I give him one thousand pounds or he would ruin our lives by reporting to the police and to the daily newspapers that I am a bigamist."

"He has not gone to South America, then?"

She shook her head. "Not yet, at any rate."

My astonishment was terrific. "You led me to believe that he'd come here only to gloat," I said, trying not to sound accusing and failing at it.

"My fondest wish was to see you uninvolved in these matters."

"You think so little of me—that I would do anything but help you as best I could?

"Say rather that I thought so much of you. That the less you knew and the less you were involved the more likely you would emerge unscathed."

Her words touched me deeply. "But one thousand pounds," I cried. "How could you hope to raise such a sum?"

"I tried pawning my jewelry," she explained. "But bargain as I might, I could not secure nearly enough in exchange."

"And so?" I suggested, prompting her, unable to prevent curiosity from creeping into my voice.

"I saw that all avenues were closed to me but one. And my only solution was not perfect. It seemed that I had a choice between revealing you to be the pawn of a lady bigamist, or to be a man who had robbed his company of one thousand pounds. This afternoon, after I returned home from our luncheon, I gave the money I had taken from your safe to Harvey Maynard in exchange for his silence."

I had no trouble understanding her predicament, but one question remained. "As far as I am aware," I said, "the combination to the safe is known only to Mr. Morehouse and myself."

"Exactly," she admitted. "And so you become the robbery's chief suspect." Once more she buried her face in her hands.

"But how did you know the combination?" I asked, persisting.

With nearly the directness of a man she stared me straight in the eye. "I had no need of a combination," she said in a flat, unemotional voice. "I merely took the money from the open safe when you were out getting Mr. Morehouse's signature on those papers."

I nodded. Her explanation made sense. As she began to cry again I noted that on the morrow when the shortage was discovered, as Alice had already pointed out, I would certainly be the first person who would fall under suspicion.

I sat silently for a long while listening to her cry, and to the clatter of the oblivious traffic that passed on the street outside. Mary Anne made small tapping and shuffling sounds as she danced around the table, preparing it for dinner. Anger grew in my breast, all of it directed at Mr. Harvey Maynard, my sweet Alice's despicable first husband. I wanted to assure her that between the two of us we would find a solution to our troubles, but I had not the faintest idea how to proceed.

"What did you say, dear?" I asked.

Alice sniffled. "I said that I realize that I have made many mistakes in my life. Perhaps this robbery was another. I certainly did not think of consequences, of how this theft might ruin our lives. Only one thought ran through my brain, that I must get the money somehow. I am now ready to admit my crimes to the police and go gladly to prison for bigamy and robbery, happy to be rid of that horrible man. My only regret is for how this fiasco will affect your reputation. I care nothing for my own, which is just as well. Surely when the police learn that I committed the crimes, and that you had no part in either of them, you will not suffer too badly. I still love you, my darling, and when I am released from prison I will attempt somehow to make up this travail to you."

"Perhaps it is not too late to get the money back," I suggested. "Do you know where Mr. Harvey Maynard may be found?"

She shook her head wearily.

An idea came to me. It would require a certain subtle theatricality on my part, but it might save us both.

"There is no reason," I said, "that either of us should suffer for the actions of Harvey Maynard." I took her two small hands in mine. "Will you trust me, my dear?" I asked.

"With my life," she said.

"I am hoping our adventure will not come to that," I said. "Now, you must quickly pack and be off for your sister's in Kent."

"But—"

"Quickly, now. I will take care of everything tomorrow morning."

"Very well, dear. I leave it all to you."

While she packed I checked the train schedules. In less than an hour I put her in a hansom and she was on her way to Kensington Station.

I knew that I would arouse suspicion of my part in the robbery not only because of my knowledge of the safe's combination, but because I would not appear at my office the next morning. I had no doubt the police would look for me at home. Quickly I prepared for their arrival.

The next morning I arose early. Much to their surprise and delight I dismissed Cook and Mary Anne for the day. They did not ask me questions, but seconds later they were gone. I put on the cap and ill-fitting painter's smock I had found in the storage shed along with a gallon or two of white paint, climbed a ladder at the side of the house, and began to apply paint to the outside wall. The cap fit all right, but the smock billowed around me like a tent. Applying paint to the outside wall of my house was pleasant enough work, and I might have enjoyed it had I not known what was yet to come.

Mr. Morehouse would soon open the office and the clerks who audited the contents of the safe would report the shortage. There would be hurried discussions, first disbelieving and then furious. My absence would be noted. The police would arrive at my home, perhaps with Mr. Morehouse accompanying them. Only then would I know for sure whether my plan worked.

I did not have long to wait. A hansom drew up in front of my house followed by a drag drawn by a four-in-hand. A lean, ferretlike man leaped from the hansom, and at his direction a gang of officers emerged from the drag and spread out, surrounding the house. I stopped painting while I watched all this activity with much interest. My heart beat like a drum in my chest, and my blood churned rapids-like through my body.

The man directing the activity of the police was about to knock upon the front door of my house when he was hailed by a tall slim man who approached walking at a brisk pace. The intensity of his gaze was unlike any I have seen before or since. This was, of course, Mr. Sherlock Holmes. I had not had occasion to meet him, but one of my clients had pointed him out to me on the street. The policeman and Mr. Holmes spoke together for a moment, and then the policeman used the door knocker to announce his presence.

I climbed in at the second floor window, hurriedly threw off the painter's smock, and deposited it and the workman's cap into a chest. I tore off a mustache I had applied earlier with spirit gum, and stuck it inside the lid of the chest. I had been wearing my usual suit of clothes under the painter's attire, so it was but the work of a moment to go downstairs as myself to see who had knocked.

"Mr. James Phillimore?" the policeman asked in a loud voice.

I admitted I was that person.

"I am Inspector Lestrade of Scotland Yard. I'll have to ask you to come with me, sir."

"Why? What is the matter?"

"There has been a robbery at Morehouse & Co., sir, and you are under suspicion."

"Ridiculous."

"That remains to be seen, sir. We'd like to ask you a few questions."

"Ask away, then," I said, allowing a righteous irritation to enter my voice.

"Down at the Yard, if you please, sir."

For the sake of appearances I blustered for another minute or two, then retrieved my coat from the hall closet. During the preceding scene, Mr. Holmes had moved off to one side and carefully examined the walls and floor of the entryway—I could not imagine why.

"If you're quite finished here, Mr. Holmes," Lestrade said with a note of sarcasm in his voice.

"Quite," Mr. Holmes said, and rejoined us at the door.

I allowed myself to be escorted outside, and when we reached the street I glanced critically at the sky. "I suspect rain," I said. "Perhaps you would be so kind as to allow me to go back for my umbrella?"

"The house is surrounded," Lestrade said. "Escape out a window or a back door is impossible."

"The thoroughness of the Yard is well known," I said. "I will only be a moment. May I go?"

Lestrade grunted in assent.

Trying not to show the excitement I felt, I marched back into the house, the picture of affronted virtue. When the door was closed behind me, I ran up the stairs and into the room where I had left my painter's garb and other accouterments. I threw on the tentlike smock and the cap, carefully applied the mustache, and climbed out the window, where I once again began painting. A few minutes later I heard a disturbance in the street. The policemen swarmed all around and through the house as if it were a disturbed anthill. There was a great deal of interrogative shouting, followed by answers in the negative.

A policeman ran by and looked up at me. "Have you seen Mr. Phillimore?" he called.

"Oo?" I asked. "The bloke wha' lives 'ere in this 'ouse?"

"Yes, yes," the policeman said impatiently.

"Went back into 'is 'ouse then, didn' 'e?" I answered as if Mr. Phillimore's whereabouts were no concern of mine. "Wha d'ou want 'im for, theen? 'ee didn' 'ook it, did 'ee? The bloke still owes me money!"

"Never you mind," the policeman said, and ran on. Moments later the policemen drained out of the house like so much black water and soon all was silence. The policemen, their hansom and their drag were gone, to search for me far and wide, no doubt believing that I had somehow slipped through their professional fingers. And so it seemed that I was ". . . never more seen in this world."

I was overjoyed to think that I had been successful in my attempt to deceive the police. All that remained now was for me to join my wife in Kent. Though I had no plans beyond that, I was certain that an opportunity to ensure our safety would present itself. Perhaps someday I would even be able to return the thousand pounds Alice and I now owed to Morehouse & Co. I was about to climb back in through the window when someone hailed me from below. "Excuse me, my good man."

I looked down and was surprised to see Mr. Sherlock Holmes staring up at me and gesticulating with his stick!

"Yes, gov?"

"I'd like to speak with you," Mr. Holmes went on. "Perhaps you would be good enough to climb down here for a moment."

I could not imagine what he might want from me, but I did what any tradesman in my position would do. I climbed down and joined him on the ground.

"You succeeded in throwing off the police," he said quietly, "but I am not so easily fooled."

"What's it all about, then, gov?" I asked, not feeling so confident. I had heard of Mr. Holmes's talents—as who in London has not?—but I continued my performance because I could think of nothing else to do.

"Come, come, Mr. Phillimore," Mr. Holmes said jocularly. "A painter without splatters of paint on his shoes is a curiosity, indeed. Don't you agree?"

In shock, I looked down at my clean shoes, freshly brushed that morning. I'm afraid I looked at Mr. Holmes rather dumbly. I had been fairly caught. All that remained, I thought, were the arrest and other legal formalities.

"Things will go better for you if you return the money," Mr. Holmes said.

"Without question," I replied. "But I do not have it."

"You know where it is, then," he accused.

I had no doubt that Harvey Maynard had it. "Only in the vaguest possible sense," I admitted.

"I see." Mr. Holmes studied me for a long moment, no doubt analyzing all he could see about my body for clues. Suddenly he laughed sharply once. "Leave your disguise in the bushes there," he said, "and come along with me to my rooms. I do not believe the police will disturb us. They are out looking for you at the train stations and docks."

I did not resist when he gripped my arm tightly and guided me toward Baker Street. I could not have escaped if I'd wanted to.

Mr. Holmes and I did not discuss the topic that was then uppermost in our minds. I, because I wished to organize my thoughts and the street did not seem to me to be the proper venue for any explanation I might offer. He—well, I'm sure Mr. Holmes had his reasons. I had been told that he always did. In any case, I was silent while Mr. Holmes commented on the prospects for the weather, and the various musical entertainments that were being performed in London's many theaters. It was only after we'd reached his rooms and he'd settled me in a chair with a cup of tea that I said, "I admit that I am quite curious as to how you happened to be walking past my house this morning."

"Nothing easier to explain," Mr. Holmes said. "I have been hired by Morehouse & Co.—your employers, I understand—to retrieve the money they believe you stole."

"And yet," I said, "even after you'd guessed that I was the one painting the house, you still did not turn me over to the police." I was, frankly, astonished.

"I never guess," Mr. Holmes admonished me. He chuckled. "And I must say that I was quite charmed by your simple subterfuge."

I thought the subterfuge was quite ingenious, myself, but I did not see any profit in arguing about it with Mr. Holmes.

"Besides," Mr. Holmes continued, "there is always time to bring in the police. My main concern this morning was the return of the money."

"I don't—" I began.

Mr. Holmes interrupted me with a raised hand. "You have only the vaguest notion where it is. So you said. And it is true that a man in your position at a house such as Morehouse & Co. is not often a criminal type. I suspect that you were forced by extreme circumstances of some nature to steal from your employer. I brought you here because I am curious to hear the details of your story."

"Very well, then," I said. And as the sun rose toward noon and shadows crept across Mr. Holmes's Baker Street flat, I told him the story of Mr. Harvey Maynard as I'd heard it from Alice, holding nothing back. If Mr. Holmes was going to trust me a little, then I must trust him in return.

Mr. Holmes listened while he puffed his pipe, occasionally asking a question to clarify matters. Frequently I could see no reason for his question, but I always did my best to answer it. Perhaps he could find the money Alice had stolen, or even Mr. Harvey Maynard himself.

When I finished Mr. Holmes puffed for a few minutes more, apparently lost in one of his famous thoughtful funks. At last he spoke. "Your wife is a victim of the worst sort of small-time crook," he remarked. "And your only crime, Mr. Phillimore, is not allowing the police to suffer the embarrassment of arresting an innocent man."

I was overjoyed by Mr. Holmes's words. "You would have no objection, then, to bringing this small-time crook, Mr. Harvey Maynard, to justice?" I asked.

"None whatsoever. And I believe we may also expect to recover the money—or a good portion of it at any rate. As a matter of fact, I have already begun my investigations along those very lines."

"Your close scrutiny of my entryway?" I suggested.

"Very good, Mr. Phillimore. I believe you to be as apt a pupil as Watson, himself!"

I didn't know whether to be complimented by the comparison to Dr. Watson, or insulted by Mr. Holmes's tone.

While I was still puzzling this out, Mr. Holmes pulled a handkerchief from his pocket and unfolded it before me on a small table. "Here," he said, inviting me to look at the handkerchief more closely, "what do you make of this?"

There was a small yellow grain of something in the center of the cloth. I looked at it closely, holding my breath so has not to disturb it. "What is it?" I asked.

"It is," he said, "a single mote of sawdust. If you inhale gently of its aroma, you will no doubt notice, as I did, the stale odor of swipes."

I detected no odor of any kind, certainly not of cheap beer, but undoubtedly Mr. Holmes was correct. "Hm," was all I said.

"Since I would not presume to believe that you or anyone else in your house is in the habit of patronizing low public houses I feel safe in suggesting that this bit of sawdust was left behind by our friend, Mr. Harvey Maynard."

"Perhaps," I said cautiously. "But there must be hundreds, even thousands of such establishments in the city."

"Quite right," Mr. Holmes said. "However, I believe we can separate the wheat from the chaff." From a convenient shelf he pulled down *G. W. Bacon's New Large-Scale Ordnance Map of London & Suburbs*. Mr. Holmes opened the book and I saw that nearly every page was annotated with handwritten notes. After briefly flipping through the tome, Mr. Holmes found the page he wanted and he sighed with satisfaction.

"Here we are," he said. "You remarked that when Mr. Maynard left your house the one time you two met he passed a brace of unengaged cabs instead of hiring one of them."

"That's right. Is this fact significant?"

"It is. But only because Mr. Maynard's actions may tell us in which establishment he picked up this speck of sawdust."

I thought for a moment. "Of course," I cried. "The place must be very near my house—walking distance, you might say."

"Elementary, my dear Phillimore. Let us consult Mr. Bacon's estimable book."

We bent over the volume and Mr. Holmes ran one thin finger along the streets of St. Marylebone, stopping now and then to read a notation he'd made in his spidery hand. "Here," he soon said as he thumped the book with his peripatetic finger, "in this alley just off East Street is a low place rejoicing in the name of The Twin Lambs."

"I am astonished to hear of such an establishment near enough that we may walk there."

"Indeed," Mr. Holmes said. "It lies in a small infected abscess in the healthy tissue of our fair borough. We are fortunate there are not more commercial hotels like it in our neighborhood, not least because we would have to search all of them until we found Mr. Harvey Maynard. As things have fallen out, I am fairly certain that we will find our culprit here." He closed the book and returned it to its shelf. "Now," he said. "It is nearly noon; and though a man such as Harvey Maynard may start drinking in the morning, he will certainly still be at it in the afternoon. I believe we have time for breakfast, which I, at any rate, have not yet eaten. Would you care to join me?"

"Feeling, as I do, that the situation is now well in hand, I would be delighted."

"Then I will ring for Mrs. Hudson."

We finished our breakfast and prepared for our adventure. Mr. Holmes pocketed a pistol, and he insisted that I carry one of Dr. Watson's. "Though," he admitted, "I do not believe we will have occasion to use them."

I nodded, hoping he was correct.

"Very well, then, Mr. Phillimore. Come along. 'The game's afoot!' "

Mr. Holmes ushered me from the room and out to the street, where he walked along the sidewalk so briskly I had difficulty keeping up. Our breath plumed in the early spring air. I admit that excitement and fear mixed in my breast. I certainly wanted to bring Harvey Maynard to justice, so I felt as if I was on a virtuous mission, but I also knew my own shortcomings. My dealings with criminals and other violent types were limited to reading about them in the *Times*. How would I react when confronted with Mr. Maynard again? I had no idea. I attempted to keep the face of my dear Alice forefront in my memory. It was for her that I was doing this.

We turned up Paddington Street, along which we proceeded a short way to East Street. Almost immediately we strode into a much smaller street, nearly an alley, which made a sharp angle as it turned away from the street we'd just left. We now stood at the head of a quarter that was, as Mr. Holmes had described it earlier, indeed "a small infected abscess in the healthy tissue of our fair borough." Ramshackle houses stood cheek by jowl, interspersed with commercial establishments of increasingly forlorn aspect. How such a place might exist so close to the more refined atmosphere of Baker Street, I have no idea. I leave that question to the city planners. I do know this: Except for the errand on which we were employed I would have been pleased to return to the high street that was still only a few steps away.

"Just along here, I think," Mr. Holmes said as we walked along being eyed by poor street mongers and disheveled loafers. Much sooner than I would have liked, Mr. Holmes and I stood before a dilapidated commercial hotel with a dirty sign hanging over the door proclaiming it to be The Twin Lambs.

"Come along, Mr. Phillimore," Mr. Holmes said brightly, as if we were about to stroll through St. James Park. He took my arm, and together we entered the establishment.

The pub was a low dark place, though somewhat quieter than I would have expected. What clientele there was appeared no better than it should have been. I was frankly contemptuous of any man who hung about a pub at this early hour, for it was just after noon. The air was redolent of tobacco smoke and cheap spirits, an odor I fancy I would have recognized from the single mote of sawdust left in my entryway by Mr. Harvey Maynard had I actually been able to detect it. Being in such a place made me quite nervous—a feeling obviously not shared by my companion.

Baleful eyes watched as we approached an empty table and sat down. The tabletop was sticky with previous libations, adding disgust to my nervousness. Still, the hope that we would find Harvey Maynard here forced me to ignore my discomfort.

A waiter appeared, growled at us, took our order from Holmes, and went away.

"Are you sure we are in the right place?" I asked.

"I assure you there is no other like it anywhere nearby."

I nodded. My confidence in Mr. Holmes was absolute.

"Do you see him?" Holmes asked.

"I did not see him as we entered. He may be one of the men sitting in that dim corner."

Holmes nodded. "Then we wait," he said.

Time passed. The waiter brought two mugs of foul-smelling swipes, which I sipped at for appearances' sake. Holmes allowed his drink to sit before him untouched.

My eyes adjusted to the light in the pub, and I knew that not one of the men in corner was Harvey Maynard. I reported this fact to Holmes. He nodded.

Men came, drank down their drinks, wiped their mouths with the backs of their sleeves, and went out again. Other men stayed, seemingly as much a part of the décor as the furniture.

Suddenly, a man exploded through the closed door at the back of the room, sending large splinters of wood in all directions. The man could not get his balance, and he reeled backward onto a table, which collapsed beneath him with a loud crash. The men who'd been sitting at the table dived for cover. Immediately another man emerged from the back room, leaped upon the first man, and began to pummel him about the head and body. But the man on the floor gave as good as he got.

"That's him," I told Holmes excitedly. "The man who flew through the door first is Harvey Maynard." I stood up, preparatory to grabbing Maynard, but Holmes rested his hand on my arm and shook his head.

One of the men who had been at the table pulled Maynard's attacker off and began to punch him. Then another man began to punch *him*. Soon the entire room was involved in furious fighting. Holmes and I backed toward the door.

Maynard pulled a knife from somewhere about his person and brandished it at the man who had attacked him first. Suddenly, a shot was fired, by whom I cannot say. It could have been fired by any of a dozen rough, hulking men who were still in the room.

Everyone froze. Only Harvey Maynard moved. He crumpled to the floor, obviously mortally wounded. We heard a police whistle and then heavy running. The men who had been drinking so calmly earlier shoved past us, hurriedly leaving the room, no doubt fearing to be discovered in such a place at such a time.

I wished to follow them but Mr. Holmes set his hand upon my arm. "Wait," he said. Against every instinct in my body I waited. Soon the room was empty but for us and the Mr. Maynard, who lay silent and still on the worn dirty floor. Blood spread onto the sawdust that had been so helpful to us. Holmes quickly approached him and with a skill born of long practice, he quickly went through the man's pockets.

"Ah," Holmes said as he extracted a packet from Maynard's inside coat pocket. Inside the packet was a sheaf of ten-pound notes. The money Alice had stolen—it had to be! I was delighted. Holmes glanced at me meaningfully and pushed the packet into his own coat pocket. In one graceful motion he got to his feet and pulled me toward the door. We went outside and rushed into a mews across the way. From there we watched policemen swarm into The Twin Lambs at a gallop.

"Someone shot Maynard," I exclaimed.

"Indeed," Holmes remarked quietly. "I believe I will leave the solution of this crime to the police. The death of a cur does not much concern me."

I looked at him, shocked. Though I certainly had no love for Harvey Maynard, the attitude of Mr. Holmes was something of a surprise. But upon reflection, even at that moment, I knew my Alice and I had been visited by a merciful Providence. Mr. Holmes would return the money—all that Maynard had not already spent—to Morehouse & Co., thus bringing another of his cases to a successful conclusion. Morehouse & Co. would graciously accept the money it had lost, though no one there might ever learn the truth of why and how it was stolen. And perhaps most importantly, Alice and I were now free from the depredations of Harvey Maynard.

Holmes and I returned to his rooms, where he quickly arranged my journey to Kent to meet my wife, and from there to a ship that would soon be sailing for the United States of America. Our final destination would be San Francisco.

"I must ask you and your wife never to return to England," Holmes warned. "I ask you this as much for my sake as for your own: the police are certain to take a dim view of some of the activities performed by the three of us."

I nodded. "I cannot thank you enough for your kindness," I said as I shook his hand.

"My blushes," Holmes said, and lowered his eyes.

Wiggins, Leader of the Baker Street Irregulars

"What on earth is this?" I cried, for at this moment there came the pattering of many steps in the hall and on the stairs, accompanied by audible expressions of disgust upon the part of our landlady.

"It's the Baker Street division of the detective police force," said my companion gravely; and as he spoke there rushed into the room half a dozen of the dirtiest and most ragged street Arabs that ever I clapped eyes on.

" 'Tention!" cried Holmes, in a sharp tone, and the six dirty little scoundrels stood in a line like so many disreputable statuettes. "In future you shall send up Wiggins alone to report, and the rest of you must wait in the street. Have you found it, Wiggins?"

"No, sir, we hain't," said one of the youths.

"I hardly expected you would. You must keep on until you do. Here are your wages." He handed each of them a shilling. "Now, off you go, and come back with a better report next time."

He waved his hand, and they scampered away downstairs like so many rats, and we heard their shrill voices next moment in the street.

"There's more work to be got out of one of those little beggars than out of a dozen of the force," Holmes remarked.

—*A Study in Scarlet*

by NORMAN SCHREIBER

Call Me Wiggins

Call me Wiggins. It's how my most intimate friends address me—with the sole exception of Mr. Sherlock Holmes. He calls me "young fellow," "young man," and on certain occasions, the import of which escapes me, "Mr. Wiggins." All of these sound better to my ears than his customary description of me in the old days as his "dirty little lieutenant." That's when I was leader of that group of street urchins that Mr. Holmes was pleased to call his Baker Street Irregulars.

And yes, I do count Mr. Holmes among my friends and, if it's not too boastful to add, I know things about him that nobody else knows. Things, I believe, that his proud nature would not allow him to reveal. For example, the man is a philanthropist. Yes, he is! He created what he is pleased to call "the Wiggins Fund" and pulled me out of the gutter. I am not ashamed to say that I am a child of the streets—brought up "on the stones," as we say. Mr. Holmes has advised me to mention this rarely if at all. But it is God's truth. He contrived to alter my life—for which I am mostly grateful.

Mr. Holmes and I first encountered each other when he had just set himself up as a consulting detective. I knew right away that he was going places. I was eleven years old at the time; but I, too, was going places. And were it not for Mr. Holmes I might be in one of those places even now. My mates and I did favors—errands and the like—for various folks. We were the best and fastest at fetching beer. And if you needed someone to hold your horses while you tended to business we were the Arabs for the job. It beat crawling up chimneys for a pittance and having nothing to show for it but a coating of soot and a cough that lingered for the rest of your life. And when no moneys were to be earned we were not too picky. We might grab an apple off a pushcart or a sneezer—that's a handkerchief to you—or whatever from some geezer's pocket. Always a few pennies to be made from the contents of someone else's pocket.

The police—or at least the more intelligent members amongst that whole sorry lot—would journey to the now famous flat at 221B Baker Street for advice. Mr. Holmes, in turn, occasionally called upon the services of me and my comrades. So you might say that I was the consulting detective's consulting detective. He was generous with his gratuities. More impressively, he was fair. He employed us to be his eyes and ears. He said nobody would ever suspect waifs of being spies. I didn't fancy being called a spy. That's almost as bad as being thought a snitch. But I liked the feel of his money in my palm and the work was exciting. And in our ways we were helping people. That was good, too.

Not too many people know about the Wiggins Fund—in part because there's not really any such thing and in part because I'm the sole recipient. It happened when I already was quite advanced in years. I was at least twelve years old, possibly thirteen. I had just finished furnishing him with my latest findings in his behalf. He was sitting in that great chair of his. He scarcely seemed to be listening to me. His eyes were half-closed. What little energy he exerted seemed to spend itself on the task of throwing up great clouds of pipe smoke over his head, as if a tidy little storm were brewing.

I completed my spirited recitation about the comings and comings of a sneaky bloke and there was silence. There was not even the usual, "Well done, Wiggins," which was the kindest appellation he affixed in those days. Suddenly he rose from his chair, scattering ashes onto the floor; opened his eyes wide and stared straight into my eyes.

"If I," he said intensely, "were to give you and the boys three guineas for a month's work, how many shillings would that be?"

"First of all, sir," I said, "that would probably be shortchanging us by at least two guineas, based on the amount of commerce we do with each other." And then I added, "If you don't mind my saying so, sir."

"Answer my question," he snapped.

"I don't like the direction of this conversation, is all," I said.

"We're not talking about your income," he said. "I'm just trying to solve a problem."

Well, that was different. He excelled at the knack of talking about one topic while you were certain it was another.

"Three guineas," I said, "is sixty-three shillings."

"And twenty guineas?"

"Four hundred and twenty shillings," I shot back.

"Recite a line from Shakespeare," he said.

"Oh Romeo," I said, in a falsetto, while flailing my arms about, "Wherefore are thou, oh Romeo?"

"Where did you learn that?" he asked.

"Oh, everybody knows that one," I said.

"What does it mean?" he asked.

"Wherefore art Romeo," I tentatively offered.

"In your own words," he barked.

"I guess she's inquiring—"

"She?" roared Holmes. "Who is she?"

"Juliet," I whispered.

"Yes, go on."

"Juliet is inquiring into the whereabouts of Romeo."

" 'Wherefore' means 'why,' " Holmes barked, "not 'where.' "

"It does?"

"Yes, it does."

"Oh, then she's asking why Romeo is—is what?"

"Why Romeo is Romeo."

"Why he's named Romeo? Well, I guess that's a good question. It's a dumb name, ain't it?"

Holmes shook his head. "Young man," he said, "you're as sharp as a pin, but you're sadly in need of an education."

And he persisted.

"Now then," he asked, "why does Juliet care to know anything about Romeo?"

"Well, he's her bloke, ain't he?"

"That's good enough for me," Holmes said.

I smiled in relief, not really knowing what I was smiling at.

"You're capable of better things, young man," he said. "We're going to give you an education."

"Education." I hooted. "I've got no time for that nonsense. I've got a business to run. And besides, I can't really see myself, all fancied up like a schoolboy and sitting in a classroom."

"Who in the blazes said a word about classrooms? I said you need an education—not an incarceration," he said. "Classes come later with college."

"College," I snorted. "Me? I've got life just the way I want it. Why go muck it up with college? I go about my business. I make my rounds. I know where to get a shilling here and a shilling there. Last week it was, I got two shillings from a gentleman who needed me to hold his horses for ten minutes. Who do you know who can earn two shillings in ten minutes?"

"Let me ask you a question," said Holmes. "If you were walking down the street and you came across a half-crown coin resting, half hidden, in the filth of the gutter, what would you do?"

"I'd look about," I immediately responded, "to make sure it was not a joke because I hate to be made a fool of."

"And if it were not a joke?"

"I'd snatch it up right quick."

"Why," he asked.

"If you see something of value in the gutter," I said, "you can't just leave it there."

"Even if it's awash in mud and grime?"

"You clean it off," I said, "and then you get good use out of it."

"You are that coin, young man," said Holmes, "and you're due for a good cleaning and an education. Otherwise you will remain in the gutter and have no opportunity for improvement."

I didn't like being tricked by my own words and I stormed out. I walked around London trying to calm down. It didn't work. His words made me take notice of what was all around me: chaps who were five, ten, or even fifteen years my elder who were, to put as good a face on it as possible, faring poorly. They were no longer swift enough to run errands. They were hobbled by alcohol and atrocious injuries. They were sleeping under bridges and in railway arches. The more industrious of them concocted the vilest of appearances, the better to beg with. I had seen these scenes thousands of times and laughed at them. Thanks to Mr. Holmes, on this particular promenade I felt as if I were seeing my future.

I returned to 221B Baker Street the following day and announced my willingness to be educated. He smiled and assured me that it would not hurt much. His notions of how to educate me were as unorthodox as that brief academic examination he inflicted upon me that day that was so significant. He taught me the essentials of the disciplines in which he was well-versed. As Dr. Watson has pointed out, there is much Mr. Holmes did not know or care to know. To my new tutor's credit, he recognized that a great many fields of knowledge might serve me even if they were irrelevant to him. He engaged other tutors to school me. Apparently he solicited donations from a select few souls to pay for any and all expenses. This is what we call the Wiggins Fund.

I was given a thorough grounding in the classics. He made sure that I learned proper language and manners. He warned me never to speak in my own natural way. He said that the English were of such a peculiar nature that, despite my virtues and all that I may have attained, I would be shunned if my speech betrayed my origins. We've all got to come from somewhere and I'm not ashamed of any of it. But I was not going to put all this work in and then lose everything just because of some silly prejudice about aitches, for example.

To my surprise, I took to this new regime rather well. I discovered that much of what they call education is similar to how we navigate our lives on the street—except education frowns on the more colorful language with which we seasoned our speech. We take the facts in as we see them and use them to formulate ideas and actions—whether those ideas are about the best way to live a good life or the best way to secure the best errands. The process by which we think and act is the same. That was both depressing and reassuring.

I was admitted to Christ Church, Oxford, at the age of seventeen. I never questioned how I was able to matriculate there. I know I displayed some merit. I also know that it did not hurt to have Mr. Holmes as a champion. More than anything else I wanted to sit in a lecture where Dr. Charles Lutwidge Dodgson, whom some may know as Lewis Carroll, stood at the podium and talked about the wonders of mathematics. Unfortunately, Dodgson no longer cared to be a lecturer and had retired from the activity. He did, however, continue to give classes in logic to some lucky few, mostly high school girls. I managed to wheedle myself into a private class he conducted in the house, which is what we call Christ Church College. I had not lost my ability or instinct for doing errands and services and, quite frankly, I had ingratiated myself with Dr. Dodgson.

I took it upon myself a few years ago to introduce Holmes to Dodgson. My motive was simple. I wanted to be present at what had every promise of being the most dazzling discourse between two of our civilization's most prominent logicians.

I suppose I also wanted to show Mr. Holmes that I was moving in respectable circles, not as a mere boastful moment but rather a tribute to Mr. Holmes himself. It was he that transformed me from a street urchin into an educated man with prospects. He did it by revealing to me the world of letters and learning and he gave me a bit of artifice that would help me in the variety of social and professional situations. Thanks to his help and that of those anonymous donors, I had the wherewithal to advance to and study at Oxford. I did not know where my education would take me. Holmes made no secret of his belief that I would be a splendid consulting detective. Dodgson told me the great satisfaction that comes to he who devotes his life to the intricacies of mathematics.

I took the precaution of warning them that, disparate souls as they were, they might not like each other. I was little prepared for the result of my warning. The historic meeting took place at what Dodgson referred to as his "house," a suite of ten rooms in stairway seven of Tom Quad at Christ Church College. Its previous occupant had been Lord Bute. While Dodgson proudly made mention of his abode's noble pedigree, he was quick to point out that neither the rank nor the title had been transferred to him.

"There is no way I could be mistaken for a member of the peerage," he said with a certain degree of rue, brightly adding, "but at least it gives me the opportunity to bask in the company of similarly afflicted souls, such as yourselves."

The three of us sat at a large roomy table in his study, a chamber that always comforted and delighted all who had the good fortune to enjoy its hospitality. It was rumored that such occasions tended to be infrequent except for a rare invitation to a favored student, the visit of some noteworthy individual to the grounds of Christ Church or children under the age of ten.

Reverend Dodgson's willingness to meet with Mr. Holmes surprised me. The don possessed an extremely shy nature. Some even said he was a recluse who rarely ventured forth, except to deliver a lecture, a very occasional sermon, or to go for one of his brisk walks. I thought this to be an exaggeration.

Dodgson prepared the tea in a precise, if not eccentric, manner. As was his long-standing custom, he held the pot firmly and paced back and forth while tilting the pot first to the left and then to the right. I had time to admire the three-globed chandelier overhead, which illuminated the room with a brilliance and a warmth that, I fancied, were exceeded only by the humble genius's warmth and demeanor. I looked beyond Mr. Holmes toward the great window and its view of St. Aldate's, framed by solid curtains. On the sill was a great pile of books and monographs. To the right of the window was the noted famous Dodgson bookcase, neatly laden with all sorts of arcane treasures. To my right was the deep fireplace with its ample mantel on which rested a few ornate jars and vases. Reverend Dodgson ceased his determined parading when exactly ten minutes had elapsed and he joined us at the table.

Dodgson held up the ornate teapot and asked, "Shall I be mother?"

Holmes and I nodded, and Dr. Dodgson poured tea for each of us.

We sipped of the bracing, steeped elixir and smiled at each other. After a discreet pause, Professor Dodgson asked, "And what do you do, Holmes?"

Mr. Holmes seemed surprised by the good professor's apparent ignorance of his exploits.

"I play the violin," replied Mr. Holmes, "and as an avocation I fight the forces of evil."

"Quite a responsibility," said Dodgson.

"I suppose," said Mr. Holmes.

"After all, Bach's airs should not be fiddled with by just anyone; else Bach's heirs will be most vexed."

Mr. Holmes smiled a tight smile. Dodgson, on the other hand, warmly recommended the raspberry jam. Mr. Holmes dutifully spread the fragrant fruit compound across his biscuit.

"And," continued Dodgson, "Just how do you wage war against evil?"

"I assist my patrons, according to their needs and according to my own curiosity. I find innocent people who have been abducted. I apprehend perpetrators of fiendish crimes and see to it that they are sent to gaol where they belong."

"Ahh," said Dodgson, "you are a magician."

"Nothing of the sort," said Mr. Holmes. "My weapon is not magic but pure logic."

"People vanish and you make them materialize. You seek other people and make them vanish."

"You have a refreshing, and most unusual definition of magic," snapped Mr. Holmes.

"Just how are you faring in your war against evil?"

"I have had my share of triumphs," replied Mr. Holmes.

"What joy," said Dodgson. "Please allow me to thank you on behalf of Christendom. I know I shall sleep better tonight."

Mr. Holmes leaned forward and tapped his finger upon the table. "If you only knew how bitter the battle and resourceful the enemy, you would never dare close your eyes to sleep again, sir!"

"I do have some notion of the battle, sir; but if it weren't for sleep and the visitation of dreams, we would be bereft of ideas. More tea?"

"No, thank you," said Mr. Holmes. "I read your defense of Euclid. It seemed to be a most appropriate use of your special talent.

"Thank you."

"And are you still writing those little entertainments for the kiddies?"

"Yes," said Dodgson, "we mustn't all be scaring the children. Now, must we?"

"Why should children be spared knowledge of reality?" asked Mr. Holmes. "How does that prepare them for the responsibilities of maturity?"

"I have noticed that the people who so assuredly use the word 'maturity' are better at pronouncing it than exemplifying it. What do you think?"

"I think," said Mr. Holmes, daubing at his lips with the linen napkin and rising from his chair, "that I have urgent business elsewhere."

I was stunned.

Mr. Holmes fixed his intense eyes on me and softly said, "Well, young man, are you returning to London with me or shall you waste the afternoon by drinking tea and pretending to find virtue in the idle science of pure mathematics?"

I looked at Mr. Holmes and then at Dodgson. Each was staring at me, waiting to see whose company I would prefer for that afternoon and, it might be, forever after. Each, in his own way, has been a benefactor. Each in his own way has been a teacher. They were treating me like the stray dog that I am—a dog that must show love and obedience to one or another master.

Mr. Holmes's lip actually began to curl, not as I was prepared to expect, in contempt, but in laughter. And Dodgson, dear, sweet, shy, humble Dodgson permitted himself the barest outline of a smile.

"Well done, Reverend," said Mr. Holmes.

"The stage lost a fine actor, Mr. Holmes," said Dodgson, "when you chose to fight the forces of evil. Of course, there are those who choose to think of the stage, itself, as evil; but we can discount those poor, misguided wretches."

My shocked mien apparently changed to bafflement.

"Good God, my young friend," said Holmes. "How could you possibly believe that two such Englishmen as Reverend Dodgson and I could not find, each in the other, a worthwhile and appropriate companion? I must admit it was quite flattering to be thought of as the good don's peer."

"I meant no harm," I offered.

"Of course not," said Mr. Holmes. "And to be perfectly frank, your little foray into matchmaking pleased Reverend Dodgson and I no end, and so we decided to perform this little dramatic sketch as a thank-you."

I was scarcely in the mood to say "you're welcome," although to have two such esteemed and accomplished fellows stage a little performance especially for me did charm me in some uncharted and probably dangerous area of my psyche.

"And," added Mr. Holmes, "we derived a special pleasure from your desire to introduce us because Reverend Dodgson is one of the small band of people who have come together at my urging to help you make your way in the world."

My face reddened. I am grateful for the kindness shown to me by Mr. Holmes and, as I learned on that day Professor Dodgson, and those others whose identities were unknown to me. But I do not like the cloak of deception that forever covers me. I do not like knowing of my fraud.

Sensing my thoughts, Holmes said, "Be of good cheer, young fellow. All of us harbor secrets, some nastier than yours."

"We all are sinners," agreed Dodgson. "In my prayers, I constantly ask God to give me a new life."

"You?" I asked in disbelief.

"Does he?" asked Mr. Holmes.

"In his own mysterious manner," Dodgson sighed, "I suppose that he does. Each sunrise is an opportunity to find and walk on the righteous path with His blessing. But by the time the sun has set, we have already contrived to grasp the temptations that we had hoped to renounce."

"You lead an exemplary life, sir," I interjected.

"Only in deed," he said. "Only in deed."

"My good Reverend," said Mr. Holmes, "you are hobbled by your knowledge of God's word. We, on the other hand, are saved by our comparative ignorance. I do know, however, about the God of justice and he will not find you wanting."

Dodgson sighed again, and said, "And I in turn hope that when I arrive at the Pearly Gates for judgment, you will be there to plead my case."

"If it's not too much of a bother," said Mr. Holmes, "I prefer not to precede you on such a journey."

Dodgson refilled our teacups and said, "Actually one reason I encouraged our young friend to arrange this meeting is because of a little problem I have. I might be in need of your services, Holmes."

The great detective wiped his lips with a napkin and casually reached into his pocket for his pipe.

"Please don't smoke," said Dodgson curtly. "You know I hate smoking."

"Quite right," said Mr. Holmes, and replaced the faithful stained calabash. "Please tell me more."

"I," Dodgson began, "have been—" And here he paused—not for dramatic effect but as a victim of the stammer that had plagued him all of his life.

We looked at him expectantly. Finally the words came.

"Stung! I have been—stung. I need you to use those magical powers about which we had such a good laugh to make my good name reappear."

"My dear fellow," said Holmes, "I am hardly the scourge of gossipmongers."

"Nor do I ask your help in such a pursuit. Let me just state it flat out. Four of my diaries are missing. They cover the years 1858 to 1862. They are private musings, my daily thoughts. By reviewing the entries I am helped in striving for redemption. I fear that someone has stolen them for the purpose of profiting from the dissemination of those matters in my life which I prefer to keep hidden. I don't know what to do. I couldn't bear the thought of the whole world sharing my secrets."

"I see," said Mr. Holmes. "I shall have to ask you a few questions."

"I had better excuse myself," I said.

"No," snapped Mr. Holmes.

Both Dodgson and I looked at him in bewilderment.

"Mr. Wiggins shall stay with us and hear your entire discourse on these troubling events," said Mr. Holmes. "I have need of his assistance and he is someone we both can trust. Are we agreed?"

Dodgson nodded and so did I.

"Now then," said Mr. Holmes, "tell me about these diaries and the circumstances surrounding their disappearance."

"It has been my custom to maintain a diary in which I record thoughts, feelings, ideas, beliefs, activities, and other such items of personal interest that I may wish to consult at some future date. It is not uncommon to maintain such a document. It is my companion, confessor, mirror and yardstick. Others may use a diary to engage in small talk with themselves, or to express what if spoken would have them expelled from polite society. I, too, use my diaries for certain practical matters—to make note of the publication and date of notices about my works, to log the names of visitors or people to whom I've journeyed and the particulars of the pastime, to note payments for expenses I have incurred, and so on. But I also evaluate my efforts to serve God's purpose. In that regard, my diary is a document of my frailties and temptations—and, yes, my prayers."

"If they were unearthed," Mr. Holmes said carefully, "would they contain any entries that would get you in trouble with the law?"

"Some fates are worse than 'trouble with the law,' " said Dodgson.

"Perhaps, and we'll get to those considerations in due time," said Mr. Holmes. "But let us proceed deliberately. If the perpetrator of this assault on your property were brought to trial, could his barrister harm you by reading excerpts from your diary?"

Dodgson blanched. "Is that sort of thing done?" he asked.

"Yes," said Mr. Holmes. "The clear logic of the law holds that stealing is stealing. And punishment is meted out to the evil who prey upon the innocent. But when you have law, you have lawyers—creatures no doubt not contemplated when the Almighty was devising His plan to which you had just referred. Lawyers earn their keep by introducing as evidence any froufrou that would distract a judge and jury from the contemplation of the demands of justice. In a court of law, there certainly could be a solemn recitation of your words as an attempt to deflect wrath away from the filthy thieves and toward you. It's not right, but there you are."

"I'd be mortified. I'd be ruined. Perhaps you should not perform this favor."

"Consider the consequences," said Mr. Holmes, "if no effort is made to retrieve the precious journals."

Dodgson looked into the fireplace and seemed to be peering into his own personal hell.

"Isn't this a pretty puzzle," he said. "I can embark on the rescue of my own rightful property and thereby create the legal contraption that will ruin me; or I can let sleeping dogs lie with the grim knowledge that they will awaken some day and cruelly rip whatever remains of my reputation to shreds. One path leads to ruin whereas the other path leads to ruin."

"It's a shame," I cut in, "that you didn't burn the diaries."

Dodgson's gray eyes flickered with anger and sorrow. Mr. Holmes shot me a sharper look. Apparently I was to be seen and not heard.

"I'm sorry," I said, "I thought I was part of this."

"And, indeed you are," said Holmes. "Be assured that I will advise you of the moment when your talents are to be of use. Until then, please reward us with your patience—and your silence."

I could not help but marvel at the splendid company in which I found myself. In the old days someone simply would have told me to shut me mush.

"How could I burn them?" asked Dodgson. "They are my life, my solace and perhaps even my instrument of salvation."

"There is a third possibility," Mr. Holmes said. "Although I assist the police, I am not, nor would I care to be, an agent of the law. This allows me to provide discretion when appropriate. I would be proud to do that for you."

Dodgson flashed a pathetic smile, and said, "Thank you, Mr. Holmes, I would be most grateful if you were to continue in this matter."

"I do not care to know the particulars of your diaries. And I am sure Mr. Wiggins shares my feelings."

I soberly nodded in agreement, hoping that my face did not betray my rampant curiosity.

"However," Mr. Holmes continued, "we do need to know what the diaries look like."

"Excuse me for a moment," said Dodgson, and he rose from the table. He walked purposefully over to the bookcase, reached to the topmost shelf his hand could extend, and secured a black leather-bound volume of a size and thickness that made it identical to the remaining books on that very shelf as well as those on the shelf below.

"My mind has always been awash with ideas for stories and songs and poems and games and mathematical problems," said Dodgson, as he returned to the table. "And I suppose I wanted some convenient repository for the fragmentary ideas that I was too busy to get to. And perhaps I was a bit full of myself, thinking that the stray musings of a young man were worth logging. Anyway I started this one while I was staying at the Residence of Ripon Cathedral, where my father served as canon."

He opened the diary and read aloud, "One January 1855. Tried a little Mathematics unsuccessfully. Sketched a design for illumination in the title page of Mary's Book of Sacred Poetry. Handbells in the evening. A tedious performance."

He snapped the book shut, and sonorously proclaimed, "Thus wrote Dodgson."

"That hardly seems the stuff of scandal," said Mr. Holmes.

"No," said Dodgson, "and to answer your previous question, nothing of a criminal nature appears in my journals. I have performed no acts forbidden by law or by our Creator. That is not testament to my rectitude or discipline but rather my abject fear of breaking the commandments of God."

"We know that," said Mr. Holmes.

"Nevertheless, people gossip about me," said Dodgson. "They tsk-tsk at the thought of the hospitality I extend my child friends. They whisper about the married women who have journeyed here for picnics and dinners and such. They depict me as a naive old man with puzzles in his pocket and a hopelessly childish sense of the world. Good grief, Holmes! My parents brought eleven children into this world. There was no shelter for naiveté in my father's house. It was too small.

"Others paint me as a cunning rascal who enjoys the blessings of marriage without the sanction of marriage. My targets are said to be my female friends whose ages range from five to forty. I do love female company but I have not compromised anyone.

"I believe that to despise fame is to despise merit; but there is another side to the coin. People who do not know me feel they have license to concoct and spread stories about me. My good sister, Mary Lutwidge Collingwood, even posted me a letter about all of this gossip. I told her, 'You need not be shocked at my being spoken against. Anybody who is spoken about at all is sure to be spoken against by somebody; and any action, however innocent in itself, is liable, and not at all unlikely, to be blamed by somebody. If you limit your actions in life to things that nobody can possibly find fault with, you will not do much.' "

"A noble sentiment, indeed," said Mr. Holmes.

"Gossip is transient," said Dodgson. "But the written word remains. And the words I have written into my diaries about my reflections must not remain. My diaries describe not only what I did and said but what I thought and dreamed and of course what I prayed. I do believe that my candor on these pages helped spare me from actually taking the path that I saw in my visions. That and keeping very busy."

"At least," said Mr. Holmes, "you are spared the indignity of having a certain doctor spread the news of your most private habits to the world."

"How convenient it must be to have a doctor at your beck and call," said Dodgson. "Only one medicine helps me. I think that the more one feels one's own sin, and the wonderful goodness of God who will forgive so much, the more one longs to help others to escape the shame and misery one has brought on oneself."

"That may be," said Mr. Holmes. "I do not traffic in such thoughts. But I know that this young fellow and I will help you to escape the snares of others.

"Now, then," he continued, "when were the books taken from you?"

"About two months ago I had a thought about a word game I could devise that could teach children about logic," said Dodgson. "It reminded me of a notation for a game I made back then which I thought might assist me in this new diversion. I never finished that first game because writing about Alice consumed so much of my spare time. I went to this very book-case and it was gone, along with three of its companions."

"And," asked Holmes, "when was the last time you consulted that diary."

"I have no idea. It's been years and years."

"Who else knows about these diaries?" asked Mr. Holmes.

"Nobody," declared Dodgson. "Absolutely nobody!"

"Without being impertinent," said Mr. Holmes, "I would venture to guess that somebody does."

"Lots of people keep diaries," said Dodgson, "but I have never made any special point about them. I never discuss them. They are never in view when anyone visits with me. Nothing about their appearance invites interest. They are just dull, black books on a shelf in an aging lecturer's bookcase."

"Was anything else taken?" asked Holmes. "Any other book, an art object or trinket or some other private possession?"

"Nothing," said Dodgson.

"You are quite sure?"

"As you know," said Dodgson, "it is my habit to make lists of every-thing. I gathered my various inventories and proceeded to check. I thought of you as I proceeded. I thought you would be proud of my thoroughness and foresight. Nothing else was missing."

"I am honored by your thoughts," said Holmes. "Have you received any communications from the thief?"

"I have not," said Dodgson.

"No threats to make the contents public unless you pay a ransom or perform a service or cease from some real or imagined action."

"No," said the shocked Dodgson, "but I live in fear that a message of that sort will come to me."

"Let's see what facts we have assembled," said Mr. Holmes. "Four diaries have been taken from your bookcase. The thief took only these and nothing else, so clearly that was his purpose. The crime occurred somewhere between two months and 'years and years ago.' You've received no menacing letters or demands for money. So we do not have a motive and without a motive our search for suspects can take us anywhere."

"Prospects do not seem promising," said Dodgson.

"On the contrary, my dear Dodgson," said Holmes, "this shall be one of my easier adventures."

"It cheers me to hear that," said Dodgson, "but I don't see how that can be."

"It's simple," said Holmes. "Whoever did it is someone you know and trust. By definition, that eliminates most of the world's population."

"Most comforting," said Dodgson. "Actually, Mr. Holmes, I do feel comforted by the knowledge that you are assisting me—even if nothing comes from your labors."

"Don't worry, we shall find your diary snatcher," said Mr. Holmes. "One more thing. Would you be so kind as to furnish me with a list of people who have been in this room for years and years."

"How many years?"

"That is entirely up to you and the limits of your concentration. The more extensive the list, the greater are our chances of identifying the culprit. And do not exercise judgment. Do not exclude a name because you doubt that they could have done such a thing. Omission of the one guilty name wastes more of our time than the inclusion of a hundred innocent names. And please append to each name, a brief description of who the person is, when they might have been here, and what, if any, grounds for dispute they might have you, no matter how trivial. I will need this information tomorrow morning."

"Certainly," said Dodgson, "now that we have discussed this dreary business, you must have dinner with me in the Hall."

The thought of a good dinner cheered me.

"No," said Mr. Holmes. "This young man and I are heading to town for dinner and a room, and we will begin the hunt tomorrow."

Dodgson was crestfallen.

"There, there," said Holmes, "it scarcely would serve our enterprise to have you seen eating and drinking with a somewhat notorious consulting detective. Our young friend will appear at this door tomorrow at noon and you shall give him the list we discussed."

And so I did and so he did.

When I returned to our room in town, I ceremoniously handed the list to Mr. Holmes. He weighed it in his hand as if to judge its merit and glanced at the top page, which simply bore the title, "List of Visitors to Dodgson House at Tom Quad as Requested by Holmes and Wiggins."

Dodgson's list was fourteen pages long. With meticulous longhand he enumerated all who had entered his apartment. In addition to their names, the don added date, nature of visit, station in life, the duration of their stay, and any notation about the disposition of the visitor toward him. Asterisks marked a goodly number of entries. These denoted visitors who made more than one appearance at Mr. Dodgson's house. Mr. Holmes pressed the lengthy document back into my hand and told me to analyze it.

I wanted no part of this tedious task.

"Mustn't you examine this yourself in order to further your investigation?" I asked, mustering the best argument I could to forestall this dreary occupation. "Especially since he went to all this trouble to prepare it in accordance with your urgings."

"I've seen Dodgson's lists before, and I have no desire to burrow through one more such compendium. Some clue does lurk in that list of names, and your industry will be most helpful in recovering it. As to the other concern, Dodgson knew I would request such a list and made sure to prepare it in advance. He then affixed a title page after we left. Notice the cover sheet is rendered with broader strokes than is used on the subsequent pages. He felt no need to conserve ink."

"Why didn't he provide it yesterday?" I asked with some indignation.

"He believes that one must not even give the appearance of presuming on the good nature others, even when they are friends, as we are."

With that, Mr. Holmes grasped the handles of his worn leather satchel, said, "I trust you to give me a full report when I return," and was out the door.

With Holmes's ominous request dangling in the room's atmosphere, I attacked the list with the same gusto usually reserved for overboiled cabbage.

I must admit that, although hardly as gripping as one of those voluminous sagas penned by M. Dumas, Dodgson's list mesmerized me. It revealed a very different wonderland from the one for which he is so justly noted. It was an almanac of credos and purpose as well as quarrels, rebukes, and misunderstandings. And oh how the man loved rules. I have noticed that some of our species need the guiding lantern of clear and well-articulated instructions for every part of daily living. I have heard that this is particularly evident in those more northern countries of the continent; but I have not been. Charles Dodgson was not simply content to know and live by the rules. He restlessly devised new prescriptions for behavior, for games, for elections, and so on. And he was quick to protect the standards he lived by, his reputation, his faith, his friends, his works, and his privacy.

Dr. Dodgson reached for his pen at the first appearance of a slight or assault. From one of the greatest thinkers in English literature came a steady river of letters and essays to right the wrongs he observed and he was ready for battle with no distinction between the pure and the petty. As a result this shy man who loved to spend his time daydreaming of puzzles and their solutions found himself constantly opening his door to people who wanted to praise him or understand why he had committed to writing a list of their failures for others to consider. And he would tell them.

Various Scouts in the employ of Christ Church came to that famous sitting room. The Scouts were responsible for assorted housecleaning duties and reported directly to the House Manager. But that did not stop Dodgson from complaining that an accidental fire in this Scout's chimney made the young man a menace to the house, or that the "dangerous effluvium" coming from beneath that Scout's room required immediate attention, and this other Scout's clumsiness caused breakage among some of Dodgson's favorite pieces of glass and china. Both the Head Chef and the Hall Manager journeyed to Dr. Dodgson's apartment when he complained about, "beefsteak almost too tough to eat, Portugal onions quite underboiled and uneatable and boiled potatoes that are always mealy."

He must have had quite a tête-à-tête with J. Barclay Thompson, reader in Anatomy. Thompson was Dodgson's match when it came to voicing objections; although Thompson did not have the charm, wit, or good manners that we associate with Dodgson. The "keeper of bones," as Dodgson referred to the man, took exception to how T. Vere Bayne served as curator of the Common Room. After vigorously defending Bayne, Dodgson was elected to succeed Bayne, an outcome that Thompson took badly.

Then there was the wine merchant who supplied the Common Room. He was summoned to Dodgson's premises and informed in no uncertain terms to stop bestowing gifts upon Dodgson and to stop pestering the curator for meetings.

Nor did Dodgson spare his family from his honesty. His nephew Stuart Collingwood went away from a visit quite vexed. ("He asked me to comment on his attempts at writing with as much frankness as I could muster," noted Dodgson. "I complied fully and faithfully. Alas, my observations and suggestions did not please him.")

Actually it was a relative few who came or left in anger. Dodgson was available to students, met with fellow faculty, entertained notable personages who were visiting Christ Church and, of course, there was his female company—mostly young women under the age of twelve, often, but not always, accompanied by a parent.

And of course there was the Liddell family. As one might expect, the members of this family had gathered, like rosebuds, the greatest quantity of asterisks. Henry George Liddell was Dean of Christ Church, and the man who made all decisions controlling Dodgson's life in the community of scholars. The Dean's daughter, Alice Liddell, is part of the legend of Lewis Carroll. A married woman by the time I met Charles Dodgson, she had been the little girl for whom he named the adorable character and to whom, along with her sisters, he first told the Wonderland stories.

In his commentary about the family on the list, Dodgson wrote the following. "Henry George Liddell, who was hell bent and I do not use the term lightly to alter the look of the house against all common sense, and has taken exception to each article I have published about the architectural vulgarities he wishes to visit upon us and who has alienated the feelings of his family toward me, the lovely Alice, the poor departed Edith, the sweet Ina, and their loving and saintly mother Lorena."

I finished my notes, and looked around the room for other amusement. Holmes had left enough reading matter. But being interested in neither the daily newspaper nor the *Dictionary of Tropical Toxins*, I looked elsewhere. Holmes had left his pipe behind. Now there was an opportunity. I always wondered how smoking a pipe would affect my appearance. I suspected it would give me a quite distinguished look. This was my chance. Finding the mirror and striking what I believed to be a pensive pose, I placed the pipe between my lips as I had seen Mr. Holmes do so many times. I tilted my head just a bit for the proper touch of authority, and nearly fainted. What a foul taste! What a wretched residue. I expelled the noxious instrument from my mouth and carefully placed it back where I had found it. Finding no other recreation, I settled into the easy chair and drifted off to sleep.

Scarcely seconds later, or so it seemed, a thunderous banging on the door awakened me. Annoyed, I flung open the door and saw a mustachioed workman standing in the portal. The impudent rascal hadn't even bothered to remove his cap.

"Yes," I demanded.

"I'm here to attend to your lamp, sir."

"There's nothing wrong with the lamp," I said.

"There must be sir," he said. "They send me to fix it and they don't generally do that if they don't have to. And besides, there's something wrong with every lamp in this fine establishment."

"We don't wish to be bothered," I said.

"That's the funny thing," the workman said. "Nobody wishes to be bothered, but when something goes wrong in the middle of the night, they don't mind bothering me. Well, I needs me sleep, too, you know."

And with that, the scoundrel stepped right past me into the room.

"And another thing," he said, "don't you know it's bad manners to smoke another man's pipe?"

The workman was Mr. Holmes, of course. He tricked me once again. I don't know how many times I've seen him in one of his masquerades. Even though it's one of his favorite tactics, and even though we continue to have odd encounters at critical junctures with a blind man or beggar or driver or old lady, he fools us. Each time I vow I will see through his disguise the next time. I should stop making such vows.

"Cold ashes filled the pipe bowl when I left," said Mr. Holmes, removing his mustache and cap, "and now it's scarcely one third filled. The stem's mouthpiece is wet and it's been hours since I've enjoyed the pipe. Anyway I've been to Dodgson's home to see how vulnerable it is to burglary."

"That's why you were disguised as a workman?" I asked.

"Please don't annoy me with extraneous questions," he said. "Of course that is why I changed my appearance. I entered the building that housed his flat with ease. I applied my various helpers to his front and service door locks; but none of my instruments could pick his locks. I went back onto the Quad and with the aid of a bucket of soapy water and a rag, I tested the locks on his windows."

"How could soapy water and a rag help you test his windows locks?" I asked.

Mr. Holmes shook his head in dismay and rolled his eyes.

"I," he said, slowly, "was posing as the window washer. He now has the cleanest windows in all Christ Church. He also should have the comfort of knowing that they are quite secure against the invasion of burglars. I shall tell him when we see him. Or rather when he sees me. The window washer tried to give him the good news but by that point Dodgson had no interest in talking with the man."

"Why is that?" I asked.

"He was drawing some kind of sketch while I was outside his window," said Mr. Holmes, "and my presence apparently spoiled his concentration. He shouted but I couldn't hear him through the window and he gesticulated and I cheerfully waved back. By the time I was finished he was nearly apoplectic. And what have you learned?"

Holmes pointed to the list of Dodgson visitors.

I cleared my throat and announced the clever title I had given my report, "The Dudgeons of Dodgson," and smiled. Mr. Holmes preferred to frown.

I stated the number of names cited (482), mentioned the device of the asterisks, brought attention to the number of feuds started or furthered in these various meetings and made particular mention of the House employees and Common Room purveyors whose lives and livelihoods were subject to the whim of Professor Dodgson. I concluded with what I believed to be a cogent summary.

After a brooding silence that lasted at least two minutes, Mr. Holmes roared, "And that is all you can provide?"

"I think I acquitted myself rather well," I said.

"You think," he echoed bitingly. "You were so engaged in looking for likely suspects that you never thought to look for clues or patterns."

"I told you about all the people he had dustups with."

"Which of them had the opportunity?" he asked.

"They all, at one time or another, were in Mr. Dodgson's quarters."

"How many were there for ten minutes or less and only once?"

I took the list up, and started to tabulate such occurrences.

"Don't bother to answer that question now," thundered Holmes, "but we can exclude all of those. Whoever snatched the diaries needed time to first discover them, ascertain their worth, and then conceal them. How many felt aggrieved and may have invited to inflict revenge?"

"Ah yes," I said, "there was the wine merchant and the Scouts and—"

"You did a good job of identifying these," said Holmes.

"Thank you," I mumbled.

"Remove them from the list," he said. "They are of no interest to us. There have been no overt actions of the sort generally attributed to vengeance."

"That's a bit hasty," I said.

Mr. Holmes cocked an eyebrow at my unsolicited challenge to his reasoning.

"Go on," he said. "This may prove interesting."

"On the streets of London, if somebody trifles with me, I'll want to get him back. Taking possession of something that matters to him is one good way to show I'm a force to be reckoned with."

"Exactly!" said Holmes. "You have just enunciated the law of the street and, for that matter, the jungle and some of the finer castles and manors throughout the world. But if the other fellow doesn't know that you took his sacred possession or even that something of his was taken, where is your show of supremacy? It's a rather anemic form of revenge."

"But these are lecturers and students," I protested. "They haven't been trained in the arts of savagery. It is not that they do not care to rip their adversary's throat out. They just don't know how."

"If that's your view of the academy," said Holmes, "then this education is being wasted on you."

I ignored this.

"What remaining choice do we have?" I asked. "Obviously we should restrict our scrutiny to whose who love and admire our Mr. Dodgson, for you have excluded everybody else."

"So it would seem," said Holmes, with a smile. "But I have faith in you."

"In me?"

"Yes," said Holmes, "you're going to solve this case. You are already on your way."

His confidence depressed me. Didn't I have enough to do without having to save the good name of Dodgson? And who was the lionized consulting detective around here? Not I! And, most importantly, what if I failed? What if I failed? Still I owed too much to Professor Dodgson and Mr. Holmes. If this is what was expected of me, then this was what I must do. I felt even sorrier for Mr. Dodgson. He thought he was getting Holmes to help him, and instead he was getting the last of the Baker Street Irregulars.

"Don't worry, young man," said Mr. Holmes. "I'm not deserting Dodgson or you. I will be helping. But I believe that you have certain resources which well equip you for this case."

Here was good news.

"The most significant of which," he said warmly, "is that nobody knows who you are."

Well, that was something. To be involved with Mr. Holmes and his crusade against lawbreakers is an experience that is both unsettling and exhilarating. Usually Mr. Holmes assigns some mysterious task and we have no idea as to what we really are doing or why. He confides in us almost as much as the puppeteer confides in his marionettes. He often praises us for a job well done and we stagger into the fog wondering just what in blazes we have accomplished—but still with a certain sense of pride. In this Dodgson matter, however, I clearly was going to navigate without being blindfolded.

"Here is how you will do it," said Mr. Holmes.

I was to pose as a reporter who was commissioned by an American magazine to write an article about Dodgson, the man behind the beloved Lewis Carroll. And for this purpose my editor wanted me to seek out important people who were able to provide illuminating anecdotes about Dodgson.

"Won't they know I'm not an American?" I asked.

"Of course," Mr. Holmes said patiently. "But you're just to say the magazine selected you because you are at Christ Church and they thought that gave you a leg up."

"I can do it," I said.

Playing the part of a Christ Church scholar when in fact I really was one tickled me. It was refreshing to portray something that I was instead of something that I was not. As for the reporter part, that sounded like great fun also. I was to question them as thoroughly as possible as to the habits and vagaries of Mr. Dodgson. I was to forget everything about propriety and manners I had learned with such painstaking care. Apparently, impertinence was the mark of a respected journalist. If anyone questioned my line of inquiry, I was to allay their fears with the following explanation:

By telling me their private observations of Dodgson, they will be allowing the American public to feel as if they know him; and that will increase his book sales in America.

"These are the people to whom you shall pose questions," said Mr. Holmes, as he handed me Dodgson's list. Mr. Holmes crossed out most of the names with broad, firm strokes.

"I took the liberty," he said, "of eliminating all the obvious innocents. And what we want to know here, Mr. Wiggins, is what they know about Dodgson and what they don't know about him; what they are revealing and what they are striving to conceal."

"What questions shall I ask?" I inquired.

"Oh, you'll think of something," he said. "You'll find your 'victims' both here and in London. You'll start your inquiries in Christ Church and conclude in London. Report to me at Baker Street with your findings in no more than seven days."

Nothing prepared me for my new identity as a journalist for a great American magazine. Still it fit me as comfortably as my favorite slippers. It was not just that people award you with kindness and hospitality and little sweets and mementos. These kindnesses were not intended to influence your assessment and depiction of them, mind you. They bestowed these favors just because they liked you and wanted you to like them. What could be fairer and more natural? Of course, while brushing away the crumbs of one more serving of gâteau, you might idly wonder what they don't want you to know about themselves. But such thoughts quickly dissipate into the perfumed fog of fellowship and earnest amiability.

What I really loved was that when I asked them questions, they answered. This may seem to you like the normal pattern of discourse. But mind I still was a student. To see my betters jump at my command, to see those so universally respected strive to please me was a pleasant change and one to which I easily could get more accustomed.

In those rooms and at those times, nothing was more important than to be able to honor them with the flattering portraits they so richly deserved. I actually felt a twinge about my necessary deception.

My first encounter was with Friedrich Max Muller, Professor of Comparative Philology and Honorary Member of Christ Church. In 1876 there had been a great to-do over Muller's desire to change his academic status and Dodgson's attempt to throw a shoe into the machinery, or so Muller put it. It seems the Vice Chancellor approved of Muller's plan to stop teaching and immerse himself in scholarship, while retaining his full salary. Dean Liddell, who was a friend of Muller's, pulled a rabbit out of his administrative hat by getting a deputy professor to assume Muller's teaching responsibilities—but at half the salary.

Dodgson, who bore no particular malice toward Muller, thought that Liddell was being unjust. He held that the position should determine the fee. The voting members of the faculty endorsed Liddell's view. The affronted Muller thought that transferring his responsibilities to somebody getting half pay was ingenious and even when I interviewed him so many years after the fact could not understand Dodgson's inability to appreciate the genius of the idea. I, of course, thought Muller was a selfish boor but kept that opinion to myself. I just nodded and winked and let him talk.

"The young man who was allowed to take over my classes," said Muller, "told me what a privilege it was to be my successor. I assured him he would prove worthy of the confidence Liddell placed in him.

"You see," he continued, "in the university there were those who could not bear Liddell's towering high above them—not just because he was tall but because of his character and position. Nasty things were said and written, but everybody knew from what forge those arrows came."

"Do you mean Professor Dodgson?" I asked.

"You said his name," replied Muller. "I didn't. But you may presume what you like."

I solemnly inscribed his words in my notepad. Interviewing people was much like taking notes at a lecture, except that you asked questions and they answered.

"I will say this about the man," said Muller. "He baffles me. He makes all these outrageous comments on character and rectitude; he goes out of his way to damage a reputation and then acts as if he did nothing wrong. Last year he gave me this photograph of me he had made years before, attached a silly little rhyme based on my name and generally acted as if nothing were amiss."

"You kept the picture," I said.

"Yes, I did," said Muller. "It's a good likeness, don't you think."

Dean Liddell had only the kindest, most supportive and utterly dismissive things to say about Dodgson. I met with the Dean in his study. He sat on his imposing straight-back chair, which he had turned away from his massive rolltop desk. I sat on an adjoining fleur-de-lis-patterned sofa. His missus, Lorena Liddell, sat on a corner chair embroidering a throw pillow for one of her daughters. The Dean was a learned man and an inspiration to struggling scholars, such as myself. Framed certificates and degrees attesting to his position hung on all sections of the wall. A photograph of the Prince of Wales stood on the mantelpiece. Everyone knew the story of how the Prince of Wales had been a Christ Church student and was an occasional visitor to this very same room. Even his mum graced this room with her presence. It was bandied about that the Dean had a serious talk with HRH about the Prince's limited academic prospects. Next to the image of the Prince was a photo of a young woman.

"Is that," I asked, gesturing with my thumb, "a portrait of Alice?"

"Oh, no," said the Dean, "that is our daughter Edith."

"She looks like quite a heartbreaker," I said, wishing to ingratiate myself.

"She was an angel," replied the Dean. "The Lord saw fit to take her in 1876 in the prime of her young womanhood."

Now I've gone and done it, I thought.

"Dodgson made that portrait in 1867," said the Dean, "and gave it to us several months after Edith passed."

"That was good of him," I said.

"Yes," said the Dean.

"Yes," whispered Mrs. Liddell.

"An unexpected and touching kindness," said the Dean. "You know we had grown apart over the years—not that we ever were as close as he imagined or proclaimed. But owing to our separate roles in the University, and his penchant for adopting idiosyncratic positions, it looked to the outside world as if a once cordial and intimate relationship became strained. In all candor, that relationship was mostly professional to begin with but with all of that 'Alice' business, the world presumed what it chose to presume.

"Despite his intellect and the respect he earned here," the Dean continued, "Dodgson seemed to be a lonely man. He attached himself to our family, even conspiring to magically appear at places where he knew we would be. I suppose some good came out of those awkward moments. He did write those children's books. Although I do not fancy the whole world knowing that the books were named after my daughter Alice.

"And the children are portrayed as being mere casual listeners to the story when in fact they had a hand in the formulation of the tale. Did you know that when he was telling them the story, Alice asked if there couldn't be more than one cat in the tale because she so loved cats?"

"No," I responded with a show of astonishment. "I never knew that."

"Nobody does," he said, "and apparently nobody cares to. There's something to be put in your article."

I dutifully scribbled some notes.

"Your editors probably will excise it," he added. "That's what they do."

"No doubt that Dodgson is a clever and industrious man," continued Liddell. "He has the rare ability to immerse himself in pursuits and enterprises that the rest of the world never had thought about and is unlikely to think about in the future. He's forever offering advice about how people should go about their business. Sometimes there is even some merit to various of the rules and proscriptions he's taken it upon himself to offer. I suppose he means to be helpful, but he's constantly standing in the path of my efforts to improve this hallowed institution. And he's only gotten worse over the years."

The Dean turned to his wife.

"Mrs. Liddell," he asked, "when did we notice that he had become more obstreperous?"

She looked up from her meticulous stitching.

"He had invited himself over for dinner again," she said slowly, "and the girls were all chattering about the impending wedding of the Prince of Wales."

"That's right," said the Dean. "And Dodgson said, 'Well I'm going to marry Alice.' And then he winked at you. It was intended to be a playful wink but there was something about it that chilled us. And you spoke right up, dear."

"That's right," said Mrs. Liddell. "I said, 'You'll do no such thing, Charles Lutwidge Dodgson,' and he quickly changed the topic.

"Well," Mrs. Liddell continued. "It was unthinkable. She was just too young for him."

"That sort of arrangement," said the Dean, "is not all that uncommon, even in this modern age."

"It was more than that," said Mrs. Liddell. "He was not a fit prospect for our daughter. He had no title, no family wealth, no likelihood of advancement in Oxford. We wanted something more substantial for Alice than books and games and mechanical contraptions. Prince Leopold himself was one of her suitors."

"Whatever the cause," said the Dean, "Dodgson had become an annoyance. Not that he got his way very often; but still he made my job harder. Nevertheless some alumni include him in their lists of illustrious personages who have spent time here and a few of the students like him, and he has tenure, in accordance with Christ Church rules, so we are stuck, or blessed, with him—depending on your point of view and his crusade of the moment."

The round of interviews continued.

I sat in Ellen Terry's dressing room as she applied makeup and told me of the years in which Dodgson would not communicate with her. He disapproved of her liaisons and the issue they produced. She also gave me complimentary tickets to the performance of *As You Like It* that night because of the article she believed me to be writing. The seats were not as good as I would have liked, but perhaps with more notice she could have provided better.

Charles Collingwood, the nephew, prattled on about how Dodgson encouraged him to pursue a career of letters. I never mentioned the pointed comment on Dodgson's list about Collingwood's abilities. Instead I expressed admiration and envy. He told me how he would dedicate his life to furthering Dodgson's reputation.

To hear these and the others talk, each was the rock upon which Dodgson clung to for support or the misunderstood victim of his childish and ill-conceived crusades. I learned of his steady stream of good works. He printed copies of the Alice books at his own expense and donated them to children's hospitals. He sought employment for a friend of his, the schoolmaster T. J. Dymes. Dodgson sent out 180 letters soliciting help for the man. Dodgson went to the home of a friendless college servant who was afflicted with typhoid fever and looked after the man.

And I learned of eccentricities—list making, a nearly compulsive orderliness and absentmindedness being the most constant theme. His nephew related the most dramatic incident. Dodgson went to a children's party and after entering the house, dropped on his hands and crawled where he heard the hubbub of voices, and he started emitting strange sounds. He thought it would be amusing if he entered as if he were a bear. Unfortunately he actually had gone not to the party but in error to the house next door where a conference of females was taking place in connection with some reform movement or other. Realizing his mistake, Mr. Dodgson suddenly rose to his feet and fled the house.

And I heard the catalog of storms when his sensitivities were aroused. There were too many of these to enumerate. And he always seemed to be distributing photographs sometimes in the generous spirit of friendship and sometimes when he sought to curry favor.

I presented all these details to Mr. Holmes on the appointed day. He listened to my report impatiently. He paused a few times to relight his clay pipe. I took this to be a subtle rebuke but proceeded with my recitation.

"I hear no conclusion," he said. "Are we no better off than we started?"

"We know more," I said.

"So it would seem, and so much to the good," said Mr. Holmes.

"If I were to pick a culprit on the basis of these inquiries," I said, "it would be Collingwood."

"Interesting," said Holmes.

"It would seem that Collingwood had the most to gain from possession of the four diaries," I said. "He clearly wants to build a career on the shoulders of his uncle—establish himself as conservator of the legend and heir to the literary throne. Owning those diaries would enable him to write convincingly and knowledgeably of the intimate thoughts of his uncle during what some would call Dodgson's most creative period. And if he cared to slip a little dagger into his uncle's reputation as a revenge for Dodgson's unkind judgments of Collingwood's abilities, well, he'd have the means."

"What about Dean Liddell?" asked Mr. Holmes. "The two have been at odds for the longest of times."

"True," I said, "and he'd love nothing better but the sudden and complete departure of Charles Dodgson from Christ Church. The diaries would no doubt give him means to fulfill this petty dream. He's certainly autocratic enough to confront Dodgson with the diaries and demand his immediate departure but it hasn't happened. I conclude that poor Dean Liddell does not have the books in hand."

"Then," asked Mr. Holmes, "shall we call upon Mr. Collingwood?"

"No," I said. "I do not believe he is our thief. He doesn't have the spine or the imagination."

"Excellent," said Mr. Holmes. "And therefore?"

I let the question dangle in the air for a moment and then replied, "I have a theory both as to whom, why, and how."

Mr. Holmes beamed with a smile so broad, it would have cut a path through the densest of London fogs. "To whom do we then turn?"

"I have a theory," I replied, "but I wish to test it. Let us arrange a meeting with Mr. Dodgson."

"Capital," said Mr. Holmes. "Now, tell me, young man, isn't this fun?" I nodded and he beamed.

Three days later we were back in Dodgson's study. Instead of tea we were drinking ginger beer. After a proper review of our steps, Holmes gestured to me and bade me to speak.

"I have a theory, professor," I began, "and a hope. Your facility with the photographic arts is well known and revered. Do you, by any chance, have any photographs of this room."

"Yes," he replied. "It has been my practice to photograph this and other chambers here on a regular basis and to make appropriate notations including the date, the time of day, quality of light coming though the window and atmospheric conditions. I have approximately twenty-five such studies of this room—Actually that would be forty-two images, if you count photographs taken by students and presented to me. "You see," he added, "I stopped playing with photography in 1880 when they changed the materials. It just diminished the quality of the pictures. However some students needed help and encouragement, and so called on Dodgson."

"Would it be too much trouble to see the pictures?"

"Not at all," said Dodgson, "and as you may surmise, my archives are sufficiently organized. But you'll have to excuse me. I keep them all in my studio."

As he was leaving the room, I asked for the use of a magnifying glass."

After his exit, Mr. Holmes cast a smug glance at me and said, "A magnifier! How fascinating. Next you'll be smoking a pipe and wearing a hunting cap."

"I am dubious about the pipe," I said. "But let me tell you about my theory. If we look at the photographs, we may be able to observe a variation in the appearance of the bookcase. And according to the data Dodgson compiled, we might be able to determine when the diaries were taken, and see who Mr. Dodgson's visitors were in that period."

"An interesting hypothesis," said Mr. Holmes, "but a little too inelegant to be truly scientific."

Dodgson returned some twenty minutes later with the glass and a bulky envelope containing a sheaf of pictures. I set my eyeball to the glass and scrutinized each photograph, taking special care to concentrate on the bookcase. While I devoted myself to this tedious study Mr. Holmes and Mr. Dodgson entertained themselves with the creation of a cryptographic system that would need the services of two separate individuals, each knowing only a part of the code, to decipher it. Mr. Dodgson held that a necessary component was the elimination of vowels.

And then I found it.

"Mr. Holmes," I said, "would you please come over and have a look."

I showed him two photographs.

"I see," he said, pointing at the second photo. "These books are moved to the right. And they have new shelf companions to their left. And look here. This pile of books on the windowsill is slightly lower."

"Exactly," I said, and turned the second photo over to examine the date scrawled on the back and cross-checked against the now well-worn list of visitors.

"Mr. Dodgson," I said, "I believe I know who has your diaries. If I returned them to you without revealing the thief's name, would you be content?"

"No," he said. "I would not be content. Knowing that someone came here in the guise of friendship and took those valuable properties would forever bring me sorrow and fear that it might happen again."

He shrugged.

"But if that is the price of having them back," he said. "So be it."

"Then they shall be returned," I said.

I then turned to Mr. Holmes and said, "Let us go, Mr. Holmes. There is work to be done."

The next day when the Dean's maidservant brought me into the sitting room, Mrs. Liddell did not seem surprised to see me.

"The Dean is not here," she said.

"I was told," I replied. "But if I may, it is you with whom I wish to speak."

"Yes?"

"I have a confession and I need your help."

She gestured toward the same sofa on which I had sat the previous week. She looked at her husband's imposing chair and then decided to sit on the far end of the sofa, with a discreet space between us."

"Yes?" she asked again.

"First of all," I said, "I'm not a journalist."

"Yes," she said, once more.

"But let me tell you about my background."

I told her that I was indeed enrolled in Christ Church. But I described the strange journey to the school. I told about the Baker Street Irregulars and my early encounters with Sherlock Holmes. I told her what life was like on the stones, and what I did to survive. She was shocked to learn that a sneezer could bring a few bob to an enterprising lad. I told her how Mr. Holmes had changed my life and I hoped to make something of myself.

"I have told you all this," I said, "to give you power over me. Any time you wish to, you can turn to Mr. Liddell and tell him all that I have related to you. And that will be the end of me here and in life."

I then told her about Mr. Dodgson's diaries and how I promised him that he would have them back and that I needed her help to keep his promise.

She began to sob softly.

"I want you to know," I said, "that I know what it's like to have secrets. I know what it's like to live in fear that someone will find out the truth about you."

She nodded her head.

"We were so innocent," she said, "an accidental touch on the shoulder, an exchanged glance and that was all. But it tortured each of us and we dare not speak of it."

"And," I said, "when he went to his studio that bitter day in 1876 to retrieve the photographs of poor Edith, you went to his bookcase to pass the time and you happened to pick up one of the diaries and you read an entry in which he mentioned your name in the most endearing of terms."

"I was distraught over the death of my daughter. I didn't want to lose my marriage and my family. Charles is so unworldly. I was afraid his diaries would somehow get into the wrong hands. Without thinking I took the ones covering those sweet but strange years."

"Mr. Dodgson loved not Alice, but you."

"And I loved him," she replied. "Nobody ever knew of these feelings. We never even confessed them to each other but we both knew. But how did you come to this conclusion?"

"When we were talking last week about his announcement that he wanted to marry Alice," I said, "you explained that she was too young for him. You did not say that he was too old for her."

"The difference being?" asked Mrs. Liddell, who by this point had recovered her composure.

"At that moment, and with regard to that subject, your thoughts were for him and not for her."

"I've been a good wife," she said.

"I know," I replied.

She stepped out of the room briefly and returned with a pillowcase containing the four diaries.

"Husbands," she said, "are not known to explore armoires where wives keep their undergarments, let alone kitchens or laundries."

"I shall remember that," I said.

And that is how I solved my first and last case. I did not become a mathematician as Dodgson had hoped I might. Nor did I ever pursue the bright promise of consulting detective that Mr. Holmes envisioned for me. I do like my life as a journalist. Pursuing other people's secrets is much more desirable than revealing my own.

But on that very topic of secrets, I have devoted some considerable thought.

Isn't it odd that by protecting what you have, you lose some or all of who you are? I am in no position to know or say whether Mr. Dodgson and Mrs. Liddell should have expressed their feelings to each other and forged their private thoughts into a reality. Some have done so and have escaped or disregarded penalty. Others have been, shall we say, less fortunate. I do believe that each of these star-crossed never-to-be-lovers was separately torn apart by the exact same turmoil. It wasn't so much the knowledge that they loved someone they should not, a knowledge I am sure that sustained them and even elicited a curious smile in the darkest of nights and dreariest of days. It was that they could not tell another living soul about this feeling that was so much a part of their beings.

I understand this. I was aggrieved and still am over my efforts to keep certain parts of my life a secret from all. The cold logic from which Mr. Holmes advised silence on these matters has prevailed. I have no intention of risking what I have earned. And yet the example of those two sinful innocents is not lost on me. I am writing these words in the expectation that they will be published after I am gone, which I trust will be in the far,

far future. I hope that in that age people will have a more complex picture of who I am and what I have done, and that they may know of Mr. Holmes in his role as philanthropist. Perhaps they may also have a fuller and more understanding view of Mrs. Liddell, Mr. Dodgson, and all others who keep secrets to themselves. And when at last I pass, I pray that Mr. Holmes will be my champion at the Pearly Gates as he has been on this isle.

As to why Romeo had to be Romeo, I am still trying to answer that question.

MYCROFT HOLMES

"Art in the blood is liable to take the strangest forms."

"But how do you know that it is hereditary?"

"Because my brother Mycroft possesses it in a larger degree than I do. . . . When I say . . . that Mycroft has better powers of observation than I, you may take it that I am speaking the exact and literal truth."

"Is he your junior?"

"Seven years my senior."

"How comes it that he is unknown?"

"Oh, he is very well known in his own circle."

"Where, then?"

"Well, in the Diogenese Club, for example."

—"The Greek Interpreter"

by GARY LOVISI

Mycroft's Great Game

I enter this account, for which I have been silent all these years, to set the record straight for posterity. I have instructed my solicitors to deliver it to my heirs and descendants 100 years after my death at a time when all principals involved will have long been deceased and unaffected by the facts herein.

It really was quite unfair, you know. My little brother Sherlock always getting all the credit. He had become quite the publicity hound lately, with Watson and Doyle positively fawning at his every word. Why, sometimes it was absolutely unbearable.

Oh, I know what you are thinking. I am Mycroft Holmes, solid, stodgy, overweight minion of the eccentric Diogenes Club, renowned recluse of Pall Mall, blah, blah, blah. Utter balderdash, I tell you!

While I had carefully fostered a veil of anonymity over my affairs and personage, there was much more to my work than anyone would have ever guessed. And while the official dispatches and the popular press positively fell over themselves to laud brother Sherlock's little accomplishments in his consulting detective "hobby," I performed my work in a totally obscure capacity, completely avoiding discovery by any outsider. My great powers and directives were not even imagined by our politicians and the Fleet Street press, as I managed this vast worldwide enterprise of ours—the British Empire!

Now don't misunderstand, I dearly love my little brother, and it was hardly a matter at all for me to put up with his silly eccentricities and inconsistencies now and then, as I am sure he had so patiently put up with my own. It happens to the best of us, for we were true brothers, blood being thicker than water and all that sort of thing. Nevertheless, since our teen years we had gone our separate ways, and each in his own way, had achieved a measure of success.

I remember fondly when our guardian, Great Aunt Julia Vernet, had told young Sherlock and me on that summer day in the gazebo, "I am sure that both my wonderful Holmes boys will go far in this world and make your marks, if you do not allow your great intellects to get the better of you. Promise me you will always remember to use your powers for only good purposes."

We promised. We dearly loved Great Aunt Julia. She died not soon thereafter, leaving us alone. It was a blow to Sherlock and me that we have never forgotten.

Ah, but that fond memory was from such a long time ago. From a much simpler world that was very far away from the present cold orb we are forced to inhabit today.

Today, it is 1891! We approach the dawn of a new century, an exciting modern age and a treacherous era of changing technology, international intrigue and dangerous nationalistic expansionism.

Now I must play the "Great Game," doing my duty for the Empire I love. The Empire Great Aunt Julia so loved. Unlike brother Sherlock, I adhere to my great aunt's values. My brother feigns the vaulted Bohemian, but in reality, it was the very structures of Empire that allowed him to so indulge his activities in the criminal investigatory arena.

Rather, it is I who bore the weight of Atlas upon my shoulders. It was the life I had chosen. I had no regrets. I had little choice then, for I was in too deep. It was, however, the one career I was eminently suited for. I must say that I have been very successful at my chosen tasks, but it has forced me to cut myself off from everyone and everything that might interfere with the performance of my duty. No one, not even my dear brother—especially he—has ever been allowed more than the most cursory knowledge of my work. It was best for Sherlock, best for myself, and best for the Empire I serve. Safer that way all around. For I was engaged in the most dangerous of games. Sherlock has had some nebulous suspicion that I occasionally was involved in some kind of "work"—for lack of a better word—for what we'll call "the government." He may have even suspected my influence reached to some at the highest levels. That was certainly true, but what of it?

Could Sherlock ever fancy in his wildest dreams that I *was* the government? Of course I steadfastly denied everything. He had given that impression to Watson, and the good doctor had dutifully recorded such suppositions in his fictionalized accounts of my brother's cases. I knew Sherlock well, and I thought this was nothing but a vain little conceit of his. He was too logical, far too observant, and I had made my plans too well in this venture. My overweight and sedentary life, the Diogenes Club, the "recluse of Pall Mall" dodge, were all but elements of a clever ruse I incorporated into my overall persona. I knew, in truth, that Sherlock had no evidence of my business. Nothing. He may have said certain things for effect, and to Watson, but he surely did not *believe* them. I intended to keep it that way.

The absolute truth was hidden behind a lie I had woven so well that logical Sherlock would never believe it. It was, that aside from the public figureheads of our beloved Queen and noble PM—I was not merely some occasional influence in the government, but I was in fact, the Controlling Director behind the entire British Empire. There was a need for such a person. The monarchy gave me their trust; politicians at the highest levels were able to effect a compromise. I was the natural choice as I had no ambition for myself or any political group. Actually, the "Directorship" merely broadened my existing powers and responsibilities. Thus was born the unofficial and very secret office of Controlling Director. From hidden vaults and rooms beneath the Diogenes Club, with a small group of dedicated specialists, I managed all that was the British Empire.

Certainly it was best that Sherlock did not know much of these matters. I hid it well; the facts of my activities have always eluded him. I was sure Sherlock's delicate sensibilities would cause us to be at loggerheads had he full knowledge of the import of my work and duties. I know he would have been upset by certain of my dealings. So I shielded Sherlock as best I could, even as I indulged him as he went his merry way on his criminal problems, as long as they did not conflict with my own plans. It was not always easy being Sherlock's smarter brother.

It is an axiom that in order for our government and Empire to succeed, certain of what I call "prerequisites" must be realized and met. It is a sorry constant that occurs when one is involved in power politics—the Great Game, as it is called. However, I found myself constantly having to wander further afield to achieve objectives, often into hitherto unexplored and sometimes unsavory areas to ensure success in my numerous ventures for the Empire. I am the first to admit that at times I found it troubling. Such as this recent Moriarty affair.

The basis of this problem began some years ago. In my position as Controlling Director of the Empire, it was I who allowed Moriarty and his minions to exist, and to some degree, even prosper. I knew it would be useful to the needs of the government and the Empire I served if my influence also extended into criminal society. So I made inroads into that sorry element. I discovered a most enterprising individual and realized that under the proper control, a criminal element could be most useful. I further realized that by having crime "organized," it would better enable me to control it, thus being even more useful to my purposes. The criminal element contributes agents who readily perform the most unsavory deeds that the regular military and most members of legitimate agencies would never attempt. So you see, in this cynical and dangerous game we play, they do have their uses.

And yet, I began to feel I had made an error in this chessboard of intrigue that I play upon our worldwide stage. Not all factors can always be considered, not all results so carefully manipulated. It began to disturb me to see Sherlock's obsession with Moriarty. While it was certainly well founded, it had been steadily growing. Now it threatened certain "delicate situations" should Sherlock act too adroitly in this area, or if he found out too much information that was not within his purview to know and decided to act upon it.

My fear that this problem would come to a head was soon realized.

It was in the spring of 1891, when Sherlock came to visit me at my Pall Mall lodgings. Thus began the narrative Watson was to record months later in his fictionalized account of the situation entitled "The Final Problem." However, good Watson's account left out certain important facts, or related only my brother's own version, which was necessarily incomplete. I shall remedy all that now, and tell the true story that has never been told.

Sherlock's visit to my rooms was certainly a surprise, to be sure. My brother and I led separate lives these many years and saw each other only occasionally. Now he entered my rooms quietly, thoughtful.

Sherlock looked worn and haggard but alert with the hunt. I knew he was in his element investigating some kind of criminal case, no doubt, and loving it. I knew this could be a difficult meeting for both of us.

After niceties had quickly been exchanged, in Sherlock's customary tart manner, we got down to the purpose of the meeting. He told me, once again, of his suspicions about Moriarty's activities. He asked if I knew anything about them. I gave some vague generalizations and once again denied knowledge of everything.

"Ah!" my brother said sharply, "you know it is barely three years since the Ripper murders, Mycroft? Eighteen eighty-eight is not long ago. You did not know anything about that matter either. I did not investigate the case, as you are well aware, though I was asked to do so by the official police."

"That is outrageous!" I blew up in anger. I knew he was trying to provoke me. Inwardly I smiled at my brother's sharp boldness, but it did hurt. Once again, I denied everything.

He was silent, observing, fingers steepled, thinking.

"Just what are you implying? That I killed those women, or had them murdered? You are so out of bounds on this, Sherlock, you have no idea!"

He said nothing.

"Well?" I asked sharply.

"Nothing. I did not come here to argue. Today three years later, there is Moriarty to consider," he said. "That is my one focus now."

Here we were, back at Moriarty again. I felt his interest was bordering on obsession. I tried to dissuade him as best I could.

"I tell you, Sherlock, do not become overly involved in this Moriarty business. I do not advise you to travel to the Continent either," I told him bluntly.

"My dear Mycroft," he said with that glimmer of rich sarcasm in his cultured tones. He was being prissy with me. "I would expect nothing less from one who detests travel and all modes of circumlocution to only embrace the sedentary life."

"Nevertheless, Sherlock, you must be aware that it is a trap."

"Of course."

"And yet you persist?"

"And what is the alternative? Am I to forgo an opportunity to smash Moriarty and his organization once and for all!"

"Moriarty! Moriarty! You have the man on the brain! I tell you, in all truth, he is a rather small fish and of little consequence in the grand scheme of things," I replied, showing my annoyance.

Sherlock gave me a quizzical smile.

"No matter, Mycroft. I am off to the Continent."

"To where?" I asked, incredulous.

"Why, to Meiringen, by way of Interlaken."

"All the way to Switzerland?" I asked in obvious surprise.

"Indeed. I have a yen to see the Reichenbach Falls before I die."

This kind of talk disturbed me and, as Sherlock's brother, I realized I had made a grievous error by allowing this situation to approach a crisis point. I knew something had to be done soon. I had already set my mind to working out a plan. Now I felt linked to this situation as if by handcuffs. When my brother left, little did either of us realize what actions would be set in motion and what momentous events would transpire.

Try as I might to dissuade Sherlock of his obsession, to be fair, his assumptions about Moriarty's activities were more often correct than not. Moriarty certainly was an unsavory sort. However, not all that had been attributed to Moriarty, nor even the worst of it, by dear brother Sherlock, had been at Moriarty's cause or design. Some of it had been at my own. Which was the crux of the matter between us that I needed to keep from my brother at all costs. This information, what I tend to call "Empire business"—and the less said on that matter the better—must forever be kept from Sherlock. For my brother to find out the truth could destroy our friendship forever.

I grew concerned that events were swirling out of hand when no sooner did Sherlock leave my Pall Mall lodgings that evening to visit his good friend Dr. Watson, and I settle down to what I thought would be a relaxing thoughtful repose, than I had a surprise visitor.

Tall, thin, wiry, and furtive, he looked like some human manifestation of a ferret on the prowl, or some mongoose from the Indian subcontinent ready to devour a poisonous python. With his hunched back and bald pate, deep-set eyes that did not miss much at all, I knew the man instantly as he strode the twenty-two steps to my outer door, knocked once lightly, and was admitted by Burbage, my squire and retainer.

Professor James Moriarty stood in the doorway as I motioned him quickly inside. Sherlock's supposed "Napoleon of Crime," indeed! He was a nervous and fearful little man who knew he was breaking a dire rule in our relationship by ever approaching me directly in public or private—all our communications being done clandestinely through third and fourth parties.

I nodded. "Take a seat, if you please. Tell me what is on your mind."

"I will stand. I will be brief."

"Continue," I said firmly. My substantial girth made him seem to dwindle before me. He knew this was a dangerous breach contacting me directly—a serious breaking of the rules—but it was for an important reason, so we "got to the point," as the Americans are so fond of doing.

Moriarty sighed. "It is becoming impossible! Impossible, I tell you! Your brother is at me all the time now. The harassment, the constant investigation of my affairs. What have I ever done to interfere with him or his friends, Watson and Doyle? Why does he persecute me?"

I did not say anything for the moment. It was a serious matter to see this man so upset. He was no one to trifle with.

Moriarty continued, "I tell you, Mr. Holmes, I am at my wit's end with this affair. Call off your brother or I shall have no choice in the matter. I do not want to act, but know this; I will never stand in the dock. I will not allow your brother to be the cause of my loss of liberty. I have stayed my hand these past months out of respect for our mutual interests. I cannot do so forever."

I nodded slowly; Sherlock had certainly muddled up this affair royally.

"You spoke to my brother?" I asked Moriarty.

"Yes, and he will not see reason. Why, he actually drew a revolver and kept it handy as we spoke. I was highly insulted by that gesture."

I nodded. I could imagine the scene.

Moriarty continued, "I do not wish to interfere with our business arrangements, they have been beneficial and lucrative, so I come to you now pleading, Mr. Holmes, before things get out of hand or someone makes a terrible mistake that we shall all regret."

The subtle threat in Moriarty's words was all too evident.

"The mistake, my good Professor, would be if any harm ever came to my brother. I hope you understand that completely," I said, my eyes burning into his own.

He looked away, nodded slowly.

"Then we are in agreement on that matter, at least?" I asked, emphasizing my previous warning with all seriousness.

"Yes. No harm shall befall him, but please, this is quite out of hand now and becoming dangerous. I have come to you for advice and assistance."

"And you shall have it, Professor," I replied, more upbeat now that he was evidently willing to seek a nonviolent solution to the problem.

"So then, instruct me. What shall I do?" Moriarty asked.

"Nothing, Professor. You will do nothing."

Moriarty looked at me curiously.

"I will explain."

"Please do."

I was silent, thoughtful. Finally I had it all worked out.

"My brother is going on a little trip to Switzerland, hiking in the Interlaken area, perhaps even a visit to the majestic Reichenbach Falls? Are you familiar with the region?" I asked Moriarty.

He fidgeted, still standing before me, still refusing the seat I had offered him. He said, "I am. My knowledge and influence extends to the Continent, just as yours does. But what is the significance of your brother's travel there?"

"Ah, that is the interesting matter. Through various agencies, I have made it appear that you are, in fact, 'after Sherlock'; that you intend to remove him once and for all."

"Anticipating my future move?" Moriarty smiled, then thought better of it.

"A move you shall *not* be making, but yes, to your question." I said, adding, "Your little visit to him the other day has certainly played into brother Sherlock's fascination with your affairs. I have also been concerned because I have noticed a conflict growing between the two of you for some time."

"Not on my part, I can assure you," Moriarty asserted.

I nodded. "That may be true. Regardless, I have begun the manufacture of a scenario that will make my brother decide to leave London. Fleeing to the Continent, he believes your agents will attempt to hound him to an early demise. He will, of course sense a trap, and in doing so, quickly reverse it to trap you instead."

Moriarty's smile melted. He stood careful, waiting.

"Of course, nothing could be further from the truth," I added.

Moriarty nodded, but he looked surprised, confused. He said, "But I thought—"

"Absolutely, and that is the beauty of the plan. Sherlock will flee London in the belief that he is being chased by you and your minions. Meanwhile you will remain in London."

Moriarty smiled ferretlike, asked, "That will remove your brother's meddling from my affairs?"

"Yes, you will be free of him, and you and your organization will remain in London to perform your work for me once again, uninterrupted," I added.

"Then your brother will be sent on a wild goose chase?" Moriarty said with a grin.

"He needs the rest, a nice hike in the Alps shall do him good. Don't you think? Watson will accompany him," I added.

"I am still concerned that he plans a confrontation of some kind."

I smiled. "He absolutely does. But nothing of the kind shall occur. Since you will be safely ensconced in London, that confrontation cannot possibly take place. You see, I know my brother Sherlock's mind too well. He may fantasize about some titanic struggle abroad, perhaps even at the Falls of the Reichenbach. The opportunities for melodramatic heroics, I am sure, will not be lost on Sherlock. But it will be a nonevent. Instead, Sherlock will be traipsing abroad, safe and out of your hair, and you shall be safe in London, unhampered, and never the twain shall meet."

Moriarty nodded. "I am satisfied. I appreciate your assistance in the nullification of this danger to my person."

"That is just as well, Professor. Now you may rest easy. By tomorrow, Sherlock and Watson will begin their grand tour, and you shall be free and unencumbered once again. We will work out details in the coming months and I shall convince Sherlock to drop the matter before he returns."

"I thank you, Mr. Holmes. I knew that coming to you with this problem was the appropriate way to attain satisfaction."

Burbage let Professor Moriarty out and carefully closed the door behind him. We were alone now.

I looked to my aide. Burbage was as taciturn as ever, his lips sealed tight, but I felt the thoughts going round in his head. Alexander Burbage, late of the Indian Army, marksman, secret agent, Afghani scout, and now my manservant, confidential secretary, bodyguard, and sometimes man-of-action.

"Well?" I asked. I could see he was fairly bursting to speak his mind but would never do so unless I prompted him.

"I fear your brother will never leave London," he said matter-of-factly.

"He will certainly think seriously about it after you set fire to his rooms at 221B later tonight!" I said.

"I, set fire to his rooms? Are you serious?"

"Oh, absolutely, but Watson and he will not be there, of course. And it will be, after all, a very minor fire that will do no lasting damage—it will look far worse than it actually is. You can manage that, can you not? I shall instruct you later. It will, of course, be blamed on Moriarty and his 'gang'— all part of my plan to pressure my dear brother to leave London."

"But I was here when he visited you earlier today. I am sure I heard him tell you that he already planned to leave London for the Continent," Burbage replied, confused now.

"Aye, Burbage, you heard correctly," I said carefully. "So Sherlock would have me *believe*. In fact, that was all a ruse. You see, Sherlock has suspicions about my place and work, but no hard facts. Our little association on the Affair of the Naval Treaty notwithstanding did not begin to display the length and extent of my interests. So he tempts me with a plan where he proposes to do exactly what I would like him to do. And I, playing his game, dutifully reply with all earnestness that I do not like the idea at all. I further state the obvious, that he is desperately needed here in London. Now would be the worst possible time for him to leave. And he knows it. For truth to tell, we have each noticed that it tends to cause an unnatural excitement in the criminal classes when Sherlock is not in the city."

Burbage shook his head as if to clear the cobwebs of gamesmanship. He was a man of action, not used to the intellectual double thinking and conundrums required when chess pieces are moved in this Great Game of ours.

"Now, let me see if I understand this," he said finally. "Sherlock feigns a trip to the Continent, though he has no actual intent of going. He says this all just to gain your attention and see your reaction. Meanwhile, you do not give him satisfaction; instead you react in the reverse of what you actually want and intend. Which is the reverse of what Sherlock believes that you want. It seems like the reverse of logic to me. My poor head hurts from the thought of it all!"

I laughed. "You have it absolutely! And there you see the beauty. For as you are perplexed, imagine poor Sherlock! I will gently prod my little brother into accepting the validity of his initial idea—that a trip to the Continent is just what he needs now. He will come to the realization that London is too hot to hold him. That is why I had you perform several highly convincing but absolutely unsuccessful attempts upon his life recently— obviously the work of this dread 'Moriarty gang.' Sherlock will leave London convinced that the gang is hot on his trail and will seek a confrontation on the Continent. He will set a trap for Moriarty at Reichenbach. He believes that then he will solve the Moriarty problem once and for all. One way or another."

"Aye, and in the meantime, he will be out of London and out of your hair," Burbage said with a smile.

"Yes. You see I dearly love my brother, but I do not take Moriarty lightly, and my brother will not drop the matter. That places him in dire peril. While Moriarty is a useful agent, I have no illusions about this situation. Sherlock has enmeshed himself in a serious game. When a dangerous man is in fear of his liberty, unless something is done to remedy that situation, panic cannot be far behind. And during panic, a man will lash out and perform actions that may not be in his best interest. Moriarty values our alliance, but he values his freedom more and Sherlock is trimming his sails appreciably. Lately my brother has been stepping up his efforts to destroy the entire Moriarty organization. That put each man in danger from the other. An unacceptable situation. A remedy was needed. Now I can never countenance any attack by Moriarty on my dear brother. Nor Sherlock doing anything against our vital interests with Moriarty. Both men must remain safe and allowed to continue to operate. Therefore, my plan. As things stand now, this appears to be an acceptable solution to protect both men and at the same time continue my business with Moriarty. As you know, his people have become most useful lately in ferreting out and exposing anarchists and agents provocateurs who seek to throw our nation into socialist revolution. Through their efforts we have uncovered three bomb plots and broken up two cells of saboteurs and spies, all dutifully handled without police or press interference."

The next morning I was at the hansom cab stand that Watson frequented. I was the driver of the third rig, suitably disguised. That talent runs in the Holmes family, as Sherlock often makes use of it in his investigations, and Watson chronicles the same in his little detection stories. I knew Sherlock would instruct Watson to pass the first and second cab and take the third one. I smiled to myself as I saw the good doctor approach.

"Aye, guv, where to?" I barked in an indistinguishable cockney growl. Now, I ask you, good reader, had I been the entirely sedentary and reclusive creature I was made out to be, would I have been a part of such activity? Would I have even been capable of doing such a thing? Truth to tell, I often acted as my own agent in certain delicate matters such as this.

"Victoria Station, my good man, if you please," Watson said, getting in the cab. "There's an extra guinea in it for you if you make all haste and follow my directions." Then he sat back quiet, thoughtful. He hardly noticed me at all, his attention concentrated on possible watchers and followers. And while he was in absolutely no danger, I'm sure he felt as if danger were surrounding him and following his every move. I was careful to remember that my brother had certainly instructed Watson to carry his old service revolver. So I had to act with care as I knew my passenger was quite nervous and must be armed.

I climbed down and loaded the good doctor's trunks and baggage. All loaded up, with a grunt I gave the old mare a taste of the stick and we were off.

I've always enjoyed a good ride through the London streets at dawn but actually driving the cab was a real thrill for me. I get away so infrequently these days that donning a disguise and fooling poor old Watson so handily was a bit of a lark. I even played gruff conversation with him, until he barked at me, "Please! Drive the cab!" Then muttering to himself, "The man simply does not know his place!"

I smiled to myself. On Watson's part, I could see the concern and worry in his face as he tried to sit silently in the backseat, thinking dark thoughts of what the next few days might bring. I felt for him then, but realized that my deceit was protecting Sherlock and him from danger. I knew he would approve, if only for the safely of my brother, his good friend.

Of course, Watson supposed, as did Sherlock, that Moriarty and his henchmen were hotly after them at that very moment. The fire last night in the rooms at 221B had shocked Sherlock, as I knew it would. Burbage's work had certainly done the trick. This morning both men were hurrying out of London to catch the boat-train to the Continent. I sighed and allowed myself a satisfied grin as I drove the cab quickly through the empty London streets. I had averted a possible fatal confrontation between my brother and Moriarty. I was quite satisfied with the matter at the present time.

Being Sherlock's smarter brother sometimes leads me to a slight overconfidence in our relationship and my talents. Even, I daresay, an uncommon arrogance on my part. That was to prove my undoing, as well as events from a hitherto unforeseen source by the name of Colonel Sebastian

Moran. Little did I realize that all my fine underhanded plans would crash down upon my head before I knew it.

After I deposited Watson at Victoria Station, I watched with some amusement as he went about the place as inconspicuous as possible—or as inconspicuous as possible for good Watson—frightfully amusing, let me tell you. From a safe distance, still in my disguise, I watched when Sherlock and Watson finally boarded the 7:11 Continental express. When the train pulled out, I waited to be sure that my brother did not perform one of his little "double-back" tricks. When I was sure no one had left the train, I drove off, back to Pall Mall. I was happy that my brother and Watson were now on their way to the Continent. Out of London, safe from Moriarty.

The next morning Burbage woke me early with alarming news. Moriarty was still in London as we agreed, but he had secretly sent his most trusted man, Colonel Sebastian Moran, to follow my brother and Watson. Moriarty had sent a note saying it was "just a simple precaution to be sure my brother does not return to London." However, Moriarty's "simple precaution" now upset the applecart and had thrown all my plans into disarray. For I knew that once Sherlock discovered he was being followed—and he surely would—he would seek the very confrontation I had worked so hard to avoid.

"That maniac with an air gun is stalking my brother!" I fairly shouted at Burbage. "He's Moriarty's chief henchman. He is not a member of the gang, so our people did not watch him like the others. Moriarty keeps him on separate status for use in delicate and special cases. Now he has slipped away. This is an outrage, Alex. Very bad!"

My man, Alex Burbage, nodded grimly. "I can be ready to leave within the hour, sir."

I looked up at Alex. "It will be dangerous. While I thought I could reason with Moriarty—after all, this was all in his own self-interest—Moran is altogether something different. He is a killer. If he gets it in his mind, he will kill whoever is in his way—Sherlock, Watson, or you—and Moriarty's restrictions on him be damned!"

Burbage smiled, said, "A little travel, the prospect of action, it sounds like fun. I will leave immediately, sir."

"Thank you, Alex. Good man!" I said, touched by his loyalty and willingness to help. We shook hands. I said, "Be careful, Alex. Follow Sherlock and Watson, make no contact, just observe and report back to me via coded telegram each evening. And keep a sharp eye on Moran! He's a bad one, and while ostensibly under the thumb of our professor friend not to take violent action, he likes to freelance too much for his own good. Keep me informed."

Burbage was a good man. I felt entirely confident with him on the case. His talents in combat and with weapons were superior to Moran's. His loyalty was unquestioned. He was just the man for the job, my eyes and ears in this matter on the Continent.

The first report from Burbage was brought to me next evening on a silver salver where I sat reading the *Times* in my chair at the Diogenes Club.

Without a word, Wilson placed the salver down upon my reading table and then quietly departed. I saw a folded piece of foolscap that had been sent upstairs to me from the secret offices below by my chief of Intelligence, Captain Hargrove. Already deciphered, I opened the paper and read Burbage's first telegraphed report carefully.

It read:

> M.
>
> HAVE REACHED YOUR BROTHER AND W STOP ALL APPEARS WELL STOP NO SIGN OF M STOP TOMORROW INTERLAKEN AND FALLS STOP WILL REPORT NEXT EVENING STOP
>
> AB

That was the last time I heard from Alexander Burbage. By the next evening, when there had been no report from him, I became concerned. The next day I dispatched two agents from Special Branch to follow him. Two days later their report, pieced together with Dr. Watson's added comments, formed the picture of what really transpired on that foggy morning at the Reichenbach Falls.

My brother always expected that someone would be following him. Had my original plan gone into effect unhampered, all would have been fine. There would have been no pursuit. Sherlock would have been perplexed, but finding no evidence of anyone tracking him, he would have been relegated to nothing more sinister than a harmless tourist. Moran changed all that by his very presence. Whether he meant my brother harm or not, whether he was stalking with murderous intent or just to observe, neither I nor Sherlock could have known for certain. Unfortunately, while Moran stalked Sherlock, he also set himself up as bait. So as Moran watched my brother, my man Burbage watched both of them. It was not long before wily Sherlock doubled back on his tracks and soon stood to confront Colonel Sebastian Moran on the heights over the Reichenbach.

A terrible fight ensued.

Watson told me later that he was on his way back from the hotel, where he had been called away on a medical emergency. A subterfuge by Moran to get Watson out of the picture, with my brother's obvious compliance to protect his friend. But good Watson realized the trick and raced back just in time to see two figures locked in a death struggle at the height of the fog-enshrouded falls. Watson could see my brother plainly fighting for his life against a man whom he took for Moriarty. The thick fog obscured what happened next. Suddenly, out of the swirling mist a body hurled downward to the roiling waters below. Watson gasped. Was it Sherlock? Was it Moriarty?

Watson frantically raced to where he had seen the body land. It appeared the man had fallen into the turbulent river, badly injured; he had made his way to the shore only to die. Watson ran over to the man, naturally fearing it was Sherlock. He frantically turned the man over, faceup, surprised to gaze upon a face that he did not know.

Sherlock then came out of the shrubbery and Watson, surprised and relieved, let out a shout of joy.

"Holmes! You're alive!"

"Indeed, Watson, though there are those who would be disappointed with that fact."

"What happened?" Watson had asked.

Sherlock said nothing as he went over to examine the body.

Both were surprised the man was still alive, though barely. Watson did what he could, but it was obvious without serious medical attention the man would soon be dead.

Sherlock said, "Good Burbage, you saved my life. I don't know how to thank you."

"You know the man, Holmes?" Watson had asked.

It was, of course, Burbage. He had also seen the fight but was far closer and stepped in to save Sherlock's life. It was Burbage who Moran had caused to drop off the Falls as he made his escape.

"Yes, Watson. I sense my brother Mycroft's involvement here."

"Mycroft?"

Sherlock nodded grimly, then said to the injured man, "Tell me, Burbage, what were you doing here?"

Burbage coughed, tried to steady his gaze. "Moriarty betrayed your brother, sent Moran. I had to stop him."

Moriarty betrayed Mycroft? Naturally Sherlock thought the answer odd and so he questioned Burbage further.

Burbage, dying, sick with delirium and in great pain, told Sherlock all he knew about the plan to cause him to leave London. Sherlock was obviously upset by this deceit on my part, but what my man said next actually enraged him. For before Burbage died, he babbled a long detailed account of the alliance between myself and Moriarty and of some of our common projects. When Burbage died, Watson told me the look on Sherlock's face appeared as if he had died as well. The look of pained betrayal was hard set in his eyes and it was terrible to see.

Watson told me that when Sherlock first heard this news, he could see my brother's face turn ashen, and Sherlock shouted my name in rage. Sherlock had lost control and was furious. "I have been betrayed, Watson!" he shouted angrily. "Not only is my brother allied with the same forces that I have risked my life to fight, dedicated my profession to destroy, but it is now obvious that he has been working with them all along. This is just too much!"

Of course, not being there to give Sherlock my side of the story, I was at a considerable disadvantage. But Sherlock would not have listened anyway.

Watson told me later, "I have never seen your brother so upset. It was most unlike him. He had lost all composure and even commented that not even the cocaine needle could assuage his pain this time. He actually used profanity in conjunction with your name. He said he was finished with you, London, and the Empire and that he would never come back."

I was shattered by this news. Sherlock now knew that I had not only used Moriarty on certain matters, but that some of the "Napoleon of Crime's" activities were in fact, attributed to *me*! That would be an affront I knew my brother could never accept. I feared his reaction, for I knew it would be extreme.

"Then," Watson continued, "your brother gave me instructions on what I must do and say about this matter before he told me good-bye."

"What did he say?" I asked Watson.

"As far as anyone knows, Sherlock Holmes met his death at the Reichenbach. This is the last case I shall write. I am to write no more of his cases for publication in the popular press," Watson said, adding, "He told me he will travel the globe, see the pyramids, perhaps seek an audience or studies with the Dalai Lama."

I harrumphed my displeasure. Of course it was utter nonsense.

Watson shrugged. "I tried to convince Sherlock to return but upon his death, Burbage told your brother such information that caused him great anger and distress."

Indeed! Sherlock finding out that some of the actions taken by Moriarty, had in fact, been at my direction and design was the one thing I feared the most. I was crushed. *I* was the reason Sherlock was never coming back to London. It was because *I* was in London! I grew despondent and morose.

Watson shook his head sadly, added, "Aside from Moriarty and Moran, you and I are the only ones who know that Sherlock is still alive. I haven't even told Doyle the truth. He never liked your brother anyway."

I nodded; there was nothing to do about it now. Once Sherlock had made up his mind it was set in stone. I had damaged his pride, but far worse, I had betrayed him. Even if it was for his own good, I had deceived him and now he knows the worst of it. My involvement with Moriarty. It was terrible!

Watson, afterwards, began to write his last Sherlock Holmes story for the *Strand,* as directed by my brother, calling it "The Final Problem"— ending with Sherlock's death at the Reichenbach at the hands of Moriarty. And that, as Sherlock told Watson before he came home to London, was the end of that!

I made the prerequisite funds available to Mrs. Hudson to keep up the rooms at 221B. I hoped Sherlock would be back someday, once he dropped this silly notion of anger at what I had done. After all, everything I had done was for his protection and England's. Well, most of it, at any rate. As time went by, though, I began to realize how wrong I had been.

I used my agents from time to time to carry cash and letters of explanation to my brother. His travels seemed varied and eclectic. His use of the name "Sigerson," claiming to be a Norwegian explorer, did not put me off his track. Wily Sherlock kept the money but always returned the letters to my agents unread. He made it clear to me it was over between us.

But it was not over for me. Since that day the rift between Sherlock and me weighed heavily upon me. I wanted to mend that break at any cost and bring Sherlock back to London. So from that day on, I worked on a plan with Watson that I hoped would set everything right.

Three years passed since Sherlock left and I missed him. Though we were always separated, there was always a connection that resonated between us. Two great intellects. The last two Holmes brothers left alive. It was a shame it had come to this.

In the meantime I continued my work for the Empire. It was a struggle, but rewarding in its own way. The Empire was now at its height and my work progressed well. Over the last months, through my various agents, including Moriarty's organization, there had been many successes. I had managed to defuse one revolution, end two minor wars, begin one invasion, annex new territory, free a dozen hostages, cause distress among the French, confound the Germans, foster an alliance with the Czar, succeed in three assassinations and prevent two others. This string of successes ended with the murder of young Ronald Adair in London on March 30, 1894.

Much had been made of the murder of this young dilettante and scion of the lesser nobility in the popular press, but would it shock you to know that he was one of my most able agents?

His tragic murder by Colonel Sebastian Moran, up to his dirty tricks once again, had been doubly troublesome for me, for it precipitated what I had feared most in recent months, conflict between Moriarty's gang and my own Special Branch people.

It seemed that without Sherlock in London, the criminal classes—and the organized criminals in particular, of which Professor Moriarty had lately achieved an impressive consolidation of control—were making their own play for power. I began to realize I had created a monster. It is times like these that I especially miss the services of my brother and men like Burbage. I felt more alone than ever.

It was early April when virtual warfare between our two organizations broke out. My operatives in the Special Branch called it "The Silent War." There were serious political problems, probably instigated by Moriarty, and they took my full attention so that I did not notice the connection with his other actions. We missed some telling clues early on, all beneath the vision of the press and the police. So very British. I really must compliment Moriarty. It began with an inconsequential fall, then an accident by hansom cab, a heart ailment; later there was a suicide or a lovers' quarrel gone bad. Before we knew what was happening, we had lost half a dozen prime operatives and I found myself under siege.

Now I dare not even return to my lodgings across the street at Pall Mall. Should I do so and some attempt be made upon my person that is successful or causes some public spectacle, it would cause undo questions, which cannot be allowed. Thus I cannot leave the confines of the Diogenes Club. So long as I remain in this secure bastion, I am safe from Moriarty and his minions. The sad irony of this situation is not lost on me. My brother's attempt to destroy Moriarty and his entire organization three years ago had been the correct thing to do. I should never have stopped him. Sherlock always understood the criminal mind far better than I. He knew there was no reasoning with such people. I knew then it was time to cut my ties with Moriarty for good altogether.

The situation had become serious when I heard from Dr. Watson. I had not seen him since that day he had come back from the Continent after my brother had let out on his travels. Watson told me the most astounding and welcome news; Sherlock was back in London! The Adair murder had called him back, for Sherlock realized the meaning of such a bold move and the danger that it placed me in. It was an alarm to us that Moriarty was making his move. Watson said that my brother was back to help me and that he wanted to meet with me later at his rooms at 221B.

That's wonderful news!" I told Watson. "This is a perfect time for us to start our plan. Leak a message of this meeting so Moriarty is sure to find out. I will do the rest."

I must admit that the prospect of seeing Sherlock again and our reconciliation did much to improve my spirits and I eagerly looked forward to our meeting later that evening. I knew leaving the confines of the club could be dangerous, but I took precautions. I had Hargrove see to it that Lestrade sent over two of his best men from Scotland Yard to accompany me.

All was going well until we turned onto Baker Street and I realized the two plainclothes police were in the employ of Moriarty. Though in disguise, and their papers had all been quite correct—their reputation had preceded them. I finally recognized them as Scottish specialists in murder, Jamison and Conner. This, I am afraid, was not what I had planned, but by then it was too late. They had a weapon on me and I had no choice but to allow them to bring me to the destination where I knew I was to be assassinated. It was the empty house across from 221B. The very house my brother Sherlock used for some of his more clandestine activities.

I was brought into the house, and taken upstairs at gunpoint.

"Aye, guv, someone of great importance wants to see you. On the upper floor," Connor said, prodding me up the steps. His partner, Jamison, following behind quietly.

When I reached the top of the stairs I was confronted by the sinister figure of Professor James Moriarty.

"Welcome, Mr. Holmes. It is so good to see you could actually bring yourself to leave the protection of your club to join us here tonight. It has been a number of years since our last meeting. At that time I seem to remember there were numerous issues left unresolved. I believe I can promise you that they shall all be settled this evening."

"Where is my brother?" I asked defiantly.

Moriarty smiled. "How sad. The vaunted reunion of the Holmes Brothers finally after so many years. There will be no meeting, but you shall see your brother presently, I assure you."

His dark words put a dread feeling upon me. I began to realize that Moriarty had a far more sinister plan in mind than just my own murder.

"What have you done to him? You'll hang for this, Professor!" I growled.

Moriarty nodded, motioning his men to gag me and bring me forward into the next room. There I saw Colonel Sebastian Moran at the front window. He was aiming his notorious air gun at a figure silhouetted in the window across the street from us. I realized that the window was the front room of the top apartment at 221B Baker Street, and the figure silhouetted in the center window was that of my brother, Sherlock.

"Tonight, Mr. Holmes, I clean up all loose ends in this affair. It has been a long road for us to get to this point. Beginning with your meddlesome brother, Sherlock. He eluded Colonel Moran at the Falls. He'll not get away this time."

I watched the silhouette of my brother in the window across the street, wishing that he would get up and move safely out of range. I saw him move slightly, turn his head a bit, but he still presented a full shot for Moran's murderous weapon.

I wanted to shout out to Sherlock in warning, but the gun pressed tightly in my back by Conner and the gag stuffed in my mouth by Jamison made it impossible. Moriarty's men held me firmly. So I just stood there watching with dreadful fear. Here I had come to meet Sherlock and there he was, waiting for me patiently, and I would never see him again. I felt like crying when I saw Moran take aim. Moriarty rubbed his hands together in anticipation.

Moriarty said, "Colonel Moran, you may fire when ready."

Moran smiled, savoring the bloody moment, and said, "Yes, Professor." Then he slowly squeezed off a shot. There was a slight whoosh, and a moment later I saw a tiny explosion in the center of the silhouette of my brother's head.

Moran put down his weapon, stood up and said proudly, "Sherlock Holmes is dead finally, once and for all, Professor."

My heart sank. A tear streamed down my cheek. My brother dead? It was inconceivable. Terrible! I cried, knowing I would soon join him in death. That was the reunion Moriarty had planned for us.

"Good," Moriarty said, satisfied, then added, "Sherlock's brother, Mycroft, will soon join him."

"Not so fast, Professor Moriarty!" A voice boomed from the doorway at the other end of the room. It was my brother, Sherlock, standing tall and bold, and beside him was good old Watson, Inspector Lestrade, and a host of armed Scotland Yard detectives.

The trap was sprung and the rats were left with no place to hide now.

The men from Scotland Yard were upon Jamison and Conner immediately. They were disarmed, put in irons, and taken away.

Lestrade commented, "A pretty pair, those two, wanted for murder throughout the High Country. It'll be the assizes for them soon enough in Edinburgh."

Moran, seeing the way the wind was blowing, raised his hands in surrender. Lestrade's men took him into custody and held him.

Moriarty, enraged at the sudden reversal of his fortunes, quickly drew a knife and came at me before anyone could act. He held me in an iron grip with the blade to my neck. "I'll slit his throat if you don't all back off!" he ordered.

Everyone held back, waiting, fearing the worst.

Sherlock calmly said, "Let me have your revolver, please, Watson."

I saw Watson put the weapon in my brother's hand.

Sherlock cocked the hammer back, even as I could feel Moriarty's knife tickle the folds of flesh at my throat. This had *not* been in my plan for the events of the evening.

I saw Sherlock take careful aim.

Everyone was frozen, waiting to see what would happen next.

Moriarty barked at Sherlock, "I will certainly kill your brother if you do not drop your weapon and stand back!"

I watched fascinated as Sherlock held his arm out steady and straight, extended with Watson's revolver aimed at Moriarty's head.

"Drop the knife, Professor. It is over. Harm Mycroft and you will not live to hang," Sherlock said sternly.

The face-off was incredible, the tension in the room, electric. Everyone held their breath.

Moriarty lowered the knife. He was an intelligent man, surely common sense was to prevail. I could feel the blade move away from my throat. I let out a breath of profound relief, and then I saw what was in Moriarty's eyes. The hatred that was there shocked me. It was like looking into his soul and it was ugly. Repulsive. The gag still prevented me from talking, but with my eyes I implored Sherlock to shoot. Could Sherlock not see that Moriarty wanted us all to believe he was coming to reason, that he would soon surrender? All the time he was planning to slit my throat in one quick gesture, then hurl his knife into Sherlock's chest as soon as he saw the opportunity. Moriarty lowered the knife further. . . .

Sherlock did not buy the bait. He did not lower his weapon. He did not waver.

Moriarty saw all was lost. He quickly moved his arm upward, bringing the knife back to my throat for the killing blow.

One loud report issued from the revolver in Sherlock's hand!

The explosion was ear-shattering and terrible.

Moriarty froze, as did everyone in the room.

I tried to move, to get away.

Moriarty still held me tightly. I remember thinking, had Sherlock missed? It was inconceivable, but . . .

Then Moriarty's arm continued upward once again, the blade of his knife touching my throat. I remember feeling the coldness of the steel, seeing Sherlock's and Watson's terrified faces. Why did not Sherlock take another shot? What had happened? Then suddenly the knife left Moriarty's hand to fall and clatter on the floor, and his hold on me loosened and fell away. I turned and saw his surprised face, the coldness of his reptilian eyes as the fire in those eyes seemed to dissolve before me. His great criminal intellect melting away in death as I watched. There was a tiny hole in the center of his forehead and drops of blood now began suddenly pouring down his face. Then Moriarty collapsed to the floor dead, and I sighed with relief as Sherlock and Watson ran to my side.

"Good shot, Sherlock!" I said, once I had taken the gag out of my mouth and regained my composure somewhat. "You saved my life. Thank you."

"You mean to tell me this was not a part of your and Watson's plan?" he said with a smile.

I shrugged. "Indeed. However, I am relieved that you were able to improvise a correction so handily. But how did you know I had been taken hostage?"

"Good Watson here kept an eye on you after he gave you the news of our meeting. He alerted me to the fact that Moriarty's men had abducted you. I confess, I expected some such action from our enemy. The one thing you can count on in any plan, no matter how well formulated, is that something will always go wrong. The criminal mind is a dark and devious morass but it functions at a rather primordial level. So accordingly, I made my own plan, and here we are!"

"I thought Moran had murdered you," I said. "I saw your head, the silhouette moved, so I thought . . ."

"Aye, and so did Moran, and that's what convinced him and Moriarty. It was a pretty setup, Moriarty literally champing at the bit at the prospect of murdering both Holmes Brothers in the same evening when they were so close to meeting and reconciling their differences. It was a master plan, worthy of the Napoleon of crime."

I nodded. "Indeed, it was an evil plan. I will never understand the criminal mind as you do. I am just relieved we are all safe and have concluded this Moriarty business once and for all."

At that moment, Moran was dragged past us by two stout bobbies. He shouted, "Why? Why am I being arrested? I did not kill Sherlock Holmes! He is alive and here!"

Lestrade held up his hand. Then Sherlock brought over the air gun and gave it to Lestrade, saying, "Here, Inspector, I believe this rather unique gun will prove to be the weapon used in the murder of the Honorable Ronald Adair."

"Aye, Holmes," Lestrade said, "I'm sure that it will."

"And, Inspector," I added, "that should be quite enough evidence to send Colonel Moran to the gallows. He has eluded the hangman for far too long."

Lestrade nodded. "So it will, Mr. Holmes, eh, Mr. Mycroft Holmes."

Sherlock and I smiled.

Moran struggled and shouted threats.

Lestrade barked to his men, "Get him out of here!"

Sherlock and I joined Watson as he performed the final examination on the body of the late Professor James Moriarty.

"Official cause of death," Watson said, getting up from the corpse, "one bullet in the head. Death was almost instantaneous." Then to the waiting bobbies, "You men can take the body away now."

Sherlock, Watson and I sat in the rooms at 221B an hour later.

"I see you had Mrs. Hudson keep our rooms just as they were. I thank you, Mycroft."

"It was the least I could do," I said.

Sherlock nodded. "It certainly was. Especially after you had your man Burbage set fire to them!"

"Now, Sherlock . . . ," I said carefully, "It was really, after all, a very minor fire."

Sherlock laughed. "Fear not, older brother, my anger is gone and I know that in your own way, you tried to protect me, even as you protected your own interests."

"It seemed the best course open at the time," I replied.

"And anyway, we have a celebration! Watson, break out that bottle of Napoleon brandy you have kept for a special occasion. For there can be no occasion more special than this one—the end of Moriarty and the liberation of the world from his grasp—and we have a bonus! The capture and future hanging of Colonel Moran . . ."

"Not to mention you saved my life, Sherlock," I added.

"Quite right, Mycroft. Glad to be of service. You and Watson had a good plan, the use of both Holmes Brothers as bait could not fail to bring out Moriarty and Moran where we could finally get at them. Your mistake was failing to realize that no plan, no matter how brilliant, is a solid item. It is fluid, always open to change and amendment. You saw a chance to bring out our enemies; they saw an opportunity to twist your plan against you. However, they neglected to factor in my own action. So the wax bust to mark me as an easy target as I waited to meet you in these very rooms. It was a situation I knew Moriarty could not resist. And while our enemies concentrated on the image in this window, Watson, Lestrade and I, with a triple brace of good London bobbies, were quietly entering the house from the backyard."

"Mrs. Hudson helped," Watson added, pouring brandy and passing it out. "She bravely stayed in here moving the wax bust of Sherlock to trick Moran and not make him suspicious."

"Good Mrs. Hudson," Sherlock said, gently sipping his brandy.

"When Moriarty thought you were dead," I said to Sherlock, "he became confident. Even I noticed how he grew lax and did not post a guard, and that is how you were able to move up the stairs undetected. It was the perfect time to make your move," I added. "But even you did not know he would take me hostage with a knife to my throat?"

"Why, Mycroft, you continually surprise me! Actually I did. But the game was up for him no matter what and he knew it. He wanted me dead, not you. He could not get at me with a knife and I had Watson's revolver and knew how to use it. He gave me no choice, so I fired. Your eyes told me what I must do."

I nodded. It was all becoming clear to me now and I gained new respect for my little brother and his great talents.

"But I did not think you had it in you, Mycroft, lowering yourself to actual ratiocination. This uncommon interest in the criminal mind bodes well for you," Sherlock told me with a laugh and a gleam in his eye. "Why, I believe I'll make a detective of you yet."

"Your acid wit has returned, I see," I said.

"It never left, brother," Sherlock replied sternly.

"Well, I think it is time I return to my club; there are matters that need my direct attention," I said.

"Indeed," Sherlock said tartly. "Are you already thinking of a replacement for Moriarty?"

I sighed. I had no anger left in me. "No, Sherlock, that is over. I am truly sorry for deceiving you. These last three years have made me realize much and I hope that the rift I have opened between us can now be mended. I will go back to the club, tidy up a few matters, confer with Captain Hargrove, and then tender my resignation. I believe retirement is in order and, frankly, I look forward to it now."

Sherlock was surprised but pleased. He came over to me and shook my hand, saying, "Mycroft, you did what you thought best. A man, no man, should be chastised for that. I know Great Aunt Julia would have been proud of you for all you have done over the years. I am proud of you for what you did today and for what you just said."

A tear came to my eye then and I saw it mirrored in Sherlock's own eyes.

Sherlock wrapped his arms around me and we hugged each other silently for one brief endless moment as Watson watched in wonder.

"You know, I, too, think I shall retire, some day, Mycroft. Perhaps to the Sussex Downs and a study of bee culture? It can be most fascinating."

"Is that wise, Holmes?" Watson interjected with evident concern as my brother and I both looked at him and smiled.

"With Moriarty and Moran gone," Sherlock answered contritely, "I am afraid that London's criminal element will be reduced to the banal and the inept. Lestrade will be well within his depth, I am sure."

Watson and I nodded, knowing all too well of my brother's opinion of the official police.

"However, Mycroft," Sherlock added seriously, "while I am the first to admit that your 'work' has been a serious bone of contention between us for years, with your retirement I fear the Empire has lost its most successful advocate and protector. Know this, our vaulted 'Pax Britannia' exists in no small part due to your tireless effort. That is a considerable accomplishment, even if it can never be made public. With you gone from the scene, the politicians will be in charge again and God alone knows what horrors they'll perpetuate upon the body politic. For instance, I see ugly war brewing in South Africa among the Boers in years to come. I see a tragedy coming our way there. But far worse, without your direction of our ship of state, I fear within twenty short years we will find ourselves engaged in a worldwide conflagration the likes of which this world has never seen before."

I nodded. "I am aware of the projections."

"Then you know the politicians will only expand the length and depth of the misery and carnage," Sherlock added.

"Yes, brother, I know that and it saddens me, for I have worked for the Empire all my life and I do not want to see the approaching sunset. Nevertheless, the Empire is changing, and so, too, the world, and we must all change with it. Or be left behind. It is time for me to move on, and for you . . . to study bees in Sussex? Indeed!"

I took another sip of Watson's excellent brandy.

"Well, Watson, surely this has been a case worthy of your efforts for the popular press?" Sherlock said.

"Yes, I would like your permission to write it up for the *Strand*."

"Indeed, certainly, but with certain restrictions. Of course all mention of my brother and his 'government' service must be deleted. I'm afraid you will have to leave Moriarty out of the story as well. Knowledge of his surviving Reichenbach will not only contradict your previously published narrative of this case, making you look rather foolish, but it will cause fear and chaos in the criminal underground and among the public. Moran can easily fit the bill of your villain, and he is the actual murderer of young Adair. But Watson, do not publish the story for at least ten years. I see 1904 as an adequate date for the appearance to the public of such a tale. What do you think?" Sherlock asked.

"Of course, I shall abide by your wishes," Watson replied.

"Good. Thank you, old friend. I rather like the thought of being dead, at least where the public and popular press are concerned. And it certainly will surprise the criminal element who believe that I am no more, when I appear and confront them with their crimes," Sherlock added with a grin.

I nodded. "It sounds like it would make an interesting case, Doctor. I shall look forward to reading it in the *Strand* . . . some day."

"Hah! Ably put, Mycroft!" Sherlock said. "And who knows, between now and then—two Holmes Brothers, retired, on our own and left to our devices—why, we may even join forces on occasion when a particularly complex or interesting problem may arise, eh, Mycroft?"

I smiled at my brother. "I don't see why not, Sherlock. *Holmes and Holmes, Consultants*. It does have a certain ring to it, don't you think?"

BILLY

It was pleasant for Dr. Watson to find himself once more in the untidy room of the first floor in Baker Street which had been the starting point of so many remarkable adventures. . . . His eyes came round to the fresh and smiling face of Billy, the young but very wise and tactful page who had helped a little to fill up the gap of loneliness and isolation which surrounded the saturnine figure of the great detective.

—"The Adventure of the Mazarin Stone"

by GERARD DOLE

The Witch of Greenwich

[To Dave Stuart Smith]

During the years I had the luck and privilege to be the page boy of Mr. Sherlock Holmes, I ushered many an illustrious client into his old study in Baker Street. I also had the chance to witness his amazing reasoning and observational abilities, which made me dream to practice one day in turn as a consulting detective. It was a great honor, then, when in the last years preceding his retirement to Sussex my master asked me to become his assistant and began teaching me fully the art of detection. Tonight I am looking back and reminiscing about the first case I followed with Mr. Sherlock Holmes that showed me I had the deductive abilities to become a detective myself. The master referred to it as The Witch of Greenwich, an astounding story which put Londoners' security at stake. Now that all the other protagonists are gone, I dare to put on paper these lines. I unfortunately do not have the skill and literary style of the late Dr. John Watson, but I shall nevertheless strive to relate all I saw and heard in the most accurate manner.

—BILLY "PAGE BOY" CHAPLIN

PROLOGUE

Swains Lane, near Highgate Cemetery's side entrance, late at night

"Come along, Frenchie!" I said in very low voice, giving the man a slight tap on the shoulder.

Despite the freezing air the stranger was crouching against the rusty gate of the old graveyard, staring blankly at a great tomb of marble which lay a short distance beyond, as if impelled by some sort of morbid fascination. At the touch of my fingers, he gave a violent start and turned round swiftly, clenching his fists, ready to fight for his life.

"*Bon sang d'bon soir,* Billy!" he cried reproachfully. "Pah! You gave me the creeps, you know!"

I sneered at him. "Keep an eye out, next time. I could have slaughtered you as easily as a sheep, Monsieur Le Villard!"

Le Villard—or to tell the reader his full name, François Le Villard— had reached the top a long time ago in the French detective service, and worked with Scotland Yard on many occasions. He had thus built up a deep friendship with my master, Mr. Sherlock Holmes, who said of him that he had all the Celtic power of quick intuition but was deficient in the wide range of exact knowledge which was essential to the higher developments of his art. At the moment the Frenchman was carrying out a most astounding investigation which had brought him to London.

"*Mon cher ami—*" he went on, but I cut him off.

"Later . . . and don't you speak so loud!" I said bluntly, casting a careful glance around. "Let's get away from here while we can."

"But I have to get some proof first," pleaded Le Villard, showing the Kodak he was hiding in his lap.

"A goner doesn't need any. My master told you before it was sheer folly to hang about here late at night, but as usual, Monsieur Le Villard, you didn't listen to him. Now, move on!"

"*Mais,* Billy . . ."

"Sorry, old man, don't harp on it. We'd better stir our stumps!"

I took the French detective's arm in nervous haste and dragged him along down Swains Lane.

"Pray she has not spotted us already," I whispered, looking up anxiously at the great ranges of funereal trees leaning over the long, half-crumbled wall which encircled the cemetery.

Le Villard gave me a wink and patted a bulge in his jacket at heart level. "My revolver, *mon bon vieil ami,*" he boasted, "ready to give six nice kisses from France."

"Hem! A toy gun would be just as useful at the moment, I'm afraid. Once again, we'd better hurry."

We went down Highgate Hill at a very quick pace. Mist had settled over the place, obscuring the faint light of the stars. There was something weird, uncanny, threatening in the aspect of the interminable cemetery wall which lined the lane. And to make things worse, it grew more and more vague and shapeless, until it became part of the haze. Eerily, through the tense silence, a sudden yell rang out in the air.

Le Villard's face fell.

"Hey! What's that cry?" he gasped.

"Who knows? A raven's call?" I replied in uneasy tone.

In fact, I thought of something more abominable. The truly awful feeling that a monstrosity is lying in wait was strong upon me, though my composed, resolute face showed no sign of flinching. I was grimly prepared for the worst but my hope was to gain a hansom before it happened. So I said in commanding tones:

"Now run, Monsieur Le Villard! For God's sake, run!"

The French detective had no time for more than a passing glance round as I was already racing down the lane, but what he caught sight of on top of the wall was so ghastly that he hurled himself forward in my wake, awestruck.

We flew down Swains Lane, dashed across Oakeshott Avenue, and attained Highgate Road with heaving heart and panting breath.

"To that cab!" I ordered, pointing towards a hansom waiting close by.

We reached it in double quick time without mishap, and I climbed in with a sigh of deep relief.

The hansom cab was rattling over the cobbled streets through the fog-shrouded night. The streetlamps made great ghostly blurs as they melted in the distance and the passing houses were dark and gloomy as so many tombs.

I said to the Frenchman sitting by my side: "Creepy, wasn't it?"

"*Tu parles!* Never was I so scared in my whole life."

I gave him a nod and asked in a half-voice:

"Just what did you see, Monsieur?"

Le Villard's voice shook. "*Bon Dieu!* Billy, I saw a shrouded corpse floating above the graveyard wall. . . . *Oo la la! Horrible!*"

"Countess Vetcha!" I sniffed. " 'Diamond of the first water,' her wooers used to whisper when they saw her, their eyes shining with desire. A very fair Hungarian lady indeed who lived in a wonderful mansion at Eltham.

The neighborhood, though, gave her another kind of name. 'The Witch of Greenwich,' they used to call her. . . .

"In her lifetime, of course!" I added with a shrug.

CHAPTER 1
THE BLACK DEATH

Greenwich, a few hours later, some time before daybreak

"Fire! Fire!"

The cry rose up startlingly in the deep silence of the very early hour, arousing Constables Curland and Flanders, who were peacefully patrolling Churchbury Road. They turned back as one man and looked up anxiously around.

"Hey! It's all ablaze over there!" exclaimed the first one, pointing at a vivid red glare in the northern sky which threw some nearby chimneys into strong relief.

"Rats! Not half!" replied the other in harsh tones, "but say, where d'you think it is, Curland?"

"Don't know. Eltham Palace Road? . . . Kings Round? . . . Can't say for sure. Can you, Flanders?"

"Nay. Let's go and see!"

The two policemen hurried back up the hill towards the fire, using the increasing glare as a guide, its glow on the clouds waxing and waning as the flames shot up or temporarily died down, and after a while, they came in sight of a huge column of smoke.

"It's in Queenscroft Road!" cried Constable Flanders.

They covered some two hundred yards at a breakneck pace and were at last within view of a large house built in an antiquated style, blazing fiercely in the middle of a fallow park. "Holy Angels! It's the late Countess Vetcha's residence!" exclaimed Constable Curland.

His mate nodded gravely as he recognized the place also. "Yes. But thank God it's been unoccupied for over thirty years," he said with a note of relief in his hoarse voice.

The Metropolitan Fire Brigade had preceded the two bobbies and its brave men were already at work, their bright helmets glinting everywhere. Some, lost on ladders, amid smoke, poured a torrent of water on the burning and seething premises, while others used all their energy working the engines set back on the lawn.

A few neighbors had joined the aged warden who was staring in utter sadness at the already tottering walls of the once-proud mansion. The old man looked a heartrending, sorry sight, probably evoking in himself the bygone days when the park was full of carriages which pulled up one by one before the house, brilliantly illuminated in a far less dramatic way, when fur-lined cloaks and coats, dress uniforms, sumptuous gowns, passed in procession before a gigantic footman who made deep bows.

Queenscroft Road, usually so quiet, was in an unbelievable turmoil: the intense glare, the shooting flames which darted viciously out and upwards, the puff and clank of the engines, the rushing and hissing of the water, the roar of the fire, and the columns of smoke which in heavy sulky masses hung gloating over the blazing mansion, gave it a weird and tragic aspect. Suddenly, Constable Curland who, like his mate, had been gazing eagerly at the firemen's fierce struggle, uttered a wild cry.

"Hang me! There's a woman inside the house."

Indeed a female form had appeared at an upper window, framed in flame, curtained with smoke, but it vanished on the spot, as if swallowed by the noxious fumes. The small party of bystanders reacted as one:

"Save her! Save her!"

Women twisted their hands with shrill cries, men clenched their fists and swore. The old warden alone stood rigid, transfixed with bewilderment.

"Mercy me! . . . I can't believe it. . . . I . . . it can't be!" he faltered out, his lips parted, his eyes distended, his face frightened and white.

"Say, are you sick, my good man?" inquired Constable Flanders solicitously, having noticed his distorted features.

"No . . . no . . . nothing much . . . the heat probably. Thank you, Constable."

In the meantime, a fire sergeant had climbed up a ladder and leaped into the open window. He was swallowed up in a moment and lost sight of. Everyone beneath held his breath, wondering if he would ever come out of the furnace. Deadly seconds elapsed and at last, here he was again at the window, bearing a lifeless female form. A mighty cheer arose. He was greeted with great shouts of joy. But the people should not have crowed so hastily over his victory for, as we shall see now, it was what may be called a Pyrrhic one. The first to realize that there was something not quite right with the sergeant was Constable Curland.

"Hey, look at him!" he exclaimed. "What's up? Has he got the fidgets or what?" Indeed, oddly enough, the sergeant gave the impression of having a sudden fit of frenzy, most similar to St. Vitus's dance. He looked like a wild contortionist lost in a sea of flame and smoke, and it was extremely weird to watch him twisting and shaking all over in the glare of the conflagration. Obviously the poor man had grown suddenly mad. That thought and a thousand troubled others passed through everyone's mind.

Already, two firemen were rushing up ladders to give him help. Alas, they were hardly halfway up when he abruptly dropped the senseless woman back into the blaze and hurled himself headfirst out of the window with an unearthly yell. Constables, neighbors, and firemen alike were horror stricken. Women gave screams and fainted, men dashed mechanically forward with oaths, but there was nothing to be done, and the next moment, while the unknown woman was probably heaped in a small pile of ashes inside, the fire sergeant lay lifeless on the lawn like a broken puppet.

The sergeant's corpse was now lying on a stretcher, waiting to be taken away. Suddenly, the old warden who had just approached and was leaning over it as so many others did, gave a violent start. Pointing a trembling finger at the dead man's face, he cried in tones of pure horror:

"The Black Death! Mercy me! . . . The Black Death!"

Then, ridden by intense fear, he sprang back and most unexpectedly ran away, yelling all the more: "The Black Death! The Black Death!"

An expression of deep horror had suddenly come over Constables Curland's and Flanders' faces. They both had been soldiers in India and both had heard this blood-chilling announcement while on campaign in Bengal. They looked at each other aghast.

The Black Death! . . . or, in other words . . . bubonic plague!

CHAPTER 2
THE EMPTY COFFIN

Inspector Gregson sat in his office at Scotland Yard, perusing a report which bore the stamp of the police mortuary. He turned it over in utter perplexity, pursed his lips and groaned inwardly:

"He's always been a man of sound advice . . . why not ring him, then?" He took up the receiver on his desk with some brusqueness and dialed Sherlock Holmes's number. My master answered immediately.

"Holmes speaking."

"Hullo! It's Gregson."

There was a chuckle at the other end of the line.

"Dear me, we must be kindred spirits, Greg'. I was on the point of calling you. I read in the morning paper that the late Countess Vetcha's mansion in Eltham burned to the ground last night. I am deeply interested in the matter, you know. . . ."

It was Gregson's turn to be pleased. My master's unexpected words immediately put him in a good mood and he replied with great friendliness: "You still don't know the best, Mr. Holmes. Did you read about Sergeant McLean?"

"The brave fireman who found death on duty? Indeed yes, why?"

"Well, the press didn't report the whole story. You'd better cling to your chair, sir!"

The inspector paused for a couple of seconds. He declared at last with some emphasis: "Sergeant McLean's body and face bore stigmata of bubonic plague!"

"Oh? And about time, too!" was my master's brief, stolid reply. Gregson was totally discountenanced by it. He gave a gasp of appalled surprise and almost dropped the phone.

"Don't . . . don't tell me you expected it, Mr Holmes!" he stammered out.

"Of course I did! Sorry to spoil your little surprise, Greg'!"

The inspector passed a trembling hand over his forehead. "How on earth could you—" he began in tones of pure astonishment, but my master cut him off.

"The explanations will come at the proper time, Greg'," Holmes said. "There is no time to waste, believe me. Londoners' security is at stake. I must interview the mansion's caretaker at once. Tell me, where can I find him?"

"I don't know. He ran away."

"Ran away?"

"Yes. You see, he'd hardly looked at the fireman's face when he made off, bawling like a banshee. Nobody's seen him since."

"Too bad. The main trail is lost," muttered my master bitterly. "Well, I'll have to do without him, then," he added after a brief silence.

"Look here, Mr. Holmes, you spoke of Londoners' security. . . . Are you serious?"

"Most serious, alas! The situation could rapidly become tragic."

"Hey! What do you mean?"

"Hem! I would trigger off a panic in Scotland Yard if I told you. . . . Sorry, Greg'," apologized Sherlock Holmes. And most impolitely, to cut short the inspector's questioning, he rang off.

The shadowy twilight was deepening into night. My master and François Le Villard were carefully moving through Highgate Cemetery's dismal wilderness. They passed many half-ruined, moss-grown cenotaphs and decayed chapels whose stained-glass windows were smashed; they zigzagged in a maze of flat-topped tombs with buddleia and fern sprouting from crevices, until they came into view of a huge yew casting its broad, black, outstretched limbs athwart a massive mausoleum of marble, as if to protect it from the chill breezes which now and again came sighing and sobbing through its interlacing branches. Sherlock Holmes then gently touched his companion's shoulder and pointed to the white monument. The Frenchman gave a nod and looked carefully around. They waited a while in the long, dank grass, caught in the eddying current of the keen night air, and then stole towards the great tomb. At last they reached its rusty iron gate. My master gently opened it with a latchkey he had produced from his pocket and stepped in. He found his bearings instantly, as far as the lingering light would admit it, to a narrow stone staircase and climbed down as stealthily as possible, followed by Le Villard. They reached the bottom rapidly and my master flashed his pocket lantern full onto a small sepulcher whose center was occupied by a single oak coffin. The smell of rot there was almost unbearable. Nevertheless they stepped to the coffin and read the following epitaph, inscribed on a large brass plate:

> KAROLINA SZOKOLI
> COUNTESS VETCHA
> WHO DEPARTED THIS LIFE
> 18 MAY 1871
> IN HER 24TH YEAR

"Well, let's see now what's left of her," said my master grimly. Putting then the lantern into Le Villard's hands, he produced a screwdriver and began to remove the many screws. Soon the lid was loose. He lifted it with disgust and a low exclamation broke from the Frenchman's lips:

"*Bon sang.* . . . It's empty!"

"I expected it," said Holmes.

He breathed a sigh, wagged his head from side to side in utter despondency, and declared loudly, in sepulchral tones: "So, here is the definite proof. . . ."

After a moment's silence, he continued in the same way: "Karolina Szokoli was married when in her teens to Count Vetcha, who so utterly crushed her young life by his continued cruelty and excesses that she died while yet in the very heyday of her youth and beauty. . . ."

Oddly enough, as he was delivering this funereal oration, my master had carefully fitted his hands with thin but very solid leather gloves. Much to Le Villard's surprise, he produced then a very tiny pair of forceps and scrutinized the coffin's decayed satin lining. All of a sudden, very swiftly, he picked up something minuscule and thrust it into a small test tube he had also produced from his waistcoat. ". . . And she has ever since haunted the estates of the illustrious Hungarian family to which she belongs."

My master pocketed the tweezers and test tube with a surreptitious smile of satisfaction, and added in the same grim voice: "We know now that Countess Vetcha is one of the living dead and we had better take our leave before she turns back. It's the Church's business to exorcise the place, not ours. Let's get out of here, François!"

CHAPTER 3
BOG TOWN

Bog Town. Search as minutely as you could on a London map, you would not have found it, even on the most detailed one. And yet it well and truly existed not so long ago. On paper, it was but a mere blank, at the outermost bounds of Lewisham, between Deptford Church Street and Norman Road. Scotland Yard itself had but a rather vague layout of this (at least officially) nameless district. There, on every side of a strip of fallow land watered by Deptford Creek, big heaps of waste and rubbish alternated with rows of rickety shanties—the dingy abode of the great metropolis's rag-picking population.

In Bog Town, all day long, you found numbers of tattered women seated in front of their shabby dwellings, with bushel baskets full of refuse by their side. They probed and examined, in the most pernickety manner, the squalid loot that their men had brought back from their early morning's dustbin round, sorting out whatever could be worth a bob, a tanner, or even a brass farthing. Bands of ragged kids were gamboling around and shouting in merriment under the amused gaze of careworn patriarchs seated by the side of their windows. The only pub in the neighborhood was always thronged with motley groups of rag-and-bone men loafing about the bar, drinking, chatting, and smoking their pipes. On Saturday evenings in the taproom could be seen Curly the squeeze-box player, with a dozen couples enjoying the dance and singing over their gin-and-water. To sum up, Bog Town's inhabitants, though very poor, formed a cheerful and happy lot until that fatal day when they suddenly all became . . . plague-struck!

There was a mist round Bog Town when my master, Inspector Gregson, and myself found it, one of those strange, fugitive fogs that drift like ghosts at night in the hollows. Instantly, a tall fellow with a red nose and bushy whiskers put in an appearance with the suddenness of a specter, and gave them a military salute. He was Constable Miles, dispatched to us by the Lewisham Police, and had been watching out for our arrival a very long time in the cold with dutiful resignation. In the mist, his lantern was a glowworm and I told myself with a shudder that it would soon become a frail guide in the acrid fog.

"The quarantine line . . . fully operational, Constable?" Gregson asked the bobby point blank.

"Yes, sir. Since nightfall, sir."

"The ill?"

"Taken away to hospital."

"The dead?"

"Removed to the last, sir."

"The doctors, the nurses?"

"They all left."

"Which means the four of us will be the only living ones tonight in Bog Town?"

The constable's voice shook: "In . . . indeed yes, sir."

A few hours before, Bog Town had been shut by a barbed-wire fence which endowed it with the grim aspect of concentration camp. Each fifty yards hung large boards with "Danger. No trespassing." in red. The only possible entry was through a gate guarded by policemen in arms. Just past it, a tent had been pitched for sanitary purposes. There, we found the proper safety clothes for our visit. They consisted of black rubber robes which, reaching down to the ground, rose to a point above the head, entirely concealing form and face, except for the eye holes. Goggles, rubber gloves, and boots completed the equipment.

"The Holy Mother Church hath need of thee, Great Inquisitor!" I jested, bowing at my master who had just arrayed himself in the gloomy robe.

Holmes quelled me with a glance. "Stop cracking jokes and put on yours, too, my boy," he said in acid voice while grinning secretly at Gregson who, in the black outfit, because of his very big stomach, looked like a corpulent rubber doll.

We were now slowly passing through the foggy pall that overspread Bog Town. No doubt that, in other circumstances, our figures would have made an onlooker's blood run cold, so ghostly we appeared in the gleam of the policeman's lantern, seeming to glide without perceptible effort over the muddy ground. In fact, it was our lot to be scared in this deadly immensity, in the midst of the great, somber-hued heaps of refuse which rose menacingly, and we summoned every ounce of courage we possessed to move on without trembling knees.

"It started Sunday morning . . . ," began Constable Miles as we passed a row of wretched, tumbledown hovels, just to break the unbearable silence which hung upon Bog Town. But the effect was even worse for, through the rubber mask, his voice sounded deep and sepulchral. He broke off on the spot.

"Please go on, Constable," invited my master, laying a comforting hand upon his shoulder.

Miles nodded and waved his arms, briefly resembling a hulking crow. He resumed:

"Many ragmen were taken very sick all of a sudden. After a while, some fell dead on the ground without warning, but others had great sufferings; you heard them groan and cry. It was heartbreaking, you know. There were desperate fellows who ran screaming around. I have heard of an old woman in violent pain who broke out naked and ran direct to Deptford Creek, where she drowned herself. The disease spread very quickly and in the evening dead bodies were lying upon the ground all about the place. . . . Frightful! Doctors were sent for too late, you see; they could save only a few people. They told us it was some kind of very violent and infectious fever."

"A white lie, to prevent a panic," whispered Holmes to my ear.

"What a pity!" went on the policeman. "They were nice folks; sometimes a little bit rough, but nice, very nice."

He shook his head mournfully and added: "Think that the night before, they had a ball . . . music . . . fireworks!"

"Fireworks?" I wondered.

"Yes, fired from Deptford Bridge, and there was an organ, too. . . . It played polkas and waltzes."

Constable Miles drew a long breath and ceased to speak. For some time on, he led us round about Bog Town, and not a sound was to be heard, except the soft squelch of our footsteps in the mud.

At one moment, my master climbed up a big junk heap and looked into the night. It was dark and foggy, and he could only catch sight of the vague shimmering of a stagnant pool down below. There was no point to remain any longer in these grim and repellent surroundings. Holmes shrugged his shoulders and told me that brandy, tobacco, and a hot bath would be most welcomed back home.

CHAPTER 4
MONSIEUR VICTOR

My master was just on his way down when suddenly, with eyes accustomed to the darkness of the night, he noticed several moving figures noiselessly deploying themselves out towards his companions. We were waiting quietly for him at the foot of the mound, totally unaware of what was going on, and did not see the shadowy forms slowly creeping around us in deadly silence. At once Holmes knew the full extent of the danger and he shouted with stentorian lungs: "Lads, watch out!"

We were startled by his command but, at first, we did not understand what it meant. So we turned round and stared at him blankly. However, we were not long in realizing the situation, for a mere second had elapsed when came a wild yell, followed by a rustle in the mud, and the attack of a posse of fiends. They were ten or twelve, perhaps more. Their faces were shriveled, their eyes bloodshot and glaring, their long hair disheveled, tangled, and matted.

"Lord bless me!" groaned Gregson.

Indeed, the sight of these repulsive creatures, dashing at us from nowhere in this empty, forbidden place, was truly nightmarish. The inspector sprang back, searching for his gun, and I did the same, but conversely, dropping his lantern, Constable Miles made a couple of swift strides forward. Before the assailants could react, he had seized the first one by his throat and belt, lifted him high in the air, swung him round, and hurled him clean into the others, who toppled and fell down. This clever and courageous action averted immediate danger and helped to gain a little time.

"Here, lads! Come up! Quick!" cried Holmes.

It was a steep climb to the top of the rubbish heap, one of the tallest in Bog Town, and the rubber outfits were not meant for such sport; nevertheless, the three of us did reach it in a few moments.

"Thanks, Master! I'm glad to be with you again," I said to Sherlock Holmes, who had offered me a helping hand, "and a thousand thanks more for your warning. What would have happened without it?"

"Billy's right, thank you, Mr. Holmes," said Gregson in turn, "but phew! Speak of a mad rush!"

He panted and coughed, and then said to Miles, who stood stolidly by his side: "Thank you, too, Constable, you've been capital. But damn it! What a scrapper you are!"

The latter nodded unpretentiously with a slight laugh.

For a long time Sherlock Holmes kept peering carefully into the night. The wild men who had attacked us had not pursued us up the mound, and they were now hardly visible in the gloom. It seemed, though, that they were standing round it, dreary and motionless, with their eyes fixed on the top.

"What are we waiting for, Mr. Holmes?" asked the inspector at last. "Can't we draw our guns and pitch into these freaks?"

"That would be the last thing to do, Inspector."

"Why?"

"Too dangerous!"

Gregson shrugged his shoulders and said somewhat angrily: "I don't follow you, Mr. Holmes. Aren't these just a bunch of ragmen off their chumps?

"Who really knows?" replied Holmes evasively.

Miles, who had been prying around during all that time, suddenly fell on his knees and started digging the ground vigorously with his gloved hands, like a dog in search of a bone. Two or three minutes later, he gave a great cry of triumph.

"What did you find?" asked Holmes, laying his hand upon the constable's shoulder.

"Light your lantern and point it here, Mr. Holmes!"

"All right."

My master followed Miles's instructions. He whistled a long, low sound of wonderment and exclaimed: "Well, I'm damned! An interesting find indeed, Constable!"

Amongst quantities of broken glass, splinters, rotten vegetables, and undescribable odds and ends, Miles had discovered a hidden passage, a sort of dark pit with a rickety ladder which seemed to plunge into immeasurable depths.

"They are coming up!" warned Miles, pointing a finger at the shadowy forms that had just begun to ascend the great dust heap.

"That settles it," declared Holmes sternly, "we must risk it down the pit!" Then turning to me, he added: "Go down first, my boy, and watch out. Here is my pocket lantern: wave it three times when you reach the bottom; we will then follow you."

Sherlock Holmes, Gregson, and Miles looked eagerly down the gloomy pit. At last they saw my faint light far below. "Let's go!" said the master quietly. He clung to the ladder, and with a few encouraging words, bade his companions to follow. Slowly and cautiously they descended, the frail ladder oscillating violently with them in the pitchy darkness. At last they reached the bottom, and found themselves at what was the end of a rocky passage, which had been roughly hewn out and sloped upwards. Vague draughts seemed to prove that it communicated with the outside. Only half reassured about the exit, but knowing that the only chance to stop our opponents was at that price, Holmes pulled down the ladder, whose rotten wood easily crumbled into pieces. We all walked swiftly then, in Indian file, through the passage. My master's lantern led the way, awakening bats whose rustle and squeak broke for once the unearthly silence that brooded in there. After some fifty or sixty yards, we reached a large cave, and though

it shone dimly in the inky darkness, the light given by the lantern was sufficient to show the nature of our new surroundings. The place was empty
save for a deep layer of dust and a strange object that filled half the chamber.
It looked at first sight like some enormous insect, lying upon its back, with
long twisted legs extended in the air above it, and a glimmering body of
irregular shape beneath them. But closer investigation brought a truer
explanation. The bent and twisted bands of metal were all that remained of
what had once been a huge, iron-bound chest of wood.

"The people who broke it open were in a great hurry," declared Sherlock Holmes.

"Was it full of riches, Master?" I asked him.

"I think so, my boy. No wonder then that . . ."

Holmes left the sentence unfinished, for at that moment came a sound
as of a stifled moan from the other end of the cave. He turned round and
flashing his lantern in that direction, he discovered a man lying on his back,
in the thick dust of the floor, his body covered with blood. He had very
dark hair and a black, waxed mustache, which brought out the extreme
paleness of his face.

"Hey! He's at death's door!" exclaimed Gregson.

At once, we all knelt by his side, and my master gently raised his head.

"You'll give him a little brandy, Billy," he said. "Here is the flask."

The stranger opened his eyes. "*Merci, mon vieux*," he muttered in
French, with a painful attempt at a smile. He drank greedily and a little
color came back to his cheeks. For a moment he stared silently, then delirium seized him and he said, or rather shouted: "*L'or! . . . ratissé l'or! . . . et
puis pan pan dans les tripes! . . . Tout d'même, me faire ça à moi, Victor! . . .
Môssieu Victor, le roi des dompteurs de puces!*" He stopped abruptly and
drew a deep breath, his last one, for the next moment, he was dead.

Silence fell upon the little group. Bats could be heard again, squeaking
around in the cave. Then Gregson cleared his throat and questioned:

"Tell me, Mr. Holmes, what was all that twaddle the Frenchman said?
Can you translate it for me?"

"Hm!" replied my master, setting his hand to his brow. "You see
Greg', he simply meant that someone stole the gold kept in the chest, and
fired a pistol at him, Victor . . . Mr. Victor, king of the flea trainers!"

CHAPTER 5
FIREWORKS

"In Paris," began François Le Villard, "the Folies Bergère and the Moulin Rouge are large music halls that draw crowds of wealthy night birds; but less sophisticatedly, on the boulevard, to the four winds of heaven, stand the small booths, *petites baraques*, as we call them. Here, there is a zest in the air which is absent from more expensive places, and a diversity of entertainments that is truly amazing. Think that, without spending a centime, you can dawdle along from parade to parade, and gaze at such performers as monkeys riding bicycles, plumed wizards crunching glass or swallowing swords, Arabian girls doing the belly dance with enormous snakes around their neck, cavemen eating fire, Chinese spitting it ... and many, many more!"

The French detective paused. He leaned back in his armchair and for some minutes enjoyed silently the glass of sherry wine my master had served him. But I, who was all ears, and could not wait to know the rest, asked: "Tell me, Monsieur, was Monsieur Victor one of these entertainers?"

"Yes indeed," said Le Villard, gazing with half-closed eyes at the liquor through the finely carved crystal, "and not the least one, believe me, young man! His show attracted a lot of people in Montmartre. You gave twelve pence to a blond girl who sat behind a brass grille, and you entered the booth: it was a plain, rather cramped place with no chairs, lit *a giorno* by a big electric bulb hanging from the roof. In the center, on a table, was laid a sort of fish tank—but an empty one—which had the shape of a large suitcase and was shut by a glass lid. When some twenty people had been admitted, an invisible barrel organ started playing a lively march and Monsieur Victor came in. He bowed at the audience, smiled, twisted his waxed mustache, did this and that, then rolled up his left sleeve. When the music was over, he took a pair of tweezers, opened a pillbox, picked up a few black tiny things which looked like pinheads, and laid them carefully on his arm. . . . These were fleas."

"Fleas?" I exclaimed.

"Yes, and that's how he fed them."

"You mean, with his own blood?"

"Well, a good drink never harmed anybody, you know!" retorted the French detective with a mischievous smile. He finished his sherry wine and went on: "Now the show really began. Monsieur Victor plucked off the fleas one by one with the tweezers, and put them in the fish tank. All sort of minuscule accessories were displayed in it, like a tiny cardboard sleigh or a cart built with toothpicks and four collar buttons: well, he'd hitch up couple of fleas with hair to one or the other, and make them draw it on a distance of a few inches; or he'd pick up two fat ones and make them ride a seesaw; he might also organize a race between half a dozen others; sometimes he'd make them jump over obstacles like a small pile of matches or through a wedding ring. . . . It was very clever indeed."

"Are you serious, Monsieur?" I wondered.

"Most serious, Billy. It may be staggering, but it is the honest truth. Monsieur Victor really deserved the title of 'king of the flea trainers,' and the audience always gave him a big hand."

I would probably have asked many more questions about the man we had found agonizing in a cave the night before, if Mrs. Hudson had not appeared at that very moment. She stood in the doorway, her hands on her hips, with indignation in her eye.

"What's the matter, Mrs. Hudson?" asked Sherlock Holmes with a smile.

"Pah! They'll muck up the roofs fifty yards around and break our tiles, no doubt!"

"What with?" wondered my master.

"Fireworks!" she sniffed.

"Fireworks?" I exclaimed. "What do you mean, Mrs. Hudson?"

"Pshaw! Don't you play the fool with me, young man! It's yourself who gave them permission this morning to put in the whole kit and caboodle on the roof."

My jaw dropped. "Me?"

"You!"

"I don't understand," said I.

"Damn it! I do!" cried Holmes abruptly.

"But . . . but . . . what's going on, old man?" wondered Le Villard in turn.

"Most abominable things! Presto! Follow me, François!"

Pushing Mrs. Hudson aside in his haste, my master reached the door in one single stride and rushed up the stairs all the way to the attic; there he climbed up a ladder at breakneck pace, banged open a skylight, and landed on the terrace roof. It was pitch dark outside and at first, he could see absolutely nothing.

"I've got a lantern, let me light it, *saperlotte*!" exclaimed Le Villard, who had just joined him; but, at the very second, he was bumped into by someone or something and he collapsed on the ground with a cry of pain. Strangely enough, a second shrill cry echoed to his in the gloom, a short distance away.

Just then the moon came out from behind a great bank of clouds and flooded the sky with its brilliant and ethereal radiance. To his great amazement, my master found himself in the presence of a young girl wearing a nightgown. She looked terrified.

"What are you doing up here, miss?" he asked gently.

"I . . . I don't know. . . . I'm a bit of a sleepwalker at times. . . . I woke up here a moment ago . . . and . . . Oh my God!"

A shudder of terror passed through her frame as she cried, pointing a trembling finger at something behind the detective's back: "Look! It's coming back!"

Sherlock Holmes turned round. He could not help giving a start for what he had seen was truly abominable: somewhere in the distance, its huge figure outlined against the sky, a dreadful creature was floating over the rooftops, waving menacingly at him. It had a white, fleshless face—almost a skull—with two greenish glows deep in the eye sockets and long, long red hair flowing like flame all around it.

Bang, bang, went my master's gun.

The ghost shook violently then flew away into the air with a hiss of anger. Reaching St. Pancras, it ascended its steeple at great speed, up to the lightning conductor. It whirled round it for three or four seconds, then impaled itself on its spike most violently.

"Devil-a-bit!" cursed Sherlock Holmes. His face had hardened, and for a long time, he stood up silently in the wind-battered night, casting circular glances upon the one thousand and one roofs of London which glimmered faintly in the misty moonshine. When at last he turned back to tell the fair sleepwalker a few comforting words, he felt mystified and puzzled, for he realized at once that she had made the most of his confusion to disappear.

CHAPTER 6

PLAGUE OVER LONDON

Sherlock Holmes, François Le Villard, and myself were seated in Gregson's office at Scotland Yard. The inspector had greeted us warmly and called for a pot of tea.

"Well, it's time to have a good chat, isn't it?" he said, looking about him as in search of approval.

My master nodded. He lit his pipe and began: "A fortnight ago, my excellent friend Chief Inspector François Le Villard paid a call on me to seek my help. He meant to confound a French fairground entertainer called Monsieur Victor, for he knew the fellow was in fact a trafficker in all sorts of illegal goods, and he thought that he was coming to London for some very fishy reasons."

"Hem, may I ask what they were?" said Gregson.

"*Eh bien*, you see, Inspector," replied Le Villard, "in Paris, Victor was involved in a very big business of body snatching. Fairgrounds offered him great opportunities: there are so many *misérables* and down-and-out people hovering about, whose disappearance goes unnoticed. His underworld friends gave him a helping hand when it came to bringing fresh corpses to dissecting tables. All in all, a simple, easy and very profitable trade, *parbleu!*"

The Frenchman sipped his tea and resumed:

"Victor was a very clever rascal, and the Sûreté could never collect serious proofs against him. Nevertheless, I kept a watchful eye on him and lately, by searching once again his caravan while he was out, I came across a most interesting document: this was a half-burnt letter in the stove; it made allusions to an appointment Victor had with a certain Karolina Szokoli at Highgate Cemetery's side entrance, late at night. *Diable!* For me, it undoubtedly meant body snatching, and I told myself that, at last, here was my chance to confound him. The date of the appointment was missing, having being written on the burnt part of the letter, but something told me it would take place soon, probably on one of the nights of the forthcoming week. So I packed up my things and crossed the Channel at once."

"When François pronounced the name of Karolina Szokoli," intervened Sherlock Holmes, "I suspected foul play: the lady Monsieur Victor was supposed to meet at Highgate Cemetery was nobody else than Countess Vetcha, known by her disparagers as the 'Witch of Greenwich' ... and the lady had been moldering in her grave for over thirty years!" My master took a puff at his pipe and added in an offhand tone: "At least, that's what she was supposed to be doing!"

Gregson regarded him uncomprehendingly.

"Hey, what on earth are you telling me?" he asked.

"Well, I just meant the Countess didn't lie in her coffin. . . ."

"The devil!"

"You couldn't use a better word, Greg'," agreed Holmes, grinning from ear to ear.

"*Ah, Bon Dieu, oui!*" Le Villard broke in. "I saw her ghost floating over the graveyard's wall!"

"Gho . . . ghost?" faltered Gregson.

"*Mais si!* Moreover Billy saw it, too. Am I not right, *mon vieux*?"

"Quite so, Monsieur!" I answered laconically.

Sherlock Holmes gave a dry chuckle, then turning to me: "The tube, please," he ordered, "but just be careful, my boy."

I opened the leather bag on my lap and produced a test tube shut by a cork sealed with a broad circle of wax; I handed it to my master with the greatest precaution. He put it under Gregson's nose and said:

"What do you see inside it, Inspector?"

"Err . . . bug . . . a small, black bug . . . a flea, I think."

"Exactly. For your guidance, I'll tell you that I picked it up in Countess Vetcha's coffin. Now . . ." and Sherlock Holmes's tone became icy, "do you realize what formidable danger it represents?"

"Well . . . no."

"I'll tell you."

My master shook the test tube and one could see the flea jumping up and down, slightly magnified by the thick glass. He declared: "This insect, at the moment, is the most dangerous creature in the world! The tarantula's or the asp's bite is a kiss by comparison!"

"By jingo! What do you mean, Mr. Holmes?"

"I mean that this flea carries . . . bubonic plague!"

The inspector's eyes opened in terror.

"Black . . . black death?" he said, in an awestricken whisper.

My master nodded gravely. He handed me back the test tube and resumed: "It is obvious to me that the responsibility for this most dreadful deed falls in first place upon Monsieur Victor's head. I imagine that, through his foul acquaintances at the *Faculté de Médecine* in Paris, he obtained some infected fleas. It was very, very easy then to make them multiply by the hundred, the thousand. . . ."

"The thousand?" exclaimed Gregson in tones of pure horror.

"Indeed. The buyer of Victor's deadly parcel had a most ambitious and deadly scheme. In fact, something unseen in London since 1665!"

"Wait . . . wait, Mr. Holmes! All this goes too fast for me. Please tell me at first who he was!"

"She rather, Greg'! Well, she was—or pretended to be—the Witch of Greenwich."

"Gug-gug-great Scott!" cried the inspector, jumping to his feet. He fidgeted about the room for a minute or so, then asked abruptly:

"What about that dirty plan she had cooked up?"

My master stood up in turn, and, casting his eyes into Gregson's, declared in a voice in which was no note of a doubt: "To spread bubonic plague all over London!"

Gregson's blood ran cold. "Mercy me!" he gasped, staring blankly at Sherlock Holmes.

There was a dead, flat, stricken silence, then my master declared in a solemn tone, as if addressing the Queen, whose picture hung on the wall:

"I have seen right through the Witch's plans and this shall never happen. I swear it!"

He sat back, obviously full of mingled perplexities. For a while, he kept entirely motionless and Gregson, Le Villard and I did the same. At last, as the clock was striking six, he moved a little and spoke again:

"The wretched lady had a first try over Bog Town with the atrocious results we have witnessed. Who could think of a better place to spread plague with infected parasites? Fleas are the unfriendly but common companions of rag-and-bone people. Besides, the Witch knew—though I still don't know how—that there was a large oak chest filled with gold, hidden deep under one of the big rubbish heaps. Why not use Victor to open it and carry the riches away, then get rid of him with a good pistol shot. That's what she did in cold blood."

"But how did the Witch manage to slaughter the entire rag-picking population at once, Master?" I wondered.

"By an abominable but most clever trick, Billy. I have read somewhere recently that in ancient China, Prince Tsin used the same tactic against

Mongol invaders in the year of our Lord 296. You see, Tsin had the brilliant idea to tie pouches full of infected fleas to fuses set on rods. He had but to fire them then at the menacing host of foes to decimate them."

Sherlock Holmes made a slight pause. He cast a glance round and then said: "In the present case, the Witch used some kind of . . . fireworks!"

"Fireworks?" exclaimed the three of us like a single man.

"Yes, great explosive balls whose fragments, when they burst, cover a radius of a quarter of a mile. I think she hid them for a while in her family tomb at Highgate Cemetery and brought them into the vicinity of Bog Town, with the help of Monsieur Victor, on the intended night. They were let off from Deptford Bridge, as Constable Miles told us casually."

"Bon Dieu!" exclaimed Le Villard; "Good Lord!" echoed Gregson.

Sherlock Holmes nodded. He knocked the ashes from his pipe and began to refill it slowly.

As he was proceeding to light it, I remarked indignantly: "I presume that, to sweeten the pill for the good folk of Bog Town, the she-devil played the organ while the fireworks were lighting up the sky!"

My master agreed with a very bitter smile. He drew a heavy puff at his pipe and declared, looking past me into the face of the setting sun that was sinking, red and angry and somber, beyond great ranges of Victorian houses:

"Fairy lights and sweet music . . . Who could dream of a more sadistic way of spreading the Black Death over London again!"

CHAPTER 7

HORROR IN A LONDON FOG

I was moving through the jaundiced mists of the London fog. Walking up Oxford Street, I occasionally overtook the vague shape of an automobile guided at a snail's pace by an invisible driver. In the neighborhood of Old Cavendish Street, I caught a quick glance of a bearded character lighting a cigarette; I chuckled in comparing him to Captain Nemo at the controls of his Nautilus lost in a sea of impenetrable thickness. Farther on, as the street lamps provided scant illumination, I gave myself a delicious shiver by imagining that their flames were jack-o'-lanterns which misled the overconfident passerby to bottomless sewer pits. Then, turning back to more serious thoughts, I evoked mentally the many appalling crimes committed under the fog's sheltering cloak: men and women had been waylaid, girls raped, children torn from their mothers and wives from their husbands.

I was nearing Baker Street when, abruptly, out of the mist came white things, like so many figures on a magic-lantern screen. In the midair they wavered, assuming shapes beyond comprehension. At the same time, from Soho Square, came a sound as of a stifled sob, immediately followed by weird, unearthly groans. All this was so blunt, so gruesome, so menacing, that it made my heart thump like a steam engine. Then, all of a sudden, in a phosphorescence all its own, a most abominable ghost rose from the gray folds of mist. Its black, putrid face was purely atrocious: no trace of a nose, empty eye sockets fringed with filth, and a large, toothless mouth grinning bestially. The horror of its presence shattered nerve and reason: Could it be the Black Death itself, riding the fog-drenched night with a posse of fiends? Such was the mad idea that came to me as I tried to turn back and run away. Unfortunately, my legs failed me and I remained aghast on the pavement.

With arms upraised, as if declaring vengeance, the abominable apparition was glaring at me while the other specters were starting a wild saraband around me.

"I'm done for!" I thought, trembling in all my limbs.

Actually, the situation was desperate and, barring a deus ex machina, I seemed condemned to the flames of hell. But, as improbable as it may seem, the deus came. And it came under the very human shape of . . . Sherlock Holmes!

"Courage, Billy!" cried my master as he dashed out of the fog, "Courage, my boy!" He planted himself in front of me to shield me with his body, and he cast a fierce, scornful glance at his vapory opponents.

"I've had enough of this ghastly farce!" he roared, suddenly producing an automatic pistol. He made two steps forward and, without warning, started firing at them.

Bang! Bang! Bang! . . . Plof! Plof! Plof! . . .

Three ghosts, one by one, blew up in the air.

"Rubber dummies!" I exclaimed, totally bewildered.

"Yes! Inflated with helium gas! I was played the trick twice before, recently," retorted Holmes with blazing eyes.

Bang! Bang! . . . Plof!

The last pseudo-specter exploded under the detective's well targeted bullets and the street was rid of all aberration again.

My heart bouncing with joy this time, I searched for the proper words to tell my master my gratitude, but I didn't even have time to open my lips: indeed, the gun's last report had hardly faded away when Sherlock Holmes called out, with challenge in his voice:

"Will you dare show yourself now, Countess?"

No reply came.

"Cowardess!" scowled the detective.

No reply again.

A couple of seconds elapsed, then, through the gray curtain of mist, a tall, white figure moved slowly forward—a pale, transparent form—which seemed to carry the light along with it. Billy could see loose strands of golden hair, floating from the creature's upright head. It glided like a moonbeam, as if wafted by the faint breeze. But this time, there could be no mistake, the apparition was a flesh-and-blood person, and a most handsome one: a young girl, not over twenty. Holmes, at her sight, could not help giving a start, for she was none else than the fair damsel in nightgown that he had briefly met on his terrace roof, the evening before.

"Is . . . is she Countess Vetcha, the . . . the Witch of Greenwich, Master?" I asked him in low, uneasy voice.

"No, Billy, certainly not."

I gave a sigh of relief.

"Thank God! But in that case, what's this poor one doing out alone here?"

"Can't you guess?"

"Well . . ."

I looked up into her face. The wide open, vacant eyes, the rigid features, told their own story: the girl was sleepwalking. As if he had read into my mind, Sherlock Holmes said in a whisper: "Yes, she is! But don't you wake her up, my boy; it could be fatal."

"What shall we do, then, Master?"

"Hem! Just let her go her own way."

The fair sleepwalker went past us without paying us the slightest notice, and vanished into the mist. "Where is she going and why is she up?" I wondered. It was all very mystifying, but I did not have time to ask myself more questions, for, at that very moment, an old man came out of the fog: he was small, rawboned, with a rather stupid-looking face, side whiskers, and a round, bald skull. He seemed in a great hurry.

"Pardon me, gentlemen," he asked politely, "have you seen a fair-haired girl just now, er . . ."

"Sleepwalking in the street? Yes, we have, my good man!" replied Holmes with a strange little grin.

"Thank God! I feared I had lost her. But please, sir, could you tell me which way she went?"

Instead of answering the stranger, my master looked him over and asked:

"You were Countess Vetcha's warden, weren't you?"

An expression of surprise and apprehension came over the old man's face.

"Indeed, sir," he said, "but how do you know it?"

"I have seen your photograph on an identification sheet at Scotland Yard. My name is Sherlock Holmes!"

The old man bowed servilely. "Sherlock Holmes, the famous detective," he said with downcast eyes. "I understand now. As you probably know, sir, I am called Beresford."

My master nodded. "Beresford, yes," he said thoughtfully. For a moment, he stared keenly at the old servant, then, all of a sudden, to my amazement, he advanced upon him, crying in tones of great disgust:

"Alias . . . the Witch of Greenwich!"

The warden's attitude changed the minute he heard that name; it shifted from servility to ferocity, and there he stood in the fog-sodden street, facing Sherlock Holmes with strained eyes and bestially gnashing teeth. He crouched as my master ran in upon him, but, as he had little the advantage of the latter in size or weight, there seemed to be no great misgivings as to the outcome. They closed. As the warden's muscles tightened on his, Sherlock Holmes knew, with a sudden, daunting shock, that he had met the strength of fury. For a moment the two men strained, then with a rabid scream the warden dashed his face into my master's shoulder and bit through shirt and flesh until his teeth grated on the shoulder blade. Now, upon the outrage of that assault a fury not less insane than that of his opponent fired Holmes, and, clutching at the throat, he tore that hideous face from his shoulder. Another moment and he should have strangled him but a female voice appealed:

"In Heaven's name, don't kill him!"

Holmes's hold relaxed and the warden collapsed, unconscious, on the pavement. My master shook himself painfully and took a glance over his shoulder: by my side stood the fair sleepwalker, looking at him with a painful attempt at a smile, fully awake now.

EPILOGUE

"When, in the early nineties, Count Vetcha married young and fair Karolina Szokoli," told my master later to François Le Villard and Inspector Gregson, "he made an excellent deal: indeed, he was the heir of a most illustrious Bohemian family, but he was totally penniless, while, an orphan, she was at the head of a huge fortune. Greed dazzled the Count, and when his bride gave birth to a girl, he ruthlessly tore the baby away from her. Then he began living a life of perpetual orgies in their mansion at Queenscroft Road. For wicked reasons, he confined Karolina and began to impersonate her, propagating infamous excesses under that dressing-up: thus was born the legend of the Witch of Greenwich. Worn out by grief, poor Karolina died a premature death, and the Count squandered the remains of his wife's fortune in the following years. At last, wanted by Scotland Yard for a nasty episode related to his scandalous habits, the Count disappeared and was never heard of ever again."

Sherlock Holmes took a puff at his pipe and resumed: "In fact, he never left Queenscroft Road: under a very clever disguise, he quite simply became Beresford, the warden. Besides, he put up a highly organized gang of housebreakers, chosing his accomplices mostly amongst rag-and-bone men. Over some twenty years, the rascals accumulated a tremendous loot in silver, gold, and jewels, kept in a huge iron-bound chest of wood that was hidden in a secret chamber, deep beneath a dust heap in Bog Town."

"I understand now," intervened Le Villard. "The Count, wanting to get hold of the riches for himself, found no better way than to kill the entire population of Bog Town."

"Right, François," replied Holmes, "with the help of Mr. Victor and . . . his daughter."

"Hey, hey!" exclaimed Gregson, "we had forgotten the girl!"

Holmes nodded. "A grown-up by now, but a poor maiden out of her mind at times."

"You are speaking of the fair sleepwalker, aren't you, Master?" said I.

"Yes, my boy. An honest girl she was, but because of her intermittent lunacy, it became very simple for her wicked father to use her, against her will of course, at such simple tasks as lighting the fireworks or playing the barrel organ."

Sherlock Holmes took more puffs at his pipe and added:

"Now, the ragmen's loot was not enough for the Count. It had worked so nicely so far, why not, then, make hay and do the same on a larger, much larger scale. After having burnt down his mansion to annihilate every trace of the past, the rascal planned to spread plague over London to get hold of the multiple riches of the metropolis."

"Such as the Crown Jewels?" hazarded the inspector.

"Yes, Gregson, and much more!"

Holmes paused, then, as if addressing a fly on the ceiling: "Since we caught him," he said, "the Count—or the Witch, as you like to call him—has been declared a very dangerous lunatic by the doctors. Justice won't do anything against him, but he shall remain shut for the rest of his life in a padded cell at Bedlam. His daughter is cared upon by the best specialists and no doubt she will recover in the near future."

"But what about the ragmen's riches, Mr. Holmes?" asked Gregson.

"Lost!" was my master's brief reply. But in saying this, he gave me a wink, and I answered with a slight, surreptitious smile. Le Villard, quick-witted as most Frenchmen, had no difficulty in understanding the trick, and he thought with an inward chuckle that the unclaimed loot might one day become the dowry of the Count's unfortunate daughter. To divert the inspector's possible suspicions, he stood up abruptly and said with a French accent, purposely heavier than usual:

"*Bon sang!* To get rid of Mr. Victor and all the ragmen at the same time is what you British may call, er . . . 'killing two birds with one stone'!"

Gregson fell into the trap. He could not help cracking a joke, retorting with a big laugh: "With one flea, rather! . . . With one flea, my friend!"

PROFESSOR JAMES MORIARTY, PH.D., F.R.A.S.

"The famous scientific criminal, as famous among crooks as—"

"My blushes, Watson," Holmes murmured, in a depreciating voice.

"I was about to say 'as he is unknown to the public.'"

"A touch—a distinct touch!" cried Holmes. "You are developing a certain unexpected vein of pawky humor, Watson, against which I must learn to guard myself. But in calling Moriarty a criminal you are uttering libel in the eyes of the law, and there lies the glory and the wonder of it. The greatest schemer of all time, the organizer of every devilry, the controlling brain of the underworld—a brain which might have made or marred the destiny of nations. That's the man. But so aloof is he from criticism—so admirable in his management and self-effacement, that for those very words that you have uttered he could hale you to a court and emerge with your year's pension as a lolatium for his wounded character. Is he not the celebrated author of *The Dynamics of an Asteroid*—a book which ascends to such rarefied heights of mure mathematics that it is said that there was no man in the scientific press capable of criticizing it? Is this a man to traduce?"

—*The Valley of Fear*

by MICHAEL KURLAND

Years Ago and in a Different Place

My name is Professor James Clovis Moriarty, Ph.D., F.R.A.S. You may have heard of me. I have been the author of a number of well-regarded scientific monographs and journal articles over the past few decades, including a treatise on the Binomial Theorem, and a monograph titled "The Dynamics of an Asteroid," which was well received in scientific circles both in Great Britain and on the continent. My recent paper in the *British Astronomical Journal*, "Observations on the July 1889 Eclipse of Mercury with Some Speculations Concerning the Effect of Gravity on Light Waves," has occasioned some comment among those few who could understand its implications.

But I fear that if you know my name, it is, in all probability, not through any of my published scientific papers. Further, my current, shall I say, notoriety, was not of my own doing and most assuredly not by my choice. I am by nature a retiring, some would have it secretive, person.

Over the past few years narratives from the memoirs of a certain Dr. John Watson concerning that jackanapes who calls himself a "consulting detective," Mr. Sherlock Holmes, have been appearing in the *Strand* magazine and elsewhere with increasing frequency, and have attained a, to my mind, most unwarranted popularity. Students of the "higher criticism," as those insufferable pedants who devote their lives to picking over minuscule details of Dr. Watson's stories call their ridiculous avocation, have analyzed Watson's rather pedestrian prose with the avid attention gourmands pay to mounds of goose-liver pâté. They extract hidden meanings from every word, and extrapolate facts not in evidence from every paragraph. Which leads them unfailingly to conclusions even more specious than those in which Holmes himself indulges.

Entirely too much of this misdirected musing concerns me and my relationship with the self-anointed master detective. Amateur detection enthusiasts have wasted much time and energy in speculation as to how Sherlock Holmes and I first met, and just what caused the usually unflappable Holmes to describe me as "the Napoleon of crime" without supplying the slightest evidence to support this blatant canard.

I propose to tell that story now, both to satisfy this misplaced curiosity and to put an end to the various speculations which have appeared in certain privately circulated monographs. To set the record straight: Holmes and I are *not* related; I have *not* had improper relations with any of his female relatives; I did *not* steal his childhood inamorata away from him. Neither did he, to the best of my knowledge, perform any of these services for me or anyone in my family.

In any case, I assure you that I will no longer take such accusations lightly. Privately distributed though these monographs may be, their authors will have to answer for them in a court of law if this continues.

Shortly before that ridiculous episode at the Reichenbach Falls, Holmes had the temerity to describe me to his befuddled amanuensis as "organizer of half that is evil and nearly all that is undetected in this great city." (By which he meant London, of course.) What crimes I had supposedly committed he was curiously silent about. Watson did not ask for specifics, and none were offered. The good doctor took Holmes's unsupported word for this unsupportable insult. Had Holmes not chosen to disappear for three years after his foul accusation, I most assuredly would have had him in the dock for slander.

And then, when Holmes returned from his extended vacation, during which time he did not have the kindness, the decency, to pass on one word that would let his dear companion know that he was not dead, he gave an account of our "struggle" at the falls that any child of nine would have recognized as a complete work of fiction—but it fooled Watson.

The truth about the Reichenbach incident—but no, that is not for this narrative. Just permit me a brief pause, the merest aside in this chronicle before I go on, so that I may draw your attention to some of the details of that story that should have alerted the merest tyro to the fact that he was being diddled—but that Watson swallowed whole.

In the narrative that he published under the name "The Final Problem," Watson relates that Holmes appeared in his consulting room one day in April of 1891 and told him that he was being threatened by Professor Moriarty—myself—and that he had already been attacked twice that day by my agents and expected to be attacked again, probably by a man using an air rifle. If that were so, was it not thoughtful of him to go to the residence of his close friend and thus place him, also, in deadly peril?

At that meeting Holmes declares that in three days he will be able to place "the Professor, with all the principal members of his gang," in the hands of the police. Why wait? Holmes gives no coherent reason. But until then, Holmes avers, he is in grave danger. Well now! If this were so, would not Scotland Yard gladly have given Holmes a room, nay a suite of rooms, in the hotel of his choosing—or in the Yard itself—to keep him safe for the next three days? But Holmes says that nothing will do but that he must flee the country, and once again Watson believes him. Is not unquestioning friendship a wonderful thing?

Holmes then arranges for Watson to join him in this supposedly hasty flight. They meet at Victoria Station the next morning, where Watson has trouble recognizing Holmes, who has disguised himself as a "venerable Italian priest," presumably to fool pursuers. This assumes that Holmes's enemies can recognize the great detective, but have no idea what his good friend Dr. Watson, who wears no disguise, who indeed is congenitally incapable of disguise, looks like.

Again note that after a six-month absence, during which Holmes and I—but no, it is not my secret to tell—at any rate, six months after I was assumed to be dead I returned to my home on Russell Square and went about my business as usual, and Watson affected not to notice. After all, Holmes had killed me, and that was good enough for Watson.

I could go on. Indeed, it is with remarkable restraint that I do not. To describe me as a master criminal is actionable; and then to compound matters by making me out to be such a bungler as to be fooled by Holmes's juvenile antics is quite intolerable. It should be clear to all that the events leading up to that day at Reichenbach Falls, if they occurred as described, were designed by Holmes to fool his amiable companion, and not "the Napoleon of crime."

But I have digressed enough. In this brief paper I will describe how the relationship between Holmes and myself came to be, and perhaps supply some insight into how and why Holmes developed an entirely unwarranted antagonism toward me that has lasted these many years.

I first met Sherlock Holmes in the early 1870s—I shall be no more precise than that. At the time I was a senior lecturer in mathematics at, I shall call it, "Queens College," one of the six venerable colleges making up a small inland university which I shall call "Wexleigh" to preserve the anonymity of the events I am about to describe. I shall also alter the names of the persons who figure in this episode, save only those of Holmes and myself, as those who were involved surely have no desire to be reminded of the episode or pestered by the press for more details. You may, of course, apply to Holmes for the true names of these people, although I imagine that he will be no more forthcoming than I.

Let me also point out that memories are not entirely reliable recorders of events. Over time they convolute, they conflate, they manufacture, and they discard, until what remains may bear only a passing resemblance to the original event. So if you happen to be one of the people whose lives crossed those of Holmes and myself at "Queens" at this time, and your memory of some of the details of these events differs from mine, I assure you that in all probability we are both wrong.

Wexleigh University was of respectable antiquity, with respectable ecclesiastical underpinnings. Most of the dons at Queens were churchmen of one description or another. Latin and Greek were still considered the foundations upon which an education should be constructed. The "modern" side of the university had come into existence a mere decade before, and the Classics dons still looked with mixed amazement and scorn at the Science instructors and the courses offered, which they insisted on describing as "Stinks and Bangs."

Holmes was an underclassman at the time. His presence had provoked a certain amount of interest among the faculty, many of whom remembered his brother Mycroft, who had attended the university some six years previously. Mycroft had spent most of his three years at Queens in his room, coming out only for meals and to gather armsful of books from the library and retreat back to his room. When he did appear in the lecture hall it would often be to correct the instructor on some error of fact or pedagogy that had lain unnoticed, sometimes for years, in one of his lectures. Mycroft had departed the university without completing the requirements for a degree, stating with some justification that he had received all the institution had to offer, and he saw no point in remaining.

Holmes had few friends among his fellow underclassmen and seemed to prefer it that way. His interests were varied but transient, as he dipped first into one field of study and then another, trying to find something that stimulated him sufficiently for him to make it his life's work; something to which he could apply his powerful intellect and his capacity for close and accurate observation, which was even then apparent, if not fully developed.

An odd sort of amity soon grew between myself and this intense young man. On looking back I would describe it as a cerebral bond, based mostly on the shared snobbery of the highly intelligent against those whom they deem as their intellectual inferiors. I confess to that weakness in my youth, and my only defense against a charge of hubris is that those whom we went out of our way to ignore were just as anxious to avoid us.

The incident I am about to relate occurred in the fall, shortly after Holmes returned to begin his second year. A new don joined the college, occupying the newly created chair of Moral Philosophy, a chair which had been endowed by a midlands mill owner who made it a practice to employ as many children under twelve in his mills as his agents could sweep up off the streets. Thus, I suppose, his interest in Moral Philosophy.

The new man's name was—well, for the purposes of this tale let us call him Professor Charles Maples. He was, I would judge, in his mid-forties; a stout, sharp-nosed, myopic, amiable man who strutted and bobbed slightly when he walked. His voice was high and intense, and his mannerisms were complex. His speech was accompanied by elaborate hand motions, as though he would mold the air into a semblance of what he was describing. When one saw him crossing the quad in the distance, with his gray master of arts gown flapping about him, waving the mahogany walking stick with the brass duck's-head handle that he was never without, and gesticulating to the empty air, he resembled nothing so much as a corpulent king pigeon.

Moral Philosophy was a fit subject for Maples. No one could say exactly what it encompassed, and so he was free to speak on whatever caught his interest at the moment. And his interests seemed to be of the moment: he took intellectual nourishment from whatever flower of knowledge seemed brightest to him in the morning, and had tired of it ere night drew nigh. Excuse the vaguely poetic turn of phrase; speaking of Maples seems to bring that out in one.

I do not mean to suggest the Maples was intellectually inferior; far from it. He had a piercing intellect, an incisive clarity of expression, and a sarcastic wit that occasionally broke through his mild façade. Maples spoke on the Greek and Roman concept of manliness, and made one regret that we lived in these decadent times. He lectured on the nineteenth-century penchant for substituting a surface prudery for morality, and left his students with a vivid image of unnamed immorality seething and billowing not very far beneath the surface. He spoke on this and that and created in his students with an abiding enthusiasm for this, and an unremitting loathing for that.

There was still an unspoken presumption about the college that celibacy was the proper model for the students, and so only the unmarried, and presumably celibate, dons were lodged in one or another of the various buildings within the college walls. Those few with wives found housing around town where they could, preferably a respectable distance from the university. Maples was numbered among the domestic ones, and he and his wife, Andrea, had taken a house with fairly extensive grounds on Barleymore Road not far from the college, which they shared with Andrea's sister, Lucinda Moys, and a physical education instructor named Crisboy, who, choosing to live away from the college for reasons of his own, rented a pair of rooms on the top floor. There was a small guest house at the far end of the property which was untenanted. The owner of the property, who had moved to Glasgow some years previously, kept it for his own use on his occasional visits to town. The Mapleses employed a cook and a maid, both of whom were day help, sleeping in their own homes at night.

Andrea was a fine-looking woman who appeared to be fearlessly approaching thirty, with intelligent brown eyes set in a broad face and a head of thick, brown hair, which fell down her back to somewhere below her waist when she didn't have it tied up in a sort of oversized bun circling her head. She was of a solid appearance and decisive character.

Her sister, "Lucy" to all who knew her, was somewhat younger and more ethereal in nature. She was a slim, golden-haired creature of mercurial moods: usually bright and confident and more than capable of handling anything the mean old world could throw at her, but on occasion dark and sullen and angry at the rest of the world for not measuring up to her standards. When one of her moods overtook her, she retired to her room and refused to see anyone until it passed, which for some reason the young men of the college found intensely romantic. She had a manner of gazing at you while you conversed, as though your words were the only things of importance in the world at that instant, and she felt privileged to be listening. This caused several of the underclassmen to fall instantly in love with her, as she was perhaps the first person, certainly the first woman aside from their mothers, who had ever paid serious attention to anything they said.

One of the underclassmen who was attracted by Miss Lucy's obvious charms was Mr. Sherlock Holmes. She gazed at him wide-eyed while he spoke earnestly, as young men speak, of things that I'm sure must have interested her not in the least. Was it perhaps Holmes himself who interested the pert young lady? I certainly hoped so, for his sake. Holmes had no sisters, and a man who grows up without sisters has few defenses against those wiles, those innocent wiles of body, speech, and motion, with which nature has provided young females in its blind desire to propagate the species.

I was not a close observer of the amorous affairs of Lucy Moys, but as far as I could see she treated all her suitors the same; neither encouraging them nor discouraging them, but enjoying their company and keeping them at a great enough distance, both physically and emotionally, to satisfy the most demanding duenna. She seemed to me to find all her young gentlemen vaguely amusing, regarding them with the sort of detachment one finds in the heroines of Oscar Wilde's plays, to use a modern simile.

Professor Maples took the in loco parentis role of the teacher a bit further than most of the faculty, and certainly further than I would have cared to, befriending his students, and for that matter any students who desired to be befriended, earnestly, sincerely, and kindly. But then he seemed to truly care about the needs and welfare of the young men of Wexleigh. Personally I felt that attempting to educate most of them in the lecture hall and at tutorials was quite enough. For the most part they cared for nothing but sports, except for those who cared for nothing but religion, and were content to allow the sciences and mathematics to remain dark mysteries.

Maples and his wife had "at home" afternoon teas twice a month, the second and fourth Tuesdays, and quite soon these events became very popular with the students. His sister-in-law, who was invariably present, was certainly part of the reason, as was the supply of tea cakes, scones, fruit tarts, and other assorted edibles. I attended several of these, and was soon struck by an indefinable feeling that something was not what it seemed. I say "indefinable" because I could not put my finger on just what it was that puzzled me about the events. I did not attach too much importance to it at the time. It was only later that it seemed significant. I will try to give you a word picture of the last of these events that I attended; the last one, as it happens, before the tragedy.

It was Holmes who suggested that we attend Professor Maples's tea that day. I had been trying to impress upon him a rudimentary understanding of the calculus, and he had demanded of me an example of some situation in which such knowledge might be of use. I outlined three problems, one from astronomy, involving the search for the planet Vulcan, said to lie inside the orbit of Mercury; one from physics, relating to determining magnetic lines of force when an electric current is applied; and one based on some thoughts of my own regarding Professor Malthus's notions on population control.

Holmes waved them all aside. "Yes, I am sure they are very interesting in their own way," he said, "but, frankly, they do not concern me. It does not matter to me whether the Earth goes around the Sun or the Sun goes around the Earth, as long as whichever does whatever keeps on doing it reliably."

"You have no intellectual curiosity regarding the world around you?" I asked in some surprise.

"On the contrary," Holmes averred. "I have an immense curiosity, but I have no more interest in the Binomial Theorem than it has in me. I feel that I must confine my curiosity to those subjects that will be of some use to me in the future. There is so much to learn on the path I have chosen that I fear that I dare not venture very far along side roads."

"Ah!" I said. "I was not aware that you have started down your chosen road, or indeed that you have chosen a road down which to trod."

Holmes and I were sitting in an otherwise unoccupied lecture hall, and at my words he rose and began pacing restlessly about the front of the room. "I wouldn't say that I have chosen the road, exactly," he said, "to continue with this, I suppose, inescapable metaphor. But I have an idea of the direction in which I wish to travel"—he made a point of his right forefinger and thrust it forcefully in front of him—"and I feel I must carefully limit my steps to paths that go in that direction."

"Is it that pile of erasers or the wastebasket at the end of the room at which you hope to arrive?" I asked, and then quickly raised a conciliatory hand. "No, no, I take it back. I'm glad you have formulated a goal in life, even if it doesn't include the calculus. What is the direction of this city on a hill toward which you strive?"

Holmes glowered at me for a moment and then looked thoughtful. "It's still slightly vague," he told me. "I can see it in outline only. A man—" He gathered his ideas. "A man should strive to do something larger than himself. To cure disease, or eradicate hunger or poverty or crime."

"Ah!" I said. "Noble thoughts." I fancied that I could hear the lovely voice of Miss Lucy earnestly saying that, or something similar, to Holmes within the week. When a man is suddenly struck by noble ambitions it is usually a woman who does the striking. But I decided it would be wiser not to mention this deduction, which, at any rate, was rather tentative and not based on any hard evidence.

"It's Professor Maples's afternoon tea day today," Holmes commented. "And I had thought of going."

"Why so it is," I said. "And so we should. And, in one last effort to interest you in the sort of detail for which you find no immediate utility, I call to your attention the shape of Lucinda Moys's ear. Considered properly, it presents an interesting question. You should have an opportunity to observe it, perhaps even fairly closely, this afternoon."

"Which ear?"

"Either will do."

"What's the matter with Miss Lucy's ear?" Holmes demanded.

"Why, nothing. It's a delightful ear. Well formed. Flat, rather oblate lobes. I've never seen another quite like it. Very attractive, if it comes to that."

"All right, then," Holmes said.

I closed the few books I had been using and put them in my book sack. "I hereby renounce any future attempt to teach you higher mathematics," I told him. "I propose we adjourn and head toward the professor's house and his tea cakes."

And so we did.

The Mapleses' event was from three in the afternoon until six in the evening, although some arrived a bit earlier, and some I believe stayed quite a bit later. The weather was surprisingly mild for mid-October, and Holmes and I arrived around half past three that day to find the professor and his household and their dozen or so guests scattered about the lawn behind the house in predictable clumps. The vice chancellor of the university was present, relaxing in a lawn chair with a cup of tea and a plate of scones. Classical Greece was represented by Dean Herbert McCuthers, an elderly man of intense sobriety and respectability, who was at that moment rolling up his trouser legs preparatory to wading in the small artificial pond with Andrea

Maples, who had removed her shoes and hoisted her skirts in a delicate balance between wet clothing and propriety.

Crisboy, the physical education instructor who roomed with the Mapleses, a large, muscular, and pugnacious-looking man in his late twenties, was standing in one corner of the lawn with a games coach named Faulting, a young man with the build and general appearance of one of the lithe athletes depicted by ancient Greek statuary, if you can picture a young Greek athlete clad in baggy gray flannels. The comparison was one that Faulting was well aware of, judging by his practice of posing heroically whenever he thought anyone was looking at him.

The pair of them were standing near the house, swinging athletic clubs with muscular wild abandon, and discussing the finer details of last Saturday's football match, surrounded by a bevy of admiring underclassmen. There are those students at every university who are more interested in games than education. They spend years afterward talking about this or that cricket match against their mortal foes at the next school over, or some particularly eventful football game. It never seems to bother them, or perhaps even occur to them, that they are engaged in pursuits at which a suitably trained three-year-old chimpanzee or orang-utan could best them. And, for some reason that eludes me, these men are allowed to vote and to breed. But, once again, I digress.

Maples was walking magisterially across the lawn, his gray master's gown billowing about his fundament, his hands clasped behind him holding his walking stick, which jutted out to his rear like a tail, followed by a gaggle of young gentlemen in their dark brown scholars' gowns, with their mortarboards tucked under their arms, most of them giving their professor the subtle homage of imitating his walk and his posture. "The ideal of the university," Maples was saying in a voice that would brook no dispute, obviously warming up to his theme, "is the Aristotelean *stadium* as filtered through the medieval monastic schools."

He nodded to me as he reached me, and then wheeled about and headed back whence he had come, embroidering on his theme. "Those students who hungered for something more than a religious education, who perhaps wanted to learn the law, or what there was of medicine, headed toward the larger cities, where savants fit to instruct them could be found. Paris, Bologna, York, London; here the students gathered, often traveling from city to city in search of just the right teacher. After a century or two the instruction became formalized, and the schools came into official existence, receiving charters from the local monarch, and perhaps from the pope."

Maples suddenly froze in midstep and wheeled around to face his entourage. "But make no mistake!" he enjoined them, waving his cane pointedly in front of him, its duck-faced head pointed first at one student and then another, "a university is not made up of its buildings, its colleges, its lecture halls, or its playing fields. No, not even its playing fields. A university is made up of the people—teachers and students—that come together in its name. *Universitas scholarium*, is how the charters read, providing for a, shall I say, guild of students. Or, as in the case of the University of Paris, a *universitas magistrorum*, a guild of teachers. So we are co-equal, you and I. Tuck your shirt more firmly into your trousers, Mr. Pomfrit; you are becoming all disassembled."

He turned and continued his journey across the greensward, his voice fading with distance. His students, no doubt impressed with their new-found equality, trotted along behind him.

Lucy Moys glided onto the lawn just then, coming through the French doors at the back of the house, bringing a fresh platter of pastries to the parasol-covered table. Behind her trotted the maid, bringing a pitcher full of steaming hot water to refill the teapot. Sherlock Holmes left my side and wandered casually across the lawn, contriving to arrive by Miss Lucy's side just in time to help her distribute the pastries about the table. Whether he took any special interest in her ear, I could not observe.

I acquired a cup of tea and a slice of tea cake and assumed my accustomed role as an observer of phenomena. This has been my natural inclination for years, and I have enhanced whatever ability I began with by a conscious effort to accurately take note of what I see. I had practiced this for long enough, even then, that it had become second nature to me. I could not sit opposite a man on a railway car without, for example, noticing by his watch fob that he was a Rosicrucian, let us say, and by the wear marks on his left cuff that he was a note cashier or an order clerk. A smudge of ink on his right thumb would favor the note cashier hypothesis, while the state of his boots might show that he had not been at work that day. The note case that he kept clutched to his body might indicate that he was transferring notes to a branch bank, or possibly that he was absconding with the bank's funds. And so on. I go into this only to show that my observations were not made in anticipation of tragedy, but were merely the result of my fixed habit.

I walked about the lawn for the next hour or so, stopping here and there to nod hello to this student or that professor. I lingered at the edge of this group, and listened for a while to a spirited critique of Wilkie Collin's recent novel, *The Moonstone*, and how it represented an entirely new sort of fiction. I paused by that cluster to hear a young man earnestly explicating on the good works being done by Mr. William Booth and his Christian Revival Association in the slums of our larger cities. I have always distrusted earnest, pious, loud young men. If they are sincere, they're insufferable. If they are not sincere, they're dangerous.

I observed Andrea Maples, who had dried her feet and lowered her skirts, take a platter of pastries and wander around the lawn, offering a cruller here and a tea cake there, whispering intimate comments to accompany the pastry. Mrs. Maples had a gift for instant intimacy, for creating the illusion that you and she shared wonderful, if unimportant, secrets. She sidled by Crisboy, who was now busy leading five or six of his athletic protégés in doing push-ups, and whispered something to young Faulting, the games coach, and he laughed. And then she was up on her tiptoes whispering some more. After perhaps a minute, which is a long time to be whispering, she danced a few steps back and paused, and Faulting blushed. Blushing has quite gone out of fashion now, but it was quite the thing for both men and women back in the seventies. Although how something that is believed to be an involuntary physiological reaction can be either in or out of fashion demands more study by Dr. Freud and his fellow psycho-analysts.

Crisboy gathered himself and leaped to his feet. "Stay on your own side of the street!" he yapped at Andrea Maples, which startled both her and the young gamesmen, two of whom rolled over and stared up at the scene, while the other three or four continued doing push-ups at a frantic pace, as though there were nothing remarkable happening above them. After a second Mrs. Maples laughed and thrust the plate of pastries out at him.

Professor Maples turned to stare at the little group some twenty feet away from him and his hands tightened around his walking stick. Although he strove to remain calm, he was clearly in the grip of some powerful emotion for a few seconds before he regained control. "Now, now, my dear," he called across the lawn. "Let us not incite the athletes."

Andrea skipped over to him and leaned over to whisper in his ear. As she was facing me this time, and I had practiced lip-reading for some years,

I could make out what she said: "Perhaps I'll do you a favor, poppa bear," she whispered. His reply was not visible to me.

A few minutes later my wanderings took me over to where Sherlock Holmes was sitting by himself on one of the canvas chairs near the French windows looking disconsolate. "Well," I said, looking around, "and where is Miss Lucy?"

"She suddenly discovered that she had a sick headache and needed to go lie down. Presumably she has gone to lie down," he told me.

"I see," I said. "Leaving you to suffer alone among the multitude."

"I'm afraid it must have been something I said," Holmes confided to me.

"Really? What did you say?"

"I'm not sure. I was speaking about—well . . ." Holmes looked embarrassed, a look I had never seen him encompass before, nor have I seen it since.

"Hopes and dreams," I suggested.

"Something of that nature," he agreed. "Why is it that words that sound so—important—when one is speaking to a young lady with whom one is on close terms, would sound ridiculous when spoken to the world at large? That is, you understand, Mr. Moriarty, a rhetorical question."

"I do understand," I told him. "Shall we return to the college?"

And so we did.

The next afternoon found me in the commons room sitting in my usual chair beneath the oil painting of Sir James Walsingham, the first chancellor of Queens College, receiving the keys to the college from Queen Elizabeth. I was dividing my attention between my cup of coffee and a letter from the reverend Charles Dodgson, a fellow mathematician who was then at Oxford, in which he put forth some of his ideas concerning what we might call the mathematical constraints of logical constructions. My solitude was interrupted by Dean McCuthers, who toddled over, cup of tea in hand, looking even older than usual, and dropped into the chair next to me. "Afternoon, Moriarty," he breathed. "Isn't it dreadful?"

I put the letter aside. "Isn't what dreadful?" I asked him. "The day? The war news? Huxley's Theory of Biogenesis? Perhaps you're referring to the coffee—it is pretty dreadful today."

McCuthers shook his head sadly. "Would that I could take the news so lightly," he said. "I am always so aware, so sadly aware, of John Donne's admonishment."

"I thought Donne had done with admonishing for these past two hundred years or so," I said.

But there was no stopping McCuthers. He was determined to quote Donne, and quote he did: " 'Any man's death diminishes me, because I am involved in Mankind,' " he went on, ignoring my comment. " 'And therefore never send to know for whom the bell tolls; it tolls for thee.' "

I forbore from mentioning that the dean, a solitary man who spent most of his waking hours pondering over literature written over two thousand years before he was born, was probably less involved in mankind than any man I had ever known. "I see," I said. "The bell has tolled for someone?"

"And murder makes it so much worse," McCuthers continued. "As Lucretius puts it—"

"Who was murdered?" I asked firmly, cutting through his tour of the classics.

"Eh? You mean you don't know? Oh, dear me. This will come as something of a shock, then. It's that Professor Maples—"

"Someone has murdered Maples?"

"No, no. My thought was unfinished. Professor Maples has been arrested. His wife—Andrea—Mrs. Maples—has been murdered."

I was, I will admit it, bemused. You may substitute a stronger term if you like. I tried to get some more details from McCuthers, but the dean's involvement with the facts had not gone beyond the murder and the arrest. I finished my coffee and went off in search of more information.

Murder is a sensational crime which evokes a formidable amount of interest, even among the staid and unworldly dons of Queens College. And a murder *in mediis rebus*, or perhaps better, *in mediis universitatibus*; one that actually occurs among said staid dons, will intrude on the contemplations of even the most unworldly. The story, which spread rapidly through the college, was this:

A quartet of bicyclists, underclassmen from St. Simon's College, set out together at dawn three days a week, rain or shine, to get an hour or two's cycling in before breakfast. This morning, undeterred by the chill drizzle that had begun during the night, they went out along Barleymore Road as usual. At about eight o'clock, or shortly after, they happened to stop at the front steps to the small cottage on Professor Maples's property. One of the bicycles had throw a shoe, or something of the sort, and they had paused to repair the damage. The chain-operated bicycle had been in existence for only a few years back then, and was prone to a variety of malfunctions. I understand that bicyclists, even today, find it useful to carry about a complete set of tools in order to be prepared for the inevitable mishap.

One of the party, who was sitting on the cottage steps with his back up against the door, as much out of the rain as he could manage, indulging in a pipeful of Latakia while the damaged machine was being repaired, felt something sticky under his hand. He looked, and discovered a widening stain coming out from under the door. Now, according to which version of the story you find most to your liking, he either pointed to the stain and said, "I say, chaps, what do you suppose this is?" Or he leapt to his feet screaming, "It's blood! It's blood! Something horrible has happened here." I tend to prefer the latter version, but perhaps it's only the alliteration that appeals to me.

The young men, feeling that someone inside the cottage might require assistance, pounded on the door. When they got no response, they tried the handle and found it locked. The windows all around the building were also locked. They broke the glass in a window, unlocked it, and they all climbed through.

In the hallway leading to the front door they found Andrea Maples, in what was described as "a state of undress," lying in a pool of blood—presumably her own, as she had been badly beaten about the head. Blood splatters covered the walls and ceiling. A short distance away from the body lay what was presumably the murder weapon: a mahogany cane with a brass duck's head handle.

One of the men immediately cycled off to the police station and returned with a police sergeant and two constables. When they ascertained that the hard wood cane belonged to Professor Maples, and that he carried it about with him constantly, the policemen crossed the lawn to the main house and interviewed the professor, who was having breakfast. At the conclusion of the interview, the sergeant placed Maples under arrest and sent one of the constables off to acquire a carriage in which the professor could be conveyed to the police station.

It was about four in the afternoon when Sherlock Holmes came banging at my study door. "You've heard, of course," he said, flinging himself into my armchair. "What are we to do?"

"I've heard," I said. "And what have we to do with it?"

"That police sergeant, Meeks is his name, has arrested Professor Maples for the murder of his wife."

"So I've heard."

"He conducted no investigation, did not so much as glance at the surroundings, and failed to leave a constable behind to secure the area, so that, as soon as the rain lets up, hordes of the morbidly curious will trample about the cottage and the lawn and destroy whatever evidence there is to be found."

"Did he?" I asked. "And how do you know so much about it?"

"I was there," Holmes said. At my surprised look, he shook his head. "Oh, no, not at the time of the murder, whenever that was. When the constable came around for the carriage to take Professor Maples away, I happened to be in the stables. The hostler, Biggs is his name, is an expert single-stick fighter, and I've been taking lessons from him on occasional mornings when he has the time. So when they returned to the professor's house, Biggs drove and I sat in the carriage with the constable, who told me all about it."

"I imagine he'll be talking about it for some time," I commented. "Murders are not exactly common around here."

"Just so. Well, I went along thinking I might be of some use to Lucy. After all, her sister had just been murdered."

"Thoughtful of you," I said.

"Yes. Well, she wouldn't see me. Wouldn't see anyone. Just stayed in her room. Can't blame her, I suppose. So I listened to the sergeant questioning Professor Maples—and a damned poor job he did of it, if I'm any judge—and then went out and looked over the area—the two houses and the space between—to see if I could determine what happened. I also examined Andrea Maples's body as best I could from the doorway. I was afraid that if I got any closer Sergeant Meeks would notice and chase me away."

"And did you determine what happened?"

"I may have," Holmes said. "If you'd do me the favor of taking a walk with me, I'd like to show you what I've found. I believe I have a good idea of what took place last night—or at least some of the salient details. I've worked it out from the traces on the ground and a few details in the cottage that the sergeant didn't bother with. It seems to me that much more can be done in the investigation of crimes than the police are accustomed to do. But I'd like your opinion. Tell me what you think."

I pulled my topcoat on. "Show me," I said.

The drizzle was steady and cold, the ground was soggy, and by the time we arrived at the house the body had been removed; all of which reduced the number of curious visitors to two reporters who, having stomped about the cottage but failing to gain admittance to the main house, were huddled in a gig pulled up to the front door, waiting for someone to emerge who could be coaxed into a statement.

The main house and the cottage both fronted Barleymore Road, but as the road curved around a stand of trees between the two, the path through the property was considerably shorter. It was perhaps thirty yards from the house to the cottage by the path, and perhaps a little more than twice that by the road. I did measure the distance at the time, but I do not recollect the precise numbers.

We went around to the back of the house and knocked at the pantry door. After a few seconds' scrutiny through a side window, we were admitted by the maid.

"It's you, Mr. Holmes," she said, stepping aside to let us in. "Ain't it horrible? I've been waiting by the back door here for the man with the bunting, whose supposed to arrive shortly."

"Bunting?"

"That's right. The black bunting which we is to hang in the windows, as is only proper, considering. Ain't it horrible? We should leave the doors and windows open, in respect of the dead, only the mistress's body has been taken away, and the master has been taken away, and it's raining, and those newspaper people will come in and pester Miss Lucy if the door is open. And then there's the murderer just awaiting out there somewhere, and who knows what's on his mind."

"So you don't think Professor Maples killed his wife?" I asked.

The maid looked at me, and then at Holmes, and then back at me. "This is Mr. Moriarty, Willa," Holmes told her. "He's my friend, and a lecturer in Mathematics at the college."

"Ah," she said. "It's a pleasure, sir." And she bobbed a rudimentary curtsey in my direction. "No, sir, I don't think the professor killed the Missus. Why would he do that?"

"Why, indeed," I said.

"Miss Lucy is in the drawing room," Willa told Holmes. "I'll tell her you're here."

"I see you're well known here," I said to Holmes as the maid left.

"I have had the privilege of escorting Miss Lucy to this or that over the past few months," Holmes replied a little stiffly, as though I were accusing him of something dishonorable. "Our relationship has been very proper at all times."

I repressed a desire to say "how unfortunate," as I thought he would take it badly.

Lucinda came out to the hall to meet us. She seemed quite subdued, but her eyes were bright and her complexion was feverish. "How good—how nice to see you, Sherlock," she said quietly, offering him her hand. "And you're Mr. Moriarty, Sherlock's friend."

Holmes and I both mumbled something comforting.

"I'm sorry I didn't see you when you arrived earlier, Sherlock," Lucy told him, leading us into the sitting room and waving us to a pair of well-stuffed chairs. "I was not in a fit condition to see anyone."

"I quite understand," Holmes said.

"I am pleased that you have come to the defense of my—of Professor Maples," Lucy said, lowering herself into a straight-back chair opposite Holmes. "How anyone could suspect him of murdering my dear sister Andrea is quite beyond my comprehension."

"I have reason to believe that he is, indeed, innocent, Lucy dear," Holmes told her. "I am about to take my friend Mr. Moriarty over the grounds to show him what I have found, and to see whether he agrees with my conclusions."

"And your conclusions," Lucy asked, "what are they? Who do you believe committed this dreadful crime?"

"You have no idea?" I asked.

Lucinda recoiled as though I had struck her. "How could I?" she asked.

"I didn't mean to startle you," I said. "Did your sister have any enemies?"

"Certainly not," Lucy said. "She was outgoing, and warm, and friendly, and loved by all."

"Andrea went to the cottage to meet someone," Holmes said. "Do you have any idea who it was?"

"None," Lucy said. "I find this whole thing quite shocking." She lowered her head into her hands. "Quite shocking."

After a moment Lucy raised her head. "I have prepared a small traveling bag of Professor Maples's things. A change of linen, a shirt, a couple of collars, some handkerchiefs, his shaving cup and razor."

"I don't imagine they'll let him have his razor," Holmes commented.

"Oh!" Lucy said. "I hadn't thought of that."

"I may be wrong," Holmes said. "I will inquire."

"Could I ask you to bring the bag to him?" Lucy rose. "I have it right upstairs."

We followed her upstairs to the master bedroom to collect the bag. The room was an image of masculine disorder, with Professor Maples's bed—they for some reason had separate beds, with a night table between—rumpled and the bedclothes strewn about. Clothing was hung over various articles of furniture, and bureau drawers were pulled open. Maples had dressed hastily and, presumably, under police supervision, before being hauled off to the police station. Andrea's bed was neat and tight, and it was evident that she had not slept in it the night before.

I decided to take a quick look in the other five rooms leading off the hall. I thought I would give Holmes and Miss Lucy their moment of privacy if they desired to use it.

One of the rooms, fairly large and with a canopied bed, was obviously Lucy's. It was feminine without being overly frilly, and extremely, almost fussily, neat. There were two wardrobes in the room, across from each other, each with a collection of shoes on the bottom and a variety of female garments above.

I closed Lucy's door and knocked on the door across the hall. Getting no answer, I pushed the door open. It was one of the two rooms rented by the boarder, Crisboy, furnished as a sitting room, and I could see the door to the bedroom to the left. The young athletic instructor was sitting at his writing desk, his shoulders stooped, and his face buried in his arms on the desk. "Crisboy?" I said. 'Sorry, I didn't know you were here." Which seemed a poor excuse for bursting in on a man, but my curiosity was probably inexcusable if it came to that.

He sat up and turned around. "No matter," he said, using a small towel he was holding to wipe his face, which was red and puffy from crying. "Is there any news?" he asked me.

"Not that I am aware of," I said.

"A heck of a thing," he said. "That police person thinks that John—Professor Maples—killed Andrea. How could he think that? Professor Maples couldn't hurt anyone. Insult them, yes; criticize them, yes; pierce them with barbs of—of—irony, yes. But hit anyone with a stick? Never!"

I backed out of Crisboy's sitting room with some murmured comment and closed the door. The hall door to the left was now identified as Crisboy's bedroom. The door to the right turned out to be Andrea's dressing room, with a small couch, a bureau, a dressing table, and a connecting door to the master bedroom. The remaining door led to the lavatory.

Holmes emerged from the master bedroom with the traveling bag thrust under his arm, shook hands with Lucy, and we went downstairs and out the back door.

"Here, this way," Holmes said, taking me around to the side of the house. "There are markings on the path that, I believe, give some insight into what happened here. I have covered them over with some planks I found by the side of the house, to prevent them being washed away or tramped over."

"Clever," I said.

"Elementary," he replied.

Holmes had placed four pieces of planking on the path between the house and the cottage. We paused at the one nearest the house. "The police theory—the theory of Sergeant Meeks—is that Andrea Maples left the house to have an assignation at the cottage with an unknown suitor—if a man who trysts with a married woman may be called a suitor. They are trying to determine who he is. Professor Maples, awakening sometime during the night and finding his wife absent, went to the cottage, caught her as the suitor was leaving, or just after he left, realized what had happened by the state of her clothes, if not by other, ah, indications, and, in an uncontrollable rage, beat her to death with his walking stick."

I nodded. "That's about the way it was told to me."

"That story is contravened by the evidence," Holmes declared, carefully lifting the plank. "Observe the footsteps."

The plank covered a partial line of footsteps headed from the house to the cottage, and at least one footstep headed back to the house. The imprint in all cases was that of a woman's shoe.

"Note this indentation," Holmes said, pointing out a round hole about three-quarters of an inch across and perhaps an inch deep that was slightly forward and to the right of an outbound shoe imprint.

He sprinted over to the next plank and moved it, and then the next. "Look here," he called. "And here, and here. The same pattern."

"Yes," I said, "I see." I bent down and examined several of the footsteps closely, marking off the measurement from toe to heel and across the width of the imprint in my pocket notebook, and doing a rough sketch of what I saw, shielding the notebook as best I could from the slight drizzle.

"Notice that none of the footsteps in either direction were left by a man," Holmes said.

"Yes," I said, "I can see that." There were three sets of footsteps, two leading from the house to the cottage, and one returning.

"It proves that Professor Maples did not kill his wife," Holmes asserted.

"It certainly weakens the case against him," I admitted.

"Come now," Holmes said. "Surely you see that the entire case is predicated on the syllogism that, as Maples is never without his walking stick, and as his walking stick was used to kill Andrea Maples, then Maples must have murdered his wife."

"So it would seem," I agreed.

"A curious stick," Holmes told me. "I had occasion to examine it once. Did you know that it is actually a sword cane?"

"I did not know that," I said.

"I believe that it will prove an important fact in the case," Holmes told me.

"I assume that your conclusion is that Professor Maples was without his walking stick last night."

"That's right. Andrea Maples took it to the cottage herself. The indentations by her footsteps show that."

"What is it that you think happened?" I asked Holmes.

"As you've noted, there are three sets of footsteps," Holmes said. "Two going from the house to the cottage, and one returning to the house. As you can see, they are the footprints of a woman, and, carefully as I looked, I could find no indication of any footprints made by a man. One of the sets going seems to be slightly different in the indentation of the heel than the other sets. The returning set seems to be made up of footsteps that are further apart, and leave a deeper imprint than the others. I would say from examining them that Andrea Maples went to the cottage to meet someone. Before he arrived, she decided to arm herself and so she rushed back to the house and changed shoes—perhaps the first pair had been soaked by her stepping in a puddle—and then took her husband's walking stick—which she knew to be actually a sword cane—and returned to the cottage."

"And the person she was planning to meet?"

"He must have come by the road, as there are no markings on the path. But Professor Maples would surely have come by the path."

"So she thought herself to be in some danger?"

"So I would read it."

"So you would have it that it was not a romantic tryst?"

"Perhaps it had been," Holmes suggested. "Perhaps she had decided to break off an affair with some person, and she knew him to have a violent nature. In the event it seems that she was correct."

We had reached the cottage and, finding the back door unlocked, entered the small back pantry leading to the kitchen. Holmes dropped the traveling bag by the door and lay his topcoat and hat over a kitchen chair, and I followed suit.

"That would explain why she failed to wake up her husband and returned to the cottage by herself, although she believed herself in some danger," I said. "It neatly ties up most of the known facts. But I'm afraid that you won't be able to convince the police that you're right."

"Why not?"

"There's the fact of the disarray of Andrea Maples's clothing. As I understand it she was in her undergarments, and seems to have been dressing. It indicates that the meeting with her mysterious friend was, ah, friendly."

"Perhaps he forced himself on her."

"Perhaps. But then one would expect her clothing to be not merely loosened or removed, but stretched or torn. I did not hear that this was so. Did you have an opportunity to examine the woman's clothing?"

"Yes, I paid particular attention to the state of her clothing. She was wearing a petticoat and an over-something—another frilly white garment covering the upper part of her body. I am not very expert in the names of women's garments."

"Nor am I," I said. "I assume the remainder of her clothing was somewhere about?"

"It was in the bedroom."

We entered the parlor. The shades were drawn, keeping out even the weak light from the overcast sky. Holmes struck a match and lit an oil lamp which was sitting on a nearby table. The flickering light cast grotesque shadows about the room, creating a nebulous sense of oppression and doom. Or perhaps it was just the knowledge of what had recently transpired here that gave the room its evil character. "There," Holmes said, pointing to a large irregularly shaped bloodstain on the floor by the front door. "There is where she lay. She came from the bedroom, as the rest of her clothing was there, and was attacked in the parlor."

"Curious," I said.

"Really?" Holmes replied. "How so?"

The question was not destined to be answered, at least not then. At that moment the front door banged open and a police sergeant of immense girth, a round, red face, and a majestic handlebar mustache stomped down the hall and into the room. "Here now," he boomed. "What are you gentlemen doing in here, if I might ask?"

"Sergeant Meeks," Holmes said. "You've returned to the scene of the crime. Perhaps you are going to take my suggestion after all."

Meeks looked at Holmes with an air of benevolent curiosity. "And what suggestion might that be, young man?"

"I mentioned to you that it might be a good idea to post a constable here to keep the curiosity seekers from wandering about. It was when you were escorting Professor Maples into the carriage to take him away."

"Why so it was, Mr., ah—"

"Holmes. And this is Mr. Moriarty."

Meeks gave me a perfunctory nod, and turned his attention back to Holmes. "Yes, Mr. Holmes. So it was, and so you did. We of the regular constabulary are always grateful for any hints or suggestions as we might get from young gentlemen such as yourself. You also said something about preserving the foot marks along the lane out back, as I remember."

"That's right."

"Well I went to look at them foot marks of yours, Mr. Holmes, lifting up a couple of them boards you put down and peering under. They was just what you said they was—foot marks; and I thanks you kindly."

"From your attitude I can see that you don't attach much importance to the imprints," Holmes commented, not allowing himself to be annoyed by the sergeant's words or his sneering tone.

"We always try to plot a straight and true course when we're investigating a case," the sergeant explained. "There are always facts and circumstances around that don't seem to fit in. And that's because, if you'll excuse my saying so, they have nothing to do with the case."

"But perhaps there are times when some of these facts that you ignore actually present a clearer explanation of what really happened," Holmes suggested. "For example, Sergeant, I'm sure you noticed that the footsteps were all made by a woman. Not a single imprint of a man's foot on that path."

"If you say so, Mr. Holmes. I can't say that I examined them all that closely."

Holmes nodded. "If what I say is true," he said, "doesn't that suggest anything to you?"

Sergeant Meeks sighed a patient sigh. "It would indicate that the accused did not walk on the path. Perhaps he went by the road. Perhaps he flew. It don't really matter how he got to the cottage, it only matters what he did after he arrived."

"Did you notice the imprint of the walking stick next to the woman's footsteps?" Holmes asked. "Does that tell you nothing?"

"Nothing," the sergeant agreed. "She may have had another walking stick, or perhaps the branch from a tree."

Holmes shrugged. "I give up," he said.

"You'd be better off leaving the detecting to the professionals, young man," Meeks said. "We've done some investigating on our own already, don't think we haven't. And what we've heard pretty well wraps up the case against Professor Maples. I'm sorry, but there you have it."

"What have you heard?" Holmes demanded.

"Never you mind. That will all come out at the inquest, and that's soon enough. Now you'd best be getting out of here, the pair of you. I am taking your advice to the extent of locking the cottage up and having that broken window boarded over. We don't want curiosity seekers walking away with the furniture."

We retrieved our hats and coats and the bag with Professor Maples's fresh clothing and left the cottage. The rain had stopped, but dusk was approaching and a cold wind gusted through the trees. Holmes and I walked silently back to the college, each immersed in our own thoughts: Holmes presumably wondering what new facts had come to light, and trying to decide how to get his information before the authorities; I musing on the morality of revealing to Holmes, or to others, what I had discerned, and from that what I had surmised, or letting matters proceed without my intervention.

Holmes left me at the college to continue on to the police station, and I returned to my rooms.

The inquest was held two days later in the chapel of, let me call it, St. Elmo's College, one of our sister colleges making up the university. The chapel, a large Gothic structure with pews that would seat several hundred worshipers, had been borrowed for this more secular purpose in expectation of a rather large turnout of spectators; in which expectation the coroner was not disappointed.

The coroner, a local squire named Sir George Quick, was called upon to perform this function two or three times a year. But usually it was for an unfortunate who had drowned in the canal or fallen off a roof. Murders were quite rare in the area; or perhaps most murderers were more subtle than whoever had done in Andrea Maples.

Holmes and I sat in the audience and watched the examination proceed. Holmes had gone to the coroner before the jury was seated and asked if he could give evidence. When he explained what he wanted to say, Sir George sent him back to his seat. What he had to offer was not evidence, Sir George explained to him, but his interpretation of the evidence. "It is for the jury to interpret the evidence offered," Sir George told him, "not for you or I." Holmes's face was red with anger and mortification, and he glowered at the courtroom and everyone in it. I did my best not to notice.

Lucinda was in the front row, dressed in black. Her face wooden, she stared straight ahead through the half-veil that covered her eyes, and did not seem to be following anything that was happening around her. Crisboy sat next to her, wearing a black armband and a downcast expression. Professor Maples was sitting to one side, with a bulky constable sitting next to him and another sitting behind him. He had a bemused expression on his face, as though he couldn't really take any of this seriously.

Sir George informed the assemblage that he was going to proceed in an orderly manner, and that he would tolerate no fiddle-faddle and then called his first witness. It turned out to be the young bicyclist with the sticky fingers. "I could see that it was blood," he said, "and that it had come from beneath the door—from inside the house."

Then he described how he and his companions broke a window to gain entrance, and found Andrea Maples's body sprawled on the floor by the front door.

"And how was she dressed?" the coroner asked.

"She was not dressed, sir," came the answer.

A murmur arose in the audience, and the young man blushed and corrected himself. "That is to say, she was not *completely* dressed. She had on her, ah, undergarments, but not her dress."

"Shoes?" the coroner asked, with the bland air of one who is called upon to discuss seminaked ladies every day.

"I don't believe so, sir."

"That will be all," the coroner told him, "unless the jury have any questions?" he added, looking over at the six townsmen in the improvised jury box.

The foreman of the jury, an elderly man with a well-developed set of muttonchop whiskers, nodded and gazed out at the witness. "Could you tell us," he asked slowly, "what color were these undergarments?"

"White," the young man said.

"Now then," Sir George said, staring severely at the foreman, "that will be enough of that!"

Sergeant Meeks was called next. He sat in the improvised witness box hat in hand, his uniform and his face having both been buffed to a high shine, the very model of English propriety. The coroner led him through having been called, and arriving at the scene with his two constables, and examining the body.

"And then what did you do, Sergeant?"

"After sending Constable Gough off to Beachamshire to notify the police surgeon, I thoroughly examined the premises to see whether I could ascertain what had occurred on the, ah, premises."

"And what were your conclusions?"

"The deceased was identified to me as Mrs. Andrea Maples, wife of Professor Maples, who lived in the main house on the same property. She was dressed—"

"Yes, yes, sergeant," Sir George interrupted. "We've heard how she was dressed. Please go on."

"Very good, sir. She had been dead for some time when I examined her. I would put her death at between seven and ten hours previous, based on my experience. Which placed the time of her death at sometime around midnight."

"And on what do you base that conclusion?"

"The blood around the body was pretty well congealed, but not completely in the deeper pools, and the body appeared to be fairly well along into rigor mortis at that time.

"Very observant, Sergeant. And what else did you notice?"

"The murder weapon was lying near the body. It was a hardwood walking stick with a duck's-head handle. It had some of the victim's blood on it, and a clump of the victim's hair was affixed to the duck's head in the beak area. The stick was identified by one of the bicyclists who was still present as being the property of Professor Maples, husband of the victim."

"And what did you do then?"

"I proceeded over to the main house to question Professor Maples, who was just sitting down to breakfast when I arrived. I told him of his wife's death, and he affected to be quite disturbed at the news. I then asked him to produce his walking stick, and he spent some time affecting to look for it. I then placed him under arrest and sent Constable Parfry for a carriage to take the professor to the station house."

"Here, now!" a short, squat juror with a walrus mustache that covered his face from below his nose to below his chin, shifted in his seat and leaned belligerently forward. "What made you arrest the professor at that there moment? It seems to me that whoever the Maples woman was having an assigerna . . . —was meeting at this here cottage in the middle of the night was more likely to have done her in."

"Now, now, we'll get to that," the coroner said, fixing the fractious juror with a stern eye. "I'm trying to lay out the facts of the case in an orderly manner. We'll get to that soon enough."

The next witness was the police surgeon, who testified that the decedent had met her death as a result of multiple blunt-force blows to the head and shoulders. He couldn't say just which blow killed her, any one of several could have. And, yes, the duck-headed cane presented in evidence could have been the murder weapon.

Sir George nodded. So much for those who wanted information out of its proper order. Now . . .

Professor Maples was called next. The audience looked expectant. He testified that he had last seen his wife at about nine o'clock on the night she was killed. After which he had gone to bed, and, as he had been asleep, had not been aware of her absence.

"You did not note that she was missing when you awoke, or when you went down to breakfast?" Sir George asked.

"I assumed she had gone out early," Maples replied. "She went out early on occasion. I certainly didn't consider foul play. One doesn't, you know."

Professor Maples was excused, and the audience looked disappointed.

An acne-laden young man named Cramper was called up next. He was, he explained, employed at the local public house, the Red Garter, as a sort of general assistant. On the night of the murder he had been worked unusually late, shifting barrels of ale from one side of the cellar to the other. "It were on account of the rats," he explained.

Sir George, wisely, did not pursue that answer any further. "What time was it when you started for home?" he asked.

"Must have been going on for midnight, one side or 'nother."

Sir George stared expectantly at Cramper, and Cramper stared back complacently at Sir George.

"Well?" the coroner said finally.

"Well? Oh, what happened whilst I walked home. Well, I saw someone emerging from the old Wilstone cottage."

"That's the cottage where the murder took place?" Sir George prompted.

"Aye, that's the one, aright. Used to be a gent named Wilstone lived there. Still comes back from time to time, I believe."

"Ah!" said Sir George. "And this person you saw coming from the, ah, old Wilstone cottage?"

"Happens I know the gent. Name of Faulting. He teaches jumping and squatting, or some such, over by the college field building."

There was a murmur from the audience, which Sir George quashed with a look.

"And you could see clearly who the gentleman was, even though it was the middle of the night?"

"Ever so clearly. Aye, sir."

"And how was that?"

"Well, there were lights on in the house, and his face were all lit up by them lights."

"Well," Sir George said, looking first at the jury and then at the audience. "We will be calling Mr. Faulting next, to verify Mr. Cramper's story. And he will, gentlemen and, er, ladies. He will. Now, what else did you see, Mr. Cramper?"

"You mean in the house?"

"That's right. In the house."

"Well, I saw the lady in question—the lady who got herself killed."

"You saw Mrs. Maples in the house?"

"Aye, that's so. She were at the door, saying good-bye to this Faulting gent."

"So she was alive and well at that time?"

"Aye. That she were."

The jury foreman leaned forward. "And how were she dressed?" he called out, and then stared defiantly at the coroner, who had turned to glare at him.

"It were only for a few seconds that I saw her before she closed the door," Cramper replied. "She were wearing something white, I didn't much notice what."

"Yes, thank you. You're excused," Sir George said.

Mr. Faulting was called next, and he crept up to the witness chair like a man who knew he was having a bad dream, but didn't know how to get out of it. He admitted having been Andrea Maples's night visitor. He was not very happy about it, and most of his answers were mumbles, despite Sir George's constant admonitions to speak up. Andrea had, he informed the coroner's court, invited him to meet her in the cottage at ten o'clock.

"What about her husband?" the coroner demanded.

"I asked her that," Faulting said. "She laughed. She told me that he wouldn't object; that I was free to ask him if I liked. I, uh, I didn't speak with him."

"No," the coroner said, "I don't imagine you did."

Faulting was the last witness. The coroner reminded the jury that they were not to accuse any person of a crime, even if they thought there had been a crime; that was a job for the criminal courts. They were merely to determine cause of death. After a brief consultation, the jury returned a verdict of unlawful death.

"Thank you," Sir George said. "You have done your duty. I assume," he said, looking over at Sergeant Meeks, "that there is no need for me to suggest a course of action to the police."

"No, sir," Meeks told him. "Professor Maples will be bound over for trial at the assizes."

Sir George nodded. "Quite right," he said.

"Bah!" Holmes said to me in an undertone.

"You disagree?" I asked.

"I can think of a dozen ways Faulting could have pulled that trick," he said. "That young man—Crampe—didn't see Andrea Maples in the door-way, he saw a flash of something white."

"Perhaps," I said.

"Bah!" Holmes repeated.

When we left the building Miss Lucy came over to Holmes and pulled him away, talking to him in an earnest undertone. I walked slowly back to my rooms, trying to decide what to do. I disliked interfering with the authorities in their attempted search for justice, and I probably couldn't prove what I knew to be true, but could I stand by and allow an innocent man to be convicted of murder? And Maples would surely be convicted if he came to trial. There was no real evidence against him, but he had the appearance of guilt, and that's enough to convince nine juries out of ten.

About two hours later Holmes came over, his eyes shining. "Miss Lucy is a fine woman," he told me.

"Really?" I said.

"We talked for a while about her sister. That is, she tried to talk about Andrea, but she kept breaking down and crying before she could finish a thought."

"Not surprising," I said.

"She asked me if I thought Professor Maples was guilty," Holmes told me. "I said I was convinced he was not. She asked me if I thought he would be convicted if he came to trial. I thought I'd better be honest. I told her it seemed likely."

"You told her true," I commented.

"She is convinced of his innocence, even though it is her own sister who was killed. Many—most—people would allow emotion to override logic. And she wants to help him. She said, 'Then I know what I must do,' and she went off to see about hiring a lawyer."

"She said that?" I asked.

"She did."

"Holmes, think carefully. Did she say she was going to hire a lawyer?"

Holmes was momentarily startled at my question. "Well, let's see. She said she knew what she must do, and I said he's going to need the best lawyer and the best barrister around to clear himself of this, for all that we know he is not guilty."

"And?"

"And then she said she would not allow him to be convicted. And she—well—she kissed me on the cheek, and she said, 'Good-bye, Mr. Holmes, you have been a good friend.' And she hurried off."

"How long ago did she leave you?"

"Possibly an hour, perhaps a bit longer."

I jumped to my feet. "Come, Holmes," I said, "we must stop her."

"Stop her?"

"Before she does something foolish. Come, there's no time to waste!"

"Does what?" he asked, hurrying after me as I hastened down the hall, pulling my coat on.

"Just come!" I said. "Perhaps I'm wrong."

We raced out of the college and over to Barleymore Road, and continued in the direction of the Mapleses' house at a fast walk. It took about ten minutes to get there, and I pushed through the front door without bothering to knock.

Mr. Crisboy was sitting in the parlor, staring at the wall opposite, a study in suspended motion. In one hand was a spoon, in the other a small bottle. When we entered the room he slowly put both objects down. "Professor Maples depends on this fluid," he said. "Two spoons full before each meal." He held the bottle up for our inspection. The label read: *Peals Patented Magical Elixir of Health.* "Do you think they'd let me bring him a few bottles?"

"I'm sure they would," I told him. "Do you know where Lucy is?"

"She's upstairs in her room," Crisboy told me. "She is quite upset. But of course, we're all quite upset. She asked not to be disturbed."

I made for the staircase, Holmes close behind me. "Why this rush?" he demanded. "We can't just barge in on her."

"We must," I said. I pounded at her door, but there was no answer. The door was locked. I put my shoulder against it. After the third push it gave, and I stumbled into the room, Holmes close behind me.

There was an overturned chair in the middle of the room. From a hook in the ceiling that had once held a chandelier dangled the body of Lucy Moys.

"My God!" Holmes exclaimed.

Holmes righted the chair and pulled a small clasp knife from his pocket. I held the body steady while Holmes leaped up on the chair and sawed at the rope until it parted. We laid her carefully on the bed. It was clear from her white face and bulging, sightless eyes that she was beyond reviving. Holmes nonetheless cut the loop from around her neck. "Horrible," he said. "And you knew this was going to happen? But why? There's no reason—"

"Every reason," I said. "No, I didn't predict this, certainly not this quickly, but I did think she might do something foolish."

"But—"

"She must have left a note," I said.

We covered her body with a blanket, and Holmes went over to the writing desk. "Yes," he said. "There's an envelope here addressed to 'The Police.' And a second one—it's addressed to me!"

He ripped it open. After a few seconds he handed it to me.

> *Sherlock,*
> *It could have been different*
> *   had I been different.*
> *I like you tremendously.*
> *Think well of me.*
> *I'm so sorry.*
>
> > *Lucy*

"I don't understand," Sherlock Holmes said. "What does it mean? Why did she do this?"

"The letter to the police," I said, "what does it say?"

He opened it.

> *To whoever reads this—*
> *I am responsible for the death of my sister Andrea. I killed her in a jealous rage. I cannot live with myself, and I cannot allow Professor Maples, a sweet and innocent man, to suffer for my crime. This is best for all concerned.*
>
> > *Lucinda Moys*

"I don't understand," Holmes said. "She was jealous of Faulting? But I didn't think she even knew Faulting very well."

"She kept her secrets," I said, "even unto death."

"What secrets?"

"This household," I said, gesturing around me, "holds one big secret that is, you might say, made up of several smaller secrets."

"You knew that she had done it—that she had killed her sister?"

"I thought so, yes." I patted him on the shoulder, and he flinched as though my touch were painful. "Let us go downstairs now," I said.

"You go," Holmes said. "I'll join you in a few minutes."

I left Holmes staring down at the blanket-covered body on the bed, and went down to the parlor. "Lucy has committed suicide," I told Crisboy, who had put the bottle down but was still staring at the wall opposite. "She left a note. She killed Andrea."

"Ahhh!" he said. "Then they'll be letting the professor go."

"Yes," I said.

"She'd been acting strange the past few days. But with what happened, I never thought. . . . Hanged herself?"

"Yes," I said. "Someone must go to the police station."

"Of course." Crisboy got up. "I'll go." He went into the hall and took his overcoat off the peg. "Ahhh. Poor thing." He went out the door.

About ten minutes later Holmes came down. "How did you know?" he asked.

"The footsteps that you preserved so carefully," I said. "There were three lines: two going out to the cottage and one coming back. The single one going out was wearing different shoes, and it—she—went first. I could tell because some of the prints from the other set overlapped the first. And it was the second set going out that had the indentations from the walking stick. So someone—some woman—went out after Andrea Maples, and that woman came back. She went out with the walking stick and came back without it."

"I missed that," Holmes said.

"It's easier to tell than to observe," I told him.

"I had made up my mind about what I was going to find before I went to look," he said. "The deductive process suffers from preconceptions."

"It's a matter of eliminating the impossible," I told him. "Then whatever remains, however improbable, must be the truth."

"I shall remember that," he said. "I still cannot fathom that Lucy was that jealous of Andrea."

"She was, but not in the way you imagine," I told him.

"What do you mean?"

"Do you remember that I suggested that you notice Lucinda's ears?"

"Yes." Holmes looked puzzled. "They looked like—ears."

"Their shape was quite distinctive, and quite different from those of Andrea. The basic shape of the ear seems to be constant within a family. This was a reasonable indication that Andrea and Lucinda were not really sisters."

"Not really sisters? Then they were—what?"

"They were lovers," I told him. "There are women who fall in love with other women, just as there are men who fall in love with other men. The ancient Greeks thought it quite normal."

"Lovers?"

"Andrea preferred women to men, and Lucinda was her, ah, mate."

"But—Professor Maples is her husband."

"I assume it was truly a marriage of convenience. If you look at the bedrooms it is clear that Andrea and Lucy usually shared a bedroom—Lucy's—as they both have quantities of clothing in it. And I would assume that Professor Maples and Mr. Crisboy have a similar arrangement."

"You think the professor and Crisboy—but they . . ."

"A German professor named Ulrichs has coined a word for such unions; he calls them homo-sexual. In some societies they are accepted, and in some they are condemned. We live in the latter."

"Holmes sat down in the straight-back chair. "That is so," he said. "So you think they derived this method of keeping their relationships concealed?"

"I imagine the marriage, if there was a marriage, and Andrea's adopting Lucy as her 'sister' was established well before the ménage moved here. It was the ideal solution, each protecting the other from the scorn of society and the sting of the laws against sodomy and such behavior."

"But Andrea went to the cottage to have, ah, intimate relations with Faulting."

"She liked to flirt, you must have observed that. And she obviously wasn't picky as to which gender she flirted with, or with which gender she, let us say, consummated her flirting. There are women like that, many of them it seems unusually attractive and, ah, compelling. Augustus Caesar's daughter Julia seems to have been one of them, according to Suetonius. Andrea found Faulting attractive, and was determined to have him. My guess is that she and Lucy had words about it, but Andrea went to meet Faulting anyway, while Lucy remained in her room and worked herself into a jealous rage. She didn't intend to kill Andrea; that's shown by the fact that she didn't open the sword cane, although she must have known about it."

Holmes was silent for a minute, and I could see some powerful emotion growing within him. "You had this all figured out," he said, turning to me, his words tight and controlled.

"Much of it," I admitted. "But don't berate yourself for missing it. I was familiar with the idea of homo-sexuality through my reading, and several acquaintances of mine have told me of such relationships. I had the knowledge and you didn't."

But I had misjudged the direction of Holmes's thoughts. The fury in him suddenly exploded. "You could have stopped this," he screamed. "You let it happen!"

I backed away to avoid either of us doing something we would later regret. "I knew nothing of Andrea's tryst," I told him, "nor Lucinda's fury."

Holmes took a deep breath. "No," he said, "you couldn't have stopped the murder, but you could have stopped Lucy's suicide. Clearly you knew what she intended."

"You credit me with a prescience I do not possess," I told him.

"You were fairly clear on what she intended an hour after the event," he said. "Why couldn't you have rushed out here before?"

"I don't know," I told him. "Until you told me what she had said to you, it didn't strike me—"

"It didn't strike you!"

"You spoke to her yourself," I said, "and yet you guessed nothing."

"I didn't know what you knew," he said. "I was a fool. But you—what were you?"

I had no answer for him. Perhaps I should have guessed what Lucy intended. Perhaps I did guess. Perhaps, on some unconscious level I weighed the options of her ending her own life, or of her facing an English jury, and then being taken out one cold morning, and having the hood tied around her head and the heavy hemp rope around her neck, and hearing a pusillanimous parson murmuring homilies at her until they sprang the trap.

A few minutes later the police arrived. The next day Professor Maples was released from custody and returned home. Within a month he and Crisboy had packed up and left the college. Although nothing was ever officially said about their relationship, the rumors followed them to Maples's next position, and to the one after that, until finally they left Britain entirely. I lost track of them after that. Holmes left the college at the end of the term. I believe that, after taking a year off, he subsequently enrolled at Cambridge.

Holmes has never forgiven me for what he believes I did. He has also, it would seem, never forgiven the fair sex for the transgressions of Lucinda Moys. I did not at the time realize the depth of his feelings toward her. Perhaps he didn't either. His feeling toward me is unfortunate and has led, over the years, to some monstrous accusations on his part. I am no saint.

Indeed, as it happens I eventually found myself on the other side of the law as often as not. I am pleased to call myself England's first consulting criminal, as I indulge in breaking the laws of my country to support my scientific endeavors. But when Holmes calls me "the Napoleon of crime," is he not perhaps seeing, through the mists of time, the blanket-covered body of that unfortunate girl whose death he blames on me? And could it be that he is reflecting on the fact that the first, perhaps the only, woman he ever loved was incapable of loving him in return?

At any rate, I issue one last stern warning to those of you who repeat Holmes's foul canards about me in print, or otherwise: there are certain of the laws of our land that I embrace heartily, and the laws of libel and slander ride high on the list. Beware!

MRS. HUDSON

The table was all laid, and, just as I was about to ring, Mrs. Hudson entered with the tea and coffee. A few minutes later she brought in the covers, and we all drew up to the table. Holmes ravenous, I curious, and Phelps in the gloomiest state of depression.

"Mrs. Hudson has risen to the occasion," said Holmes, uncovering a dish of curried chicken. "Her cuisine is a little limited, but she has as good an idea of breakfast as a Scotchwoman."

—"The Naval Treaty"

by LINDA ROBERTSON

Mrs. Hudson Reminisces

As part of *English Fireside Magazine*'s ongoing series, "Unsung Heroines," I recently interviewed Mrs. Jean Hudson, once the landlady and house-keeper for the famous consulting detective Sherlock Holmes and his friend and chronicler, Dr. John Watson. After Mr. Holmes gave up sleuthing for a quieter life keeping bees in Surrey, Mrs. Hudson sold her house at 221 Baker Street, the scene of so many of the adventures recounted by Dr. Watson, and moved to a cottage in Perthshire.

I made the walk from the train station to her home on a fine May after-noon. As I reached the garden gate, I heard a low bark, followed by a men-acing growl. On the path beyond crouched an enormous black dog, baring his teeth in a convincing snarl. I was wondering how to talk him out of leaping the fence and going for my throat, when a woman appeared around the side of the house and called to me. "Hello! You must be Miss Gunn. I'm Mrs. Hudson. Do come in. It's all right, Otto, she's a friend." Otto sub-sided and moved to one side of the path as I opened the gate, but trailed after me suspiciously as I walked through the small, flower-filled garden and followed Mrs. Hudson into the cottage. Once in the sitting room, he slumped with a sigh onto the hearth rug, where he lay watching us and giv-ing an occasional wag of his tail when Mrs. Hudson glanced at him.

Despite her years, which she admits are "well over sixty," Mrs. Hudson is a commanding figure of a woman, tall and energetic, her gray hair fram-ing a kind and cheerful face. Over tea and currant cake, which she served in her comfortable sitting room, we had the following conversation:

E.F. It's a pleasure to meet you. I feel that I already know you in some way, after reading Dr. Watson's stories. I'm rather sorry to have missed see-ing 221B Baker Street, but you have a lovely place here. Such pretty light, and the garden is simply burgeoning with flowers. And Otto is certainly an impressive dog. You must feel quite safe with him guarding your house.

Mrs. H. Dear Otto—loyal to a fault, I'm afraid. I'm sorry if he gave you a scare. He was a gift from Mr. Holmes after I settled here. "There may still be enemies," he said, even though he has long since retired from detective work. I appreciated his kindness, but I can't say I worry much about such things. But about Baker Street—you needn't worry about having missed it. There wasn't anything exceptional about the house, except for its connection with Mr. Holmes. We had so many sightseers the last few years, peering in the windows and demanding to be let in, as if we were a museum. I wish I'd had Otto then. He's a Baskerville hound, you know. Do you remember Dr. Watson's story?

E.F. Oh, certainly. But I thought there was only one Hound of the Baskervilles, and he was killed at the end.

Mrs. H. Well, yes and no. There was a bit of a story around the Hound, as it turned out. I think Mr. Holmes felt a bit bad about having to shoot him and also a bit curious about the origin of such an extraordinary animal. After the mystery was solved Mr. Holmes made another visit to the dealer who had sold the hound to that horrible Mr. Stapleton and found out where they had gotten him. As it happened, the dog came from a village, Giles Tor, only twenty miles or so from Baskerville Hall. There are dozens of them there. The villagers say they're descended from some elk hunting dogs brought over by one of William the Conqueror's knights—Gilles of something-or-other Sur Mer, who settled there. His line died out centuries ago, but the dogs have thrived. After the legend of the Hound spread through the area, the local people started calling them Baskerville hounds. The villagers think that it was probably a wandering Basky that Sir Hugo and his men saw. Most of the breed are brindle, actually. Only about one in ten is black like the Hound or Otto here.

It's one of the things I miss about having Mr. Holmes around. He knows so many things! It seemed I was always learning something strange and new about the world.

E.F. Do you hear from Mr. Holmes often?

Mrs. H. Oh, yes. We've stayed good friends. He writes and sends me honey from his beehives, and sometimes pays a visit when he travels to Scotland. The rustic life in Surrey agrees with him, I think. He seems more at peace, and he tells me that he reads and does chemistry experiments now to his heart's content.

E.F. Do you know if he still does any detective work?

Mrs. H. I'm sure of it. Sometimes he comes by as a sort of surprise, you know, as though he were called up here with little warning. And on those occasions he's been a bit closemouthed about his reasons for coming to Scotland—and he has that look in his eye.

E.F. What look?

Mrs. H. I don't quite recall how Dr. Watson put it—he described it so much better than I can. That glint that used to tell us that, as Mr. Holmes like to put it, "the game is afoot."

E.F. Has he said what he's doing?

Mrs. H. Very little. He has always been quite discreet about his detective work. But I believe he is sometimes called upon by the government. Once, when he visited, he was returning from some assignment for the Sea Lord, out in the Hebrides.

E.F. And do you hear from Dr. Watson?

Mrs. H. His wife writes sometimes. He is retired, too, and Mrs. Watson says he is often troubled by the war wound in his leg—or was it his shoulder? I can't remember. Dr. Watson and I were not that close. I was just the landlady to him, a figure in the background, really—which is just as well, all things considered. As annoying as the visitors were to Baker Street, looking for Mr. Holmes, I can scarcely imagine how I would take being famous in my own right.

E.F. Was it the visitors who sent you fleeing to a village in Scotland after those years in London?

Mrs. H. Oh, no, I was born and raised in Perth, so coming here was really a bit of a homecoming. I have family nearby—my sister and her husband have the pub in the village, and another brother lives in Blair Atholl, and of course there are various nieces and nephews and their children. And after a lifetime in cities, I felt the country would be a welcome change.

E.F. Was it? I know some fellow Londoners who were never able to be comfortable outside the city.

Mrs. H. It took some time to get used to the quiet. But I stay busy with church fairs and charity work and looking after the children of my nieces and nephew, and I'm learning to raise vegetables and make preserves. I'm quite the country lady these days. Do have some more currant cake. It was one of Dr. Watson's favorites.

E.F. Thank you, I think I will have another piece. How did Sherlock Holmes become your tenant in the first place?

Mrs. H. Oh, just in the ordinary way, by answering my advertisement for rooms to let. Now that I think of it, what a dreadful year that was!

E.F. Oh, dear—what happened?

Mrs. H. A number of things. The worst was that poor Harry—my husband—had fled to the Continent, because the police were after him.

E.F. Really! Why?

Mrs. H. They suspected him of being involved in a bucket shop in Edinburgh which ended very badly. I was so worried—

E.F. A bucket shop? What's that?

Mrs. H. This one was some men selling shares in a gold mine in Canada.

E.F. I don't understand. What's the harm in that?

Mrs. H. I don't recall the details very well. Either there wasn't any gold or there was no mine, I don't remember which.

E.F. Goodness! How did your husband come to be suspected of being part of that?

Mrs. H. Well, he was in that line of work, so to speak.

E.F. Your husband was a swindler?

Mrs. H. A harsh word—but not to put too fine a point on it, I supposed that's what he was. He was "with the game," as they called it. Which means he was a confidence man, and quite good at it. Never convicted of anything, though the police in England, Scotland, Ireland, and Wales were after him, on, and off, for thirty years.

E.F. My goodness—and you weren't troubled being married to him?

Mrs. H. Honestly, no, except for worrying on account of the risk. No, Harry never did anyone any violence, and as for the money he took—well, I'm Scots, and the men he took from were mainly English and rich. As far as I'm concerned, they have a lot to answer for. My grandparents were thrown off their farm in the Clearances, and lost everything they had. Many people like them starved or were forced to emigrate. Two of my grandmother's brothers set sail with their families for New Zealand, but their ship was lost at sea. They say my grandmother died of a broken heart when she heard the news. My granddad walked with his children—my mother and her sister and brother—to Perth and found work in a mill. My father was a millworker, too, but he turned to drink and was killed in a brawl. So my mother supported us by taking in laundry, and my sisters and I worked with her. We worked from sunup to well past sundown, and seldom had warm clothing or enough to eat. As I see it, what Harry took was only what the English and the owners of the land and the mills took from us. I tell you, miss, after Harry and I were married, while my mother was alive I sent money to her every month, so that she could have a few of the comforts she could not afford when we were children. And I felt that what I was giving her was no more than she was owed.

E.F. My goodness— How did you go from those beginnings to being a London landlady?

Mrs. H. I was fortunate in some ways. I was a lively girl, with a nice singing voice and a knack for mimic. When I wasn't helping my mother wash and iron, I made a bit of extra money singing on the street. Then a friend of my uncle's who worked in a theater recommended me to the manager. I apprenticed there, more or less, singing between the acts to keep the audience in their seats while the candy butchers worked the aisles. When I grew older, I played character parts. And then I met Harry.

E.F. How did you meet Harry—er, Mr. Hudson?

Mrs. H. He was an actor, too, touring with a company from London. We met through a friend and he courted me. After he returned to London, he sent for me, and we were married there. But the theater company folded a few months later, and we were both out of work. Luckily for us, an old friend of Harry's showed up around then, and introduced him to the confidence trade. A fine and funny Irishman he was, named O'Brien, God rest his soul. Harry took to the game—his experience as an actor helped—and he did quite well.

E.F. Did you work with Mr. Hudson at his, uh, profession?

Mrs. H. Once or twice at first, in a minor way. But Harry didn't like the idea. This may sound odd, given how he made his living, but he craved respectability. He was a Cockney, born and bred, but he always had a yearning for a better life. Especially after young Harry was born, he kept us well away from his business dealings. It was Harry's idea to get us the house on Baker Street, after a particularly good score. He used to say that the house and I were his insurance and his pension. "I know that when I decide to rest from my labors, I'll have my bonnie Jean to come home to," he would say to me. "And if the worst happens, you'll at least have a place to live and an income for yourself and the bairn." Harry's always been a good man, in his way.

But you wanted to know how I met Mr. Holmes and Dr. Watson. Well, as I said, it was hard times for us. I lived in fear that Harry would be caught and tried for murder, and I truly wondered whether I would ever see him again.

E.F. My goodness! Murder?

Mrs. H. Yes. It was a nasty business. A baronet—Sir Roderick Parr, if I remember correctly—was murdered, and the story was that he was a bates who had uncovered the con and was killed because he threatened to go to the law. A peach here in London claimed that Harry was one of the men involved in the scheme.

E.F. How terrible! But what do you mean when you say that Sir Roderick was a bates?

Mrs. H. That he was one of the people being swindled.

E.F. Goodness! And what is a *peach*?

Mrs. H. Oh, dear, I fear I'm giving you an education in the ways of the criminal classes! A peach is a snitch, a police informer—a criminal who goes around tattling to the police about what his fellow criminals are up to.

E.F. Why would someone do that? One keeps hearing about honor among thieves, you know, and all that.

Mrs. H. Oh, there's little honor in the criminal element. A peach usually tells on his fellows to get some leniency from the police and the judge for his own crimes. This one didn't know anything, really, but Inspector Gregson had been trying for years to catch Harry and was only too ready to believe him. Poor Harry insisted to me that he had nothing to do with it and that he was working an entirely different game in Liverpool. But of course he couldn't tell *that* to Inspector Gregson, so he had to drop out of sight or be arrested.

Then, on top of everything else, I lost my lodger, Mr. Postlethwaite. He was caught stealing from the theater he was managing—cleared out in the middle of the night, owing most of a quarter's rent. Scotland Yard inspectors were trooping through the house for days, ransacking his rooms for clues about where he had gone and badgering me and my poor girl until she threatened to give notice. And Gregson suspected Harry somehow had a hand in that, too. They found Postlethwaite about a year later, somewhere in Yorkshire. I'm sure Mr. Holmes would have nabbed him much sooner, had he been called upon. He and I talked once or twice about Postlethwaite, and Mr. Holmes surmised that he wouldn't have left England. I can't recall why—when Postlethwaite was actually found I thought it was just a lucky guess. But as I was saying, it was a month or more before the uproar died down enough that I could advertise that the rooms were to let. I was afraid even then that no one would want rooms in my house, what with all the attention we were getting from the police. I was truly grateful when Mr. Holmes showed up.

E.F. I would imagine so, after all that. What was your first meeting with him like?

Mrs. H. I remember that he came to look at the rooms and was interested in taking them, but said he would need another lodger to share the expense. He came back the next day with Dr. Watson in tow, and they rented the rooms on the spot.

E.F. What was your first impression of Sherlock Holmes?

Mrs. H. A gentleman, nice manners, but a bit stiff and standoffish. I'd like to say I saw something about him that suggested greatness, but in all honesty, he was just a tall, thin young man, a bit formal and distant, with a rather superior attitude. I took more to Dr. Watson, actually, at first. He had a friendlier manner—though I think he was a bit shocked when he learned how his landlady's husband made his living. Mr. Holmes, though—he was a much cooler character. Even then, I don't think there was much that could surprise him.

E.F. It must have been rather disconcerting having Holmes as a tenant—the strange people visiting at all hours, the chemistry experiments, the gunplay, suspects jumping out of windows, that sort of thing.

Mrs. H. Not really. I'd had other tenants who were at least as trying. Postlethwaite, for one. And then there was the Great Ponti, a fire-eater. He decided to practice a new effect in his rooms one evening after having a bit too much wine with dinner, and set fire to the drapes. We were lucky the entire house didn't burn down. And there was M. Fleuron, with his boa constrictor that escaped and ate one of the cats. Mr. Holmes was actually fairly tame by comparison. And of course he always paid for the repairs. And he did Harry and me a great favor soon after moving in.

E.F. What was that?

Mrs. H. He cleared Harry of the murder business. He learned about it on his own. I didn't tell him or Dr. Watson about poor Harry's problem. They were gentlemen, after all, and I didn't think they would take kindly to hearing that their landlady's husband was a wanted criminal. I think I explained Harry's absence by saying something about him being a traveling man. But one day when Dr. Watson was out, as I was bringing Mr. Holmes his breakfast, he suddenly said to me, "Mrs. Hudson, how would you like to see your husband here in London again?"

I wasn't sure what he was at, so I simply said something about how it was always a pleasure when Mr. Hudson's work allowed him time with his family.

"Mrs. Hudson," he said, "I know your husband is in hiding because of trouble with the law. Inspector Gregson saw fit to tell me about Mr. Hudson and the murder of Sir Roderick Parr not long after I took these rooms. I have looked up some accounts of it in the Edinburgh papers and taken the liberty of writing to a police inspector of my acquaintance there. From what I have learned of the case I believe that your husband's claim that he is innocent of the murder may be worth looking into."

"Sir?" I said, but I felt about to faint from fear. I knew Mr. Holmes was clever and he was beginning to make a name for himself as a detective. But I couldn't tell if I could trust him. For all I knew, he was working with the police to apprehend Harry and hoping to gain my confidence to track him down. And, if the truth be known, even I had only Harry's word that he was not part of that scheme. Harry was not one to talk about what he was up to. "If you don't know, you don't have to lie," he used to say to me.

"Mrs. Hudson, please sit down," Mr. Holmes said, and I sat in Mr. Watson's chair at the table, trying to decide what to do next. I must have looked the picture of wretchedness. Mr. Holmes surprised me with the kindness of his tone. "I can see you are reluctant to trust me in this," he said, looking me in the eye, "but I am in good faith. You are a friend, and I would not betray you. Besides," he went on, with a twinkle in his eye, "consider the fact that if I did, I would have to find other lodgings, and Dr. Watson would never forgive me."

I smiled a little at this, and he continued. "I take it that you have a way of communicating with Mr. Hudson."

I thought about it a moment and then decided I could trust him at least that far. "Yes," I said, "I can get a message to him."

"Well, then, why not let him decide? Send him a letter, and enclose this with it." And he went to his desk, wrote a few words on a sheet of paper, folded it, and handed it to me.

E.F. What did he write?

Mrs. H. I waited until I was downstairs to look at the paper, even though he hadn't said not to. He had written a brief note: "Mr. Hudson: If you are indeed innocent in the death of Sir Roderick Parr, I am willing to attempt to clear you, but I will need your help. If you wish my assistance, meet me at a time and place of your choosing—Sherlock Holmes."

Well, the letters Harry and I wrote to one another took a roundabout route, because we feared that the police might be watching to see if I posted any letters to him or received any from him. I gave the letter with Mr. Holmes's note in it to Mr. McBeath, our butcher. Mr. McBeath was a friend of Harry's, and he gave my letters to another of Harry's friends, Mr. Delagnes, who was a traveler in wine. Delagnes mailed them *poste restant* to the town in Italy where Harry was staying. Harry's replies—under the name Pietro Ruvolo, if I remember—were posted to Delagnes in care of his overseas supplier in Calais. Harry told me all this afterward; at the time I didn't know how the letters got to him from the butcher. Mr. McBeath and I had a code, when a letter came from Harry. When I went to choose the meat for our dinner, he would say that the kidneys were particularly nice that day, so that I would know that a letter would be in that day's delivery and would be sure to open the package myself instead of letting the girl do it.

Weeks went by before I received a response to Mr. Holmes's note. Then a letter came to me from Harry, with a note inside it addressed to Mr. Holmes. Mr. Holmes showed it to me. It said, "Dear sir: I appreciate your efforts on my behalf. I will be in Paris for a week, beginning September 15. There is a café, Le Chien Sourd, on the Rue des Ecoles. Tell the proprietor, M. Launay, who you are, and he will send for me."

E.F. My goodness, what intrigue! Why, it's like a spy story!

Mrs. H. Well, dear Harry did a bit of that, too, later in his life. To continue, though, Mr. Holmes read the note and studied the paper, saying little but "hmm," and "indeed." I offered to pay for his passage to Paris, but he declined. Before he left, though, Mr. Holmes asked me for a photograph of Harry. The only one I had was from his acting days—Harry didn't want photographs of himself lying about—but I gave it to Mr. Holmes with as good a description as I could. He was gone for several days. Upon his return, he told me, "Mrs. Hudson, I have met your husband, and he is a fine, intelligent man, despite his unfortunate profession." He said nothing else about the meeting, but left again a few days later, with Dr. Watson in tow. It was well over a week before they returned. Poor Dr. Watson looked drawn and tired and said something about never having been so seasick in his life. But Mr. Holmes was all afire and as intent as a dog on a scent. He summoned me to his rooms, and said to me, "Mrs. Hudson, your husband will come here in the next evening or two, in some sort of incognito. Is your girl likely to recognize him?"

"Probably not if he is disguised, sir, but I can't be certain."

He thought for a moment and said, "Make sure that you are the one to answer the door, then. When he comes he will ask for me. If you recognize him, make no sign, but tell him that the sailor will be coming presently and show him upstairs as if he were a stranger."

I sat up that night and the next. And on the second night, some time after ten o'clock, the doorbell rang, and I ran to answer it. A worried-looking man came into the hallway, put down a carpetbag, and as he took off his hat and unbuttoned his overcoat, asked in a low, rather embarrassed voice for Mr. Holmes. "I believe he's expecting me," he said. He wore a clerical collar, and had reddish side whiskers and a fringe of hair around a bald pate. It took a moment for me to recognize the man as Harry, but hard as it was, I gave no sign that I knew him, but showed him upstairs, and told him what Mr. Holmes had said to say about the sailor. "Oh, good," he murmured, and glanced at me with a the hint of a smile.

Holmes answered the door and let him in. A few minutes later, Dr. Watson came down the stairs and said, "I'm going out to fetch another visitor, Mrs. Hudson. Mr. Holmes would like you to sit up and wait for our return."

As anxious as I was, tiredness overcame me, and I fell asleep in my chair. I was awakened by the sound of Dr. Watson's key in the door. With Dr. Watson was a tall man, dressed in workman's pants and a sailor's pea-coat, and holding his cap. He was old, but strong-looking, with angular features and a steady, direct gaze. "Mrs. Hudson, this is Peter Moodie," Dr. Watson said. "Would you please come upstairs with us?" Thoroughly mystified at this point, I followed them.

As we reached the top of the stairs, Mr. Holmes appeared on the landing. "Ah, Mr. Moodie!" he greeted him. "Come in. Mrs. H., may I have a word with you?" As Dr. Watson and Mr. Moodie passed into the sitting room, Holmes stayed with me in the hall and whispered, "It is very important that Mr. Moodie not know Mr. Hudson's identity until the proper moment. Please do not say his name or your own, until I tell you."

The room was brightly lit. Harry was sitting there, shed of his vicar's disguise, his bald spot and whiskers gone. He stood up as I entered, but gave no sign that he knew me. For all that I knew this was part of Mr. Holmes's plan, it was a bit disconcerting to see him act like a stranger. Dr.

Watson took a seat, and Mr. Holmes invited Mr. Moodie to sit also. "And, ma'am, will you please have a seat over there?" he said, indicating a chair next to Harry's.

When we were all seated, Mr. Holmes began to speak. "Mr. Moodie has generously made the long journey here from the Shetland Islands, to share with us his rather unique knowledge of certain events that took place in Edinburgh last year. Mr. Moodie, if you will?"

Peter Moodie sighed and looked down at his rough hands, still holding his cap, then looked back up at us and with an air of resolution, began speaking in a Shetland burr so thick that even I had a hard time following it at times. "It's a hard story to tell, and a harder one to have lived," he said. "Some years ago, my only daughter, Elizabeth, left our home in Lerwick to go into service in Edinburgh. She was our youngest, the child of our old age, and very precious to us. She was a good girl, but life in the Shetland Islands had not prepared her for the ways of the city, and she fell prey to Sir Roderick Parr. He seduced her with promises of marriage and then deserted her when she told him she was with child. Her shame was so great that she almost starved rather than tell us what had become of her, but a friend heard of what had happened and sent word to us, and I traveled to Edinburgh and brought her and the bairn home. My poor child! She had been a pretty young woman, but when I found her, she was so pale and thin, and her spirit was broken, sir." He stopped, and his hands clenched his cap as if they would tear it in two. "Lizzie and her child stayed with my wife and me, but she had been taken with the consumption while destitute in Edinburgh. Her baby sickened and died, and I thought it a mercy, God forgive me, given how it had come into the world. As for Lizzie, though we cared for her as best we could, the consumption took her last year. When she died, I lost my reason with grief. I had been a ship's carpenter, but I was too old any more to go to sea, and all I could think about was finding Sir Roderick, if he was still alive, and destroying him like the dog he was. I'm sorry sir, but I get so angry when I think of him—"

"It's all right," Mr. Holmes said. "Go on."

"All right. Well, Sir Roderick had some property outside Stirling, but at that time he was spending a great deal of time in Edinburgh. I found out where he was staying and began following him at a distance, finding out his movements and looking for the right moment to confront him. I soon found that he went almost every day to the office of the Yukon and Mackenzie Mining Company, and he seemed to spend a lot of time with another man from that office, named Stritch, who appeared from his accent to be from Canada. Parr was a big, rough bullying fellow, and Stritch seemed a little afraid of him.

"As I stayed in Edinburgh and watched Sir Roderick, my mind began to clear, and I realized that he was nothing more than a swaggering bully, hardly worth hanging for and leaving my poor wife with even more grief. But at the same time I began to suspect that he and this fellow Stritch were up to no good. Sir Roderick spent a great deal of time drinking in a pub near the mining company offices, so I began spending time there, too. When he was in his cups, which was often, he let drop hints that he was making a great deal of money in some underhanded manner. 'Lambs to the slaughter,' he would say sometimes, laughing and flashing a roll of banknotes. Stritch would pull him aside and tell him to be quiet, but Sir Roderick would laugh him off or get angry.

"On seeing that Sir Roderick might be involved in something criminal, I thought I might get my revenge on him by turning him in to the law. But I needed to know more of what he and Stritch were up to. So I found work doing repairs and carpentry for the owner of the building. I could come and go as I please and was as good as invisible to the tenants.

"I noticed that a third man sometimes visited the offices and that he was someone to whom Mr. Stritch appeared to be a subordinate. There was a narrow passageway behind Mr. Stritch's office where I could stand and hear conversations taking place there. I took to listening when Sir Roderick visited, and when this third man showed up I went back there to see what he had to say to Stritch.

"Stritch addressed the other man as Colfax, or sometimes Jack. He would report on how the business was going, and it seemed that they spent time going over some accounts. Stritch also complained about Sir Roderick. 'I don't care how much business he's bringing in,' he said. 'He won't shut up, and it's only a matter of time before he brings the law down on us.' The first time or two, Colfax listened and told Stritch, 'Just try to keep him quiet as best you can.' But one day Stritch said to him, 'Parr is saying he wants a bigger cut of the take or he's threatening to go to the police himself and say we've tried to swindle him.' Colfax heard him out and then said, 'We've got to get rid of him.' It was as simple as that.

A few mornings later, I came to work and found the Yukon and Mackenzie office empty and deserted, with not so much as a sign on the door to tell what had become of the company. At the pub that day I heard that Sir Roderick's body had been found in an alley in the Old Town. He had been garrotted and his money and watch taken. But his watch was found a street or two away. It had been tossed into a sewer, but the chain had caught in the grate.

"With Sir Roderick dead, I had no need for revenge, and I determined to return home. But before I did I went to the police to tell them what I knew about the Yukon and Mackenzie, thinking I might be able to help the people whose money had been taken. But I made the mistake of telling the police how I'd come to know of Sir Roderick, and instead of believing me when I told them he was one of the villains, they nearly arrested me for his murder."

"Thank you, Mr. Moodie," Mr. Holmes said. "Now, I have two questions for you. First, I would ask you to take a good look at this man over here," he said, looking over at Harry and motioning him to stand. "Did you ever see him during your stay in Edinburgh?"

Mr. Moodie turned in his chair and looked at Harry from under his pale eyebrows, for a long moment. Then he turned to Mr. Holmes and said, "No, sir, I have never seen this man before tonight."

"Does he in any way resemble Colfax or Stritch?"

"No, sir. Both of them were considerably taller, and not stout. Colfax, in particular, moved like a military man. I believe I once heard someone call him Major, in fact."

Mr. Holmes nodded, as if satisfied. "My next question to you, then, Mr. Moodie, is in the conversations that you heard among the men involved in the mining company scheme, did you ever hear the name Harry Hudson mentioned?"

Mr. Moodie looked surprised. "Why, yes, in fact." I felt as though my heart had stopped beating. I heard Mr. Holmes say, "Can you tell us what was said about him?"

"Yes. It was in one of the conversations between Stritch and Colfax. Stritch was upset and said something about how the last time he had run a store with Harry Hudson, there had been none of these problems and no d——d—pardon my language, ma'am—amateurs. Colfax answered, 'Well, you're not working with Harry Hudson, you're working with me, and you'll do as I say.'"

Mr. Holmes motioned for Harry to sit. "Thank you, Mr. Moodie," he said. "In case you are wondering, this man is Harry Hudson, and the lady next to him is his wife." Mr. Moodie, looking a bit baffled, nodded to us.

Mr. Holmes continued, "Now, if I may ask you one more favor, would you be willing to come with me tomorrow on a visit to Inspector Gregson of the local constabulary and tell your story to him?"

"Yes, sir, I would," Mr. Moodie replied.

"Well," said Mr. Holmes, sitting back in his chair. "Mr. Hudson, if Gregson is an honest man, as I believe him to be, you should be free to remain here unmolested after tomorrow. For now, I think a glass of brandy would be a good end to this evening. Watson, if you would be so kind as to bring the bottle and glasses. I think Mrs. Hudson is a bit indisposed." Because I had fallen into Harry's arms, overcome with joy and relief.

That night, after Mr. Holmes had put Mr. Moodie in a cab to the hotel where he was staying, Harry put his clergyman's disguise back on and left also. "I'm not sure I entirely trust Inspector Gregson," he said as we stood together in the hallway. "If he goes sideways, I may have to skip again. But oh, Jeannie me love, let us hope for the best." And he kissed me once and disappeared into the dark, foggy street.

You can imagine what it felt like to wait the next morning, after Mr. Holmes and Dr. Watson left to fetch Peter Moodie and keep their appointment with Inspector Gregson. To see Harry that one time and then perhaps never again was almost crueler than not to have seen him at all. I hurried back from my shopping and got hardly any work done, what with running to the front window at every sound of wheels or hooves on the street. It seemed an eternity before Holmes and Watson returned—and Harry was with them. I thought I would faint. Holmes asked us both up to his rooms, and once we were there, he explained, with an air of triumph, what had happened. "Our conversation went even better than I expected. I knew Gregson had corresponded with the police in Edinburgh regarding the case and was aware of Peter Moodie's story and his identification of Stritch and Colfax. He had already begun to doubt the story told him by the informer, and Moodie's statement made it clear to him that he had no case against Mr. Hudson. So he has promised that Mr. Hudson will not be arrested for Parr's murder, assuming no further evidence appears implicating him in the Yukon and Mackenzie Mining Company scheme. As for Colfax and Stritch, they seem to have vanished from the face of the earth."

Harry looked thoughtful. "Well, I can swear that I had no more involvement in the Yukon and Mackenzie scheme than I have told you, so unless another peach comes along with a better lie, I'll cause you no more trouble, at least about that. I hope that Stritch is all right. I've heard of Colfax. He's a cold-blooded, dangerous character, and I don't know why Stritch would have had anything to do with him. But Stritch was rather gullible—an odd thing to say of a confidence man, but true in his case. If I had to hazard a guess, Colfax is back in Canada, and I wouldn't be surprised if poor Stritch was at the bottom of the ocean somewhere—Colfax isn't kind to his partners in crime."

E.F. What a grim story!

Mrs. H.   Yes, indeed. But it brought my Harry back to me. And it turned out that Stritch was alive after all. He was nabbed in Canada, and confirmed that Harry had nothing to do with the mining scheme or the baronet's murder. Colfax was never found, as far as I know.

That day I cooked Harry's favorite dinner, roast leg of mutton, potatoes, and turnips. I asked Peter Moodie to join us, but he had been invited to stop with an old shipmate and his family. But Mr. Holmes and Dr. Watson dined with us, to celebrate Harry's safe return.

Harry said he was as pleased as could be to be tucking into a good dinner. "The grub in Italy is well and good, if you like that sort of thing," he said, "but oh, how I missed good English meat and potatoes."

He told how Mr. Holmes had met him in Paris and gained his trust— "It was clear to me that he had done more than simply accept Gregson's story. I was amazed at how much he knew about that affair in Edinburgh— a good deal more than I did, certainly." At Holmes's request Harry had had a photograph taken of himself and given it to Mr. Holmes, along with an address where Mr. Holmes could send a telegram to him. They agreed on a phrase by which Mr. Holmes would identify himself as the author. A few weeks later a telegram came from Mr. Holmes instructing Harry to come back to London. Harry did so, and you've heard the rest.

Mr. Holmes told how he and Watson had traveled first to Edinburgh, to speak with the police inspector in charge of investigating the Parr homicide and the Yukon and Mackenzie fraud. He confirmed that no one he had questioned had described anyone resembling Harry among the schemers. Mr. Holmes already knew something about Mr. Moodie from his earlier correspondence, and his importance to the case became even clearer on talking with the inspector. So Mr. Holmes and Dr. Watson took a steamer to Lerwick and spoke with Mr. Moodie in person. That interview further confirmed that Harry was not among the men involved in the scheme. Mr. Moodie kindly agreed to come with them to London, and Mr. Holmes sent his telegram to Harry before they left Lerwick.

Dr. Watson ate better than he had in days, and went on about how good the mutton was and how ill he had been on their voyage. "It was a miserable passage," he said. "I have never been so sick at sea. And when we got to the Shetland Islands, they were as barren and storm-swept an outpost as I have ever seen. Little stone huts on the moor, peat fires, cold and wind. Even the mutton tasted of fish. I was told the sheep eat seaweed, for lack of good grass to feed on, and their diet flavors their meat. I couldn't eat it. But Holmes, here, hardly seemed to notice it."

Harry offered to pay Mr. Holmes for all he had done. "It may take some time, because I have to get back on my feet," he said, "but you'll get every shilling." But Mr. Holmes wouldn't take a penny. He said he'd be amply repaid if Harry would teach him some of the techniques of confidence men and give him introductions from time to time to people who might be useful to him. Harry was more than willing to help. In fact, he and Mr. Holmes became fast friends."

E.F. Really! How was that?

Mrs. H. Mr. Holmes, of course, was a student of crime, and he found Harry and his trade intriguing. And Harry was a very intelligent man, though self-taught. They would talk together for hours, each smoking his pipe—especially after Harry left the trade and bought a wine shop with his friend Maurice—Mr. Delagnes. Harry taught Mr. Holmes a great deal about certain kinds of crimes and introduced Mr. Holmes to many people in the London underworld who were of great help to him. Mr. Holmes even called upon him now and then to help him with some of his cases. In fact, Harry and I both taught Mr. Holmes how to use stage makeup. I helped him with some of the disguises Dr. Watson wrote about. Do you remember the case Dr. Watson wrote up as "A Scandal in Bohemia"? Where Mr. Holmes first met Irene Adler?

E.F. Oh, of course.

Mrs. H. I always thought Mr. Holmes had something of a soft spot in his heart for that Miss Adler. Well, I made him up as a Nonconformist clergyman for that one, and Harry showed him how to walk. And we did an out-of-work groom, if I remember aright. Eventually he became quite good at makeup himself.

E.F. What happened to Mr. Hudson? Is he—

Mrs. H. Alive and well, my dear. At the moment, he's on an ocean liner to America. I know that sounds surprising, but Harry, dear man, just can't give up the game. He takes a sea voyage every now and then and makes the cost of it back playing cards. Just to keep his hand in, he says. Sometimes I go with him, but I don't enjoy it as much as he does. There just isn't enough to do on a ship. So this spring I decided to stay home and enjoy my garden. But my dear, it's getting late, and you have to walk to the village. Did you take the train from Edinburgh?

E.F. Yes.

Mrs. H. Then I won't keep you. If you start now, you'll be in plenty of time to catch the afternoon train. If you see Mr. Duncan, the ticket master, would you please tell him that the man who sold Otto to Mr. Holmes has another litter of pups for sale? Otto has started a bit of a craze for Baskerville dogs here—not to mention fathering some impressive puppies around the village. Several people in the neighborhood have Baskies now, and it looks as though we're likely to become another outpost for the breed. Good-bye, dear, and thank you for coming by and listening to an old lady chatter. Be careful as you pass the Murrays' farm. They have a Basky, and sometimes they let him run free on their land. Oh, I think I can hear him now.

It was true. Otto looked up and whimpered at the sound before rising to stand at Mrs. Hudson's side as she saw me out the door and waved a last good-bye. And as I passed through the gate again and turned onto the lane, I heard it again in the distance, the long, ascending howl described by Dr. Watson. Even in the clear light of a May afternoon, it seemed chilling and sinister, like the moor which showed darkly at the top of the hills behind me. As I walked back to the village, looking back from time to time to make sure I wasn't being followed by the source of that doleful cry, I thought of the surprises my interview of Mrs. Hudson had revealed, and how, in more ways than one, she had brought the dark tales of Dr. Watson and Sherlock Holmes to life in the serene fields and glens of the Scottish countryside.

IRENE ADLER

To Sherlock Holmes she is always *the* woman. I have seldom heard him mention her under any other name. In his eyes she eclipses and predominates the whole of her sex . . . there was but one woman to him, and that woman was the late Irene Adler, of dubious and questionable memory.

—"A Scandal in Bohemia"

by CARA BLACK

Cabaret aux Assassins

NICE, 1914

Neige Adler's beetle-black eyes narrowed as she paused in the shadows cast by the fringed areca palm. The woman reclined on a wicker chaise, her face sunken, her hands folded in prayer but Neige knew she'd come too late.

"I'm sorry. Very sorry," the nurse said, taking Neige's arm, guiding her across the clinic sunporch. "Your mother passed away a half hour ago. Very peacefully."

No matter their differences, she'd loved her mother. And Neige knew her mother reciprocated in her own peculiar fashion. Tears welled in the corner of her eye.

"Merci, sister."

She set down her travel portmanteau and crossed herself. Her mother looked tranquil. At last.

Eighteen-year-old Neige, wearing rimless spectacles and her chestnut hair upswept, sat down. Her shoulders slumped. In the distance, the peach-washed and tobacco-tiled buildings of Nice sloped to the turquoise Mediterranean. Hot air hovered in the cloudless Provençal sky. Outside the hospital window, small lemon-colored finches twittered on the balcony railing. Slants of light, and the scent of orange trees wafted from the garden below.

Growing up, Neige had spent little time with her mother, an actress, who once sang at La Scala but developed nodes on her vocal cords. Her mother took up acting and toured constantly. The Urals, Baden-Baden, Leipzig, but never Piccadilly or Broadway, where her schoolmates' parents attended the theater. At least that's what she'd told Neige. Neige, raised in a convent boarding school, had spent holidays with Léonie, her mother's housekeeper, or school friends.

Yet her mother's last telegram promised to answer questions about her family. The ones she'd so often asked. Finally. But now she'd never know.

Sad and disappointed, Neige pinned a stray hair into her chignon and fanned the stifling humidity. Below the window, the awninged trolley bus trundled over the cobbled street fronting the clinic.

"Sister," she said, "perhaps we should discuss funeral arrangements."

"Your mother left this for you." The sister handed her a tapestry-covered bag. "She gave this to me last week in case. . . ."

Inside lay a leather tooled journal, a sagging album of photographs and frayed theater programs. As Neige opened the journal, folded paper written in dark blue ink with her mother's concise clipped script fell out. She picked it up, smoothed the thick sheets, and began to read. Her eyes widened in surprise:

My dearest daughter, if you are reading this, I am unable to tell you this in person. So I must do so in a journal. Not my first choice, but coward that I've been, perhaps it's for the better. My darling, I know you disapprove of my lifestyle and I'm sure you'll disapprove even more as you read but then life isn't what we deserve. And thank God for that. I will get to your father but I must explain in my own way, convoluted as it appears.

Before you were born dearest, I worked as an agent for the ministry in Paris. For quite a few years later as well. And now, after all this time, the government wants to present me with a medal for my part in L'Affaire Dreyfus. A man truly the victim of infamy. So, dear Neige, please accept the small honor from the Conseil d'État on my behalf. Who knows . . . they may give you a position.

But why, you ask, a medal for an itinerant actress?

Suffice it to say, you weren't even a gleam in your father's eye when all this began. I'd fallen on my luck after the nodes developed on my vocal cords, ending my opera career. But, as my wont, I landed on my buttonhook boots in the frigid, wet Parisian winter of '96. I was a widow in dire financial straits and certain ministry officials knew I'd once outwitted Sherlock Holmes. I was *the woman,* as Holmes referred to me, after our encounter in the scandal in Bohemia.

Dr. Watson's later accounts never mentioned my involvement in the

Dreyfus Affair with Holmes. But Watson didn't like me—such a jealous and crafty man in a simian way! And he left out much of my story. If the truth be known, he made himself look good most times. I never cared to find out much of Watson's odd relationship with Holmes. But only a fool would trust their luck twice to outwit Holmes.

Thoughts of *the man,* as I often thought of Holmes, had crossed my mind . . . the only man, besides my dear, departed husband, Norton, whose mental acuity matched mine.

But I digress.

The Dreyfus case was a cause célèbre for years. Captain Alfred Dreyfus, as you probably know, was the only Jewish officer on the French General Staff in 1894, and he was accused of offering French military secrets to the Germans. He was court-martialed behind closed doors, convicted by a unanimous verdict, and sentenced to life imprisonment on Devil's Island in French Guiana.

But I've jumped ahead in my saga. In that grueling winter in Paris, after auditioning at the Théâtre Anglais, I'd landed the role of Mrs. Daventry in Oscar Wilde's play . . . then the talk of London. But it barely helped ends meet.

Holmes was in the audience. Thank God I didn't realize it until after the curtain call.

After the performance, a distinguished gray-haired man in a black opera cape appeared at my dressing room door bearing a huge bouquet of rare Canaan lilies.

"Madame Norton, please accept a modest bouquet and my compliments, past and present," he said. "Your performance ranks with the lilies in the field; pure and unsullied." The unmistakable deep voice alerted me. However, the man stood very tall, taller than I remembered Holmes. And more rounder figured. His face, wider—that of a different man.

"Why come in, Monsieur. . . . ," I said, puzzled.

"Duc de Langans," he interrupted. Swiftly he moved inside the door, belying his bulk, with a finger raised to his lips. His black eyes glittered and my heart hammered.

Sherlock Holmes!

"Pray enlighten me . . . Duc." I grinned. "My role merits not such lilies, so rare in winter. I find little comparison with myself and hothouse flowers. A hardy desert scrub, tenacious and wild, battling the wind and blossoming with the rain seems more apt."

"So would a wise man agree." Holmes smiled back. His eyes lingered. "Yet when could those of my sex be accused of wisdom?"

I glowed; I could not help myself. Such a man with wit and charm stimulated me, all outward appearance forgotten. Such a long time had passed since I'd felt this intensity of attraction. What possessed me I know not, yet when the stagehand poked his head in announcing "Encore curtain call, Madame Norton, quickly please!" I pulled Holmes or Duc de Langans close, in full backstage view, and kissed him. Hard and quickly. And more to my surprise he responded. "You're not an easy woman to forget, Irene," he said, breathing in my ear. "And you're making it more difficult." An odd look passed in his eye, whether of regret, longing, or a mingling of both I couldn't decipher.

The backstage boy tugged my sleeve, pulling me out to the wall of applause. I felt a thrill such as I had not felt since my opera triumphs at La Scala. I cared not why Holmes wore such disguise or whether his machinations involved me, which they clearly would portend to, but only for the blaze of passion and intrigue which had entered my work-sore and dull life.

Visions of a late brasserie supper with champagne and oysters danced in my mind. But when I returned from the several curtain calls, Holmes had disappeared. Curious and more disappointed than I cared to admit, I picked up the bouquet from the dressing table, littered with pots of powder.

Outside the backstage entrance, no hansom cab lay in sight. Only the yellow glow from the gaslight and wet, slick cobblestones greeted me. Depressed, I pulled the cloak around me for the trudge to my room in hilly Montmartre. Especially long and arduous in the chill drizzle. Why had Holmes appeared in disguise? Using me in a ruse, perhaps, to exit the rear of the theater. Rumors had abounded of his narcotics use but I knew he abstained when on a case. I clutched the flowers, heavy and ostentatious, ready to throw them in the trash heap. . . . I didn't relish struggling with them on my upward trek through the steep streets to Montmartre.

And then I felt the thin glass tube, capsule-like, among the lily stems. Under the rue du Louvre gaslight, I bent to relace the top of my boots. I shook out the white paper rolled inside. On it was written in small, black spidery writing;

Wait for me in place Goudeau, *s'il te plaît.*

How unlike Holmes to say please.

I knew this square, where the tree-filled place fronted the old washing house now an atelier by artists. And it lay a block from my apartment. Stuffing the paper in my boot, I stood up and hurried towards Montmartre.

Place Goudeau's dark green fountain, topped with spiked domes held by four maidens, trickled in the night. Veins of water iced the cobbles, caught in the flickering gaslight. Anxious, I found a dark doorway, and huddled in my cloak against the cold. The circular place lay deserted under the one skeletal tree, barren of leaves.

From an open skylight in a sloping rooftop drifted muffled sounds of laughter and dancing yellow light. A tall figure stole along the building. The he stood before me, silhouetted against the fretwork of black branches canopying the starless sky.

"Why the secrecy and disguise, Holmes?" I asked, catching my breath and trying to keep my excitement in check.

"Bear with my pretense, Irene, for I have only a moment." His eyes bore into me. He took in my wet bedraggled appearance so different from the costumed performer in makeup accepting accolades just shortly before.

"I had not the time to tell you before," he said. "Marie-Charles-Ferdinand Walsin Esterhazy."

"You say this name as if it means something to me, Holmes," I said, perplexed in my tiredness. My breath became staccato bursts of frost.

"Perhaps you know him as Comte Esterhazy, the paramour of Bijou the contortionist?"

"Bijou? We perform in the same revue, Holmes," I said, taken off guard, "but apart from that . . ."

"Comte Esterhazy has gambling debts," he interrupted. "Serious ones."

Gambling debts . . . is that what this was all about? My excitement on seeing Holmes crumbled.

"Keep an eye on him, Irene; find out his work habits at the Military ministry. Get invited to the gambling den on boulevard de Clichy. The den above the printmaking shop. Irene, do this. You outsmarted me once but help me now."

"But, Holmes, why . . ."

"Only you can be my eyes and ears there. No questions. Please. Do this for me. I won't ask another favor."

He palmed a wad of sous in my coat pocket. For a brief moment he found my frigid hand, clutched it with his own warm one and kissed it.

"I'll find you again," he said. And with a swirl of his cape he was gone.

His aura of intrigue and immediacy were hard to dispel. And truth to tell, Holmes's magnetism clutched me, perturbed as I felt. It always had.

This involved more than gambling, I was sure as I paused at the café below my building and purchased a few lumps of coal. The night and the long walk had chilled me to the bone. In my small garret, I stuck the Canaan lilies in a chipped decanter on the table, lit a small fire, and banked the coals. From my window the metal railing of the stairs mounting my hilly street crusted with ice. My Montmartre garret, with the slate-gray Paris rooftop view, nestled against the bricked fire flute and kept toasty. A bonus since charcoal prices soared in the frigid 1896 winter. And even in my fatigue, I felt the garret emanate a welcoming warmth. After putting my apprehensions aside until the next day, I slept.

I awoke to dead coals and tinny music coming from the street.

The barrel organ grinder, with his grinning half-wit son turning the crank, stood below on the cobbles. Many nights they slept in the nearby viaduct. I tossed them a few sous and shivered washing my face in icy water from a pitcher.

The only employment I knew was the stage. Drinking my weak morning coffee, I fingered my parents' obituary. They'd perished in a Trenton blizzard some years before. My only tie to America was gone. Back on the boards again, my old washhouse Ma would have said, your grandmother, had she lived. But it was a long way from the New Jersey shore to the Right bank of Paris. Sometimes, it felt too far. Other days, not far enough.

But that was a lifetime ago. No one's left in America for you, Neige. France, my adopted country, is your country.

I lodged in Montmartre, the bohemian center of painters, socialists, and writers. Not only did art and anarchy appeal to me. The cobbled and packed earth streets made it cheap. Dirt cheap. At that time, Montmartre was still a village ridging Paris.

But that morning I discovered an envelope under my door which I'd overlooked. Inside was written, "Finally a job for you . . . expect me in the morning. Meslay."

Startled, I rubbed a cloth over the table, put my few belongings to rights and pinched my cheeks for color. Why was this happening now . . . did it somehow connect to Holmes? These thoughts crossed my mind but I found no answers.

What Holmes didn't know, and how would he, was my connection to the French Ministry. Tenuous at best.

My first husband Norton's tragic death under the wheels of runaway carriage in Trieste had reversed my fortune. Norton's brother-in-law, Meslay, an French Army officer, had recruited him for occasional missions. Only after Norton's death did I learn, rest his soul, he'd assumed the part of unofficial liaison in Paris for an emissary to King George. But, widows without means were not included on the King's payroll.

I still had my looks; the waters in Baden-Baden were to thank for that. But I was approaching what the French politely refer to as a woman *d'un certain âge*. A bleak outlook of genteel penury in coastal St-Mâlo teaching drama to vacationing English children or amateur theatricals loomed.

Faced with such mundane prospects and reasoning it would be my last chance at theater before such a quiet retirement would alas, be enforced upon me, I'd renewed my connections in the demimonde.

This twilight world of courtesans, artists, dance halls, and café-cabarets offered sporadic employment. Yet it gave me time to audition for the "proper" theater. If only the role of Mrs. Daventry could have supported me I would have given the rest up.

But it was my brother-in-law, Meslay, the young military attaché who'd approached me some months before. We'd met once in the Tuilleries gardens and he'd mentioned he might be able to help me. But no word since then.

A loud knock sounded on the warped wooden door.

I opened it to see Meslay, my brother-in-law. His tall bearing in my cramped quarters; a blue cape masking his regimental uniform but not his glistening black boots seemed out of place. "Petit, eh, just a little work, but steady," he said, joining me in Montmartre that February day.

"I appreciate your help, Meslay. Our connection hasn't been close, since Norton's death." Meslay, in fact, owed me little, so I was grateful for any consideration.

"My patron needs an American expatriate's services in Paris," he said, smoothing his tapered mustache.

Meslay, who usually sparred with conversational counterpoints and endless discussion in the Gallic tradition, seemed unusually direct.

"Not to mention such an accomplished and beautiful one as you, Irene."

After his brief brush of charm, I hoped he'd continue his direct approach and get down to business.

"Only you can do this."

Surprised, I looked up from the stiff black taffeta bodice I was attempting to tame with a high-handled metal iron. The smoky looking glass showed my striped morning dress with bustle, the only decent one I kept, and my rag-rolled long hair looped around my head.

I felt hopeful. At least I could earn something besides the little I pocketed at the theater and from the café-cabarets. The heat dissipated from the dying embers in the iron, frustrating me. Once someone had ironed for me, all morning long; now how I appreciated such effort!

"And the work?" I asked.

"We'll make it worth your while," Meslay said.

As I hung the semi-wrinkled taffeta costume over the three-quarter dressing screen and gave him my attention, I wondered why he'd not answered my question.

Curious but feeling the need to play hostess even in a limited fashion, I set two thick-bottomed glasses on the rough wood table and poured from a carafe of vin rouge. Meslay accepted and raised his glass.

"*Salut!*" I said.

He raised his glass, clinked mine and downed the rotgut I got cheap from the bistro below. "Certain underpinnings in the Third Republic warrant scrutiny," said Meslay, his gaze on my wall with theater posters. "Ongoing surveillance, if you know what I mean."

Sounded oblique to me.

"Dear Meslay, my espionage roles have only been played on the stage." I grinned. "Norton performed those in real life, which only recently came to my knowledge, but I'm an excellent translator. . . ."

"Your acquaintances in the demimondaine are what I refer to," he interrupted. "You float among gypsy girls, pert ingenues in knickers, reclining odalisques and diaphanous veiled models riding circus horses."

Meslay made it sound exotic and lush, but little did he know that to survive the underside of this rock-hard unglamorous life, a woman needed a tenacious will, supple intelligence, and to appear submissive and alluring at the same time. Women jumped on tightropes. That way one avoided the streets. Perhaps, one could even triumph.

"*Oui,* Meslay, I'm acquainted with the milieu," I said. "*Mais* not with much else."

"But you have an entrée behind the scenes where few can go," he said. "Backstage, in the casinos and bordellos, in dens among languid addicts smoking opium, a discreet visit, of course, in a way that a man would be suspected."

His eyebrows tented in supplication.

Holmes had said much the same thing. What did Meslay want me to do?

The five-hundred-sou note in his gloved hand tempted me. My costumes were pawned, our last hotel bill from rue de la Paix still unpaid and my maid, Léonie Guérard, had gone to the workhouse when I'd been unable to afford her. My conscience nagged seeing her child begging on the street.

Now I could at last pay Léonie's overdue wages and get her child off the curbside begging.

"What specifically do you mean, Meslay?" I asked.

He set down the half-drunk glass and smoothed his mustache. "Irene, we propose for you to weave a web—you might say" —he smiled— "of informants in music halls, theaters, and the bordellos in Montmartre. Make acquaintances with concierges, cleaning women, café habitués, and restaurant maître d's."

I waited for the guillotine to drop—when he would tell me the goal of what he sought. But his rapt gaze followed the crinkled silver mist creeping over the butte hill on the right. Below us, the wood cart selling charcoal thumped over the cobbles as the seller cried "*charbon.*" He'd paused and I prodded him further.

"Meslay, to do that I must know why or I can't find the right . . ." Here I hesitated almost saying *mouchard*, but stool pigeon wasn't a nice connotation in French or any language.

He shrugged. "*D'accord.* We're interested in the habits of certain French officers. The artillery officers, their vices and peccadilloes."

My mind went again to Holmes's mysterious appearance and his begging me for information of a Comte in the military. Could this be connected . . . but how?

"With an eye to blackmail, Meslay?"

"Possibly, but more along the lines of bribery," said Meslay. "We want to know who's connected to Captain Dreyfus."

At that time, Dreyfus, a little known military officer, had been court-martialed and exiled to Devil's Island. His name was not yet a household name. This was before the infamous article by Zola, *J'accuse.*

"This seems difficult," I said. Theater crew were close-knit, a camaraderie existed in the demimonde, and irreverent humor characterized the intellectuals.

"A judicious scattering of these will help," he said, pulling a wad of tensou notes from his pocket.

He had a point and I certainly hoped so.

"Let's say your communication with me will be indicated when," he said, picking up the wine bottle, "the bottle sits on your window ledge. We shall meet here."

"Your visits could draw attention," I said, thinking of my inquisitive concierge to whom I owed a week's back rent. "Come to the bouillon de Pères, the Pigalle soup canteen run by the good fathers to save wayward souls. At least it gives a respite and something warm for the stomach." I winked. "The canteen sits between the restaurant de la Bohème and Club Boum-Boum in Place Pigalle. Père Angelo can be trusted with messages in case one of us might not make it."

"Aah, a dead-letter drop," said Meslay.

Fine, let Meslay define our arrangement as a sophisticated cloak-and-dagger routine. That bothered me little.

We arranged our next meeting then he ducked his head under the slanting timbered roof and left. I watched his long-strided gait as he turned into wet slick rue Lepic. He didn't turn back, though I'm sure he knew my eyes followed him from the window.

Finding information about this Captain Dreyfus or the Comte shouldn't prove too difficult, or so I hoped. Once I'd gathered up courage, the actual rounds in Montmartre and Pigalle proved curious. Fearing hoots of derisive laughter, I'd been taken aback at the Gallic shrug and open palm my mission received. To legitimize my quest, I implied the honor of the Prince of Wales, the future Edward VII, a known habitué of night life and certain "houses," was at stake.

So far, I'd bribed a crooked-nosed bouncer at the Cabaret aux Assassins to inform me of officers' visits, greased the palm of painters' models in Montmartre ateliers over a bottle of absinthe, enlisting the aid of Rose la Rouge, a streetwalker and occasional cabaret singer, and arranged with a pianist who entertained in an infamous Sentier brothel to keep his eyes out for officers' preferences.

I also enlisted my former maid Léonie's services. Since Esterhazy, a commissioned officer in the French army, worked at the Military ministry, Léonie, frequenting the office on the pretense of seeking work, would keep another eye on him.

To Léonie's and my good fortune, she was offered a job cleaning offices and assisting the concierge, who had a bad leg and approached retirement.

But how to get invited to the gambling den Holmes mentioned? I thought much on the way to rehearsal. I passed the round metal TABAC sign above the dark wood shop at the foot of rue Tholozé deep in thought. I pondered Holmes's words again and wondered if he and Meslay worked for the same side. Or not.

But I wondered how to gain Bijou's confidence. The brick-red *moulin* visible at the top loomed in the distance, the sails of which had long ceased to turn. I climbed the wide stairs with crownlike dark green gaslights dividing the staircase. Every so many steps grilled landings to the tall apartments and shops branched off from its spine.

By the time I reached Le Chat Noir, I felt no wiser. I forged my way backstage past clowns, ventriloquists and belly dancers towards Bijou, the revue's contortionist, limbering up. Bijou lifted her ruffled pantalooned leg straight up and notched the ankle behind her neck. After another vigorous stretch she collapsed into a full-split to my immense admiration. *"Fantastique,"* I said. "Bijou, you must be triple-jointed."

She grinned.

A bottle of expensive scent sat on the dressing table.

"Or in love," I said.

"Ask my new paramour," she said, her supple arms in an arc. "He's a grand *mec*, an aristocrat, not that you'd know it in the bedroom," said Bijou, her gap-toothed smile infectious. Bijou's boudoir philosophy seemed refreshing, if not accommodating. She loosened her dark brown topknot of curls, shook her head, then retied them. She stretched her long legs, then arched her back like a cat. "Enjoys the good life, does he?" I asked, hoping she'd rise to the bait.

"He likes the tables," she said.

"A poker or chemin de fer aficionado?"

She shrugged. "Both of course."

"I'm partial to baccarat." I let out a loud sigh. "Believe it or not, but I helped many a 'friend' at the Grand Casino. We broke the bank at Monte once. Of course, a Moldavian prince kept buying me chips. Blue ones. And I kept winning more. Piles and piles of them. At the end of the night I treated all the waiters to champagne."

"But you're down on your luck now, eh, *americaine*?" Bijou had street savvy.

"Let the chips tell the story, but when I feel lucky nothing gets in the way. Bijou, there's no other way to say it but, I attract good luck."

Chill cold emanated from the damp stone walls little dispelled by the small charcoal stove. The smell of greasepaint and fug of bodies weren't hidden by the cheap rosewater the cancan girls liberally applied.

"Why don't you introduce me, Bijou?" I said applying powder in front of the mercury glass mirror running the length of the small dressing room. "I have a gift."

"Only one?" Bijou grinned, her ruffled pantaloons frayed in places. "Eh, *americaine* . . . he might go for that. He's got friends who'd like you."

Le Chat Noir revue's curtains opened with a whistler, in a black-and-white Pierrot costume with white face and tears, whose tune rivaled the birds. Strains from an accordion wheezed in the background while Bijou and Frederique, the contortionists, performed. Then followed my skit; a parody of the English. Anglo-French relations had been rocky since the Battle of Waterloo. I pantomimed Napoleon's famous phrase that the British were a nation of shopkeepers. For the stuffy bureaucrat, I'd pick on the nearest portly gentleman in the crowd, sit on his lap and literally got him to eat peanuts out of my hand. The audiences loved it every time.

To my disappointment, there seemed no trace of Bijou's count in the audience. Nor the next day. No sign of Bijou either. Time for me to check in with my informants, loosen their tongues with more sous.

"*Ça va*, Anton?" I asked the doorman at the Cabaret aux Assassins, as I trudged through Pigalle the next evening. I joined him under the fan-shaped glass and iron awning.

"Fine, but the world looks heavy on your shoulders," said Anton.

"Nothing some interesting news won't lighten," I said, under my breath. Several bearded men emerged from the cabaret door, stamped their boots on the wet cobblestones. Anton motioned me to wait.

Good, I needed a lead or promise of one.

Surprised at the men's refusal of Anton's offer to hail them a hansom, I watched them trundle down the steep winding street.

"So those Assassins prefer to walk?" I eyed the rain dancing over the cobbles.

He grinned and his crooked nose shone in the lamplight. "Just Czechs from Prague with full bellies wanting to work off their repast," he said. "But they were inquisitive, waited for a friend. A Hungarian officer. A count."

"The Hungarian count didn't show up?" I asked, my ears perking up. The rain beat down and I hugged myself against the chill.

"This Hungarian's a commissioned French officer. No love lost there, I'd say, from their conversation."

Intrigued, I narrowed my eyes. "You speak Czechoslovakian?"

"My mother was Czech," he said. "But I don't share that with many."

"Did they mention a Comte Esterhazy?" I said. I knew Esterhazy was a Polish name.

"Esterhazy?" He tugged his beard. "Ferdinand Walsin was who they mentioned. He came, but I didn't see him leave."

Where had I heard that? I thought hard.

Of course, from Holmes! Marie-Charles-Ferdinand Walsin Esterhazy . . . Comte Esterhazy. "You didn't see him leave?"

"Don't have eyes in the back of my head when I take my dinner, do I?"

I grinned. "But I thought all doormen had another set."

At least now I knew that Esterhazy visited and others looked for him as well.

"Anton, what goes on here besides the cabaret and the food?"

"And the high-stakes chemin de fer game?" he said, in a low voice.

I nodded. "Higher stakes than the game above the printing shop in place Clichy?"

"Many an inheritance has traded hands here as dawn rose over Montmartre."

This sounded like the type of game Esterhazy would be drawn to . . . as the clichéd moth to a flame.

I pressed franc notes in his hand. "If this Walsin shows up, later or anytime. Send a runner, find me, or leave a note with my concierge."

But tramping home from Pigalle that sleeting, frigid evening I noticed a stocky side-whiskered man following me. Had been since the Bateau Lavoir, the old washhouse taken over by artists, which fronted the cobbled square. Apprehension filled me.

Past the small park, and up the steep winding cobbled streets I was followed.

I ducked into the local *alimentaire*. The man who followed me waited outside. He eyed the window but I could see his large form, through the letters painted on the shop window, heaving to and fro.

After selecting a hub of cheese, I paid the amount owing on my credit and scribbled a quick note to the proprietaire. The aproned proprietaire bagged my purchase, rubbed his hands on his stained apron, then gave a quick nod indicating the rear of the shop. And a wink.

I scooted to the shop's rear, past the tubs of brined fish, the freshly slaughtered rabbit haunches on ice, leaning flour sacks. Behind rue Lepic, the narrow cobbled street lay ice-sheathed and icicles hung from handcarts.

Relieved to see the narrow street deserted and to have lost the man, I battled the sleet to my oval courtyard in the adjoining street. After paying off my many debts, not enough had remained to find alternative lodging. So I remained, appreciative of my luck in having a warm garret.

Madame Lusard, the concierge, a wire-haired battle-ax of a woman, thrust a batch of letters in my cold hands. She pulled her shawl tight around her, opened the door of her loge, and returned to a purring cat in front of her glowing grate. My excitement crested as I mounted the grooved worn stairs of the building, feeling the embossed vellum envelopes. Surely, evidence of a wealthy sender.

Inside, I struggled out of my wet cloak, leaving puddles on the rough wood floor. After sticking scraps of newspaper in the window cracks to block the drafts, I pulled on my one dry pair of leggings and lit the gaslight. The small room warmed up quickly thanks to Madame Lusard's fire below. I hung the cloak on a peg to dry. Often, I slept by the brick radiating heat and dried my clothing in several hours. Unlike others who shivered and caught pneumonia every winter, I counted myself lucky.

I opened the thick envelope to find an upcoming audition announcement at Théâtre Anglais.

Not forgotten . . . wonderful! A secondary role in a George Bernard Shaw drawing-room farce. I knew most of the first act, could learn the rest in a day. Joy filled me. A real part and someone had thought to send it my way!

I sat down, my back against the warm brick with a glass of *vin,* the audition announcement, and full of wonder. It was then I noticed the bottle on the window ledge. Turned and indicating a meeting with Meslay. Something I was supposed to do, but he had obviously entered my garret, beat me to it.

My stomach knotted in unease. The little information I'd gleaned made me an unworthy informant. And the idea of trudging out again in the bitter cold of a dark winter's night filled me with less than anticipation.

I drained my glass. Found my nearly dry clothing and the small stone I kept warmed by the brick. For night journeys I slipped the hot stone in my muff and the warmth kept my fingers nimble.

Meslay may have arranged this meeting, but I would find out the purpose of my inquiries. Or wash my hands of it, I decided. So determined was I to make sense of this covertness that joy at my upcoming audition had withered.

I noticed Meslay, not sporting his dashing uniform but in a drab overcoat, spooning soup at a long table in the bouillon de Pères. Steamed opaque windows gave a faint glow and fairylike appearance to the seedy place Pigalle outside. Père Angelo greeted me, offering a warm handshake and a bowl. I stood in line, with the clochards, tired ladies of the night, and the assorted hungry of Montmartre. Fragrant and hot, the onion soup with thick, runny melted cheese always coated my insides.

This time I dropped some bills in the donation can, happy to be able to thank the fathers for their help.

"Why did you go in my room?" I asked, sitting down across from Meslay.

"And a good evening to you, too, Irene," he said, sipping the table wine laced with water.

"No more cat-and-mouse, I need to understand the purpose," I said. "Or count me out."

He grinned. "What about my information?"

"Good point, I don't know what I'm looking for."

"Exactement!" he said. "But be a good girl and tell me what your contacts say. Then I can prove how essential yours skills rate to my superior."

I knew Meslay wouldn't be a good contact to alienate. And after all, he paid me. I recounted a list of the informants. "See, that's all."

"But what have you heard . . . anything unusual?" He leaned forward. "No matter how small."

Time to throw in Comte Esterhazy's nonappearance. I recounted the doorman's words about the men looking for him.

His face changed. I saw his knuckles whiten on the spoon handle.

"What aren't you telling me, Irene?"

Everything around us seemed to stop. Fear rose in my throat. He knew I held back things. I remembered the man tailing me. Had Meslay had me watched . . . followed?

"It's Bijou," I said, "she's in the revue at Le Chat Noir, too. This Count Esterhazy is her paramour."

An odd smile crossed his face. He glanced at our table companions: an old woman who'd nodded out and a clochard attacking his onion soup with vigor.

"Make contact with Esterhazy," he said, his voice lowered but distinct.

"How would I do that?" I asked.

"But I've hired you, haven't I?" he said. "You figure it out."

"I'm sorry, Meslay, I know you've got a job to do and the money helps, but unless things get clearer consider my services at an end."

"Irene, the less you know . . ."

"The less I can find out for you," I finished for him. "My word and discretion is to be trusted. I think Norton would have told you that."

And from Meslay's look I think Norton had.

"We know Esterhazy was a traitor."

"Who's *we* and what did he betray?"

"He sold military secrets to Germany. Not Captain Dreyfus. What we don't know is if he copied the Balkan plan and passed it to Germany and Kaiser Wilhelm."

"The Balkan plan?"

"It's vital," he said. "If the Germans have the Balkan plan, they'll have the key to our defense strategy. Everything. But we can still change the plan and implement new strategies . . . barely. But we must know."

But how did I fit in this? And what about Holmes?

"How can I find out?"

"He's a gambler. In debt."

I knew that much from Holmes but listened.

"We know somewhere he keeps a tally of his losses, his winnings, and the secrets he holds. He's joked to his colleagues he has a 'bank of secrets.'"

"What about Captain Dreyfus," I asked. "Will the military exonerate him then?"

Meslay's dark eyes burned.

"I can only speak for my section, but Esterhazy will suffer a court-martial," he said. "But I need your help to furnish the proof whether the plan is compromised."

Loath to say his name, I knew no other way but to ask bluntly. "What of the rumor of Sherlock Holmes?" I kept my face blank with effort. "At the Théâtre Anglais I overheard a conversation. That's all. Supposedly he's in Paris."

"You've heard that, too, then, about Holmes?" he asked as if this were old news. Meslay shrugged, tore off a hunk of baguette. "He's sniffing around for the Crown. Unofficially, of course. The British want Holmes to lessen the impact of any files compromised by Esterhazy."

So Holmes worked for England and I for France.

"Does that mean he's adversarial to your ministry?"

"Tiens." Meslay crumbled the white part of his baguette, rolled the piece into small white beads. "It means England's for England and France for itself in how to keep the Kaiser at bay . . . like time immemorial. Napoleon read their intentions correctly—selfish!"

And wasn't France selfish? But maybe it was self-preservation since their home and hearth bordered Germany.

Meslay and I arranged another meeting. As I left, my heart weighed heavy. Conflicting emotions crossed through me. Here I was at odds with Holmes! Something I'd never wanted to happen again.

Yet Holmes hadn't appeared, and to be frank I had no binding obligation to England. Holmes tried to use my guilt to assist a king and country as they had used my late husband Norton.

The more and more and I thought the more I realized I had a job to do. Fortified by the hearty soup, I headed towards Le Chat Noir to find Bijou. My calling was acting. Time for me to use my skills.

"Not seen nor heard from Bijou," said Vartan, the wire-thin backstage manager, to my query. He looped his wool scarf around his neck. "Far as I'm concerned she doesn't need to come back. She's one who gets a luxury ticket and crawls back begging when it expires. Know what I mean?"

I wasn't sure but nodded.

"She borrowed a costume, some of my things. Know where she lives?"

"Doubt she's there."

"Why not?"

"Moved up in the world, hasn't she?"

Vartan had an ax to grind . . . was it jealousy?

"But at least I could inquire as to where she's gone."

He stared me up and down.

"Alors," I said. "Making a living comes hard enough without buying new costumes."

"Rue Androuët. Her mother's the concierge of the corner building. Can't miss it."

I hiked the narrow Montmartre stairs called a street and by my place there stood Léonie in the shadows.

Her matronly eyes glittered with excitement. She pulled me back into the dark recesses of the stairs. "Don't knows as I'll get me job back but I got these for you, Madame Irene." She pointed to the hem of her long skirt. "A bag of papers."

"A bag?"

"Remember the concierge with the gamey leg . . . the one I told you I help seeing as she's 'indisposed' sometimes? She don't throw away papers from the wastebaskets. . . . I found out she saves them."

"And that's what you have in the bag?"

"Mail and letters, too!" Léonie nodded. "Thinks me daft and a bit slow, she does, but that's fine by me. Like you says, I'm to keep me eyes open and not much from me mouth. So yesterday, her leg was hurting something awful, swollen up it was, too. After I lit the fires, cleaned the big reception rooms, she says, 'Fetch the contents from the baskets.' I did and as I was fixing to slag them into the furnace she screams, '*Non, non* in here!' Then she says pick up the letters from the boxes and takes some and don't distribute . . . she gave me some daft excuse but I just nodded."

"Go on, Léonie, please!"

"Then I thinks back . . . 'course, she has to have been been doing it while I'm there, too. But the kicker being these come from the military offices. Where the Comte Esterhazy worked. I only seen him the once. Yesterday. But he wrote on this here blue paper, this bordereau they calls it."

"Marvelous work, Léonie!"

"This here's a right jumble, but seein' as I had no time to sort it, I puts the blue bordereau on top."

"You're a fairy princess, Léonie!"

She grinned her lopsided way, her eyes sparkled, and I regretted how my life included her so little. I slipped a wad of franc notes in her hands, gave her a hug, and told her to stay home for a few days with her child.

In my garret I stashed the bag, knowing I'd later spread it out and try to make sense of it. The several crumpled blue bordereau I smoothed out, struck by the angular handwriting. But no signature! *Merde!*

One step forward and two steps back.

So now, all I could do was find Bijou and see if her trail led to Comte Esterhazy.

Trudging to rue Androuët, I realized it faced the Cabaret aux Assassins. . . . Was that how Bijou met the Comte?

And it rested a block away from the place Goudeau . . . where Holmes had met me!

I knocked on the concierge loge door. No answer. In the dim building courtyard, a woman bent over at the communal water spigot. She saw me and straightened up, then took halting steps with a bucket held over one arm. In the darkness, she appeared old and racked by slight shakes of palsy.

"*Oui?*" she said, wiping her other reddened hand on her none too clean apron, squinting at me.

"*Bon soir,* Madame, you must be Bijou's mother . . ."

"Older sister," she said, interrupting me.

"Aaah, of course, please forgive me. The light is nonexistent and I was told Bijou's mother is the concierge here."

But Bijou's sister could be her mother, so haggard and worn she looked. Old before her time. Too many children? Too much work at the wash-house which I could see from her painfully chapped and sore hands.

"Neither one's here. My mother's gone to Lille, and Bijou . . . eh who knows?"

I didn't believe her for a moment. About Bijou anyway. Those careworn eyes were street smart. And well they would be. Survival was tough on the butte in Montmartre. Before I could say more, I noticed the portly man who'd followed me the other night, paused in the boulangerie window opposite. He wore a bowler hat, his gold watch chain glinted in the gaslight.

A baby cried from inside the loge and Bijou's sister hurried ahead. I walked with her, then paused at the large heavy door and bid adieu. Without so much as a good-bye she trundled inside the loge.

I saw the bowler-hatted man approaching the door.

Caught between an unfriendly woman and stalking man . . . Where could I go?

The door leading to the downstairs cave lay ajar. I slipped inside, pulled it shut, figuring I'd wait until he left, then come out. But as I reached the end of the steep damp limestone steps a glow of light came from ahead. This was no dead-end cellar but a tunnel branching ahead.

Montmartre was full of limestone quarries, webbed by tunnels and full of quarried holes and pockets like cheese. Yet buildings were built over them. I followed the tunnel to the light. Could this be the adjoining cellar for Cabaret aux Assassins?

On the damp wall crude lettering indicated the street names, gas main locations written in chalk. The smell of damp mold and refuse grew stronger. Mounds of moist earth and stacked wine bottles greeted me as I entered what appeared to be the cellar of the cabaret. Trying to keep my bearings I calculated this would be the right direction.

A low hum of conversation drifted from behind a water-stained wood door, buckled and sagging. The clammy feel in the air bothered me. Grabbing a smock from a pile of dirty blue ones, I took off my coat, slipped the smock over my muslin dress, smoothed my hair back, and tied a napkin over my head, as so did many washerwomen and restaurant kitchen scrubbers, I hoped my cover would tide me over until I discovered Bijou or the Comte.

I knew I didn't have far to go when I heard a load oath.

"Damn you, Esterhazy . . . that's five thousand you owe! Settle your scores. Pay up!"

"Who are you?" A wine-laced voice hissed in my ear.

I jumped.

"The washing-up woman, sir."

"And what are you doing here?" This voice belonged to a very drunken man with stains and dribbles of food on his waistcoat. He held my elbow with a pincerlike grip.

Panicked, I looked around. "Them, sir." I said keeping my head down and pointing to a pile of dirty crockery.

"Get to it, then," he said, pinching my behind hard and chuckling.

He flung open the door. "Now, gentlemen, don't say I'm too late for the game!"

I looked up quickly. Inside, around an oval table, the air thick with cigar smoke, sat three men. Glasses and cards in their hands. Piles of colored chips and a whisky decanter were on the table.

"Always ready for a new partner," said a voice. I looked closer. Bijou, fanning herself and clearly bored, leaned on that man's shoulder. Handsome and flushed, he sported a manicured red goatee and mustache. That must be him!

"Don't get out of this, Esterhazy," one of the other men said to him. "Settle up before . . ."

"Let our friend join us," said Esterhazy, smoothing the edge of his mustache. The drunken man tottered inside.

"Clear this. Make me some room." He jerked his hand to me. "Did you hear me . . . clear up!" he thundered.

My hand shook, but I kept my head down, picked up a tray and moved into the smoky cellar room. I prayed to God Bijou wouldn't recognize me.

"Bring us some more whisky," said the man.

"Good idea," said Esterhazy. "I'll pay this time."

"And how?" queried the suspicious man.

"A promissary note."

"Like all the others?" He shot his hand forward as Esterhazy scribbled something on a napkin.

"Take this," he said pushing it in my hand. "Bring the Irish whisky and clean glasses."

"Yes, sir," I kept my voice low, my eyes down, and tried to breathe.

But servants were invisible except for easy shots of abuse. No one paid me any heed.

I swiftly loaded the tray, swiped the table with a cloth, avoiding the colored chips, and edged out.

"Hurry up! Help's become so lazy these days . . ." was the last I heard as I hurried through the cellar looking for the stairs. I put Esterhazy's napkin in my dress pocket. As I emerged behind the counter in the cabaret, I shoved the loaded tray onto the counter.

The cabaret's tables were filled. Accordion strains and tinkling glasses filled the air. As I walked, several patrons, the worse for wear from drink, asked me to clear their tables. Ignoring them, I reached the heavy velvet curtain, hung to prevent drafts from entering the door.

As I opened the door I came face-to-face with the portly gentleman in the bowler hat whom I thought I'd escaped. He stared at me. I cringed. Someone jostled him forward and I, thankful for the scarf and still wearing the smock, lowered my gaze and kept going. My heart pounded. Once outside, I ran.

Suffice it to say, as soon as I reached a covered doorway, I tore off the disguise, caught my breath, regretting my winter coat left in the cellar. Shivering in my thin muslin dress, I took a circuitous route back through Montmartre.

My concierge, Madame Lusard, handed me my mail. More bills. Inside my garret I kicked off my wet lace-up boots and set them by the warm brick.

Loud knocks sounded on the door.

Had Madame Lussard overlooked a piece of mail?

I opened the door to see the stocky side-whiskered man, his wet greatcoat crooked under his arm. His small pig eyes filled me with fear. How had he found me?

"Madame Norton?"

I nodded slowly.

"Emil Cavour," he said, doffing his rain-speckled hat, panting from exertion. "Pardon my boldness, but I assure you we have something to talk about."

"Who are you, Monsieur?"

He tugged his goatee. "A question, Madame, that the wisest philosophers ponder even to this day. If you permit me entry, we can get out of hearing of your concierge."

Peering downstairs, I saw the glow of her oil lamp on the landing.

I had no recourse but to comply.

Emil Cavour had lamb-chop side-whiskers. He made himself at home on my garret's one chair, wobbly leg and all. He surveyed the costumes hangared on nails poking from the walls, as he lit a short stubby cheroot.

"Why do you follow me, Monsieur Cavour?"

"You favor the bohemian lifestyle, it appears, Madame Norton," he said, not answering me. "Some artistic bent?"

His presumptive manner rankled me.

"Liking and having no choice aren't the same thing," I said. "How does that concern you?"

"Nice view," he said, rising and approaching the window. Pinprick lights dotted the blue-black Paris evening below. "We know Montmartre's a hotbed of anarchists, misfits seething to sabotage the Third Republic."

The startled look on my face did not go unnoticed by him. Did he follow me thinking I plotted to undermine the government? If so, how could I dissuade him without revealing Meslay's assignment? But I'd jumped ahead. . . . Who was he? . . . Where were his credentials?

And then my eye caught on the bag, under the table, Léonie had brought me. What to do?

"My concierge's son's with the police," I said, putting on the expression I once wore at the baccarat table in the Monaco casino. I opened my door. "He's helpful. Very helpful when tenants are insulted. I'll ask you to leave before I feel so inclined."

"Asking me to leave, Madame Norton?" he said, his brow crinkled in amusement.

"My manners betray me." I smiled. "I always ask before I demand."

Cavour remained at the window. "Close the door, Madame. I don't think you want the building hearing about your past."

What had this portly weasel got up his cuffed sleeve? I could bluff, too. My debts were paid. Just paid. But no matter. I earned a living—albeit a sparse one. I wouldn't reveal anything until he furnished credentials.

"A certain liaison with a then crown prince, Madame Norton, does that refresh your memory?"

I closed the door.

"Who are you?"

"Let's say I'm part of the greater good, as the military refer to themselves, safeguarding Mother France."

Some inner sense warned me to leave my brother-in-law Meslay's name unspoken. "The Prussian ignominy of 1870 and the communards tear the fabric of our society apart," he said, and his voice rose, as if addressing a crowd. He was almost comical but he knew my secrets. That made him dangerous and someone to be listened to. Had my former lover, the present king, kept me under surveillance? But I doubted that. . . . Cavour's manner and rhetoric bespoke a disappointed warhorse.

His next words surprised me even more. "Bijou, the contortionist, at le Chat Noir mentioned you."

"That's why you follow me?"

"Let's say it makes you interesting."

"Yes, of course, we're in a revue popular with the working class and the slumming aristos and bourgeoisie. Lines form down place Pigalle for the late-afternoon matinees."

"Count Esterhazy, a French officer, her paramour, interests us," he said.

"But why?"

"Be useful and I'll be useful to you," he said handing me a visiting card engraved with Emil Cavour, Office of Statistics.

"Ask Bijou yourself."

His small eyes narrowed. "Certain ministers in a certain government seem bothered by your . . ."

"Existence? The fact that I withheld compromising evidence of the said monarch, but have not and will never, use it? They don't trust me, isn't that it, since they rank as connivers and deal with liars."

Cavour made a deep bow. "They never said you were smart." When he looked up his face contorted with amusement. "Deception is the currency, as you seem aware of, in these matters."

Bizarre. I wanted him to say why me and why now.

"Madame Norton," he said. "The evidence against Dreyfus must not be compromised. I count on your utmost cooperation."

"What kind of threat is that?"

"If one military man is attacked, we all stand with him."

"But I don't understand, why didn't you defend Dreyfus, an officer . . ."

"He's a Jew, Madame," he interrupted. "They defend their own kind."

"So that's what this is all about?" Disgust rose in me.

"He was an outsider, of course; he sold secrets."

"Assuming he didn't, and someone else from the officer pool did, it would disgrace your branch. Never admit a mistake but blunder on. Isn't that the military motto?"

He raised his cane towards me. I'd scratched the truth and gone too far. "Get out before . . ."

The door opened. "I believe Madame Norton requested your departure. Of course, I'm ready to assist should you need help in that regard on the stairs."

Both Cavour and I turned. I stared into the face of Holmes, a.k.a. Duc de Langans.

Sensing trouble behind the sarcastic tone, Cavour bristled a quick "good evening," glared at me, then left.

Holmes waited until he cleared the stairs, then stepped inside. Immediately he pinched the candle wick between his fingers, my only light, and went to the window.

"He's gone. But his spy, the organ grinder, has taken over watching you."

I found it hard to feel anger. Poor man, I didn't begrudge the organ grinder any job he could find in this cold.

"I could have handled that, Holmes," I said.

"And no doubt you would have done well, Irene. I, for one, have limitless respect for your capabilities. But nothing is the way you imagine," he said. "Trust me."

He approached me, then abruptly went to the bricked-up chimney and sat down cross-legged.

"But you have told me nothing. Nothing."

I went to the window, a dark frame of sky pockmarked with stars. "All this bone-chilling weather; it's freezing and it hasn't even snowed! I've never seen Paris with snow. Can you believe that, Holmes?"

"Neither have I, Irene," he said, his tone tinged with resignation. "I owe you an explanation."

"Explanation? Why not start with who you work for and why. Then we'll go from there."

"The only problem, Irene, is that the French and we English make the strangest bedfellows."

"You forget, Holmes, I'm American."

For once he was quiet.

I sat down, curled next to him, resting my head on his shoulder. The spreading heat of the toasty warm brick and his slow, steady breathing calmed me.

We sat quietly for I don't know how long. Until Holmes made up his mind to tell me what he wished. But ahead of our very eyes, under my gouged table, sat the bag Léonie brought from the ministry with Esterhazy's bordereau. And in my pocket his promissary napkin for whisky.

Somehow that all had to tie in.

"We don't want another war. With Kaiser Wilhelm least of all," Holmes said, with a sigh. "The Royal Navy hasn't recovered from the last one. Shocking but true, the navy keeps it hush-hush. Under wraps for years. Somehow the Balkan plan, with our diminished fleet and less than sterling capabilities, is something the French know about and privately gloat over. Yet, their fleet is almost as decimated, wouldn't withstand a German naval attack, and they would rely mightily on ours. The dastardly conundrum for all is that this information might have been furnished with military secrets."

So the British were "selfish," as Meslay put it but for good reason. And so were the French.

"But how can you tell if this Esterhazy passed the Balkan plan on?"

Holmes stretched his long legs out. "Not the most imaginative fellow, he called it 'B' . . . that's all. But we don't have copies of his bordereau; seems the concierge spies for the Germans and rifles through the trash."

I wanted to tell him that his toes almost touched them. But I held back. Whether from loyalty to Meslay or anger at the past history of the British using Norton, I wasn't sure, but I couldn't give Holmes the papers. I battled the curious attraction to Holmes, my equal and more, knowing any relations with him impossible.

"What real difference, Holmes, is it if you or the French find out in the end? It's poor Dreyfus who's imprisoned."

"Think of the greater good, Irene."

"Whose greater good?"

"A wise remark," he said. "But my employer will argue against that." He looked tired. Beat. "You know, Irene, this endless chess of European politics has run its course for me. After this, I'm retiring to the Somerset Downs."

Should I believe him?

And then big, thick, white flakes danced in the darkness. I ran to the window. Snow, like confectioner's sugar, dusted the cobbles and rooftops below. A little child ran in the street shouting "*neige, neige*" until his mother called him inside.

"Look, Holmes, it's snowing. Our first Paris snow!"

He came to the window and we watched in wonder. He curved his arm around me and kept me warm.

"Seems I've grown accustomed to you beating me at the game, Irene," he said pulling me back towards the brick fireplace. "I've come to even like it."

Did he know more than he let on? But I did, too. We took up kissing where we'd left off backstage. This time we had no curtain calls to distract us. He spread my blanket on the floor and in the darkness, with only the silent falling snowflakes as witness, you, dearest Neige, were conceived. Out of love. By two people who could never live together.

Before dawn, I crept through the garret, took the few things I owned, and the bag. I turned the bottle in the window. The only thing I took from Holmes was his cape, since it was such a frigid morning. I paused at the door, pulled out one of the bordereau. The cryptic message was written in the same handwriting as on Esterhazy's napkin. The letter *B* was in the lower corner. I pulled out another, this time a *B* was in the top left-hand corner. That one I propped on the table for Holmes. I could afford to be generous.

By the time I reached the bouillon des Pères in Pigalle, I decided to convince Meslay of my need for a well-deserved vacation in the South. And I'd bring Léonie and her little girl along. And so, my dear Neige, you were born nine months later in Grasse, a perfume-making village nearby in the mountains. Holmes knows nothing of this. The last I heard, true to his word, he lived in Somerset tending bees. A beekeeper.

But armed with this knowledge and, I hope, a greater tolerance of your mother, you must decide whether to seek him out or not. Whatever your decision, my sweetest Neige, I know it will be the right one. . . . Your loving mother.

When the sister returned she found the young woman shouldering her portmanteau. "May I help you find accommodation nearby?"

"No, thank you, sister, I'm going to the station," Neige said. "If I hurry I'll catch the train that connects to the Channel ferry. I must go to England."

Colonel Sebastian Moran

"My collection of M's is a fine one," said [Holmes]. "Moriarty himself is enough to make any letter illustrious, and here is Morgan the poisoner, and Merridew of abominable memory, and Mathews, who knocked out my left canine in the waiting room at Charing Cross, and, finally, here is our friend of tonight."

He handed over the book, and I read: "*Moran, Sebastian, Colonel.* Unemployed. Formerly 1st Bengalore Pioneers. Born London, 1840. Son of Sir Augustus Moran, C.B., once British Minister to Persia. Educated Eton and Oxford. Served in Jowaki Campaign, Afghan Campaign, Charasiab (dispatches), Sherpur and Cabul. Author of *Heavy Game of the Western Himalayas,* 1881; *Three Months in the Jungle,* 1884. Address: Conduit Street. Clubs: the Anglo-Indian, the Tankerville, the Bagatelle Card Club."

On the margin was written in Holmes's precise hand: "The second most dangerous man in London."

—"The Adventure of the Empty House"

by PETER TREMAYNE

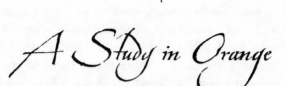

A Study in Orange

Somewhere in the vaults of the bank of Cox and Co., at Charing Cross, there is a travel-worn and battered tin dispatch box, with my name, John H. Watson, MD, late Indian Army, painted on the lid. It is filled with papers, nearly all of which are records of cases to illustrate the curious problems which Mr. Sherlock Holmes had at various times to examine.

—"THE PROBLEM OF THOR BRIDGE"

This is one of those papers.

It was my estimable friend, the consulting detective Mr. Sherlock Holmes, who drew the printing error to my attention.

"Really, my dear Watson!" he exclaimed, one morning over breakfast, as he thrust the copy of *Collier's Magazine* towards me. "How can you let something like this slip by? I have often found myself remarking on the considerable liberties that you have taken in your accounts of my cases, but this date is an error in the extreme. Detail, my dear Watson. You must pay attention to detail!"

I took the copy of the magazine from his hands and glanced at the page on which his slim forefinger had been tapping in irritation. *Collier's* had just published my account of the case of "Black Peter" in which Holmes had been able to clear young John Neligan of the accusation of murder of Captain "Black Peter" Carey. He had caused the arrest of the real culprit, Patrick Cairns. The case had occurred some eight years before, in 1895 to be precise. Indeed, it had only been with some caution that I had decided to write it at all. Although the events happened in Sussex, all three men were Irish sailors, and Holmes was always reticent when it came to allowing the public to read anything that associated him with Ireland.

This was, I must hasten to say, not due to any bigotry on the part of Holmes. It was simply a stricture of my old friend that no reference be made that might associate him with his Anglo-Irish background. He was one of the Holmes family of Galway. Like his brother Mycroft, he had started his studies at Trinity College, Dublin, before winning his demyship to Oxford following the example of his fellow Trinity student Oscar Wilde. On arrival in England, Holmes had encountered some xenophobic anti-Irish and anticolonial hostilities. Such prejudices so disturbed him that he became assiduous in his attempts to avoid any public connection with the country of his birth. This eccentricity had been heightened in later years by public prejudicial reaction to the downfall and imprisonment of the egregious Wilde, whom he had known well.

While Holmes allowed me to recount some of his early cases in Ireland such as "The Affray at the Kildare Street Club," "The Spectre of Tullyfane Abbey," and "The Kidnapping of Mycroft Holmes," purportedly by Fenians, I had faithfully promised my friend that these accounts would be placed in my bank with strict instructions that they not be released until fifty years after my death or the death of my friend, whichever was the later event.

It was, therefore, fearful of some error that I had associated him in some manner with the nationality of the three men involved in the case of "Black Peter," that I took the magazine from him and peered cautiously at the page.

"I was very careful not to mention any Irish connection in the story," I said defensively.

"It is where you pay tribute to my mental and physical faculties for the year '95 that the error occurs," Holmes replied in annoyance.

"I don't understand," I said, examining the page.

He took back the magazine from me and read with careful diction: "In this memorable year '95, a curious and congruous succession of cases had engaged his attention, ranging from his famous investigation of the sudden death of Cardinal Tosca—an inquiry which was carried out by him at the express desire of His Holiness the Pope. . . ."

He paused and looked questioningly at me.

"But the case was famous," I protested. "It was also publicly acknowledged that the Pope asked specifically for your help. I kept some of the articles that appeared in the public press. . . ."

"Then I suggest you go to your archive of tittle-tattle, Watson," he interrupted sharply. "Look up the article."

I moved to the shelves where I maintained a few scrapbooks in which I occasionally pasted such articles of interest connected with the life and career of my friend. It took me a little while to find the six column inches that had been devoted to the case by the *Morning Post*.

"There you are," I said triumphantly. "The case of Cardinal Tosca was recorded."

His stare was icy.

"And have you noticed the date of the article?"

"Of course. It is here, for the month of November 1891 . . ."

"Eighteen ninety-one?" he repeated with studied deliberation.

I suddenly realized the point that he was making.

I had set the date down as 1895. I had been four years out in my record.

"It is a long time ago," I tried to justify myself. "It is easy to forget."

"Not for me," Holmes replied grimly. "The case featured an old adversary of mine whose role I did not discover until after that man's own death while in police custody in early 1894. That was why I knew that the date that you had ascribed to the case was wrong."

I was frowning, trying to make the connection.

"An old adversary? Who could that be?"

Holmes rose abruptly and went to his little Chubb Safe, bent to it, and twiddled with the locking mechanism before extracting a wad of paper.

"This," he said, turning to me and tapping the paper with the stem of his pipe, "was what I found in my adversary's apartment when I went to search it after his death. It is a draft of a letter. Whether he sent it or not, I am not sure. Perhaps it does not matter. I believe that it was fortuitous that I found it before the police who would doubtless have made it public or, worse, it might have fallen into other hands so that the truth might never have been known to me. It is a record of my shortcomings, Watson. I will allow you to see it but no other eyes will do so during my lifetime. You may place it in that bank box of yours with your other scribbling. Perhaps after some suitable time has passed following my death, it can be opened to public scrutiny. That I shall leave to posterity."

I took the document from him and observed the spidery handwriting that filled its pages.

I regarded Holmes in bewilderment.

"What is it?"

"It is the true story of how Cardinal Tosca came by his death. You have had the goodness to claim the case as one of my successes. This will show you how I was totally outwitted. The man responsible wrote it."

My jaw dropped foolishly.

"But I was with you at the time. You solved the case to the satisfaction of Scotland Yard. Who . . . ?"

"Colonel Sebastian Moran, the man who I once told you was the second most dangerous man in London. He was my adversary and I did not know it. Read it, Watson. Read it and learn how fallible I can be."

> *The Conduit Street Club, London W1*
> *May 21, 1891*

My dear "Wolf Shield":

So he is dead! The news is emblazoned on the newspaper billboards at every street corner. His friend, Watson, has apparently given an interview to reporters in Meiringen, Switzerland, giving the bare details. Holmes and Moriarty have plunged to their deaths together over the Reichenbach Falls. Sherlock Holmes is dead and in that news I can find no grief for Moriarty, who has dispatched him to the devil! Moriarty, at his age, was no street brawler and should have sent his hirelings to do the physical work. So Moriarty's untimely end was his own fault. But that he took that sanctimonious and egocentric meddler to his death is a joy to me.

Holmes was always an irritant to me. I remember our first clash in the Kildare Street Club in Dublin, back in '73. He was but a young student then, just gone up to Oxford. He and his brother, Mycroft, who, at the time, was an official at Dublin Castle, were lunching in the club. It chanced that Moriarty and I were also lunching there. It was some paltry misunderstanding over a ridiculous toilet case with that old idiot, the Duke of Cloncurry and Straffan, that Holmes's meddling caused me to be thrown out of the Club and banned from membership.

It was not the last time that little pipsqueak irritated me and thwarted my plans. But there is one case where he was not successful in his dealings with me. Now my own ego must lay claim to having got the better of that Dublin jackeen. I proved the better man but, alas, he went to his death without knowing it. I would have given anything that he had plunged to his death knowing that Sebastian Moran of Derryna-cleigh had outwitted him while he claimed to be the greatest detective in Europe! But, my dear "Wolf Shield," let me tell you the full story, although I appreciate that you know the greater part of it. You are the only one that I can tell it to for, of course, you were ultimately responsible for the outcome.

In November of 1890 His Eminence Cardinal Giacomo Tosca, nuncio of Pope Leo XIII was found dead in bed in the home of a certain member of the British Cabinet in Gayfere Street not far from the Palace of Westminster. The facts, as you doubtless recall, created a furor. You will remember that Lord Salisbury headed a Conservative government that was not well disposed to papal connections at the time. The main reason was the government's stand against Irish Home Rule summed up in their slogan—"Home Rule is Rome Rule." That very month Parnell had been reelected leader of the Irish Party in spite of attempts to discredit him. The Irish Party controlled four-fifths of all Irish parliamentary seats in Westminster. They were considered a formidable opposition.

A doctor named Thomson, called in to examine the body of the papal nuncio, caused further speculation by refusing to sign a death certificate, as he told the police that the circumstances of the death were indistinct and suspicious. The doctor was supported in this attitude by the local coroner.

The alarums that followed this announcement were extraordinary. The popular press demanded to know whether this meant the papal nuncio was murdered. More importantly, both Tory and Liberal newspapers were demanding a statement from government on whether the nuncio had been an intermediary in some political deal being negotiated with Ireland's Catholics.

What was Cardinal Tosca doing in the house of the Conservative government Minister Sir Gibson Glassford? More speculation was thrown on the fire of rumor and scandal when it was revealed that Glassford was a cousin, albeit distant, of the Earl of Zetland, the Viceroy in Dublin. Moreover, Glassford was known to represent the moderate wing of the Tories and not unsympathetic to the cause of Irish Home Rule.

Was there some Tory plot to give the Irish self-government in spite of all their assurances of support for the Unionists? All the Tory leaders, Lord Salisbury, Arthur Balfour, Lord Hartington, and Joseph Chamberlain among them, had all sworn themselves to the Union and made many visits to Ireland declaring that Union would never be severed. Yet here was a cardinal found dead in the house of a Tory minister known to have connections with Ireland. It came as a tremendous shock to the political world.

Catholic bishops in England denied any knowledge of Cardinal Tosca being in the country. The Vatican responded by telegraph also denying that they knew that Cardinal Tosca was in England. Such denials merely fueled more speculation of clandestine negotiations.

As for Sir Gibson Glassford himself— what had he to say to all this? Well this was the truly amusing and bizarre part of the story.

Glassford denied all knowledge of the presence of Cardinal Tosca in his house. Not only the press but also the police found this hard to believe. In fact, the Liberal press greeted the Minister's statement with derision and editorials claimed that the government was covering up some dark secret. There were calls for Glassford to resign immediately. Lord Salisbury began to distance himself from his junior minister.

Glassford stated that he and his household had retired to bed at their usual hour in the evening. The household consisted of Glassford himself, his wife, two young children, a nanny, a butler called Hogan, a cook, and two housemaids. There all swore that there had been no guests staying in the house that night and certainly not His Eminence.

In the morning, one of the housemaids, descending from her room in the attic, noticed the door of the guest's room ajar and the glow of a lamp still burning. An attention to her duties prompted her to enter to extinguish the light and then she saw Cardinal Tosca. His clothes were neatly folded at the foot of the bed, his boots placed carefully under the dressing table chair. He lay in the bed clad in his nightshirt. His face was pale and his eyes wide open.

The maid was about to apologize and leave the room, thinking this was a guest whose late arrival was unknown to her, when she perceived the unnatural stillness of the body and the glazed stare of the eyes. She turned from the room and raised the butler, Hogan, who, ascertaining the man was dead, informed his master, after which the police were called.

It was not long before the clothing and a pocket book led to the identification of His Eminence.

The household was questioned strenuously but no one admitted ever seeing Cardinal Tosca on the previous night or on any other night; no one had admitted him into the house. Glassford was adamant that he and his wife had never met the Cardinal, or even heard of him, let alone extended an invitation to him to be entertained as a guest in their house.

Inquiries into the Catholic community in London discovered that Cardinal Tosca had arrived in the city incognito two days before and was staying with Father Michael, one of the priests at St. Patrick's Church in Soho Square. This was the first public Catholic Church to be opened in England since the Reformation. It had been consecrated in 1792. But Father Michael maintained that he did not know the purpose of Cardinal Tosca's visit. The Cardinal had simply told him that he had arrived from Paris by the boat train at Victoria and intended to spend two days in important meetings. He exhorted Father Michael not to mention his presence to anyone, not even to his own bishop.

Now, and this was the point that troubled the police the most, according to Father Michael, the Cardinal had retired to his room in the presbytery, that is the priest's house, in Sutton Street, Soho, at ten o'clock in the evening. Father Michael had looked in on His Eminence because the Cardinal had left his missal in the library and the priest thought he might like to have it before retiring. So he saw the Cardinal in bed in his night attire and he was looking well and fit. At seven o'clock the next morning, Cardinal Tosca was found dead by the housemaid a mile and a half away in Sir Gibson Glassford's house in Gayfere Street, Westminster.

The press redoubled their calls for the Glassford to resign and the Liberal press started to call on Lord Salisbury's entire government to offer their resignation. Riots had burst out in Belfast instigated by Unionists and various factions of the Orange Order, the sectarian Unionist movement, were on the march and the thundering of their intimidating lambeg drums was resounding through the streets of the Catholic ghettos.

The police confessed that they had no clue at all. They did, however, treat the butler, poor Hogan, to a very vigorous scrutiny and interroga-

tion and it was discovered that he had some tenuous links to the Irish Party, having some cousin in membership of the party. Glassford, a man of principle, felt he should stand by his butler and so added to the fuel of speculation.

The police admitted that they were unsure of how the Cardinal came by his death, let alone why, and unable to charge anyone with having a hand in it.

Because of the suspicion of an Irish connection, which was mere prejudice on the part of the authorities due to the Catholic connection, the case was handed over to the Special Irish Branch, which is now more popularly referred to as the Special Branch of Scotland Yard. The Police Commissioner James Monro had formed this ten years before to fight the Irish Republican terrorism. The head of the Special Branch was Chief Inspector John G. Littlechild. And it was through the private reports of Detective Inspector Gallagher that I was able to observe, in some comfort, the events that now unfolded.

It was some seven days after the revelation of Cardinal Tosca's death that Chief Inspector Littlechild received a visit from Mycroft Holmes. This was a singular event as Mycroft Holmes, being a senior government official in Whitehall, was not given to making calls on his juniors. With Mycroft Holmes came his insufferable younger brother Sherlock. My friend Gallagher, who had the information as to what had transpired directly from Littlechild himself, told me about this meeting. Littlechild had been handed an embossed envelope bearing a crest. No word was said. He opened it and found a letter entirely in Latin, a language of which he had no knowledge. It showed the arrogance of the Holmes Brothers that they did not offer a translation until the Chief Inspector made the request for one.

It was a letter from none other than Gioacchino Pecci, who for thirteen years had sat on the papal throne in Rome as Leo XIII. The letter requested that the police allow Sherlock Holmes to investigate the circumstances of the death of the papal nuncio and provide whatever support was required. Mycroft Holmes added that the Prime Minister had himself sanctioned the request, presenting a note from Lord Salisbury to that effect.

I was told that Littlechild had an intense dislike of Sherlock Holmes. Holmes had not endeared himself to Littlechild because he had often insulted some of Scotland Yard's best men—Inspector Lestrade, for example. Inspector Tobias Gregson and Inspector Stanley Hopkins had also been held up to public ridicule by Holmes's caustic tongue. But what could Littlechild do in such circumstances but accept Holmes's involvement with as good a grace as he could muster?

Holmes and his insufferable and bumbling companion, Watson, were to have carte blanche to question Sir Gibson Glassford's household and make any other inquiries he liked. Littlechild had thankfully made one condition, which was to come in handy for me. Detective Inspector Gallagher was to accompany Holmes at all times so that the matter would remain an official Scotland Yard inquiry. Thus it was that I was kept in touch with everything that the so-called Great Detective was doing while he was entirely unaware of my part in the game.

This is the part of the story that my friend Gallagher narrated to me.

The first thing that Holmes informed Gallagher of was that he had telegraphed Cardinal Tosca's secretary in Paris. The secretary confirmed that Cardinal Tosca had caught the boat train to London, promising to return within forty-eight hours. The journey had been prompted by the arrival of a stranger at Cardinal Tosca's residence in Paris late one night. The secretary had the impression that the visitor was an American by the way he spoke English with an accent. When asked his business, the man presented a small pasteboard that had a name and a symbol on it. The secretary could not remember the name but was sure that the device was harp-shaped. The man spent a few minutes with the Cardinal and the next morning the Cardinal caught the boat train. Moreover, the Cardinal insisted on traveling alone, which was highly unusual.

Inspector Gallagher pointed out that had Holmes consulted him, he would have been informed that this information was already in police hands, having consulted the Cardinal's secretary. Holmes was too conceited to be abashed by the fact. He believed that nothing was achieved unless he personally achieved it.

Gallagher accompanied Holmes and Watson in a hansom cab to their first port of call: the local mortuary where the body of the Cardinal was being preserved, much to the outcry of the Catholic Church, who felt it scandalous that His Eminence was thus prevented a lying in state and burial according to their practices.

Holmes insisted that he and Watson should examine the body, and this was done, after much argument, in the company of the original examining doctor, Thomson, and the coroner, with Gallagher looking on without enthusiasm. In fact, Gallagher found Holmes's involvement quite objectionable. He seemed to claim authority over the medical experts and leant over the corpse using a large magnifying glass as he examined it. He suddenly let out a hiss of breath and turned to his companions.

"Do you not remark on the slight bruising on this neck vein," he remarked, pointing dramatically, like one who has discovered something unique.

"I did so remark on it, Mr. Holmes," Dr. Thomson replied patiently. The coroner was clearly displeased.

"If you will read my report, that matter was made clear . . . ," he began but Holmes actually waved him into silence.

"But what of the puncture wound which is discernible under my glass. What of that, sir?" he demanded of the doctor.

"I found it irrelevant," replied Thomson. "A bite of some sort, that is all."

Holmes turned to his crony, the sycophantic Watson.

"Watson, please observe this mark and bear in mind that I have brought it to the attention of these . . . gentlemen."

Gallagher thought that he was being quite insulting and so did Dr. Thomson and the coroner, who waited with unconcealed impatience for Holmes to complete his study.

Finally, Holmes turned to Gallagher and demanded to see the clothes that had been found with His Eminence's body.

"Is there any question that these clothes found by the body belong to the Cardinal?" he asked as the parcel was handed to him.

"None whatsoever," he was assured. "Father Michael himself examined and identified them."

The Cardinal's pocket book, rosary, and pocket missal were all contained in the package.

"I presume that none of this material has been removed or tampered with?" queried Holmes.

Gallagher flushed with mortification.

"Scotland Yard, Mr. Holmes, is not in the habit of removing or altering evidence, as you well know."

Holmes seemed oblivious to his insults and he searched through the *pocket book which contained some banknotes in both French and English currencies and little else apart from two pasteboard visiting cards. They bore the name "T. W. Tone" on them and a little harp device surmounted by a crown. Holmes showed them to Watson and said quietly, "Note these well, Watson, old friend." It was as if Gallagher was not supposed to hear, but he did so and duly reported the fact to me.*

Holmes then frowned and peered closely at the bundle of clothes.

"Wasn't the Cardinal supposed to be wearing a nightshirt? Pray, where is that?"

"It was wrapped separately from the other clothing," Gallagher assured him, producing it. "As this was what the body was clad in, it was considered that it should be kept separate in case it provided any clues."

The insufferable Holmes took out the nightshirt and started to examine it. A curious expression crossed his features as he sniffed at it. Turning, he picked up the other clothing and sniffed at that. He spent so long smelling each item alternatively that Gallagher thought him mad.

"Where have these been stored during these last several days?"

"They have been placed in sacking and stored in a cupboard here in case they were needed as evidence."

"In a damp cupboard?"

"Of course not. They have been kept in a dry place."

Half an hour later saw them at Father Michael's presbytery, where His Eminence had last been seen alive. He treated the poor priest in the same brusque manner as he had the doctor and coroner. His opening remarks were, apparently, exceedingly offensive.

"Did the Cardinal take narcotics, according to your knowledge?" he demanded.

Father Michael looked astounded, so shocked that he could say nothing for a moment and then, having regained control of his sensibilities, after Holmes's brutal affront, shook his head.

"He was not in the habit of using a needle to inject himself with any noxious substance?" Holmes went on, oblivious to the outrage he had caused.

"He was not . . ."

". . . to your knowledge?" Holmes smiled insultingly. "Did the Cardinal receive any letters or messages while he was here?"

Father Michael admitted no knowledge on the matter, but, at Holmes's insistence, he summoned the housekeeper. She recalled that a man had presented himself on the door of the presbytery demanding to see His Eminence. Furthermore, the housekeeper said the man was well muffled, with hat pulled down and coat collar pulled up, thus presented no possibility of identification. She did remember that he had spoken with an Irish accent. He had presented a card with a name on it. The housekeeper could not remember the name but recalled that the card had a small device embossed on it, which she thought was a harp.

Gallagher could not forbear to point out that Scotland Yard had asked these questions prior to Holmes's involvement.

"Except the question of narcotics," replied Holmes, a patronizing expression on his face.

Holmes then demanded to see the bedroom where Father Michael had bade good night to His Eminence. He carefully examined it.

"I perceive this room is on the third floor of the house. That is irritating in the extreme."

Father Michael, Gallagher, and even Watson exchanged a puzzled glance with one another as Holmes went darting around the bedroom. In particularly, he went through Cardinal Tosca's remaining clothing, sniffing at it like some dog trying to find a scent.

Holmes then spent a good half an hour examining the presbytery from the outside, much to the irritation of Gallagher and the bemusement of Watson.

From Soho they took a hansom cab to Sir Gibson Glassford's house in Gayfere Street. Glassford was apparently close to tears when he greeted them in his study.

"My dear Holmes," he said, holding the Great Detective's hand as if he were afraid to let go of it. "Holmes, you must help me. No one will believe me; even my wife now thinks that I am not telling her all I know. Truly, Holmes, I never saw this prelate until Hogan showed me the dead body in the room. What does it mean, Holmes? What does it mean? I would resign office, if that would do any good, but I fear it would not. How can this strange mystery be resolved?"

Holmes extracted his hand with studied care and removed himself to the far side of the room.

"Patience, Minister. Patience. I can only proceed when I have facts. It is a mistake to confound strangeness with mystery. True, the circumstances of this matter are strange but they only retain their mystery until the facts are explained. Watson, you know my methods. The grand thing is to be able to reason backward."

Watson nodded, as if he understood, but looked unhappy. Inspector Gallagher was pretty certain that the bumbling doctor had not a clue of what the arrogant man was saying. Glassford looked equally bewildered and had the courage to say so.

"Facts, my dear sir!" snapped Holmes. "I have no facts yet. It is a capital mistake to theorize before one has facts. Insensibly, one begins to twist facts to suit theories, instead of theories to suit facts."

He made Glassford, his wife, and all the servants go through the evidence they had already given to the police and then demanded to see the bedchamber in which His Eminence had been found.

"I observe this bedroom is on the fourth floor of your house. How tiresome!"

Once again, he wandered around the bedroom, paying particular attention to the carpeting, exclaiming once or twice as he did so.

"Seven days, I suppose it would have been an impossibility to think anything would have remained undisturbed."

The note of accusation caused Detective Inspector Gallagher to flush in annoyance.

"We did our best to secure the evidence, Mr. Holmes," he began.

"And your best was to destroy whatever evidence there was," snapped Holmes conceitedly.

He then led the way outside the house and stood peering around as if searching for something. But he seemed to give up with a shake of his head. He was turning away when his eyes alighted on two men on the opposite side of the road who were peering down an open manhole. From the steps of the house, an elderly woman, clutching a Pekingese dog in her arms, was observing their toil, or rather lack of it, with disapproval. An expression of interest crossed Holmes's features and he went over to them.

"Good afternoon, gentlemen," he greeted the workmen. "I observe by your expression that something appears amiss here."

The workmen gaped at him, unused to being addressed as gentlemen.

"Naw, guv'nor," replied one, shaking his head. "We do reckon ain't naw'fing wrong 'ere." He glanced at the elderly lady and said in an aggrieved voice. "But seems we've gotta check, ain't we?"

The elderly lady was peering shortsighted at Holmes.

"*Young man!*" *she accosted him, in an imperial tone.* "*I don't suppose you are an employee of the local sewerage works?*"

Holmes swung round, leaving the two workmen still gazing morbidly down the hole in the road, and he smiled thinly.

"*Is there some way I can be of assistance, madam?*"

"*I have not seen eye to eye with your workmen there. They assure me that I have been imagining excavations near my house by the sewerage company. I do not imagine things. However, since these excavations have ceased, or rather the sounds of them, which have been so oppressive to my obtaining a decent night's repose, I presume that we will no longer be bothered by these nightly disturbances?*"

"*Nightly disturbances?*" *Holmes asked with quickening interest.*

When she confirmed that she had complained a fortnight prior to the sewerage company of nightly disturbances caused by vibration and muffled banging under the street, causing her house to shake, one of the workmen summoned courage to come forward. He raised a finger to his cap.

"*Begging' yer pardon, lady, but wiv all due respect an' that, ain't bin none of our lads a digging dahn 'ere. No work bin done in this 'ere area fer months naw.*"

Holmes stood regarding the old woman and the workmen for a moment, and then with a cry of "*Of course!*" *he bounded back to Glassford's house and his knocking brought Hogan, the butler, to the door again.*

"*Show me your cellar,*" *he ordered the startled man.*

Sir Gibson emerged from his study, disturbed by the noise of Holmes's reentry into the house, and looked astounded.

"*Why, what is it, Mr. Holmes?*"

"*The cellar, man,*" *snapped Holmes dictatorially, totally disregarding the fact that Glassford was a member of the government.*

In a body they trooped down into the cellar. In fact, several cellars ran under the big house and Hogan, who had now brought a lamp, was ordered to proceed them through the wine racks, a coal storage area, a boiler room, and areas filled with bric-a-brac and assorted discarded furniture along one wall.

"*Have any underground excavations disturbed you of late? These would have been during the night.*" *Holmes asked as he examined the cellar walls. Glassford looked perplexed.*

"Not at all," he replied, and then turned to his butler. "Your room is above here at the back of the house, isn't it, Hogan? Have you been disturbed?"

The butler shook his head.

"Does the Underground railway run in this vicinity?" Holmes pressed.

"We are not disturbed by the Underground here," replied Sir Gibson. "The Circle Line, which was completed six years ago, is quite a distance to the north of here."

"That wall would be to the north," Holmes muttered, and turning to Hogan ordered the man to bring the lamp close while he began examining the wall. He was there fully fifteen minutes before he gave up in irritation. Inspector Gallagher was smiling to himself and could not help making the thrust: "Your theory not turning out as you would hope, Mr. Holmes?"

Holmes scowled at him.

"We will return to Father Michael's," he almost snarled.

At the presbytery he demanded to see the priest, and being shown into the study asked without preamble: "Do you have a cellar?"

Father Michael nodded.

"Pray precede me to it," demanded Holmes arrogantly.

The priest did so, with Holmes behind him and Watson and Gallagher trailing in the rear. It was an ordinary cellar, mostly used for the storage of coal and with wine racks along one side. Holmes moved hither and thither through it like a ferret until he came to a rusting iron door.

"Where does this lead?" he demanded.

Father Michael shrugged.

"It leads into the new crypt. As you know, we are rebuilding the church and creating a crypt. The door used to lead into another cell, but it has not been opened ever since I have been here."

"Which is how long?" asked Holmes, examining it carefully.

"Ten years."

"I see," muttered the Great Detective. Then he smiled broadly. "I see." He said it again almost as if to impress everyone that he had spotted some solution to the mystery.

"And does an Underground railway run near here?"

Father Michael shook his head.

"Our architect ascertained that before we began to rebuild the church. We needed to ensure strong foundations."

Gallagher felt he could have done a dance at the crestfallen expression on Holmes's face. It lasted only a moment and then Holmes had swung round on him.

"I want to see the Metropolitan Commissioner of Sewers and maps of the system under London."

Gallagher felt he was dealing with a maniac now. It seemed that Holmes had devised some theory that he was determined to prove at all cost.

Mr. Bert Small, the manager of sewerage system, agreed to see Holmes and provide plans of the area at the company's Canon Row offices, just opposite the Palace of Westminster on the corner of Parliament Street.

"I cannot see the connection I wish to make," Holmes in resignation said, pushing the plans away from him in disgust. "There seems no way that one could negotiate the sewers from Soho Square to Gayfere Street, at least not directly in a short place of time. And the Underground railway does not run anywhere near Father Michael's nor Glassford's houses."

It was then that Bert Small came to the rescue of Holmes, demonstrating that it was not intellect alone that helped him solve his cases but good fortune and coincidence.

"Maybe you are looking at the wrong underground system, Mr. Holmes," he suggested. "There are many other underground systems under London apart from sewers and the new railway system."

Holmes regarded him with raised eyebrows.

"There is another system of tunnels that runs under Westminster?"

Mr. Small rose and took down some keys, smiling with superiority.

"I will show you."

It took but a few minutes for Mr. Bert Small—the man of the moment, as Gallagher cynically described him—to lead them from his office around the corner to Westminster Bridge. Here Mr. Small led them down a flight of steps to the Embankment to the base of the statute of Queen Boadicea, in her chariot with her two daughters. There was a small iron door here, which he unlocked and suggested that they follow him.

A flight of iron steps led them into a tunnel. Mr. Small seemed to swell with pride and he pointed out that it was situated just above the lower-level interceptory sewer which ran below the level of the Thames. They could see that it was built of brickwork but arched rather than circular and was about six feet high. It was designed, said Mr. Small, to carry cast-iron pipes with water and gas.

He took a lantern and shone it along the dark, forbidding way.

Gallagher was conscious of the river seeping through the brickwork, dripping down the walls on either side and, above all, he was aware of the smell, the putrid stench of the river and the echoing tunnel before them. Holmes began to sniff with a sigh of satisfaction.

Mr. Small pointed down the tunnel.

"These tunnels run from here along the river as far as the Bank of England, Mr. Holmes. These are Sir Joseph Bazalgette's tunnels, which he completed fifteen years ago," he said proudly. "You have probably seen, gentlemen, that Sir Joseph died a few months ago. The tunnel system under London was his finest achievement and . . ."

Holmes was not interested in the eulogy of the civil engineer who had built the tunnels.

"And are there other connections?"

"Altogether there are eleven and a half miles of these sorts of tunnels. They fan out through the city," replied Mr. Small, blinking at being cut short.

"Do they connect with Soho Square and Gayfere Street?" Holmes demanded.

"There are none of these tunnels that would connect directly. You would have to go from Soho Square down to Shaftesbury Avenue to find an entrance and then you would have to exit here and walk to Gayfere Street."

"Then that's no good to me," snapped Holmes irritably. "Let's return to the surface."

Detective Inspector Gallagher smiled to see the Great Detective so put out that whatever theory he had could not be sustained.

As they emerged onto the Embankment, Mr. Small, perhaps seeking to mollify Holmes's bad humor, was prompted to make another suggestion.

"There is yet another tunnel system, Mr. Holmes," he finally ven-

tured. "*That might pass in the general direction that you have indicated, but I am not sure. I do have a plan of it back at the office. But it has been closed down for over a decade now.*"

Holmes asserted that he would like to see the plans.

Gallagher believed that Holmes was off on another wild goose chase and, being just across the road from his office at Scotland Yard, he left Holmes and Watson with Mr. Small. He returned to report the progress to his chief, Littlechild. It was two hours later that Gallagher received a curt note from Holmes asking him to meet him at Glassford's house within half an hour and bring a posse of armed police officers, who were to station themselves in the front and back of the building.

Gallagher reluctantly carried out Holmes's orders after consulting with Chief Inspector Littlechild, who checked with the Commissioner.

Holmes met Gallagher at the door of Glassford's house and immediately took him down into the cellar. The first thing that Gallagher noticed was an aperture to the south side of the cellar that had previously been covered by the piles of old furniture. Beyond this hole was a tunnel of some ten feet in length, dug through the London clay. But within ten feet it met a well-constructed brick-lined tunnel. It was of arched brickwork some four and a half feet in height and four feet wide and a small-gauge railway line ran through it. Gallagher was puzzled, for this was certainly not a tunnel connected with the rail system. Holmes ordered a policeman to be stationed as a guard at this point and then invited Gallagher to join him in Sir Gibson Glassford's study.

Holmes had gathered everyone in Glassford's study. There was the Minister himself, his wife, and all the servants, nanny, cook, housemaids, and the butler, Hogan. The Great Detective was looking pleased as punch with himself and Gallagher reported that the spectacle was repulsive in the extreme.

"The case was simple," exclaimed Holmes in his usual pedantic style. "I drew your attention to the bruising and puncture mark over the vein in the Cardinal's neck. To most people who have dealt with the administration of narcotics, the puncture mark was the sign of a hypodermic syringe. Usually, this is the method by which a medication or drugs is introduced under the skin of the patient by means . . ."

"I think we know the method, Holmes," muttered Gallagher. "Dr. Thomson did not agree with you. Indeed, he conducted tests which showed no sign of any foreign substance, let alone narcotics or poison, *being introduced into the body of the Cardinal which would cause death."*

"There was no need to introduce such foreign matter," Holmes went on, looking like a cat that has devoured cream. "The hypodermic contained no substance whatsoever."

"But how . . . ?" began Sir Gibson.

"It contained nothing but air," went on Holmes. "It caused an air embolism—a bubble of air—to be introduced into the bloodstream. That was fatal. Cardinal Tosca was murdered."

Gallagher sighed deeply.

"We already suspected that . . . ," he protested.

"I have now demonstrated your suspicion to be a fact," replied Holmes scornfully. "Now that we know the method, the next question is how was the body transported here?"

"You have been at pains to prove your theory that there is a passage through the underground sewers from Soho Square to here," muttered Gallagher.

Holmes smiled condescendingly.

"As you have now observed, it is no theory. It was obvious that the body had to be removed from Soho Square to Gayfere Place. Hardly through the streets in full view, I think, eh, Watson?" Holmes chuckled at his own humor. "It was clear to me that the body had been removed through a dank, smelly sewer. A tunnel where the clothes the body was being transported in, in this case, his nightshirt, had come into contact with the excretions running from the walls. The odors were still apparent after some days in police storage. There was no odor on the Cardinal's other clothing. Those transporting the body had carried them wrapped separately in a bag or some other casing, which protected them. The only question was—through what manner of tunneling was this achieved?"

He paused, presumably to bask in their admiration of his logic. He met only bemusement.

"The body was transported not through the sewers as it happened, Gallagher. In 1861 the Pneumatic Dispatch Company built an underground rail system. The plan was to transport only mail. However, two years later the Post Office opened its own system and this, coupled with the fact that the Pneumatic system had begun to develop mechanical faults and air leakage, caused the plans to extend it to be shelved. Ten years ago that entire system was abandoned and was also forgotten."

Holmes paused, waiting like a conjuror about to pull a rabbit from a hat.

"Except by Mr. Small," *pointed out Gallagher, not wishing Holmes to claim the approbation.*

"And by the group of people intent on mischief. The body of the Cardinal was carried, with his clothing, from his bedroom in the presbytery down to the cellar. In spite of assurances that the door had not been opened in ten years, I observed scuff marks showing that it had been opened recently. The body was removed into the new crypt where workman had, in their excavations, made contact with the old Pneumatic tunnel. The tunnel came directly towards Westminster. In preparation for this ghastly event, which had been well planned, a tunnel had been excavated in advance into the cellar of Sir Gibson's house. I was alerted by the complaints that had been made to the local sewerage company by the old lady opposite who had been disturbed by it. I subsequently found out that, being elderly, she had removed her bedroom to a lower floor, near ground level. That was how she had been disturbed in the night. I found it curious that her concerns were not shared by anyone in this house."

"But I have already told you that only the butler lives on the lower floor," *pointed out Sir Gibson,* "and Hogan has not complained of any such noises. Have you, Hogan?"

The man shook his head morosely.

"Well," *went on Holmes obliviously,* "our conspirators, for that is what they are, had enticed their victim from France on the pretense that he was wanted to mediate in some negotiations between this government and members of the Irish Republican Brotherhood. The idea appealed to Cardinal Tosca's vanity and he came here obeying the conspirators' exhortation not to tell anyone else. He was killed and the body brought through this underground system."

"But for what purpose?" *demanded Glassford.* "Why was he killed and placed in my house?"

"The purpose was to achieve exactly what this has nearly achieved. An attempt to discredit you as a member of government, and to stir up antagonism against any movement by the Irish Party to press forward again with its political campaign in parliament."

"I don't understand."

"What group of people would best benefit by discrediting both a gov-

ernment pledged to the Unionist cause and to those who seek only Home Rule within the United Kingdom? Both those objectives would receive an irrevocable blow by the involvement of a Tory Minister in the murder of a Cardinal and the suspicion of some conspiracy between them? Where would sympathy go to?"

"I presume the more extreme Irish Nationalists—the Republicans."

"Watson, your revolver!" cried Holmes suddenly.

It was too late. Hogan had pulled his own revolver.

"Everyone stay where they are!" he shouted.

"Don't be a fool, Hogan," snapped Gallagher, moving forward, but Hogan waved his weapon threateningly.

"I am not a fool," the butler cried. "I can see where this is leading and I shall not suffer alone."

"You'll not escape," cried Holmes. "The police have already surrounded this place."

Hogan simply ignored them.

He stepped swiftly back, removing the key from the lock of the study door. Then he slammed the door shut, turned the key, and they heard him exiting the house.

When Gallagher threw his weight again the door, Holmes ordered him to desist.

"He'll not get far."

In fact, Hogan hardly reached the corner of the street before members of the Special Branch called him to stop and surrender. When he opened fire, he was shot and died immediately. Which was, from my viewpoint, my dear "Wolf Shield," just as well.

Holmes had reseated himself with that supercilious look of the type he assumed when he thought he had tied up all the loose ends.

"Hogan was a member of the Irish Republican Brotherhood, the Fenians. He had ingratiated himself into your employ, Sir Gibson, and was told to wait for orders. The diabolical plot was to use the murder of His Eminence to bring about the fall of your government."

"And we know the name of the man who lured the Cardinal here," Watson intervened importantly, speaking almost for the first time in the entire investigation. "We should be able to track him down and arrest him."

Holmes looked at his acolyte with pity.

"Do we know his name, Watson?"

"Why, indeed! He overlooked the fact that he left his card behind. T. W. Tone. Remember?"

"T. W. Tone—Theobald Wolfe Tone is the name of the man led the Irish uprising of 1798," Sir Gibson intervened in a hollow voice. Watson's was red with chagrin. Sir Gibson glanced at Holmes. "Can we find out who the others were in this plot, Mr. Holmes?"

"That will be up to the Special Branch," Holmes replied, almost in a dismissive fashion. "I fear, however, that they will not have much success. I suspect those who were involved in this matter are already out of the country by now."

"Why did Hogan remain?"

"I presume that he thought himself safe or that he remained to report firsthand on the effects of the plot."

Glassford crossed to Holmes with an outstretched hand.

"My dear sir," he said, "my dear, dear sir. I . . . the country . . . owe you a great debt."

Holmes's deprecating manner was quite nauseating. Gallagher told me that he found his false modesty was truly revolting.

It is true that when the government released the facts of the plot, as Holmes had given it to them, the case of the death of Cardinal Tosca became a cause célèbre. Holmes was even offered a small pension by the government, and he refused, perhaps more on account of its smallness than any modesty on his part. He even declined a papal knighthood from the grateful Bishop of Rome.

Sickening, my dear "Wolf Shield." It was all quite sickening.

But, as you well know, the truth was that Holmes did not come near to resolving this matter. Oh, I grant you that he was able to work out the method by which I killed Cardinal Tosca. I admit that I had thought it rather an ingenious method. I had stumbled on it while attending a lecture in my youth at Trinity College. It was given by Dr. Robert MacDonnell, who had begun the first blood transfusions in 1865. MacDonnell had given up the use of the syringe because of the dangers of embolism or the air bubble which causes fatality when introduced into the bloodstream. My method in the dispatch of the Cardinal was simple, first a whiff of chloroform to prevent struggle and then the injection.

My men were waiting and we transferred the body in the method Holmes described. Yes, I'll give him credit as to method and means. He forced Hogan to disclose himself. Hogan was one of my best agents. He *met his death bravely. But Holmes achieved little else. . . . We know the reason, my dear "Wolf Shield," don't we?*

Well, now that Holmes has gone to his death over the Reichenbach Falls, I would imagine that you might think that there is little chance of the truth emerging? I have thought a great deal about that. Indeed, this is why I am writing this full account in the form of this letter to you. The original I shall deposit in a safe place. You see, I need some insurance to prevent any misfortune befalling me. As well you know, it would be scandalous should the real truth be known of who was behind the death of Cardinal Tosca and why it was done.

With that bumptious irritant Sherlock Holmes out of the way, I hope to lead a healthy and long life. Believe me—

Sebastian Moran (Colonel)

[Extra note attached by Watson.]

Having read this extraordinary document I questioned Holmes whether he had any doubts about its authenticity.

"Oh, there is no doubt that it is in Moran's hand and in his style of writing. You observe that I still have two of his books on my shelves? Heavy Game of the Western Himalayas *and* Three Months in the Jungle.*"*

I remembered that Holmes had purchased these volumes soon after the affair of "The Empty House."

"Moran was many things, but he was no coward. He might even have been a patriot in a peculiar and perverted way. His family came from Conamara and had become Anglicans after the Williamite Conquest of Ireland. His father was, in fact, Sir Augustus Moran, Commander of the Bath, once British Minister to Persia. Young Moran went through Eton, Trinity College, Dublin, and Oxford. The family estate was at Derrynacleigh. All this you knew about him at the time of our encounter in the affair of 'The Empty House.' I do not mean to imply that he was without faults when I said Moran was no coward and a type of patriot. He had a criminal mind. He was a rather impecunious young man, given to gambling, womanizing, petty crime, and the good life.

"He bought himself a commission in the India Army and served in the 1st Bengalore Pioneers. He fought in several campaigns and was mentioned in dispatches. He spent most of his army career in India and

I understand that he had quite a reputation as a big-game hunter. I recall that there was a Bengal tiger mounted in the hall of the Kildare Street Club, before he was expelled from it, which he killed. The story was that he crawled down a drain after it when he had wounded it. That takes iron nerve."

I shook my head in bewilderment.

"You call him a patriot? Do you mean he was working for the Irish Republicans?"

Holmes smiled.

"He was a patriot. I said that Moran had criminal tendencies but was no coward. Unfortunately the talents of such people are often used by the State to further their own ends. You have observed that Moran admits that Inspector Gallagher kept him informed of our every move in the case. Unfortunately Gallagher was killed in the course of duty not long after these events, so we are not able to get confirmation from him. I think we may believe Moran, though. So why was Moran kept informed? Colonel Moran was working for the Secret Service."

I was aghast.

"You don't mean to say that he worked for our own Secret Service? Good Lord, Holmes, this is amazing. Do you mean that our own Secret Service ordered the Cardinal to be killed? That's preposterous. Immoral. Our government would not stand for it."

"If, indeed, the government knew anything about it. Unfortunately, when you have a Secret Service then it becomes answerable to no one. I believe that even behind the Secret Service there was another organization with which Moran became involved."

"I don't follow, Holmes."

"I believe that Moran and those who ordered him to do this thing were members of some an extreme Orange faction."

"Orange faction? I don't understand." I threw up my hands in mystification.

"The Orange Order was formed in 1796 to maintain the position of the Anglican Ascendancy in Ireland and prevent the union of the Dublin colonial parliament with the parliament of Great Britain. However, the Union took place in 1801 and the Orange Order then lost support. Its patrons, including Royal Dukes and titled landowners, quickly accepted the new status quo being either paid off with new titles or financial bribes. The remaining aristocratic support was withdrawn when the Order was involved in a conspiracy to prevent Victoria inheriting the throne and attempting to place its Imperial Grand Master, His Royal Highness, the Duke of Cumberland, on the throne instead. The failure of the coup, Catholic Emancipation 1829, the removal of many of the restrictions placed on members of that religion, as well as the Reform Acts, extending more civil rights to people, all but caused the Orange Order to disappear.

"Those struggling to keep the sectarian movement alive realized it needed to be a more broad-based movement and it opened its membership to all Dissenting Protestants, so that soon its ranks were flooded by Ulster Presbyterians who had previously been excluded from it. Threatened by the idea that in a self-governing Ireland the majority would be Catholic, these Dissenters became more bigoted and extreme.

"The attempt to destroy the Irish Party seeking Home Rule, which is now supported by the Liberals, was addressed by diehard Unionists in the Tory Party like Lord Randolph Churchill, who advised the party to 'play the Orange Card.' The support of Churchill and the Tories made the Orange Order respectable again and Ascendancy aristocrats and leading Tories, who had previously disassociated themselves from the Order, now felt able to rejoin it. The Earl of Enniskillen was installed as Grand Master of the Order two years before these events and, with the aid of the Tories, continued to dedicate the Order to the Union and Protestant supremacy."

"But why would they plan this elaborate charade?" I asked.

"Remember what had happened in that November of 1890? The rift in the Irish Party was healing and Parnell had been reelected its leader. Once more they were going to present a united front in Parliament and Lord Salisbury was faced with going to the country soon. Something needed to be done to discredit the moderates within Salisbury's Cabinet to bring them back 'on side' with the Unionists against any plans to give Ireland home rule to help them remain in power."

"But to kill a Cardinal . . ."

". . . having enticed him from Paris to this country thinking he was going to meet with members of the Irish Nationalists," interposed Holmes.

". . . to deliberately kill a Cardinal to cause such alarms and . . . why, Holmes, it is diabolical."

"Unfortunately, my dear Watson, this becomes the nature of govern-

ments who maintain secret organizations that are not accountable to anyone. I was tried and found wanting, Watson. This case was my biggest singular failure."

"Oh come, Holmes, you could not have known . . ."

Holmes gave me a pitying look.

"You must take Moran's gibes and insults from whence they came. You could do no more," I assured him.

He looked at me with steely eyes.

"Oh yes I could. I told you about how important it is to pay attention to detail. From the start I committed the most inexcusable inattention to detail. Had I been more vigilant, I could have laid this crime at the right door. It is there in Moran's text, a fact made known to me right from the start and which I ignored."

I pondered over the text but could find no enlightenment.

"The visitor's cards, Watson. The mistake over the visitor's cards presented by the mysterious caller to the Cardinal."

"Mistake? Oh, you mean the name being T. W. Tone, the name of someone long dead? I didn't realize that it was a false name."

"The name was merely to confirm the notion that we were supposed to be dealing with Irish Republicans. No, it was not that. It was the harp device, which was also meant to lead us into thinking that it was presented by an Irish nationalist, being the Irish national symbol. The fact was that the harp was surmounted by a crown—that is the symbol of our colonial administration in Ireland. No nationalist could bear the sight of a crown above the harp. I should have realized it."

Holmes sat shaking his head for a while and then he continued:

"Place the case of Cardinal Tosca in your trunk, Watson. I don't want to hear about it ever again."

Even then I hesitated.

"Granted that Moran worked for some superior—have you, in retrospect, come to any conclusion as to who Moran's superior was? Who was the man who gave him the order and to whom he was writing his letter?"

Holmes was very serious as he glanced back at me.

"Yes, I know who he was. He died in the same year that Moran was arrested for the murder of Lord Maynooth's son. You recall that Moran died in police custody after his arrest? It was supposed to be a suicide. I realized that should have been questioned. But then I heard of the death

of . . ." He paused and sighed. "Moran's superior was a brilliant politician but a ruthless one. He, more than most, reawakened the Orange hatreds against the Catholic Irish in order to maintain the Union."

"He was a member of the government?" I cried, aghast.

"He had been until just prior to this event but he was still influential."

"And this code name 'Wolf Shield'? You were able to tell who it was by that?"

"That part was simple. The name, sounding so Anglo-Saxon, I simply translated "Wolf Shield" back into Anglo-Saxon and the man's name became immediately recognizable. But let him now rest where his prejudices cannot lacerate his judgment any more."

In deference to my old friend's wishes, I have kept these papers safely, appending this brief note of how they fell into my hands. It was Holmes, with his biting sense of humor, who suggested I file it as "A Study in Orange," being his way of gentle rebuke for what he deemed as my melodramatic title of the first case of his with which I was involved. With this note, I have placed Moran's manuscript into my traveling box, which is now deposited in my bank at Charing Cross. I have agreed with Holmes's instructions that my executors should not open it until at least fifty years have passed from the dates of our demise.

The one thing that I have not placed here is the name of Moran's superior, but that which anyone with knowledge of Anglo-Saxon personal names could reveal.

THE SECOND MRS. WATSON

I find from my notebook that it was in January 1903, just after the conclusion of the Boer War, that I had my visit from Mr. James M. Dodd, a big, fresh, sunburned, upstanding Briton. The good Watson had at that time deserted me for a wife, the only selfish action which I can recall in our association. I was alone.

—"The Adventure of the Blanched Soldier"

by MICHAEL MALLORY

The Riddle of the Young Protestor

"Mum, a coach has stopped outside, and a man is getting out," our maid Missy announced, as she peered through the curtains of the front window. Coaches—as opposed to hansoms, growlers, or those new motorized, double-decked monstrosities—are somewhat rare in our street, which is a respectable, but hardly opulent, neighborhood of northwest London. "He's coming to the door!" Missy cried, excitedly.

Her excitement having fueled my own curiosity, I stepped to the window to watch with her. Of the man in question, I could see nothing, though stopped at the curb was a stylish deep green phaeton drawn by two magnificent horses, which were kept in rein by a stern-looking, high-hatted driver.

I was not expecting anyone this morning, and if the visitor was looking for my husband, Dr. John H. Watson, he was destined for disappointment. John was off on another of his lecture tours, this one through Scotland. According to his last letter, even the dour Scots were devouring the recountings of his long association with his erratic friend Sherlock Holmes. John had been taking his increasingly flamboyant tales of his life with the great detective to the masses for nearly six months, and the public's appetite for all things Holmes seemed insatiable. I daresay that the only place in the Empire where the litany of Holmes, Holmes, Holmes, Holmes, Holmes had worn out its welcome was right here at 17 Queen Anne Street. But I do not intend to spoil a perfectly good day with ruminations about Sherlock Holmes.

A rapid knocking was heard at the door, and Missy sprang away to answer it. I confess that I was equally interested in seeing who our mysterious visitor might be, though I was in no way prepared for the revelation.

Missy led the man into the dayroom. He was of middle age and diminutive—barely five feet tall, if even that—and dressed in a fine pearl gray suit with matching gloves and homburg hat. Once the hat was doffed, I could see that his dark hair was oiled and neatly parted in the middle. He regarded me with an air of upper-class superiority that would have carried to the furthest balcony of an opera house.

"This gentleman is here to see you, mum," Missy said, with as much propriety as she could muster.

Once the shock at the man's appearance had subsided, I began to laugh. "Harry!" I cried.

"Hello, ducks!" he said, a broad, lopsided grin spreading over his elfin face. "Never expected to see ol' Harry all toffed up like some bloomin' duke, did you, my girl?"

Harry's sudden transformation from upper-class dandy to Cockney jester left Missy clearly taken aback. I came to her rescue. "Missy, I know you have heard me speak of my friend Harry Benbow. More years ago than I care to remember, he and I were on the stage with the Delancey Amateur Players. Harry was the company comedian, while I was an ingénue. Harry, this is our maid, Missy."

"Hello, love," Harry said to her, waggling his eyebrows. "How about gettin' ol' Harry a cup o' water, my girl? I ain't had a chance to stop for my mornin' pint today, so I've worked up a thirst."

Missy retired to the kitchen to get the water.

"Sit down, Harry," I offered.

"Like to, ducks, but I don't have much time," he said. "The coachman won't wait forever."

"I hope you at least have enough time to explain this entrance and that outfit." The last time I saw Harry he had been in considerably more modest circumstances, and was busking for coins in Victoria Station. "Have you discovered buried treasure?"

"Funny you should say that," he replied, as Missy returned with the water, which he downed in one gulp, and handed back the glass. "You are now looking at Havilland Beaumont, Esquire, expert in antiques."

"Is this a joke, Harry?"

"Not a bit of it. See, long 'bout a month ago, I was mindin' my own business, makin' a bob wearin' a sandwich sign for this new coffee shop down in Covent Garden. As I was walkin' around the garden, takin' in the booths and whatnot, I see this table with a set o' old dishes that were dead ringers for the ones my granny used to have. Her proudest possessions, they was. Then I see that this cove is callin' 'em antiques and sellin' 'em for nine prices. First chance I get, I crawl out o' my sign and have a look at 'em, and as I'm lookin' the cove starts givin' me all kinds of rabbit-and-pork about when they were made, who made 'em, and where—only he's got it all wrong. So I start repeatin' what my granny used to tell me about 'em, and before you can say Bob's-your-Uncle, he starts askin' how 'tis that I know so much about antique plates. So, ducks, what am I supposed to say? That I'm just a bloke whose dear ol' gran learned him about plates, and thank you very much for not callin' the peelers on me, guv? Not on your nellie. So I says, 'Well, sir, I got this twin brother who's a downright expert on antiques—' "

"Oh, Harry, you didn't!" I interrupted.

"I didn't think it would hurt nothing. But then the cove starts humming and hemming, and before you know it, he hands me a card and says to go tell my brother to show up at an antiques shop in Mayfair that's run by a friend o' his. So I leave my sandwich sign right where sits and run over to the Hammersmith Theatre, where the doorman's a mate, and he lets me into the costume room. I walk in there as plain ol' Harry Benbow, and walk out as Havilland Beaumont, Esquire."

As he spoke the last three words, Harry appeared to grow two full inches in height, and his natural Cockney accent disappeared so completely into the proper tones of an upper-class gentleman that he could have fooled a Member of Parliament. Whatever else Harry Benbow might or might not be, he was a first-rate actor.

"I rushed over to the address the cove'd given me," he went on, "and next thing I know, I'm bein' taken on as a consultant by the right honorable firm of Edward Chippenham and Company, dealer in matters antiquarian." He spoke the last word as if practicing its pronunciation. "I had to return the costume to the theater, of course, but with all the bees-and-honey they're payin' me just to show up, I went out and got one o' my own!" He raised his arms and spun around, displaying the outfit proudly. "Matchin' turtles and titfer to boot!" he added, holding up his gloves and hat. "And I get to use the boss's coach whenever I need to."

"And so you have come here to preen like a peacock, is that it, Harry?"

"*Gor,* Amelia, I wish it was as simple as that. I don't mind tellin' you I've really put a foot in it this time."

This was hardly a surprise, since every time I saw Harry, he was in some kind of trouble. "What have you done now, Harry?"

"Well, everything was goin' swimmin' until this woman came into the shop with this old family document that she wanted to know all about, and Mr. Chippenham himself puts me on the job. Now both of them and her are expecting me to figure this thing out, and I can't make tops-or-tails out of it! Well, I sat down and said to myself, 'Harry, if there's anyone who can dig me out o' this hole, it's your friend Amelia's pal Sherlock Holmes.' So here I am. Let's go see the ol' boy. I can take you in the coach."

I tried not to bristle. "Mr. Holmes has moved out of Baker Street and I have no way of contacting him," I said quickly. "I'm sorry."

In strictest terms, that was the truth. Mr. Holmes had indeed left 221B Baker Street not long after John had abdicated his position as the great detective's live-in biographer, preferring to become my husband. It was a move that Mr. Holmes continued to view as an act of desertion. It was equally true that I could not immediately put anyone in contact with Mr. Holmes, though what I was holding back from Harry was that I might have been able to locate him through his brother in Whitehall, Mycroft, with whom I had, strangely enough, developed a cordial acquaintance over the past year. But I was still too angry to even consider it.

Neither had I any intention of informing Harry about the incident that had taken place in our home not a week prior, only a day or two after John had left on his tour. I was returning home from a visit to the lending library, and I knew Missy to be out shopping. Yet when I arrived at our home, I found the front door unlocked! Thinking that perhaps Missy had returned early, or had forgotten something, I threw caution away and strode in. "Missy?" I called, but she did not answer. Entering our rooms, I noticed the door to John's and my bedroom ajar, and started for it. "Missy, why are you cleaning today? You are supposed to be—"

The shock I experienced at beholding Mr. Sherlock Holmes, inside my bedroom, gazing into my mirror, bedecked in my best green velveteen dress, is difficult, if not impossible, to communicate. After I emitted a gasp that sounded more like a shriek, Mr. Holmes turned casually toward me. "Mrs. Watson, how are you?" he asked, calmly.

"Mr. Holmes . . . what . . . how . . ." I stammered. "How did . . . did Missy let you in?"

"Your girl was nowhere to be found," he replied. "But even if she were here, it would make little difference. I have a key."

"You have a *what*?" I cried.

He fished through the pocket of his trousers, which had been carelessly thrown across our bed and withdrew a key, which he held up. "The good Watson gave it to me, and offered me use of your home whenever I needed it."

Oh, this was too much! I would definitely be having words with John about this. But my thoughts were immediately wrenched away by the sound of seams ripping. "My dress!" I cried. "Why? . . ."

"You know that my work sometimes necessitates a disguise, and occasionally, expedience dictates that the most effective disguise is that of a woman," he said, once more looking into the glass and adjusting the shoulders of the dress. "I can hardly be expected to walk into the nearest couturier and try on the new Paris fashions. Fortune has it that the combination of your tallness and my leanness means that garments made for you are destined to likewise fit me, particularly if I crouch."

"But couldn't you at least ask *me* first?"

"If time were not of the essence, I would not have come here in this way. I beg of you to step out of the room, Mrs. Watson, for I must change back into my regular clothes, and your continued presence will do nothing but ensure that you become more knowledgeable about my private physical characteristics than any member of your sex, save my mother."

My jaw dropped and I fear my face flushed, and I was unable to utter a word. Silently, though inwardly seething, I stepped into the dayroom, slamming the bedroom door behind me.

I was still angrily pacing when Mr. Holmes emerged a few minutes later, my good dress wrapped about his arm like a rag, and without so much as a nod, headed for the door. "This is *intolerable!*" I shouted, trotting behind him.

Stopping, he turned to face me. The excitement that flared in his piercing gray eyes warred with his expression of grim determination. "So is crime, Mrs. Watson," he said, quietly, and left.

I had not seen or heard from Mr. Holmes since that day, nor did I wish to—except to guarantee the safe return of my velveteen dress. But enough of Sherlock Holmes; I had to deal presently with Harry Benbow.

"Gor," Harry was muttering, dejectedly. His disappointment over losing the counsel of Sherlock Holmes, however, was short-lived. Within seconds,

his face broke into a broad smile again. "That's all right, Amelia," he said, jauntily. "Who needs Sherlock Holmes anyway? You can help my client instead."

"*Me?* Harry, I'm not—"

"There you go again, my girl, selling yourself short," he *tsk-tsked*. "I know how many problems you've solved for people all on your own. *Gor,* Amelia, if it weren't for you, I might still be singin' myself to sleep each night in the clink, 'cause o' that nasty business with those two little tykes."

In the previous year, I had managed to help rescue Harry from gaol when he had been accused of kidnapping, but that had been done as a friend. I hardly considered myself a detective, for consultation or otherwise. That, however, did not stop Harry.

"Why, if I didn't know better, I'd say you were Sherlock Holmes's longlost cousin."

"*Please,* Harry," I groaned. "Having him for an acquaintance is challenge enough. But honestly, I know nothing about antiques."

"You don't have to know anything about antiques," he said. "It's an old document with some kind of poem or nursery rhyme on it. The lady who brought it in calls it a riddle. So it ain't the document that's valuable, it's the words that are on it."

"The words?"

"Right. An' if I know you, you'll be able to come up with the answer to this riddle faster 'n you can unlock a door lock with a horseshoe nail. Not that I'd know how to do that, o' course."

"Of course," I said, with a smile. "Well, I suppose it would do no harm to look—"

"That's the girl!" he cried, clapping his hands together. "Now, you just leave everything to me, I'll set the whole thing up, don't you worry about a thing."

After doing another little dance, he flipped his hat through the air and deftly caught it on his head, and reached for the doorknob. "Got to go now, ducks." Then, once more affecting the high-born accent, he added: "I shall be in touch, my deah," and disappeared from the room.

Still reeling from the sudden appearance of Harry, I did not realize that Missy had reentered the room until she said: "You know some of the most interesting people, mum."

"Don't I, though?" I muttered.

She stepped back to the window to watch the coach drive off. "What did he want?"

"One can never be quite sure where Mr. Benbow is concerned, dear, though I am certain I will find shortly find out."

I did indeed find out two days later when the phaeton arrived once more in front of our home, and this time the driver knocked on the door and handed Missy a note that read: *Amelia, put on your best jewels and go with the driver. HB.* "My best jewels?" I wondered aloud. With equal parts of curiosity and foreboding, I retired to my bedroom, emerging a few minutes later, adorned with a string of pearls and matching earrings, I followed the driver outside to the coach and rode to the exact destination I had expected, the Mayfair shop of Edward Chippenham and Co.

Harry greeted me at the door. "So good of you to come," he intoned, punctuating his words with a wink. Leading me through the shop, which was heavily populated with staff, but surprisingly barren of actual items for sale, we ended up in a plush, paneled meeting room in the back. There, seated at a long, highly polished, table was a pleasant-looking young woman—almost a girl, really—who rose and smiled self-consciously as I entered. Closing the door behind us, Harry gestured toward the woman and said: "This is Mrs. Jane Ramsay. Mrs. Ramsay, this is our documents expert, Lady Amelia Pettigrew."

Lady Amelia Pettigrew? I struggled to keep my mouth from flying open at the news of my admittance into the peerage. It was true that I was born Amelia Pettigrew, and I like believe that I am a lady at all times, but only Harry Benbow could take such simple truths and twist them into such a massive deceit.

"Please do be seated, Lady Pettigrew," he bid me in his faux Mayfair accent.

"Thank you," I said through clenched teeth, taking a seat opposite the young woman.

"Thank you for agreeing to help me, Lady Pettigrew," Mrs. Ramsay said. "Mr. Beaumont told me that you would be able to answer all of my questions. I hope you can."

"As do I, my dear," I replied, casting a sidelong glance at Harry.

From a small handbag, Mrs. Ramsay produced what appeared to be a letter-sized piece of vellum, which she laid it on the table in front of me. On it, in fading, archaic letters, was written a most peculiar verse:

In the place where Earl and Queen both neale,
Befor the blesing of St. Andrews cross,
Where Lion meets the Mercer shal reveal
A relick of the young Protestors loss.
Upper Tower
Riseing Dudley
Slopeing King
And Castle do surounde
The time at which the relick maye be founde.

"What can you tell me about it?" she asked, eagerly.

"I can tell you that whoever wrote it could not spell," I replied. "Where did this come from?"

"Charles, my husband, refers to this simply as 'the riddle.' Apparently it has been in his family for years and years, handed down from one generation to another for as long as anyone can remember, yet its meaning remains unknown. I am taking something of a chance by bringing it here, but I merely wish to surprise him."

"Surprise him how?" I asked.

"By finding the solution to the riddle. You see, Charles and I have been married only a short time. He is considerably older than I, and . . . well, he is not the easiest man to live with. But I do so want to please him. In the short time we have been together, I have heard him speak of this riddle with almost a sense of reverence, but he continues to puzzle over its meaning. It is not much of an exaggeration to say that this scrap of parchment is the most important thing in his life. It is my hope that by finding the solution, I will be able to make him happy."

The poor girl was so young, so innocent, so sincere in her desires, that I had to wonder exactly what kind of marriage it was.

I read over the riddle again. Harry was absolutely right; it did read like a nursery rhyme. A lost verse of Mother Goose, perhaps?

"There is one more thing you should know, Lady Pettigrew," Mrs. Ramsay went on. "There is a reason that this rhyme is so important within the family. I know this will sound quite fanciful, but the 'relick' referred to in the verse is thought to be some kind of lost treasure. In fact, it is my belief that Charles views this document as some kind of treasure map."

I looked up at her, and then over at Harry, whose lips were pursed in a wry smile. "A treasure map," I mused. "That is how your husband described this document to you?"

"Actually, no, not in so many words. The truth is, Lady Pettigrew, Charles has never brought it up directly or spoken of it with me in any context. But I have overheard him talking with Mary, his daughter through his first marriage."

"And have you spoken directly with her regarding this?"

The woman appeared suddenly discomfited. "I am afraid that Mary and I have yet to become friends. She is only a couple of years younger than I am, you see, and quite headstrong."

"I take it that the first Mrs. Ramsay is no longer alive?"

"Of course not. Charles is a strict Catholic, Lady Pettigrew, and as you know, the Church does not countenance divorce. I would not be his wife unless his first wife was dead. Perhaps it is the fact that I am Mary's replacement mother that has erected the barrier between her and me—I don't know. But I do hope you will be able to advise me, even though I cannot afford to pay you much for your time."

"Not to worry, Mrs. Ramsay," Harry interrupted. "We work on commission."

I had to admit that this peculiar rhyme and this tale of hidden treasure had captivated my interest—as I am certain Harry knew it would. I asked if I could keep the vellum and Mrs. Ramsay once more showed signs of discomfort.

"I suppose that would be all right," she said, "but Charles does not know that I have taken it. It would hardly be a surprise if he had known, after all. So please, Lady Pettigrew, take care that nothing happens to it. I would not want Charles to be cross."

My heart went out to the poor girl. How difficult was her situation at home? Perhaps I could say something to make her feel a bit more at ease.

"I shall take every precaution," I assured her. "And I hope you will not think me untoward by telling you this, my dear, but I can empathize somewhat with your situation. I am likewise my husband's second wife."

"Then you must know what it is like," she blurted out. "Forgive me, Lady Pettigrew, I don't presume to compare my situation to yours, but do you sometimes feel as though you are living in the shadow of your husband's former wife?"

"There is nothing to forgive, my dear," I said, "and yes, I often feel the

presence of the one with whom my husband had previously shared his life."
And occasionally, John also speaks of his first wife, Mary, I thought, but held
my tongue.

The young woman smiled. "Oh, you have no idea how much better it
makes me feel to know that my situation is not unique. Thank you, Lady
Pettigrew." She rose and offered her hand, which I took. Then Harry
escorted her out of the room. When he returned, he looked like a kid who
had just won ownership of a candy shop in a sweepstakes. "Well, Amelia,
what d'you think?"

"Frankly, Harry, I feel slightly criminal presenting myself to the poor
girl as something I am not. Lady Pettigrew, indeed!"

"Nonsense, ducks, just look at how much better you made her feel by
talkin' to her."

"I suppose so," I acknowledged. "But I have no idea if I can actually
help her." I glanced at the piece of vellum again. "The only lines that make
any kind sense are those in the last part of the verse. The references to
Tower, Dudley, King and Castle seem to point to young Lord Dudley, the
husband of Lady Jane Grey."

"Lord and Lady Who?"

"Lady Jane Grey was an unfortunate teenaged girl who got caught up in
the political and religious machinations of Lord Dudley's father, Northumberland, who was an advisor to Edward the . . . Sixth, was it? Yes, the
Sixth . . . who was himself a mere boy. As a result, Lady Jane was proclaimed Queen of England. This was before the time of Elizabeth, before
any woman had actually been crowned as sovereign, so the idea was still
somewhat novel. But the plot fell to pieces when Bloody Mary, the eldest
daughter of Henry the Eighth, ascended to the throne. Both Lady Jane and
Dudley were arrested as traitors, imprisoned in the Tower of London, and
executed."

Harry looked confused. "I must've missed that day o' school."

I smiled. "This comes not so much from school, Harry, as from my
years as a governess. History was always my favorite subject, next to literature. Perhaps one day I shall take you on as a pupil."

"So, is that it, then? The riddle's about this Dudley Grey bloke?"

"I do not know, Harry. Some of the references seem to fit, but others do
not. 'Castle' is clear enough—whatever else the Tower of London may be,
it is first and foremost a castle. 'Upper Tower' would seem to refer to the
place where the prisoners would have been lodged. And 'Riseing Dudley' is

likely the young lord, who nearly rose to the status of prince. It would be logical to assume that 'King' is a reference to Edward the Sixth, though why he should be 'Slopeing' is anyone's guess, unless there is an archaic meaning to the word. 'Queen' could signify either Lady Jane or Mary, though 'Earl' is puzzling. It might mean Northumberland, though if memory serves, he was a duke, not an earl. As for the references to 'St. Andrew,' 'Lion' and 'the Mercer,' I'm afraid I haven't a clue."

"But you'll get it, ducks," Harry said, giving me a wink. "I 'ave complete confidence in you."

I sighed. Harry was perhaps my oldest friend, and I was loath to hurt or disappoint him in any way, but inwardly, I prayed that this latest scheme of his would not lead to trouble.

Harry was able to secure the services of the phaeton to take me back home. Once there, I pulled down from our shelf an old book of English history and began to pore over it, hoping that a clue might leap out from the pages to help identify the references in the riddle. Yet the more I read, the more mysterious the lines became.

One of the phrases that continued to puzzle me was "the young Protestor," which implied a figure who was actively fighting against a reigning monarch, perhaps even a usurper. Neither Lord Dudley nor Lady Jane fitted that description, since others attempted the usurpation on their unwitting behalf. The reference to "Lion" might stand for England itself, though "the Mercer" made little sense. Could it be a name? I glanced through the index of the book to see if I could find any notable personages named "Mercer." I found none, though several entries down I came across a name that sent a bolt of realization through my mind: *Monmouth*.

I quickly turned to the pages indicated and skimmed down the history, augmenting what I already knew about the failed attempt to usurp the throne from James II. In 1685, the Duke of Monmouth, the illegitimate son of Charles II, had staged an uprising against James that was as much a Holy War as a battle over the throne, with James on the one side holding strong Catholic sympathies, while the rebellious Duke championed the Protestant cause. The Monmouth rebellion was quickly quelled and the Duke was tried and executed. This appeared to satisfy the riddle's phrase "the young Protestors loss" far more than did the story of Lady Jane Grey. The association with Monmouth also gave new significance to the fact that 'Protestors' was capitalized—not only did it mean one who was protesting the reigning monarch's right to the throne, but one who was a *Protestant*.

What's more, the reference to "St. Andrews cross," which was the symbol of Scotland, could now be seen as representing James II, who was also King of the Scots. But then, what of "Dudley"? How on earth did he fit into the Monmouth rebellion?

After another hour or so of fruitless research, with little to show for the effort except tired eyes and a headache, I decided to put the riddle to rest for the evening.

The next morning, after dressing and breakfasting, feeling quite refreshed, I picked up the vellum once more and resumed work on it, but quickly came to the same stone wall of confusion. It was becoming clear my best course of action was to seek the assistance of a professional scholar.

After informing Missy that I was going out, I stepped out into a sunny and comfortably temperate autumn day, and embarked on a very pleasant walk past shouting news vendors and pungent fish shops, down to Oxford Street, where I caught the bus and rode it nearly to the impressive doorstep of my destination, the British Museum. Hurrying inside, along with a throng of other Londoners, I went straight to the reading room, located in the building's enormous rotunda, and looked around until I located a gaunt, white-haired man whose stooped frame and thick spectacles bespoke of a lifetime spent among the volumes. From my previous visits, I knew that he was a member of the library's staff, though I had never discovered his name. He was, however, so much a fixture of the reading room that I would not have been surprised to learn that, instead of retreating to his home at day's end, he nightly shelved himself along with the books.

Edging close to him, I whispered: "Pardon me, but I need some assistance."

He slowly turned my way. "Yes?"

"I need to find some information about Monmouth."

"Oh, yes, Monmouth," he said slowly, savoring the words. "Are you interested in the Duke or the street?"

"The Duke. I doubt the street would help me."

"Quite so," the librarian sniffed. "Please follow me."

He led me to one particular shelf, where I saw in nearly a dozen volumes devoted solely to the Duke and his imprint upon history. Almost without looking, he selected two volumes in particular, slid them off the shelf, and deposited them in my hands. "These would be the best from which to begin," he said.

I groaned inwardly as I glanced at the remaining volumes, knowing that it would take a fortnight to comb each book for clues. But dutifully I carried the first two tomes to the nearest desk, while the librarian disappeared into the maze of shelves.

After an hour's worth of reading, I had gained no more insight than that with which I had walked in, except for the discovery that one of my favorite aromas in life, the delicate but unmistakable scent of printed pages in a book, managed to antagonize my nose when the pages in question were aged and dusty enough. I sneezed and snapped the book shut at the same time. This was futile. Perhaps I would have been better off dousing my anger at Mr. Holmes long enough to throw this infernal conundrum onto his plate, like Harry had requested in the first place.

"How are we doing?" a voice behind me asked, and I turned to see that my friend, the librarian, had returned.

"Not well," I admitted. "Perhaps I should have asked for the street after all."

"Hmmp," he snorted. "I do not even understand why they would give a street a name so connected to a known traitor. There was really no need to change it. I can see nothing wrong with the name St. Andrews Street. But that, it seems, is the foundation upon which this August city is built: continual change, and most of it merely for the sake of change. If you are interested in this, I could direct you to a copy of *Vanished London.*"

He looked at me as though awaiting a response, but I could form none. Had I heard correctly? "I'm sorry, but would you repeat that?" I finally managed.

"I was suggesting the book *Vanished London,* a capital collection of photographs taken of buildings and landmarks right before they were demolished."

"No, I mean about Monmouth Street and St. Andrews Street."

"Oh, that," he sniffed. "Simply that the thoroughfare now known as Monmouth Street was once called St. Andrews Street. I thought *everybody* knew that."

"Oh," I uttered, raising a hand to my head. All this time I had been taking of the phrase *St. Andrews cross* in the riddle to mean a representation of the actual cross upon which the saint had been martyred. But what if was not a religious cross at all? What if it signified one street crossing another? Heavens, could it be that the riddle was literally a road map that pointed the way to its secret?

"Madam, are you unwell?" the librarian asked.

"What? No, I am fine, thank you," I quickly replied, "but would you happen to have a map showing the street when it was called St. Andrews?"

"I am positive we do," he said. "We pride ourselves here that, given enough time, we can produce anything." He disappeared into a back room and returned some ten minutes later, proving himself to be as good as his word. "Here we are," he said, holding a folded map of the city of London. "This is dated a mere forty-five years ago, but it is already a repository of obsolete information. I believe you will find what you are seeking here."

Carrying the map to a nearby table, he carefully unfolded and examined it, his bony finger poised and hovering over a section in the middle. "Ah, there we are," he said, dropping his finger on a particular spot. As I examined it, my heart leapt.

After questioning the librarian some more, and making notes of the details of the map, I headed back home. There I telephoned Harry at the offices of Chippenham and Co.

"I have it!" I shouted into the telephone box, a device I normally loathe, but one that, at times, does prove convenient. "I've solved the riddle!"

"*Gor* . . . I mean, *my word,* it didn't take you long."

"Honestly, Harry, it came about as much from chance as anything. But I have it."

I looked down at the sketch I had made from the map, the one that depicted St. Andrews Street crossing not only Earl and Queen Streets, but also Mercer Street, where it met its northwesterly extension, White Lion Street. This series of crossings was completely encased by a diamond made up of Tower Street, which moved upward to Dudley, which in turn rose to King Street, which sloped back down to Castle Street. "The words of the rhyme were all London street names, Harry, pinpointing the last place anyone would look for wealth. The are the streets leading to and surrounding *Seven Dials.*"

"Seven Dials? *Blimey!*" he cried, then caught himself, presumably for the benefit of anyone else at the offices of Edward Chippenham and Co., who might be within listening range. "Uh, I mean, do tell, Lady Pettigrew," he uttered in high English.

I continued describing the clues I had found on the map, still marveling at both the solution to the riddle, and the cleverness of its creator. Seven Dials was the area immediately surrounding the convergence of seven streets into a hub, which at one time was marked by a tall column containing seven sundial faces—hence its name. It had originally been an attempt at creating a fashionable neighborhood, but it rapidly fell into disrepair, and eventually became one of the worst and most crime-ridden slums the city ever had. Recent attempts to rehabilitate the area had helped, but it was still a place to be avoided after dark.

"The most significant clue of the entire riddle," I told Harry, "was the one we completely ignored: the word 'neale,' which I took to be a misspelling. But the man who laid out Seven Dials in the late 1600s was named Thomas *Neale*."

"And there's been a treasure hidden under the bloomin' rookery ever since," he mused. "All this time and no one ever knew."

"That gets into the most fascinating part, Harry. According to the librarian at the British Museum, the column was torn down by a mob in the 1770s because of the rumor that a treasure was buried underneath it. It seems probably that the source of that rumor was the riddle, which helps confirm that it is indeed as old as Mrs. Ramsay states."

"*Gor,*" Harry said again, and this time he did not even bother to correct himself. "Did they find anything when they toppled it?"

"History says no. What's more, the pieces of the column were later taken to Surrey and reassembled about a hundred years later. If anything had been hidden within the stones themselves, it surely would have been discovered already."

"So it's just a fairy tale after all?"

"Not necessarily. My friend at the museum also happened to mention that, in addition to the seven sundials on top, the column itself acted as a gigantic sundial, casting shadows over the neighboring buildings that served to chart the time of day. And what does the riddle say? That 'the time' at which the relic shall be found would be revealed? I believe that something was buried in Seven Dials, and that it was deliberately placed at a specific 'time,' as reflected by the shadow of the column. If we knew what the precise time was, we might be able to pinpoint the location. It would certainly not be easy, since the column is no longer there, but it could be done through mathematical calculations."

"Amelia, you're a blinkin' genius!" Harry crowed. "Mrs. Ramsay is goin' to be flyin' over the moon when she hears this. I'll give her a shout right now! I want you to be the one to give her the news, so I'll let you know when to come. Better yet, I'll send the coach 'round again. *Gor* bless you, ducks!"

The line quickly went dead. After replacing the receiver of the wretched device, I once again studied the riddle. There could be little doubt that the solution I had derived was the correct one. The fact that all the names mentioned in the riddle corresponded perfectly with the streets of Seven Dials could not be a coincidence. The timing also made sense. The column had been erected in 1694, a mere nine years after the Monmouth Rebellion. Perhaps the 'relick' had been kept in a temporary hiding place during the interim, and then its holders decided to secret it in a more permanent location. Burying it in Seven Dials must have been a simple matter, given the construction that was taking place in the area at that time. The only lack of foresight on the part of the riddle's composer were the assumptions that the column would remain standing forever and the street names would never change.

It all made such perfect sense. Even Mr. Holmes would have had to agree with that. Why, then, did I feel a tiny note of unease about my deduction, as though there were a serious flaw with the analysis that I could not identify? Perhaps I was simply thinking about it too much.

I resolved to set aside all thoughts of the riddle and picked up a book instead. This escapade of Harry's, while it had been intriguing, had put me grievously behind in my reading.

I had gotten through less than one chapter of *Our Mutual Friend,* by my favorite author, Mr. Dickens, when the annoying jangle of the telephone shook me out of my peaceful concentration. Rising from my chair, I marched over to thing and barked into it: "Yes, hello."

It was Harry. "Amelia, Mrs. Ramsay's gone."

"Gone? Where?"

"I don't know. I tried to ring her up at the number she gave me, and ask her to come down to the shop, but she wasn't there. Instead I got some girl told me Mrs. Ramsay's went away somewhere, but she don't know where."

The daughter, Mary, no doubt.

"Why would she leave like that without telling anyone?"

"I'm thinkin', maybe she didn't," Harry said, grimly.

"What on earth do you mean?"

"Well, this girl starts askin' me who I am, and what I wanted with Mrs. Ramsay, and when I identifies myself—at least who I'm pretendin' to be—

she gets all a'dither, and starts askin' things like whether I have the riddle on me, and where the shop is. Then she says I had no right to take that piece o' parchment from the family, like I'd stolen the bloomin' thing!"

"I don't like the way this is sounding, Harry. Why don't you come over here, just in case the girls raises some kind of trouble at the shop?"

"Right, ducks, I'll be over in two shakes."

Once again, the line went dead.

At that moment, Missy came into the room, and only when I saw that she was dressed in her personal clothes did I remember that I had promised her the evening off, with the suggestion that she attend a new play at a theater in Leicester Square. I knew, of course, that she would instead end up at the music hall, but it mattered little. She was a devoted worker and deserved a night out, even if her taste in entertainment ran the gamut from low to positively philistine. Such, I fear, is the mark of today's youth.

"Do you need anything before I go, mum?" she asked, clearly eager to be on her way.

"No, dear. Enjoy yourself, but do not stay out too late."

"Right, mum," she said, breezing through the door.

I began collecting up my notes and put them, along with the vellum page, into a neat stack on the dayroom table. It was then, amidst the complete quiet that had descended upon the house, that the flaw in my reasoning regarding the riddle's solution, which had been dancing elusively at the edges of my mind, taunting me, came into clear focus. My identification of the Duke of Monmouth as "the young Protestor," combined with the chance discovery that the present-day Monmouth Street was once named St. Andrews Street, was the key that had unlocked the riddle—but how was the writer of the riddle able to look two centuries into the future and know that St. Andrews Street was going to be renamed for the Duke?

Was it merely coincidence? Divine revelation? Was the writer of the riddle some kind of seer, a Restoration version of Nostradamus? Or was the riddle itself a clever modern forgery? For all I knew of the process of dating paper and ink, the lines could have been penned a fortnight ago, drawn from an ancient legend. But a forgery to what end? It appeared that the riddle of Seven Dials had not yet given up all of its secrets.

I stepped to the window. The sky was beginning to darken. Harry should be here soon, I thought. But an hour passed and I was still awaiting his arrival. Where on earth was he? After another anxious hour, my state of nervousness and impatience had become so great that I nearly jumped bodily out of my chair when the sharp knocking came to the door. Finally, Harry had arrived. "Missy, the door," I called, and then remembered that she had gone. Stepping to the front door, I swung it open, only to find that it was not my diminutive friend standing there, but rather a tall, distinguished looking man of indeterminate middle age.

"I'm from Chippenham's, madam," he said. "The coach is waiting out front." It was not the same driver who had come previously.

"Really? I take it, then, that Mrs. Ramsay arrived at the shop."

"Yes, madam, she is there now. I will take you there."

"Let me get a wrap first," I said, leaving the man at the door while I went back inside.

"And madam, I'm to make sure that you do not forget to bring the riddle with you," he called.

"Thank you," I called back, throwing on a jacket. Then, after stopping to pick up the stack of papers from the table, I headed back to the door. Once outside the man led me to a common hansom cab. "What happened to the phaeton?" I asked.

"In use, madam. Mr. Benbow arranged for this one."

"I see," I muttered, starting toward the cab. Then stopped suddenly, feeling a chill inside me. "Mr. Benbow arranged for this, you say?" I asked.

"Yes, ma'am. Is there a problem?

Indeed there was. I spun around and started back for the front door. "I think I shall go back and telephone Chippenham's to let them know I am on my way," I told the man.

"I think not," the man said, rushing to head me off. From his pocket he withdrew a small silver pistol.

"Who are you?" I demanded, striving for a defiant tone that was not supported by my emotions. "You are not from Chippenham's." Had the man in reality been an employee of the company, he would have referred to Harry as Mr. *Beaumont,* not Mr. *Benbow.*

"Your questions will be answered in due course," the man said. "For now, get in the cab."

"I could scream, you know."

"And I could shoot."

Deciding that reasoning with the brute was out of the question, as was any attempt at escaping, I had no choice but to do as he said. Stepping into the cab, I sat stiffly against the seat, feeling the barrel of his gun pressed into my side. He knocked on the roof of the cab and it lurched into action.

"Give me the riddle, if you please," he said, holding out his free hand, into which I placed the papers, including the vellum. He quickly shoved them into his coat pocket.

"Where are you taking me?" I asked.

"To my castle," he replied.

"Your castle?"

"Every man's home is his castle, don't you agree?"

It struck me then. "You are Charles Ramsay."

The man nodded in agreement.

"Where is your wife?"

"That stupid creature I honored with my family name?" he spat, his voice rising dangerously. "You will not be hearing from her again."

"What have you done with her?" I asked, feeling chilled by more than the night air.

"She betrayed me, Mrs. Watson, and I am not a man with a stomach for betrayal. No doubt she sobbed on your shoulder about me, told you that I was some kind of cold and heartless beast. I have reasons for my actions, just as I have certain established certain rules governing my home. The most important rule is that what is mine is not to be placed in the hands of others. That applies nowhere more strongly than to that piece of parchment she took from me and gave to you. Jane committed the unpardonable; she removed the riddle from the house without my knowledge and shared its information with others."

"She only wanted to make you happy," I said.

"I did not wed her for happiness, but for what she could give me. The common little fool never realized that."

I faced straight ahead as we careened through the narrow streets toward our destination. "What is going to happen to me?" I asked, my fear tempered with indignation.

"You possess knowledge that I require," he said. "After I have obtained that knowledge, you will have fulfilled your usefulness to me and will be discarded."

"Discarded?" I cried, indignantly.

He pushed the pistol deeper into my side. "Careful, madam. You would be wrong to assume that I will not shoot you if I have to, whether I have retrieved your information or not. Mr. Benbow has told me enough about the solution to the riddle to convince me that I could piece together the rest myself."

"Where is Harry?"

"He is safe. For the time being."

I glanced up at the ceiling, but the wretch beside me seemed to read my very thoughts. "Do not waste your time wondering if you could alert the driver," he said. "I have taken the liberty of telling him that you were mentally unstable. He has been instructed—and paid—to ignore whatever he might hear emanating from inside the cab."

We drove on in nerve-racking silence for another three-quarters of an hour, and then the cab began to slow. "Here we are," Ramsay said. "I appreciate the fact that you did not try to do anything foolish. A woman with common sense is a rare thing these days, Mrs. Watson, and I congratulate you."

"You may keep your congratulations to yourself!" I bristled.

My rising anger made Ramsay smile. Or perhaps it was my rising helplessness. "Now then," he said, "I will get out first, keeping the pistol trained on you, and then you will emerge slowly and walk beside me, straight to the door."

I remained silent as he stepped out of the cab and, hiding the pistol from the driver, paid for the ride. Then following his demands, I slowly stepped down and remained at his side. Together, we watched the cab disappear down the dark street, which was empty, except for the presence of another hansom that was stopped at the curb several houses down. I knew that any attempt to race down the street and alert the driver of that cab would meet with disaster.

Ramsay's "castle" turned out to be a modest brick dwelling in Lambeth, into which he ushered me. As soon as we were inside the house, I heard Harry's voice calling: "Amelia, are you all right?"

Another voice bellowed, "Shut up, you!" That was followed by the sound of a hard slap.

"Harry!" I shouted.

"He is in there," Ramsay said, nudging me with the pistol. "Go on."

I stepped into a comfortably furnished, though dimly lit, room. Harry Benbow was tied to a chair, his hair plastered against his forehead with perspiration. Standing over him was a young girl whose face bore a scowling expression, and who was looking at me with the most lifeless eyes I had ever seen.

"I'm sorry, Amelia," Harry moaned. "They forced me to tell 'em where to find you. I'm sorry for everything, ducks."

I directed my gaze back upon the girl. "You are Mary Ramsay, I presume."

The girl sneered.

"Mary, show some manners," Ramsay commanded, prompting her to perform a parody of a smile, one that revealed large, crooked teeth. "How d'you do?" she growled.

Ramsay pulled a chair to the center of the room and pushed me into it, and instructed the girl to tie me up as she had Harry. All the while he kept the pistol trained on me. Mary Ramsay carried out her task with deliberate roughness, and the ropes painfully chafed my wrists. "Must they be so tight?" I groaned to Ramsay.

"They must," he replied. "I am a not a man who can afford to take chances."

"You are not a man at all, you are *swine*," I riposted, but then cried out as the girl grabbed a handful of my hair and yanked it, wrenching my head backwards.

"I don't think you know who you're talking to," she said. "You should be down on the floor, scraping before your sovereign, the rightful King of England!"

Thankfully, she let go of my hair, and I rested my pained gaze upon Ramsay again. "You are the rightful King of England?"

He bowed. "As was my father, and his father, and every male member of my family since the time of William of Orange, the usurper who turned the country inexorably away from the True Church." He paced before me, taking slow, measured steps. "I am a direct lineal descendant of James the Second, the last Catholic King of the realm, and the last true monarch. Even though my family name is not to be found on any accepted genealogical chart, my descent from James is a fact."

"In other words, your ancestor was illegitimate," I said.

"I could tell right off he was a bastard," Harry added, then with an abashed glance to me, added: "Pardon my tongue, Amelia."

Poor Harry's misplaced concern with propriety in the face of such grave danger drew from me a helpless, mirthless chuckle. Unfortunately, the wretched girl behind me mistook my laughter as a comment on her father's statement, and grabbed my hair once more, giving my head a vicious twist.

"Mary!" Ramsay shouted. "How many times must I tell you: noblesse oblige." The girl let go.

I shook my aching head. "What do you want from me, *Your Majesty*?" I invested as much venom as possible into the last two words. If Ramsay took offense, he did not show it.

"The final answer to the riddle," he replied. "The exact location of the treasure."

"Why are you so certain there is a treasure?" I asked.

"Oh, it is there, Mrs. Watson. That which the riddle terms a 'relick' is actually the remainder of the fortune in gold and jewels that was raised to finance the Monmouth Rebellion. When the unfortunate duke lost his bid to become king—as well as his head—what was left of his war chest was secreted, with the knowledge that one day, the rightful monarch, the one destined by God to rule this empire, would rise up and retake the throne from the bloodline of pretenders. I am ready to fulfill that destiny, and the destiny of the True Church. That treasure will finance this ascension." He stopped and smiled. "Ironic, is it not? That the wealth that was gathered by a Protestant in an attempt to overthrow the last Catholic king will now be used to restore the status of the Catholic Church in the Empire?"

"Insane would be my description," I replied. "You cannot seriously believe that you will be crowned."

"I? Alas, no. Perhaps if one of my forebears had seen fit to accept his God-bestowed destiny, I might have been, but I have resigned myself to the likelihood that I will never sit on the throne of England. It is not for myself that I do this, Mrs. Watson, but rather for my son. Properly used and invested, the treasure could reap wealth beyond even my dreams, and with wealth comes power. Imagine, a male of royal blood being born into that kind of wealth and power. What could not that blessed boy accomplish?"

Suddenly I realized how this mad plot was hinged. "It is not simply the treasure that you are lacking, is it?" I said. "You do not have a son either, do you, Mr. Ramsay? That is the reason you married such a young woman, so you could breed a male heir. That was the thing she could give you."

"And it is the reason I will marry another young woman, and another after her, and another after her, if that is what it takes," Ramsay declared.

"I *will* have a son! I will not suffer the fates of James and the heretic Henry, with only daughters to carry on after me." He cast a contemptuous glance at Mary.

"And if they do not produce a son, you will kill them so you can marry again."

"What are a few individual lives compared to the restoration of the True Church?" he shouted. "The lives of those women mean nothing."

"How *dare* you purport to be a man of faith?" I spat. "You are sickening, a disgrace—"

"That is enough!" he thundered, quieting me. "I have no interest in wasting any more time on a debate whose outcome has already been decided. You have been very clever in solving the riddle, Mrs. Watson, I will give you that. While I am certain that I would have eventually been able to decipher it myself, you have saved me valuable time, and I am not ungrateful. But now I need the last piece of the puzzle." He knelt down before me, pushing his face close to mine, placing the barrel of the pistol against my heart. "Where is the treasure buried?"

"I . . . do not . . . know," I stammered, struggling to overcome my revulsion and fear. "Leave her be!" Harry cried out, prompting Mary to rushed over to his chair and viciously cuff him across the face.

"I do not know!" I shouted. "The solution to the riddle is Seven Dials, and I believe that at a certain time of the day the column of Seven Dials cast a shadow over the hiding place of the treasure, but what time, I do not know!"

Ramsay rose to his feet and backed away, and I was relieved to be spared the unpleasant heat of his breath. "I believe you, Mrs. Watson. You have convinced me that neither you nor Benbow have the information I seek. For me, that is a small setback. It does, however, mean that the two of you are no longer needed." He spun around to Harry and leveled the pistol at his chest. Harry's eyes widened and he struggled helplessly against his bounds. I turned my head away and closed my eyes. I could not watch. I waited for the dreadful sound of the bullet.

But instead of the shot, I heard another sound: a loud pounding on the door of the house. I opened my eyes to see Ramsay glance toward his daughter, who had started toward the door. "Ignore it, ignore it!" he demanded, raising the gun again. But the pounding continued, only now it came from two different directions.

"They're at the back, too!" Mary cried.

I heard a muffled cry that very nearly reduced me to tears of joy: *"Police, open up!"*

"*Gor,* the peelers!" Harry cried, jubilantly.

I dared not to even wonder why the police had chosen this particular time to descend upon the Ramsay house, for fear they might go away again!

Clearly as confused and frightened as they were angered by the development, Ramsay and Mary looked at each other, as though uncertain as to what to do next. A moment later we heard the splintering sound of a door being burst open, and a second after that, a half-dozen uniformed PC's entered the room, batons poised. In front of the brigade was a sergeant who trained his pistol on the stunned Ramsay and easily disarmed him. Mary was not so acquiescent. Fighting like a madwoman, she required the combined force of three constables to hold her. Despite everything, I could not bring myself to hate the wretched girl. She was a creature of her demented father's making, and as such probably never had a chance.

Another officer was working to untie Harry and I. My arms, when released, felt like molten lead. A bruise was forming on Harry's cheek, where Mary had struck him. When the situation was under control, the sergeant turned to me. "You must be Mrs. Watson," he said.

"Yes, but how on earth . . . how . . . ?" For one of the few times in my life, I was speechless.

"Come along outside, madam. You, too, sir," he beckoned to Harry.

As the constables were escorting both Ramsays to a police wagon, I overheard Charles Ramsay ranting to no one in particular: "This is not the end! I will have a son! If he be born in prison, so be it!" I shook my head, feeling an uneasy mix of pity and revulsion.

I was still puzzling over the perfectly timed arrival of the police when I looked up and saw something even more puzzling: there, before me, stood Sherlock Holmes! He trod over to where I was standing, the expression on his face a conflicting mixture of concern and something resembling embarrassment. For a brief moment, I thought he was going to reach out and lay a comforting hand on my arm, but if that was his inclination, he fought it. "I trust you are unharmed, Mrs. Watson?" he said, awkwardly.

"Barely," I gasped, feeling weak. "And I must assume that you are the means of my escape from the hands of a madman, but how on earth did you know where to find me? How did you even know I was in trouble?"

"I happened to arrive in front of your home in time to witness you being threatened by the man who was just placed into custody," he answered. "I could tell immediately that something was amiss by the tension and rigidity in your body. What's more, the man was standing far to close to you for this to be an innocent conversation. I secreted myself in the shadows and watched until I discerned a glint of metal from the man's hand, which I immediately recognized as the barrel of a pistol. After you were forced into the cab, I hailed one of my own and instructed the driver to follow you, which we did the entire way here."

"Then that was your cab I saw at the end of the street," I said.

"Yes. Once more I watched as you were forced to enter the house, and no sooner were you inside than I sent the driver to fetch the police while keeping watch outside. The constables quickly arrived, and the rest you know."

"Oh, Heaven help me," I moaned, now fearing I might collapse. The only thing that kept me upright was my refusal to faint away in a womanish swoon in front of Mr. Holmes.

"Perhaps Heaven already has," he uttered. "While I am not a fervent believer in the hand of Providence interfering with the affairs of mortals, I have to question whether the influence of a mightier force was not involved in placing me at right place at exactly the right time to facilitate your delivery."

"Mr. Holmes, don't tell me you believe you were directed to Queen Anne Street by the will of God!" I said, startled the admission.

"It is only the timing that gives me pause for thought," the detective replied. Then, lowering his voice, so that none of the constables hovering about the scene would be able to hear, he said: "The reason for coming to your home was far more commonplace: I came to return your dress."

I stared at him for a moment, and then burst out in loud, nearly hysterical laughter. "Mr. Holmes," I gasped, "you may keep the dress."

He regarded me with a startled expression, and then likewise broke into an explosive laugh. It was the first time I had ever seen such a sign of mirth coming from Sherlock Holmes.

A moment later, he regained control of himself. "I have no wish to detain you further, Mrs. Watson," he said, a sardonic smile curling his thin lips. "That is the job of the police. Good evening." With that, he turned around, strode almost invisibly through the crowd that had started to collect on the street, and disappeared into the night. The next thing I knew, Harry, who had finished regaling the police with the story of his abduction, came to my side.

"*Gor,* ducks," he said, looking into the milling crowd, "was that *him* you was talkin' to?"

I nodded. "That was Sherlock Holmes."

"So you found out a way to contact him?"

"Yes, from now on I shall leave a note for him at my cleaners," I said, and then I began to giggle helplessly again, much to the puzzlement of my old friend.

After being fully questioned by the police, I was finally allowed to go home. It was nearly midnight by the time I returned to Queen Anne Street, where I was welcomed with open arms by Missy, who had come home early from the music hall, found the house empty, and spent the last two hours working herself nearly to distraction over my unexplained absence. After offering slightly more assurance than I actually felt that I was fine, I retired to my bed, where I slept well into the next morning.

Not surprisingly, Harry turned up at our door that day. The fancy dress suit was now gone, and instead he wore his more familiar threadbare brown jacket and battered bowler hat. I expected him to report that he had been let go by the firm of Chippenham and Co., which by now must have learned the details of his deception, but instead he told me that he had resigned. "Hobnobbin' with them upper-class toffs'll land you in trouble every time," he said, with a grin.

The story of the Ramsays received little press coverage until the body of Jane Ramsay was uncovered inside their Lambeth home, two days later. After that, the story was on the front page of every newspaper—the headline in the *Illustrated London News* read, *The Man Who Would Be King,* with no apologies whatsoever to Mr. Kipling—and reporters began collecting and swarming in front of our home. Despite my best attempts to minimize it, they naturally played to the hilt my association with my ultimate savior, Sherlock Holmes. Reporters will write what they will write, of course, though I cannot say that Harry was much help to my cause. Reveling in the spotlight, like any good actor, he took every opportunity to publicly characterize me as the natural successor to Mr. Holmes, whom, he was quick to point out, became involved in the case only after I had done the crucial work involved in solving the puzzle. What Mr. Holmes thought of all this I have no idea.

Within a week, the furor had died down sufficiently to allow Missy and me to go about our normal routines without being accosted by packs of men carrying notebooks and pens. But I could not divest myself of the memory of Mr. Holmes's words. Had, indeed, Providence become involved? Had it somehow chosen the exact moment for Sherlock Holmes to come to our home, knowing that either a minute earlier or later would have meant that both Harry and I would now be lying in hidden graves? Were we, as human beings, engaged in some kind of grand design that was beyond our comprehension?

Or was Mr. Holmes's sudden arrival merely a fortunate happenstance of chance? Were we, after all, simply slaves to the random acts of every other human being? How different would all of history, indeed, all of civilization, be if any one of the million tiny, individual acts and decisions that are carried out each day, had been carried out differently? It was staggering to contemplate.

I was not able to push the riddle of the Young Protestor out of my mind until John's arrival back from his lecture tour (and while I still intended to take up the matter of his providing Mr. Holmes with a key to our home with him, it somehow seemed less imperative to do so at once). I had striven to completely banish it from my thoughts, and for the most part had succeeded. Or so I believed.

It was not until some two months after the events had transpired, when the pleasant crispness of autumn had given way to the gray wetness of winter, that I suddenly lurched up in bed, having been thrust out of a particularly vivid dream in which I was once more studying the vellum page containing the riddle. The document in my dream was identical to the real thing, except that the phrase *St. Andrews cross* had been set apart in vibrant golden letters. "St. Andrew's cross," I uttered aloud in bed, hoping that my sudden rising did not awaken John.

Unlike the Calvary cross, St. Andrew's cross was in the shape of an **X**. Or, in Roman numerals—which was the style of number most likely to be found on a sundial—*ten*.

The time at which the relick may be founde.

It had to be the missing piece of the puzzle. When the sun struck the column precisely at ten o'clock in the morning—ten in the evening not having sufficient sunlight, even in midsummer—its shadow would point like a finger directly to the "relick's" burial location.

"I must inform Harry of this!

But in the next instant, another vivid image appeared in my mind. I saw Harry bedecked in pirate's garb, toting a shovel in one hand and a pickax in the other. "*X marks the spot, my girl*," I could hear him saying. "*And who knows what kind of bloodthirsty excitement we'll find this time around?*"

I laughed and shuddered at the same time.

John moaned and rolled over, but did not awaken.

"I'm sorry, Harry," I whispered, "but this secret will remain with me."

With that, I settled down and drifted back to sleep.

REGINALD MUSGRAVE

"Reginald Musgrave had been in the same college as myself, and I had some slight acquaintance with him. He was not generally popular among the undergraduates, though it always seemed to me that what was set down as pride was really an attempt to cover extreme natural diffidence. In appearance he was a man of an exceedingly aristocratic type, thin, high-nosed, and large-eyed, with languid and yet courtly manners. . . . Now and again we drifted into talk, and I can remember that more than once he expressed a keen interest in my methods of observation and inference."

—"The Musgrave Ritual"

by GEORGE ALEC EFFINGER

The Adventure of the Celestial Snows

My name is Reginald Musgrave. More than fifty years ago I attended Cambridge University, where I had the great privilege of forming a lifelong friendship with Mr. Sherlock Holmes. Dr. John H. Watson recorded one incident in our evolving friendship in "The Musgrave Ritual." Although Holmes and I maintained our connection throughout the years, Watson never mentioned my name again in his accounts. I have a private theory about why this is so, but it has little to do with the present narrative and so I will leave it for another occasion. The events I am about to relate take place in 1875, before Holmes and Watson had their famous first meeting as recorded in *A Study in Scarlet.* The reader must bear in mind that Holmes and I were still lads at the time, and he had not yet become the Sherlock Holmes familiar to every reader of Watson's writings.

The episode began near the end of the school term. I recall that Holmes was in the boxing ring, sparring against a lad whose name I've entirely forgotten, but whose pugilistic style has stayed in my memory for half a century. He was not as tall as Holmes, but he was built more powerfully and seemed to be possessed of great speed. He was light on his feet and made rather a good show of dancing around the ring, bobbing, ducking, all that sort of thing. He may have been fast but Holmes was quicker, and in boxing, so I'm told, quickness counts the more. Speed is for running, which many of Holmes's opponents over the years eventually took up to avoid his punishing jabs.

Whatever this boy's name was, he bounced about the enclosure with a rather queer grin on his face. I wondered myself what he was about. When he had impressed us all with his agility, he moved closer to Holmes, began a long, looping swing with his right fist that was destined never to meet its target, and caught a straight, powerful left full in the face. The fellow staggered back a step or two and then sat down heavily. Holmes looked inquiringly at the dazed lad, who massaged his face with one hand and waved with the other to indicate that he was not seriously hurt but had decided to bring the contest to an early conclusion.

"What do you think?" Holmes asked me as he climbed from the ring.

"I think you must have a difficult time finding adequate competition here," I said.

"No, not about the match. About that Chinese fellow I told you about. Ch'ing Chuan-Fu, in Caius College."

"You told me someone's taken a brass box from him and he desperately wants to get it back. I wouldn't be surprised to learn that this mysterious box is worth a small fortune in whatever they use for money in China."

Holmes and I walked to the athletes' dressing room. "You may be doing him an injustice, Musgrave," he said.

"No doubt."

"I received the impression that Mr. Ch'ing is not overly concerned about his finances, despite all appearances."

I shrugged. "Then finding his precious brass box may well be worth your while."

Holmes considered for a moment. "Will you wait? I'd like to talk with you some more about this. Perhaps you'd care to accompany me when I call on Mr. Ch'ing in London."

"Certainly, Holmes. I had no real plans in any event."

And just that innocently I stepped into the deadly web of a Chinese fiend. How could we, mere students, know of the perilous trail this blithe decision would force us to follow? From the safety and security of the university's medieval walls across the continents to the ancient strongholds of the Orient—such a journey as I never in my most fevered moments wished to make. Seeking a brass box we would go, feeling the destinies of two mighty empires on our shoulders, knowing that lives, perhaps uncountable lives, depended on our actions. In retrospect it was indeed better that we didn't know what waited for us in London. Perhaps Holmes would have gone regardless, but I am forced to wonder about myself. I think I might have found a more restful occupation for those summer months.

The remainder of the school term passed without incident. I took my degree and Holmes successfully concluded the year's studies. On the third of July we met in London, where I hired a cab to take us to Ch'ing's house in Great Bowman Street. When we arrived, before Holmes could rap upon the door, it was opened by a young Chinese woman. Behind her stood a gigantic man. He looked like nothing so much as a court eunuch, the sort of creature who populates fairy tales of mysterious lands. He towered over me, over Holmes as well, and was dressed only in loose black trousers. His massive chest was bare and his glistening arms looked strong enough to lift us each with one hand. His sallow face was plump and soft-looking, and perspiration shone on his bald, shaved head. His great black mustache and the ferocity of his black eyes suggested that, should we prove so lacking in sense, he would be quite capable of suppressing whatever small annoyance the two of us together might create.

The young woman held a small silver tray, and Holmes had already placed his calling card upon it. I did the same, and as she turned to deliver the cards to her master, by some misadventure she lost her balance and dropped both tray and cards. As closely as thunder rolls upon a lightning flash, the bare-chested giant struck the young woman with enough force to send her sprawling to the floor.

I was shocked, but I was not powerless to respond. When the huge man raised his hand to hit her again, I caught hold of his wrist. He turned his menacing gaze on me, and for the space of several dismaying heartbeats we glared at each other.

I felt Holmes's light touch upon my shoulder. "Have a care, Musgrave," he murmured. He was correct to caution me, of course. My outrage was not yet spent, but I released the man's hand and turned to help the young woman.

"Forgive me," I said to her. "I apologize for my clumsiness, for striking the tray and causing you to drop it. It was my fault, not yours." That was not strictly true. I was only trying to shield her from further punishment.

I helped her to her feet, but then she glanced at me with such savage anger that something within me, something vulnerable that had never before been touched, was wounded in the most agonizing manner imaginable. She turned quickly away and hurried from the front hall. Holmes and

I were now alone with the strongman who guarded the door. The giant moved one immense hand to indicate that we should follow him, and follow him we did, into the oddly scented interior of that foreboding place.

We were led to a sitting room that was decorated in keeping with the tastes of the Orient. The furniture was low and of a non-English sparseness, as if Queen Victoria and her era had never been permitted within this house. Painted scrolls hung upon the walls, depicting tigers and groves of bamboo, laughing monkeys or odd, fat, bald men. These themes were often repeated in the rich embroidered hangings that dominated the spaces unadorned by scrolls. There were porcelain vases and carved ivory figures; gods and sages and beasts of bronze, jade, and silver; idols of cunningly worked wood decorated with glittering red and blue stones; and here and there the unmistakable, untarnished glow of gold.

I was astonished. "The brass box that was stolen must have belonged to Confucius himself."

"What did you say, Musgrave?" Holmes asked.

I looked up, surprised that he had heard me. "I was only thinking that if someone stole something from this house, he might have chosen better than a small brass box."

"Quite so. However, until we have more information, there is no use in wondering about the thief's motives."

Our huge guide showed us to European-style chairs in a dimly lighted room, facing a set of pale green damask draperies. A serving girl brought us tea and cakes—the tea was English, but very weak—as though we had been invited to enjoy an evening's entertainment at the home of a good friend.

It hadn't yet occurred to me that we were helpless. No one knew where we were should we be in need of rescue, and we didn't know how many others in the house might be arrayed against us should we need to escape. To me this was still but a curious interlude, an interesting experience before I took up the serious responsibilities of adulthood. I had no inkling of the danger that waited nearby.

There was a bright, reverberating stroke of a gong, and the draperies parted. I stifled a gasp. Seated on a magnificent raised chair was a man dressed in a long coat and trousers of yellow silk. On his feet were simple black slippers, on his head a mandarin cap with a ruby button. The coat's sleeves were long and the man's hands were hidden within. As I watched, he reached out slowly and rested his long, bony fingers upon the heads of the ornately carved Chinese dragons that formed the chair's armrests.

I looked at Holmes. He nodded. Yes, this was my first glimpse of Ch'ing Chuan-Fu. He had a high forehead and domelike head, blazing green eyes, and the serenity and indolence I would soon learn to recognize as a sign of the habitual opium user. When he gestured to us, I saw that on a few of his fingers he wore long artificial fingernails of hammered gold. "Mr. Holmes," he said in a low voice.

"Mr. Ch'ing, please permit me to introduce my companion—"

"Mr. Holmes, at the university I was quite at the mercy of your people and your customs. I was obliged to use the name by which you knew me. Ch'ing, the surname I chose to use, is the name of the ruling dynasty in China, often referred to in the West as the Manchu Dynasty. They have been in power for two hundred and forty years. Here in my modest house, however, I prefer that you address me by my true name and title—a trifling whim of mine, but you will do well to humor me in it. You will call me Fu Manchu. *Doctor* Fu Manchu."

It is impossible to explain how, but the moment he pronounced those words I knew that he was mad.

"Now, Mr. Holmes," he went on, "as to your friend. Perhaps I ought to be vexed that you brought someone with you uninvited, but it means nothing. A hostess at one of your wearying English dinner parties would be fatally inconvenienced, but I am rather pleased to make his acquaintance." He directed his attention towards me, and when he gave me his fearsome, humorless smile, I felt my heart rate increase. "Your name?" he demanded.

"Musgrave, Doctor. Reginald Musgrave."

"Of the Sussex Musgraves?" he asked. "You are recently graduated from the university, are you not?"

"Why, yes." I was seized with a great foreboding. I had come along with Holmes expecting to meet an interesting foreign gentleman and perhaps learn a little about the exotic ways of the East. I had not anticipated this robed bedlamite seated on a fantastic throne. I felt then, as ever I did in his presence, that he would take from me what he wanted and I was helpless to resist.

Not so Holmes. "I suggest, Mr. Ch'ing, or Dr. Fu Manchu," he said, "that you tell us what you expect of us, and speedily. We are not Chinese, nor are we in China. This is England, and if we are to conduct business we must do it in the English manner. Both Mr. Musgrave and I have other matters that need our attention."

Fu Manchu smiled and waved an indolent hand. "Insolent puppies," he said in a voice barely above a whisper. "I know that what you say is not true, but little matter; it will be as you wish, Mr. Holmes. Since our last meeting my small problem has almost resolved itself. Even this morning my servants brought to me the man I suspect of removing the brass box from this house. It was too late for me to send word to you that your visit was no longer necessary—I hope you will forgive me. I do have some amusement prepared for you nonetheless, and I am sure you will find it most edifying."

I was about to say that what I most wanted was to leave that house as soon as possible, but Holmes spoke first. "Then you now have the box in your possession?" he said.

I saw Fu Manchu's long fingers clench into a fist. His placid smile disappeared in an instant, replaced with a scowl. His brows drew down over his burning green eyes. "No," he said, his voice almost a growl, "I do not have the box, but I shall!" He raised his fist as if swearing an oath before his heathen gods.

There was silence for a moment, and then he rose a trifle unsteadily from his monstrous chair and beckoned us to follow him. "Come," he said, "I will show you how we distill the truth in China." Beyond the archway stood two more gigantic yellow-skinned men, each armed with a great glistening blade. The proper name for such a weapon in the Hindu lands is *kuttar*; but whatever the Chinese name for their weapons, the half-naked giants would surely have put an instantaneous end to any sudden decision of ours to leave Fu Manchu's company without his blessing.

We followed a passageway lighted only by torches placed at widely spaced intervals. There were rooms on either side, but each was closed off from the corridor by a stout oaken door; several of these rooms were guarded by Fu Manchu's underlings. I heard low moans coming from one chamber as I passed. I turned to Holmes, my eyes wide with fear, but he only nodded and placed one forefinger briefly upon his lips.

Down a narrow flight of stairs we went, and then another, into the building's cellar. How unusual, I thought, to find so large a vault beneath a London house. Then I realized that Fu Manchu must also own the houses on either side of this one, and that their foundations had been connected by tunnels. I began to imagine the terrible scenes that could be enacted in this madman's Chinese enclave. As I learned later, my imagination proved unequal to the task; never in ten lifetimes could I have conceived tableaux of such cruelty and depravity as those Fu Manchu would show to me in the weeks to come.

We left the main room of the cellar and went along a narrow, damp-smelling way to what appeared to be Fu Manchu's private torture chamber. A moment before I entered the cell, I heard the anguished cry of some unfortunate person; so racked with pain was the voice that I could not tell if it came from a man or a woman. I shuddered and halted my steps. "Come along, Musgrave," Holmes whispered in my ear. "Pluck up your courage. I may need you yet."

God save us both if he should need me, I thought. Holmes went by me, turned a corner, and entered the cell during a moment of ominous silence. A huge hand clutched at my shoulder and I must have cried out, because the hand's mate clapped me across the mouth. I could not turn to see, but I knew one of those glistening hairless statues had come to life behind me. I was thrust forward in Holmes's footsteps, and with each pace my heart beat louder in my ears. Until that moment I had never experienced such utter helplessness and desolation.

I paused in the doorway, unable to make much sense of what I saw. The room was dominated by madly dancing shadows, cast upon the walls by torches placed in sockets. The air was close and foul and smoky; I choked and looked about for Holmes. He stood beside Fu Manchu, gazing with some reluctance at a form upon the far wall.

Again I was pushed ahead. This time when I caught my balance I turned, either to strike my tormentor or, at least, to let him know the full extent of my displeasure. There was no one there.

I quickly joined Holmes, not wishing to be separated by even a few yards from the last vestige of sanity within reach. "By all the saints, Holmes!" I cried. "What have we got ourselves into?"

Holmes tried to appear calm, but I could see that he—even he—was having difficulty controlling his emotions. In later years, his coolness in times of danger would be his hallmark; this is something he owed in no small way to his experiences with Fu Manchu. "Observe," said Holmes with obvious distaste. "Evidently the Chinese technique."

I looked where he was pointing. A man hung upon the wall, his face turned to the damp, fetid stones, his chest and arms embracing the wall as though he were trying to scale it. His wrists were locked into shackles some seven feet above the floor, set wide apart, giving him the appearance of a man in ecstasy shouting his thanks to a benevolent god. In truth the weight of his body was slowly pulling his arms and shoulders apart. He cried out again and I knew that I could not bear very much more.

"Holmes," I said, "three years of translating Greek dramatists did not prepare me for this."

I spoke no more. From behind me, suddenly, like the final thunderclap of a dreadful storm, a great hand bludgeoned me at the base of the skull and I fell senseless to the dirt floor of the torture chamber of Fu Manchu.

When I regained consciousness I didn't want to open my eyes. I knew I was either mortally wounded or straightaway dead, and I was in no particular hurry to learn which. I tried to relax, hoping the throbbing in my head would diminish after a while, but it showed no inclination to do so. I prayed that I might fall again into unconsciousness, to awaken to find the dreadful suffering relieved or else myself in Heaven, where other matters would occupy my attention. Eventually I told myself that spending the rest of my life upon this hard floor was not why I'd gone up to Cambridge, and a Cambridge man did not let the side down in any case.

Now, the university is almost seven hundred years old and so replete with traditions that there's barely room left for scholars. However, exhort myself as I might by thinking of the glory of the university, I still could not raise up a single inch. I found myself overcome by nausea, which only increased the terrible anguish in my head. It seemed like an age before I managed to roll over on my back. The agony eased a little and I could think more clearly. It was only good fortune that had saved me from a crushed skull and an early grave. As it was, I feared the possibility of concussion.

There was something horribly wrong here. I had been attacked in the prison beneath Dr. Fu Manchu's London house, where the only light had come from smoky, sputtering torches. Now the bright light of the afternoon sun streamed full in my face. I had been unconscious for some time, during which someone had carried me upstairs again into the house.

Apprehension grew in me. Looking about, I found myself in a small room, empty but for a plain gray blanket on which I lay. Otherwise the room was quite bare. Beyond a window grew a young plum tree, its branches waving slowly in the wind, tapping against the glass. The hollow sound exaggerated my feelings of desolation and dread.

I went to the room's single exit and put my hand carefully upon the doorknob. Laying my ear close upon the heavy door, I heard nothing at all. Unpleasant words occurred to me—*the silence of a tomb*. I do not know what I expected to hear—screams perhaps, emanating from the torture chamber below. Seconds passed slowly, as is their way in desperate circumstances. Finally, with a mounting feeling of cold fear, I took a deep breath and turned the knob in my hand.

The iron-bound wooden door swung open slightly, creaking only a little, and I peered into the corridor beyond. I took a few steps and saw that I was in the passageway that led to the staircase down to the dungeon. There was no one about. I turned to the right, toward the rear of the house. Perhaps the wise thing would have been to turn the other way, to pass through the sitting room and foyer and escape into the street, but I could not flee before I'd learned of the fate of my friend Sherlock Holmes. I will not claim any innate courage. Rather, I recall thinking at the time that if it came to the worst, Holmes and I would fare better together than either of us might alone.

Although I did not have the daring to test the doors along the passage and look inside, I guessed that the rooms were as deserted as the one in which I'd awakened. What had Fu Manchu done with his prisoners? Had he ended their torment by execution, and was he preparing my own?

I came to the end of the corridor and began to descend. My anxiety increased as I imagined being captured again, then suffering the slowest, most agonizing tortures. Still I found myself creeping farther into the flickering torchlight from below.

Cautiously I peered around the corner of the arched entrance. Here, where I had witnessed a tormented prisoner shackled to the wall, again there was nothing. Torches guttered in their sockets, their feeble light glistening on the drops of water that coursed down the ancient, reeking stones. Holmes and Fu Manchu had disappeared. Only the empty iron staples and a few eloquent streaks of blood gave proof that anyone had ever endured Fu Manchu's cruel hospitality.

The unnatural stillness enveloped me as I explored beyond that room, looking into one prison cell after another. At last, having found nothing useful, I broke off the investigation, retracing my steps to the house's ground floor and passing through the sitting room into the front parlor. There was nothing there, although only hours before it had been decorated magnificently with rare treasures from the Orient. The painted scrolls had been taken down, the embroidered hangings had been removed, and the carved furniture was gone as well. Missing, too, were the decorative vases and ivory figures, the pieces fashioned of silver and gold, and the many jade idols. Everything had been carried away as though the elaborate room had been merely a stage set struck after a final performance. The emptiness made the room seem much larger and infinitely more lonely.

I looked around in wonder. There was not the slightest sign that anyone or anything had occupied this house for some time, not so much as a discolored place upon the wall to testify that a picture or scroll had lately hung there.

It was evident that Holmes and I had been lured to this house and drawn into a trap—but for what purpose? This afternoon's events had been carefully planned to allow Fu Manchu's servants to complete their tasks with speed and precision. I could not imagine how Sherlock Holmes and I fitted into Fu Manchu's scheme, whatever it might be. I did not even wish to speculate about why I'd been left behind at the house in Great Bowman Street.

Then with a terrible thud the front door beyond the foyer crashed open. I confess to uttering a cry of alarm, so startled was I by the sudden noise. Two men rushed into the vestibule, one with his pistol drawn.

The first intruder was a short, well-fed, florid-faced man who, despite the summer season, wore a long black coat and carried a high silk hat. In his other hand he held a walking stick with an ornate silver head. He halted a few paces into the parlor, looked around quickly, and pointed at me with his cane. "Damn me!" he cried. "An Englishman!"

I stood up straight. "Quite so," I said. "We're in London."

"Who are you, sir?" the portly fellow demanded.

"I'm Reginald Musgrave. If I may ask, who are you?"

The man frowned but did not deign to reply. The handsome lad carrying the revolver spoke up. "This is Lord Mayfield, Queen's Commissioner for special investigations."

Lord Mayfield turned to him. "Make a note of it, Powers," he said. "Then let's have a look about this place. Mangrove, did you say?"

I corrected him. "Musgrave. And you'll find nothing here."

It was Powers who replied. "Have you looked around then, sir?" he asked me. Lord Mayfield did not appear to have heard me.

"Yes," I said, "I had just completed my inspection when you came in."

"All the rooms as empty as this?"

"Yes."

Powers's expression hardened, but he put his pistol away and said nothing more. Lord Mayfield poked around with his silver-headed stick, tapping the walls and the floor, touring the deserted parlor with a thoughtful look on his plump features. He stood before me and examined me with frank mistrust. "May I ask, sir," he said suspiciously, "how you came to be here?"

"I accompanied a friend who'd received an invitation," I replied.

"A friend, you say. An *invitation*. The devil you say! Do you know who owns this house?"

I'd taken an instant dislike to this Lord Mayfield, Queen's Commissioner or not. I wasn't going to offer more information than he required. It was a foolish attitude, but I was very young and not used to such disregard. "Yes," I said, "it is the residence of Dr. Fu Manchu."

The effect on Mayfield was astonishing. "Damn me!" he cried, dropping his walking stick to the floor and grabbing the lapel of my coat. "How can you say such a thing in so cool a voice? Are you then one of his pawns? Powers, give me your pistol, and quickly!"

I disengaged the man's fist from my clothing. "I say it quite simply. Dr. Fu Manchu became acquainted with my friend at Cambridge. He invited us here in order to ask Holmes's aid in recovering some stolen object."

Mayfield's mouth worked futilely for a moment, unable to decide how to express his amazement. Powers saved him the effort. "What did you find when you arrived?" he asked.

I shrugged. "This room was filled with Chinese furniture and artwork. Fu Manchu showed us about the house, letting us get an idea of the extent of his wealth and influence. There was a brief interview and then Fu Manchu guided us downstairs, where he maintained a torture chamber and an extensive dungeon. There we saw a prisoner unknown to us, half-naked and bound to a dripping stone wall. Before I could voice my outrage I was struck from behind. I woke some time later to find the house deserted. My friend Sherlock Holmes is now missing, and Dr. Fu Manchu with his entire Chinese retinue have gone I know not where."

Lord Mayfield bent to retrieve his walking stick. "You claim you were struck," he said dubiously. "I suppose the evidence of this violence is visible upon your person?"

"You doubt me, sir?" I said in a cold voice.

Powers came between Lord Mayfield and me. "No, no," the young man said softly. "We've learned to be very careful when we mix in Fu Manchu's affairs. Lord Mayfield and I have followed his trail halfway across the world, and our lives have been threatened more than once. You ought to know that Fu Manchu isn't the kind of person whose invitations one receives with pleasure."

"I understand," I said. "Yes, the back of my head is bloody and still quite painful."

Powers glanced briefly. "You're lucky there was no fracture," he said. He put his hand out. "I suppose it's time to introduce myself. I'm Willard Powers."

"Pleased to make your acquaintance." We shook hands. He was a sturdy blond young man, well set-up, dressed in clothing chosen as much for comfort as fashion.

"As young Powers mentioned," Mayfield said, "we tend to be vigilant and wary of strangers. I trust you take my meaning, as you've seen Dr. Fu Manchu firsthand. Now I must examine every square inch of this house."

In the meantime, the Chinese genius of evil was escaping. I started to object. "But shouldn't—"

The Queen's Commissioner cut me off with a curt gesture. "Patience, Mangrove," he said. "There is undoubtedly vital evidence you've overlooked. I follow established procedure here. We're just as eager to go after that monster, but our actions must be sound. The fate of your friend, the fate of *England* may depend on what we do next. Do you see what I mean?"

I hated being patronized and I chafed at the delay, but essentially Lord Mayfield's plan was sound. I agreed reluctantly.

Behind Mayfield's back, Powers signaled me to stay calm. Given my state of mind just then, it was almost too much to ask. "If nothing else," I said, "I demand an explanation."

"Damn me, sir, no!" the older man bellowed. "I do not explain myself to schoolboys! Look here, you simply have no idea of Fu Manchu's malignant force. This affair you must leave to your government. We are already in close pursuit, and I have promised my queen that Fu Manchu will be returned to England and made to stand trial for his crimes. For your own sake and that of your friend, I cannot permit you to become further involved." He waved his stick vaguely to include the bare room and a world of mystery beyond it. I wondered if Lord Mayfield himself knew what he was talking about.

My fury rose as I listened to his speech. "Involved, you say? I beg to submit that I *am* involved, and inextricably so. You have an obligation to share your information with me. If Sherlock Holmes has been harmed, then together we will bring Fu Manchu to justice."

Lord Mayfield closed one eye and tilted his head a bit. "Plucky lad," he said. "I admire that in a boy. Wish my own son had a bit of it. Still, the point is that a stout heart is not all of it. Fu Manchu is no mere dockside pickpocket. Why, he's the very Genghis Khan of crime. Young Mr. Powers here can tell you. Do not doubt that you have my sincere good wishes, sir, but I won't let you to endanger yourself or others in this pursuit."

Powers raised both hands in a placating gesture. "Please, gentlemen, we must press on. There's nothing of interest in this parlor, but there may be something downstairs."

Lord Mayfield nodded. "If there is, Mr. Powers, I trust you will find it. For my own part, I'll complete my investigation of the ground-floor rooms."

As Powers followed me to the underground vaults, I had a question for him. "He said Fu Manchu would be returned to England for trial. Is he so certain the madman will flee the country?"

"I guess he is. Fu Manchu came to England to research particular matters of biology and chemistry at Cambridge. When we arrived here from Cairo, we lost his trail for a short time. We knew only that he intended to leave England soon. Lord Mayfield supposes this stolen object kept him here until now."

"In my short experience," I said, "I've come to doubt Lord Mayfield's ability to find his left foot in the dark."

"Don't judge him so harshly. He's a trifle stubborn and he has his prejudices, but he's lived most of his life in the Far East. He's not one for action, but he's dedicated beyond doubt. He'd rather die himself than have one of Fu Manchu's dacoits harm a single hair on the queen's head."

"Dacoits?" I'd never heard the word before.

"We've met them in Burma, India, and in all the underworlds of the Orient. Thieves and murderers. They take Fu Manchu's pay, but they're more frightened of him than of death itself."

I shuddered. "With good reason," I said.

We had reached the torture chamber and Powers surveyed the room. His expression told me that every one of his senses was offended. "I wish I could just—"

He was interrupted by a single shout coming faintly from above. Powers raced to the stairs and I was close behind.

The house's front door stood open. We ran out into the street and saw a terrible scene being played out. Lord Mayfield, still clothed in his heavy black coat, was wrestling with a short, lithe Asian in black pajamalike clothes. To be more accurate, Lord Mayfield was bent back against an iron gate while the dacoit clutched at the Commissioner's throat. Mayfield tried futilely to break the slender man's grip, striking him weakly on the head with his stick. Slowly, inexorably, the slave of Fu Manchu was choking the life from him.

Powers took this in more quickly than I. In an instant, he had come to the older man's aid. He grasped the dacoit's wrists in his powerful hands and tore them loose from Lord Mayfield's neck. I heard the Burmese man grunt and mutter something incomprehensible. Powers spun him around and swung a fist brutally into the dacoit's midsection, and followed that blow with another aimed perfectly at the point of the dacoit's chin. The Oriental fellow sprawled unmoving upon the pavement.

Three more of Fu Manchu's thugs arrived. One grabbed and held me so strongly that I didn't have the least hope of escaping, another immobilized Powers in the same manner, and the third man held a dagger with a golden hilt to the my throat.

Lord Mayfield tried to speak, but his abused vocal cords barely functioned. "Must be . . . Holmes," he whispered in a croaking voice.

"Where?" I demanded.

Lord Mayfield could only point. Farther down the street four of Fu Manchu's hoodlums had surrounded Holmes. They closed in on him slowly and warily. Powers and I struggled with our captors, but we could only watch in helpless frustration.

"Why don't they rush him?" Powers asked. "What are they playing at?"

"No doubt they've learned how well he can take care of himself," I said. "Yes, perhaps, but four against one? Not even—"

Just then, one of the dacoits made the mistake of attacking my friend Holmes. He sidestepped easily, then struck the man's face a sharp and crushing blow. The Oriental howled in shock and pain. Holmes had broken his nose, and blood streamed down his face. The other dacoits glanced at him, then proceeded even more cautiously against Holmes.

One of the three drew a knife, and I recall that my friend actually smiled in amusement. The dacoit moved forward boldly, brandishing his weapon. Holmes stepped toward him and made a quarter turn to the right, at the same time blocking his opponent's outstretched arm with his. Then he grasped the wrist of the man's knife hand and forced it backward, while twisting the wrist completely over. The dacoit cried out and let the knife fall to the ground. Holmes swung around again while applying pressure to the man's wrist, and I watched in astonishment as the burly attacker fell heavily to the ground. He gave a single harsh grunt and then lay motionless at Holmes's feet, now also well out of the fight.

"By all the saints!" I said.

"Your Mr. Holmes doesn't make a very good victim," Powers said with a laugh. "Fu Manchu's men look like they've never seen that Japanese *baritsu* before."

Holmes seemed perfectly composed. Now the third and fourth attackers were ready to try their luck. One circled Holmes cautiously, and my friend turned slowly to face him. When his back was to the fourth man, that scoundrel reached into a pocket and brought out a small glass ball. He covered his nose and mouth with a cloth and threw the glass ball to the pavement, where it shattered. Wisps of lavender-colored mist curled up from the cobblestones. In a moment both Holmes and his third opponent sagged to their knees. Then they dropped roughly to the ground, unconscious or dead.

"What was that?" I cried, dismayed.

"Chinese magic," Lord Mayfield said. "It seems to have trumped Japanese science."

Again Powers and I struggled furiously against our captors, but we had no more success than before. The fourth black-clad dacoit dragged Sherlock Holmes's limp, unresisting form along the street. One man threw open the door of a four-wheeler, and they carried Holmes inside. Our guards released us and ran toward a second carriage. They paused only long enough to collect their fallen comrades, but in a moment strong horses were pulling our enemies and their prisoner farther away with every furious stride. Just before the carriage turned a corner, I heard what I took to be a cry of outrage and defiance from Sherlock Holmes. It would be weeks and many hard miles before I heard his voice again.

I need not dwell on a description of the mood that prevailed as we completed our search of the house in Great Nordham Street. Let it suffice to say that we found nothing more. The household of Fu Manchu had vanished as if no one had ever occupied that building, leaving not the slightest clue to their destination.

"This is not the first time I've been so thwarted by that devil," Lord

Mayfield said. He bashed the wall angrily with his walking stick. "If I could, I'd damn him and all his depraved minions to the blackest pit of Hell. He is like nothing so much as Lucifer let loose again in the world, wreaking destruction for the sheer amusement of it."

"You arrived only a matter of a few hours too late," I said, trying to console him.

"Where Fu Manchu is concerned, the matter of an hour is the difference between peace and sanity on one hand, and absolute ruin and madness on the other. We followed him from Pingyüan to Kunming, where there is a regional headquarters of his secret underground society. In Kunming our Chinese guide was murdered, poisoned. From Kunming we went south and east to Canton and then Macao. We boarded a Dutch ship there and sailed through the Indies, the rumor of Fu Manchu leading us westward. We stopped in Malaya, then in Ceylon, and up the coast of India to Bombay. Everywhere we put in we asked of Fu Manchu, and everywhere his name brought a shudder and a cold look, yet no one had the courage to direct us. One by one our crew and our servants died as if by some supernatural hand—some poisoned, some strangled, some fell mysteriously without any mark or sign of injury. We crossed the Arabian Sea and entered the Gulf of Aden. As far as Suez, whenever we mentioned Fu Manchu we got the same treatment: suddenly our informants remembered nothing, suddenly they had somewhere else to go, suddenly we were no longer welcome. We felt more assured when we sailed upon the blue waters of the Mediterranean, but we were wrong. Seamen went missing overboard, and our valets dropped dead of the bites of unknown insects. The curse, if such it was, followed us until we berthed here in London, and it does not seem to have lifted yet. We could well be the next victims!"

Willard Powers gestured impatiently. "Fearing a curse is futile," he said. "There's no curse but the work of Dr. Fu Manchu, a mortal human being. He's powerful and resourceful, but after all he's only a man. He *can* be defeated, but not unless we go after him, and right now."

"I quite agree," I said. "But why was Holmes his target?"

"I cannot imagine," Lord Mayfield said.

"The important thing," Powers said slowly, "is that Holmes was kidnapped, not murdered as the others were. He was taken alive for some purpose."

"So that we'd follow," I suggested. "He could be the bait in some strange intricate trap."

Lord Mayfield squinted at me. "Perhaps you're right," he admitted grudgingly. "In that case, how are we to know where to go next, eh?"

"We should inform Scotland Yard," I said innocently, "because today's attack surely falls under their jurisdiction."

Powers waved away the suggestion. "The police haven't been much help till now, Mr. Musgrave. They refuse to believe in the existence of Dr. Fu Manchu. They tell us that we're dreaming, that we've been reading too many sensational novels. They're the ones who sleep—the police, I mean—with Fu Manchu plotting right under their very noses. Go down by the river in the evening, through the maze of waterfront streets and back alleys, and you'll see his servants slinking through the pale fog on their errands of intrigue. The Metropolitan Police prefer to think the Oriental gangs confine their crimes to assaults on their own kind, and that there's no need to mix in it. If the police had any idea how near London's placid surface these schemers operate, it would cause a general panic. By ignoring the situation the police hope it will vanish, but it will not go away. You've seen for yourself."

"Yes," I said, "I have seen."

Powers shook his head. "Lord Mayfield has the support of knowledgeable men in the Foreign Office, but even those men feel it best not to arouse widespread fear. That means that our resources are very limited. The fight against Fu Manchu, who has the vast wealth of the Far East at his disposal, is carried on by a handful of dedicated people. We few are trying to stem the onrushing tide of Fu Manchu's imperial ambitions, and with our bare hands."

"Sooner or later even the great Fu Manchu may make a fatal error," I said.

"He toys with us," Lord Mayfield said. "He plays with us the way a cat plays with a crippled mouse. This may well drive me insane before long, but I swear I'll get him before . . ." His voice trailed off. The look of grim determination on his face astonished me.

I offered another bit of information. "Fu Manchu told us a story about a stolen brass box. Do you know what it might contain?"

"A brass box?" Lord Mayfield said. "Dear me, the contents of that box are very valuable. There are wonderful medical secrets locked away in it, medicines and chemicals which could benefit all of civilization. Fu Manchu calls them the Celestial Snows. He could eliminate a great part of the anguish in our hospitals merely by sharing the rare alkaloids he possesses.

That means nothing to him, for he is hardened to other people's suffering—indeed, I think he rather enjoys it. Such a small thing, yet that brass
box is responsible for torture, abduction, and murder."

"Well," Powers said, "in any event, we must decide on our course of
action."

"I have the day's *Times,*" Mayfield said, taking the newspaper from a
pocket in his overcoat. "I'll see if any vessels bound for China are departing
tonight. Yes, by God! There's a ship leaving the London and Foochow Tea
Company docks at Limehouse just after midnight. Can we make our prepa-
rations and arrive at the wharf before the ship weighs anchor?"

I was struck by a chilling thought. "Lord Mayfield," I said, "with all due
respect, aren't you making the rather large assumption that Fu Manchu is
taking Holmes back to China? We have no evidence at all concerning his
destination."

Mayfield laughed explosively. "My dear sir," he said, "I fancy I have
more experience with that Asian rascal than you. I've tracked him from one
corner of the map to the other. He eludes me, yes, I grant that, but—damn
me, sir!—he has yet to render me helpless. I have anticipated each of his
diabolical pitfalls, and I'm still eagerly on his trail. For reasons I don't yet
comprehend, he wants me to pursue him to China. For the moment that's
all I can do. When I've caught up with him at last, then he'll learn with
whom he's been dealing this long while!"

I don't believe I have ever seen such a display of ignorance and bravado.
I saw Powers shudder at His Lordship's words. "What is the name of that
tea ship?" he asked.

"The *Eldred Tamarind*," Mayfield said.

"Sir," Powers said, "I don't believe Fu Manchu will be aboard her. He
will send most of his household back to China aboard ship, but it will be a
Chinese-owned ship with a Chinese crew, and it will not be listed in the
Times. Fu Manchu himself will travel in some more invisible way, along a
route chosen to disguise his identity and discourage his pursuers."

"If he wishes to discourage us," I said, "why is he carefully leading us
on?"

"Ah," Lord Mayfield said, "as on previous occasions, he wishes us to
follow, but he desires that we be entirely exhausted when we reach our
goal. Then we will be in his territory and at his mercy, with our strength
and our will to resist depleted. He will have the luxury of destroying us at

his leisure, in what seems to him the most entertaining manner." He looked around at us, smiling broadly, looking like a pleased-as-Punch schoolboy who had just stumbled upon the correct answer to a difficult sum. He wore that same expression only moments before he died, and it is how I always remember him in my thoughts.

"I like this less and less," I said.

"Remember, though," Powers said, "that you're under no obligation to travel with us. You've made this affair your own, and you're at liberty to lay that burden down at any time."

"Then it is to Limehouse," I said, despite a somber foreboding. And so I joined the mission against the ruthless Dr. Fu Manchu, and changed my life forever.

We left the house in Great Nordham Street and hailed a growler. We took care of our several obligations and arrived at the *Eldred Tamarind*'s berth well before midnight. It was a matter of a few minutes' haggling to secure two cabins aboard her. Lord Mayfield showed some official credentials that succeeded only in driving up the price of our passage, I have no doubt. It was clear that all of the peer's limited success against Fu Manchu was due not to his resourcefulness, but to the competence of Willard Powers.

Hours later I awoke to the sudden lurching of the cabin, which I shared Willard Powers. I sat up in my bunk. "We're under way," I said. The ship passed down the Thames, and upon the breast of the tide we were borne into the English Channel. I experienced a curious elation where I should have felt fear, as if some magnificent prize awaited me in China.

I stood with Willard Powers on the deck of the *Eldred Tamarind* as we sailed past Gibraltar. Lord Mayfield, his florid face grown deathly pale, was indisposed below in his cabin. "In a few days we will be in Port Said," Powers said. "It's the season of the *khamsin*, storms that blot out the sun with dust and sand. Everything in the port comes to a stop when they howl, so we'll waste one day idle for every day of business."

Powers knew Port Said well. A week later he and I strolled through a bazaar near the city's waterfront, wearing cotton scarves to keep the fine sand out of our mouths and noses. I suppose we were a fine pair of fools, dressed neither for the location nor the climate. I was making some comment to him when a peculiar noise interrupted me. I'd heard that sound before and Powers knew it, too—the uncanny, ululating warning cry of Fu

Manchu's dacoits. Just then the roar of the wind grew stronger and I thought perhaps I'd imagined the cry, but beside me Powers was as full of dread as any man I've ever seen. "We must dash for the ship," he said.

I nodded. The wharf was not far, and when we arrived we hurried up the gangplank. I turned toward the bow of the *Eldred Tamarind*, but Powers grabbed at me and shoved me down against the deck, behind a quantity of coiled towing cable. I raised my head enough to see seven black-clad Orientals, all carrying some sort of evil-looking edged weapon. One pointed toward the stern of the ship and two of the dacoits hurried that way. The leader said something more and a third man ran back down the gangplank on some errand. A fourth and fifth were ordered to the ship's bow. Finally the dacoit in charge pointed directly where we huddled in concealment. He and the seventh assassin moved straight toward us.

I pressed back as far as possible into the shadows. Shutting my eyes, I breathed a brief prayer, and when I looked again the dacoits were gone. "By all the saints," I murmured, "why aren't we dead?"

Powers was still crouched beside me. "There are two possibilities," he said quietly. "The first is that they didn't see us and the second is that they didn't mean to murder us *now*. Always remember that where Dr. Fu Manchu is concerned, nothing is ever sane or simple. Until we get to our destination, not an event will happen nor a word spoken that won't be reported to our enemy."

Days passed, and we passed through Suez into the Red Sea, then across the Arabian Sea to Bombay. It was eerie to know that seven brutal killers were watching our every move, waiting for some unknown signal, yet we couldn't even detect their presence. Powers and I decided it best to keep Lord Mayfield ignorant of these circumstances, at least for the present. If the dacoits were merely spying on us, then no good purpose would be served by upsetting him. In retrospect, with the kind of infallible reasoning that derives from knowing what happened next, I think we two young heroes showed damnable arrogance in making that decision. Headstrong and sometimes ill-advised Lord Mayfield might have been, but in 1875 there was no one in the world with his experience in the ways of the Far East in general and Dr. Fu Manchu in particular.

We should have consulted with him aboard the *Eldred Tamarind*, sharing our facts with him, and we should have let him participate in the plans then and later in Peking. Because Powers and I felt wise enough to proceed without him, I've always felt as if in part we contrived the unlucky man's demise.

Of the voyage there is much to say but little that is directly connected to my account of Sherlock Holmes, so I may leave the rest of it to the imagination of my patient audience.

Nothing further delayed us. Hours later the merchant ship left India behind, rounded Dondra Head, and made for Burma. Many more days passed in ominous silence. Powers and I vowed to remain watchful, knowing full well that Fu Manchu's dacoits were still aboard. Late summer became autumn, and the *Eldred Tamarind* went from port to port, from Rangoon to George Town in Malaya, Batavia on Sumatra, and Singapore. Then we headed up through the South China Sea, stopping for several days first at Hong Kong, then at Shanghai. At last, as winter began to threaten our hope of success, in early December we navigated the Yellow Sea and put in at Tientsin, a great crossroads port on the Pei River, about as far inland as London is along the Thames.

Trouble could begin at any moment, now that we were finally on Chinese soil. Lord Mayfield knew the city of Tientsin well, and over a splendid Chinese meal, he and Powers debated the best way to proceed. As for myself, I felt I had little to contribute and I preferred to listen. As it happened, however, it was my suggestion that ultimately led to the confrontation with the array of forces now gathered in China. It was as if my presence had been needed as a catalyst. In all innocence I unleashed the struggle that would decide who would live and who would die, who would gain power and who would retire in defeat. It was not only Sherlock Holmes who had invited me to accompany him to the house of Fu Manchu—Fate had played a part, too.

Lord Mayfield obtained a coach in which we could ride the rest of the way to Peking. Most travel in China at this time was in open carts, crude vehicles with solid wooden wheels and no system of springs to lessen the shocks of the road. Carriages were a European luxury, and the Chinese considered them shameless wastes of material and horses.

As we approached the Outer City of Peking, we discussed our immediate goals. "We should inquire of the legation," Powers said. "We need all the information they've got concerning Fu Manchu's activities. We don't know anything about what he's been up to, or what he may be planning."

"I have already so directed the driver," Lord Mayfield said. "The

British embassy is housed near the Gate of Heavenly Peace. *Heavenly Peace!* The names of these streets and buildings might be amusing if they weren't so hideously at odds with the true nature of these people."

"Not all Chinese are as cruel and mad as Dr. Fu Manchu," Powers said quietly.

The Queen's Commissioner did not seem to hear. "After we conclude our business there, we will pay a call on Dr. Fu Manchu himself!"

And that is what transpired. For more than two hours, Lord Mayfield engaged the British diplomats in a heated wrangle concerning official policy, and then we were back in the coach, rattling our way toward the Peking residence of Dr. Fu Manchu. He most certainly knew of our arrival in the Chinese capital, and he must be biding his time. I stared through the coach's windows as the city revealed itself to me, strikingly beautiful but horrifying, too. Peking makes each man many promises; if the man is fortunate, few of those promises are kept.

"I intend to control Fu Manchu," Lord Mayfield said. "Just as he tried to control me, I will show him the strength of my will. I have suffered great indignities at his hands. These things must be repaid. Stop here."

The driver pulled the horses to a halt about fifty yards from the house. We stepped down from the carriage and ordered the driver to wait. With Powers in the lead, we advanced on the building. All three of us were armed with pistols, but they seemed terribly inadequate to me. We were rushing into the lion's den.

We were fools.

At the estate's front gates, Lord Mayfield spoke angrily with one of Fu Manchu's great eunuch guards. It was obvious that the guard did not understand a word of the tirade, and he prevented us from going in. Thus frustrated, Mayfield did not argue further; he aimed his revolver and shot the eunuch twice. "Come with me if you would save your friend," Mayfield cried. Then he turned and ran into the building.

There was nothing for it but to follow him. We plunged into the cold, dimly lighted house. I saw no one, heard no one, and was aware only of an eerie feeling of emptiness. I felt that we had just made a massive and irreparable error. Mayfield led us deeper into the small palace. "There's no one here," he admitted at last.

"If I know him," Powers said, "he has a secret exit from this rat's nest."

"That is quite correct," came the sibilant voice of Dr. Fu Manchu. He came toward us with a platoon of armed women. We'd been surrounded in the gloom.

They quickly disarmed us. "This is most interesting to me," Fu Manchu said, showing that hellish smile of his. "I predicted your arrival for Tuesday of last week. I suspect that the unusual weather in the Yellow Sea delayed your ship. No matter. I did not predict this futile and deluded attack upon my property and my person. Now your destiny is mine to choose, and while I decide your fate I must request that you accept my hospitality." He gestured to his female soldiers.

They led us down a flight of stairs and through the long, dark tunnel to the subterranean court beneath the Palace of the Opal Moon. We were separated and thrust roughly in different directions. Isolated from Willard Powers and Lord Mayfield, I was led through the twisting underground ways until I became hopelessly lost. There was a barred door shut with an old iron lock. A eunuch unlocked it and swung open the portal. There was no light inside. He pushed me forward and I fell into the cell. Someone grabbed my wrists and manacled me to the damp, stinking wall.

After what must have been many minutes I began to be aware that I was not alone in the cell. There was another prisoner, chained to the opposite wall. He man was gaunt and unkempt, exhausted and starved. He was wearing a long fleece-lined coat, such as my cousin Talbot brought back from the Near East during his short tour there on behalf of the Foreign Office. I did not know who this wretched prisoner of Fu Manchu was, but I did not doubt that in a short while I would come to resemble him. The thought made me shudder; my courage had all but seeped away.

Then the man spoke to me. "Musgrave?" he said. His voice was so cracked and weak, it took me a moment to recognize it. It was Holmes. I felt a flood of tears wash down my cheeks. I don't know which emotion caused them: relief, terror, pity? He looked beyond all hope. He and I were dressed so incongruously; we had obviously taken much different routes to this same damnable end.

"Yes, Holmes. You have been in Afghanistan, I perceive." He never let me forget that foolish statement.

Only a few yards of stone floor separated us, yet in the gloom I could not see his face well. As it was, he aroused my compassion and sympathy, though I knew he had little use for such feelings. He drooped in his chains, rattling them softly now and then as he tried to make himself more comfortable. That was impossible. All these decades later, my body still complains of the abuse it endured beneath the Forbidden City of Peking.

We were visited only by eunuch guards and an ancient, bowed Chinese woman who brought us our daily rations of thin fish soup and rice. I spent endless hours dreaming of food, all kinds of food, even such things as I'd never before desired. My thoughts of escape centered on the huge feasts I would devour afterward.

Holmes and I passed the time relating the wonders and hardships we'd experienced in our separate journeys to Peking. I had learned that Holmes never forgot a single detail of any experience he wished to retain. Now he went over every conversation, every hard-won bit of information, but the exact nature of Fu Manchu's malevolent scheme still eluded him.

One day I was startled when a tall, muscular Arab entered our cell. "Kind sirs," he said, "I am Ali as-Salaam, a servant of Dr. Fu Manchu. My master regrets the nature of your accommodations and I bring his apologies. He has spared your lives against the direct order of Madame Tzu Hsi, the mother of our emperor. Be assured that Dr. Fu Manchu is working tirelessly to have your death sentences removed and your freedom restored."

Holmes and I glanced at each other. "We are most grateful," he said sardonically.

"Tell me about the others," I said.

Ali turned to me. "Now, Mr. Musgrave, have no fears in behalf of your associates. Lord Mayfield is comfortable in the palace of my master, learning much about Chinese civilization and the problems this land is having with certain European states. Willard Powers has been incarcerated for reasons similar to those that force your own captivity."

Holmes's chains rattled. "I fear to ask for details," he said. "Lord Mayfield is 'comfortable,' in your words. Who knows but that you'd describe *our* condition as comfortable."

Ali shrugged sadly. "My good sirs, forgive these circumlocutions. You find them unpleasant, but I seek only to avoid unnecessary pain."

The only response was a short, barking laugh from Holmes.

"Again, good sirs, I am sorry," Ali said. He lifted his torch high and looked at us both. "I will return again to give you further news. In the meantime I will report that you are both well." He left the cell and a eunuch slammed the door closed behind him. Once again we were delivered into darkness. Neither Holmes nor I spoke for a long while.

The next day—I call it that because I reckoned time according to the twice-daily meals—Holmes tried to engage the old woman in conversation. I supposed it a futile effort, because it was unlikely that this withered old grandmother could speak English, and less likely that she would speak in the presence of one of the eunuchs. "I would like a better look at this rice," Holmes said. "I am sure there are all manner of vermin crawling through my food. I know—I feel them in my stomach, creeping in my body. I demand that you bring that torch here!"

Holmes's voice frightened me. I realized how much I depended on his strength and wisdom. If he'd finally given up to the horror of our confinement, then I was truly alone.

"You are afraid to let me see!" he shrieked, with a shrill cackle. It made me shudder. The old woman spoke a few words in Chinese to the guard with the torch. The eunuch stepped nearer, letting the firelight fall upon the bowl of rice in her hands. Holmes stared at the food, then looked into the woman's face. "When do I learn all of the puzzle?" he asked. Now his voice was firm and strong, as it always had been.

The old woman pretended she didn't understand. She shoved the rice bowl forward.

"You brought me here to solve a riddle," Holmes said. "What has this prison cell to do with it?"

The old woman straightened her fragile body. She seemed taller, stronger, younger. "I must believe that you are ready," Fu Manchu said. "We will begin the task immediately, if you wish. I am sorry that I cannot release you until you present an acceptable solution. That is the will of my emperor." In reality it was the will of Madame Tzu Hsi. History proved me correct on this point: Tzu Hsi ruled China with absolute and ruthless power until her death under questionable circumstances in 1908, the day after the emperor's own death.

"I would prefer a more comfortable consultation," Holmes said, "but quite evidently my wishes are of little importance."

Fu Manchu bowed low. "On the contrary, my English friend, I hold you in the greatest esteem. It is only that in this matter I am powerless."

"I will ignore your rhetorical falsehood," Holmes said. "Please begin."

Dr. Fu Manchu spread his hands. "China is compelled to accept the goods and services—and the principles—of the European and American invaders. We may not need these things, but we cannot hide from them.

How do we rid China of foreign influences, cleanse China and restore the purity of the past? Peaceful means have failed. Your government doesn't even realize how hated it is in Peking."

"I care very little for politics," Holmes said. "What is your problem?"

"Someone within the Forbidden City is in alliance with these pirates," Fu Manchu said.

"Then we must decide who has most to gain thereby," Holmes said.

"The only product the English exploit that has grown more popular in China is opium," Fu Manchu said. "The Empress Dowager is publicly against the opium trade. However, in truth she permits it to flourish because the habit renders her subjects docile and easier to rule. There is a saying: 'As long as there is opium, there will be no revolution.' Nevertheless, I am of the opinion that the Manchu saying is wrong, and that there shall be a revolution whether the people smoke opium or not. In the event of an overthrow, power will fall to those who are familiar with the necessities of government, but who are denied true power under our present system."

"You mean the eunuchs," Holmes said.

Fu Manchu spread his bony, clawlike fingers. "It is possible," he said. "I suspect that An Li, the Grand Eunuch, is as much aware of this problem as I, and that he is making his own plans."

"What about the Imperial Princes?"

"Possible, although doubtful. The Emperor, after all, is not the son but the nephew of the Dowager Empress. There are princes whose claims to the throne are, like my own, certainly plausible. I am sure that Tzu Hsi is wary of Prince Kung and Prince Chuang. Could one of these men be plotting with the foreign big noses to remove her? Great Britain, Prussia, and even the United States may be helping to install a more sympathetic ruler in Peking. Someone has contacted the Chinese secret societies, the White Lotus and the Triads, and has begun negotiations that would bring them all together beneath a single banner."

The desolate sound of Holmes's chains rang out while he thought about these things. "What is it that you fear from them?" he asked.

"I fear nothing, as I told you before. I need to know what is happening in China and what will happen, so that I am not caught unprepared by the winds of change."

"The others must feel the same," Holmes said.

"The brass box I sought is again in my possession, and it contains several Celestial Snows which may aid you in your contemplation. I wish I could offer you a more congenial setting, but I will fulfill your needs and Mr. Musgrave's while you are my guests."

"I require your promise that you will also protect our friends," Holmes said.

The odd film covered Fu Manchu's heavy-lidded green eyes. He made wolf's teeth and said, "I assure you that I will give each of them my personal attention, and attend to them as each requires." Then we were suddenly alone. Fu Manchu and the eunuch guard had gone.

"How many different ways can you interpret his last remark?" I asked my friend.

Holmes shook his head sadly. It was not necessary to say anything.

Thus began Holmes's use of cocaine, which was one of the white powders in the brass box. The identification of the other alkaloids is still a mystery to Western medical science. I watched Holmes submit more often to the lure of Fu Manchu's assortment of Celestial Snows. His moods changed rapidly, swinging from intense concentration to a curious lassitude. I ascribed these changes to the chemical substances, but eventually I learned that the moods were the cause and not the effect of his use of these compounds. He turned to one to focus his mental abilities; he chose another to relax or to chase boredom.

"You must realize that these substances are a great weapon of his," I warned. "They are one of his means of controlling the minds of his enemies."

"I intend to use them sparingly, for quite legitimate purposes," he said. "I am not going to abuse them to the point of harming my body or my mind."

"I pray you know when you are nearing that point," I said. This is the same concern that was voiced years later by Dr. Watson, who watched Holmes poison himself with cocaine, morphine, and opium whenever Holmes felt the situation warranted.

Each day Fu Manchu, having abandoned his disguise, brought Holmes more information about the noblemen and eunuchs who were the principal candidates in the conspiracy to overthrow the rule of Madame Tzu Hsi. Holmes asked short, specific questions about each man: What was his birth? Has he felt adequately rewarded for his services to the government? Did he belong to one of the secret societies? Did he have any personal quarrel against the Imperial family? Fu Manchu answered the questions briefly but completely. The two men, perhaps the two most agile minds I have ever known, discarded many of the suspects easily. They agreed finally that the guilty man was either An Li the Grand Eunuch, or Prince Kung, an enemy of An Li and son of the Emperor Tao Kuang.

"I must speak with both these men," Holmes said. "Perhaps then I may find a solution. At this moment I believe the threat comes from Prince Kung, who may have enlisted the aid of the Grand Eunuch. An Li, acting by himself, may not be able to find sufficient support beyond the walls of the Forbidden City. He is, after all, a eunuch. It does not seem likely to me that a eunuch could be made ruler of China. He would not have the blessing of the wealthy and powerful Mandarin class, whatever the force of his personality."

"Nevertheless, Mr. Holmes," Fu Manchu said languidly, "you must learn never to make preliminary judgments without complete data. Yet in principle I agree with your theory, and we shall see if the future confirms it. I will arrange for An Li and Prince Kung to visit you soon. On those occasions, I will instruct you on the role you must play; these men cannot be lured to this dungeon to speak to a chained prisoner. Therefore I will devise a suitable fiction in a more agreeable setting."

After the departure of Fu Manchu, Holmes began to discuss the matter with me. I objected that I had few pertinent contributions to make, but Holmes was not really seeking my advice. It was his habit to examine his puzzles by going over each facet of it aloud. I did make an observation that later proved to be of some importance. "You agree with that yellow-robed monster that the threat to the Dowager Empress must be either An Li or this Prince Kung?"

"No, not at all," Holmes said. "I avoided making that declaration. Instead, I told Fu Manchu that on his list of possible suspects, those two were the only likely candidates."

"Is it possible the true enemy is someone not on Fu Manchu's list?"

"Exactly, Musgrave." Holmes laughed softly. "I believe it is our only genuine hope for escape. Fu Manchu does not plan to let us leave this place alive, but if I can discover the answer to his riddle, I may be able to use it to win our freedom. If his secret rival were An Li or Prince Kung, surely Fu Manchu would be certain of it by now. His opponent is someone he does not suspect, perhaps someone he is unable to suspect. That is the reason he sought advice from me: I am an outsider with a foreigner's way of looking at things. The doctor hopes that I will be able to see a pattern where he is unable to see anything at all."

Hours later the cell door opened and Ali came in carrying a torch, unaccompanied by eunuch guards. At the time I didn't think that unusual. "Good evening, good sirs," he said.

"Is it evening?" asked Holmes.

"I bring you word from your countrymen. Mr. Holmes, I have never lied to you, yet I have deceived you. It is time to make some important matters clear to you. I bring word from the British legation."

"The legation!" Holmes cried. "But surely Fu Manchu—"

"I am Fu Manchu's trusted servant," Ali said, "but I am also a loyal servant of Queen Victoria's emissaries in Peking. I have been gathering information here for many years. I have been sent to tell you to have no fear. Intense efforts are proceeding through lofty diplomatic channels to have you released by decree of the Empress Dowager herself. The British legate can bring a certain amount of pressure to bear. I must say that the meddling efforts of your Lord Mayfield have caused no little embarrassment for both sides in this negotiation. Nevertheless, an agreement should be reached very soon."

"Ali," I said, "you put yourself at risk for us."

He bowed to me. "I am a servant of the big noses, Mr. Musgrave, and as such I would be hated everywhere in Peking. My work has been secret, and I must ask you to honor that arrangement. My life would be forfeit otherwise."

"You have my word, of course," I said.

"I also have some hope of learning Fu Manchu's secrets of the Celestial Snows, particularly the ancient Elixir of Immortality."

"An elixir of immortality," Holmes said. "So Oriental geniuses waste their lives in that vain pursuit, too."

Ali shrugged. "Fu Manchu has almost perfected it. The difficulty is that ancient texts describe the ingredients in very ambiguous, poetic terms. Fu Manchu must yet learn what the wise old ones meant by Flower of Cinnabar and Red Stone Fat. The third thing is honey, but honey produced from the nectar of a particular flower. The name of that flower is meaningless to modern scholars."

Holmes laughed. "I'm glad to hear there's a rational explanation for Fu Manchu's actions. He is only a deluded Chinese doctor who believes he can live forever."

"Perhaps he is deluded, but if his experiments are successful, a descendant of Tzu Hsi will soon wear the crown in Buckingham Palace."

There was a long silence in the dungeon. "We British will make Fu Manchu regret that he ever came to our shores," Holmes said at last.

Ali shook his head. "The future shall be as God wills." He turned his back and left us again in darkness.

Did I then fall unconscious, did I sleep and dream? The voice of Dr. Fu Manchu roused me. "May I assume, Mr. Holmes," the Chinese doctor asked, "that you are near a solution?"

"I must conduct one or two further interviews, of course," Holmes said.

Our captor bowed his head, and at his gesture two of his slaves began to loosen our bonds. Fu Manchu, along with his female soldiers and his eunuch guards, escorted us up the stone steps to his stronghold in the Palace of the Opal Moon. His residence and its precious contents would never be suspected by the eunuchs of the Great Within, yet every word spoken there was whispered in Fu Manchu's ear. He dwelt within the bounds of the Forbidden City because he considered himself the rightful emperor of all China—and who was there to dispute him?

We were bathed and clothed and fed, made comfortable, and left alone. A young woman arrived to announce that Prince Kung would receive us within the hour. "It must be daylight in the world," Holmes said in a curious musing tone.

Not long thereafter we were conducted into the presence of Prince Kung, brother to the former emperor and the current emperor's finance minister. He was the most powerful of all the imperial princes. He'd been a close ally of Madame Tzu Hsi in years past, but a rift had grown between them. Prince Kung, with his yellow jacket proclaiming his immediate connection to the imperial family and his hat's ruby button marking his exalted rank, sat grimly in an audience chamber of the Hall of Placid Contemplation. He indicated that we should take seats, and tea was served. Fu Manchu sat beside Holmes to translate the proceedings.

The prince spoke briefly. He was frankly puzzled why this foreign gentleman with no diplomatic rank should want to see an imperial prince. Unspoken was his true meaning: Why should an imperial prince want to see this foreign gentleman?

Holmes bowed his head. "Even far away in England, where our Queen Victoria sits like an English image of the Empress Dowager of China, we have men who plot to betray the heaven-guided hands of our great ruler. Prince Kung, I pray that you have measured me as a humble but honest and truthful man. I would ask one question of you, and your answer may help to make China the great nation you have always desired her to be."

Fu Manchu translated this speech, one more elaborate than anything I'd ever heard Holmes say in all the time I'd known him.

Prince Kung spoke. Fu Manchu merely turned to Holmes and said, "You may ask your question. The imperial prince will consider replying."

Holmes bowed again. "Prince Kung," he said, "in an ancient city in Europe there is a monastery. The monks who live in this place are honest, decent followers of God. They tend their gardens and practice their devotions, and their one pride is a tree older than any other tree in the land. It was standing before the monastery was built around it. This marvelous tree blooms only once in ten years, and its flowers are the most beautiful that anyone has ever seen. It gives fruit only once in a hundred years, and those who taste it are said to be granted a glimpse of Paradise. Now one day a bolt of lightning struck this magnificent tree and started a fire in its whispering boughs. The monks ran from their cells, anxious and afraid. This is my question, Prince Kung: Did the monks rescue the tree or its indescribable fruit?"

There was silence in the hall for a few long moments. Then a hint of a smile touched Prince Kung's face, and he nodded his head in apparent satisfaction.

Fu Manchu spoke. "Your audience is over, Prince Kung welcomes you to China." Holmes bowed low. The prince gave another fleeting smile, stood up, and walked from the hall with great dignity.

I was perplexed. "A nice little story, Holmes. Where did you hear it?"

"I invented it," my friend replied. "I had plenty of time for quiet games of the mind while you worked so futilely at breaking your iron bonds day after day."

I gave a derisive snort. "Did you learn anything from his answer?"

Holmes glanced quickly at Fu Manchu. "I learned something, of course. Tomorrow I will discover how much, when I interview An Li, the Grand Eunuch."

In the morning a messenger arrived, saying that Fu Manchu awaited us in the Palace of the Opal Moon. The green-eyed villain joined us shortly thereafter. "Your interview with An Li will not be as pleasant as your conversation with Prince Kung," he told Holmes.

"I anticipate that," my friend said. "Yet I must ask him a question and observe his manner when he replies."

Fu Manchu nodded. He signaled to his servants, an armed woman and a sword-bearing eunuch. We formed a procession and left the small palace, walking beneath the drab, cold Chinese sky toward the peaked roofs of the Forbidden City.

An Li had no royal blood, so our interview would not be conducted in any of the imperial buildings. We had been scheduled for a mere quarter of an hour in an anteroom of the Hall of the Memory of Glory, An Li's headquarters. This is where he drew up the daily agenda for the emperor and his intimidating regent, Tzu Hsi.

We waited many minutes beyond the time appointed for our interview. An Li burst into the chamber looking harried and displeased. He made a brief, sour acknowledgment of Fu Manchu's rank, gave Holmes and myself a contemptuous glance, and sank into a luxuriously stuffed dragon chair. He said nothing, but waited for my friend to get quickly to the point.

"Master An Li," Holmes said, "the emperor is the Son of Heaven. Yet at the same time he is the custodian of his people, like the caretaker of a temple that belongs to an invisible god. The temple is the caretaker's in a sense, for he protects it and draws strength from it. Yet his obligation never lessens, for if he lays down this burden the temple will soon be no more. Then from where will the caretaker derive his strength? What fortune will he have left?"

An Li frowned. "Dr. Fu Manchu brought you to Peking from the western edge of the world just to say this foolish thing?" he asked irritably.

Holmes smiled. "I would ask you another question," he said.

"Yes, speak."

"The caretaker of the temple has a servant. If the caretaker abandons the temple, what blame is there for the servant?"

An Li's eyes narrowed. He saw that he had underestimated Holmes. "If the caretaker abandons the temple," An Li said slowly, "there are other temples and other caretakers. There is no blame for the servant." He indicated that he was much too busy to give us any more time, so Fu Manchu led us out of the Hall of the Memory of Glory.

"Now, what have you learned?" asked Fu Manchu, as calmly as if the future of China did not depend on the results of these meetings.

"There is still one more interview I must conduct," Holmes said. "I must pose a question to the Dowager Empress, and then I shall tell her the identity of your hidden enemy."

Fu Manchu bowed his head in genuine respect. "It will be done," he said. "We shall dine this evening with the emperor's regent." As I write this in 1927, it no longer seems marvelous that Fu Manchu could promise a dinner audience with Madame Tzu Hsi on such short notice. We came to expect such things from that mad genius.

When we were properly costumed and groomed, Ali led us to the Hall of Assured Harmony. An Li, the Grand Eunuch, showed us to our places. We made our kowtows, waited for Tzu Hsi and the boy emperor to be seated, and the dinner progressed. Never in my life, before or since, have I been so overwhelmed by a banquet.

Hours later, after the final course had been served, Tzu Hsi spoke to Fu Manchu, who presented Holmes and myself. I think she had the same distrust and contempt for Europeans held by most Chinese noblemen. Further, I don't think Tzu Hsi understood just what Holmes was doing at her court. Fu Manchu had not fully prepared her to understand what was about to happen.

Holmes stood and faced the Dowager Empress, then made the triple kowtow to her nephew. "I have been told that you have a secret enemy in your court," he said. "I believe I can uncover the source of this disloyalty by asking a single question. If that is so, I will tell you who your traitor is. Then I shall ask that my friends and I be permitted to return safely to our homes."

Fu Manchu paused and looked at Holmes. The Dowager Empress said something, perhaps demanding that Fu Manchu translate Holmes's words. Fu Manchu spoke for a few moments. Tzu Hsi replied. "She is interested in hearing your thoughts," Fu Manchu said.

Holmes turned and bowed to the Empress Dowager. "A king who has built a great palace will not destroy it because a workman damages some tiles upon the roof. He may dismiss the workman, but then he must hire another to take the first one's place. Who is to say that the second workman may not do more damage than the first? Yet is it right for the king to mount to his roof and repair the damage himself?"

Tzu Hsi did not answer. Instead, An Li rose to face Holmes. He spoke and Fu Manchu translated. "The king has many servants," the eunuch said. "He may order any of the servants to work upon the roof. In a well-run kingdom the king will not even know of this matter. It is the duty of his chamberlain to attend to such trivial things. Why do you fret the Son of Heaven with such foolishness? Is this how you annoy your own queen? You Europeans must learn that we do not enjoy your riddles."

Tzu Hsi spoke a few words. "She says you are ten thousand times more wise than her Grand Eunuch," Fu Manchu said. "She warns you that you must speak again now, and that your words will decide if you live or you die. It is that simple."

Holmes permitted himself a brief smile. "Then I am correct, after all. Please inform the great lady that the traitor is with us in this room. It is she herself, the Dowager Empress Tzu Hsi, who bargains with both the Western powers and the secret societies. She is plotting the overthrow of her own dynasty."

I stared at Holmes. Ali said nothing. I think that even Fu Manchu was a bit stunned. He turned to the dais and spoke. There was a terrible commotion as the meaning of Fu Manchu's words sank in. The Grand Eunuch's face turned as red as wine, and he began to shriek in a ghastly, high-pitched voice that was neither male nor female. The guards moved nearer. The atmosphere in the hall was cold and murderous.

Ali leaned forward between Holmes and myself. "Fu Manchu did not translate your words," he said in a low voice. "He told her that An Li was her traitor. The Empress Dowager will accept that. It will save both her and the young emperor. An Li will die. The fate of China itself is on no one's mind at the moment, good sirs."

Fu Manchu turned and cast a fierce expression upon Ali. He pointed one long, gaunt arm and cried a few words. The Mongol guards hurried towards us.

"He has condemned me, good sirs," Ali said bravely. "I will—" The Mongols pinned Ali's arms behind him and led him quickly from the chamber. We never saw that good man again.

"He was a spy for the British," Fu Manchu said by way of casual explanation. "No doubt you were well aware of that. However, An Li, worthless dog, will also be removed, and I will use my influence with Tzu Hsi to restore this nation. My power in China is now almost absolute."

That night I fell into an exhausted sleep, troubled by terrifying dreams of torture. I awoke in darkness, a hand covering my mouth. "Be still," a low voice whispered in my ear. I was relieved to see Willard Powers and Lord Mayfield, both of whom I had thought dead.

"We must move quickly," Powers said. "The British territorial army is attacking Fu Manchu's house. Everything is in confusion, and this could be our only chance to escape. If we wait too long, we could be cut off."

"Then let us go," Holmes said. "China holds no more fascination for me."

Lord Mayfield seemed dull and besotted. He wore a foolish half-smile on his unshaven face, and he didn't seem to be listening to our discussion. "I think we've been dead wrong about opium," he said. "It's rather pleasant in its way, isn't it?" We all turned to look at him, but no one said a word.

Powers looked at me. "Mayfield will be useless if it comes to a fight," the young American said. "Worse than useless, because someone will have to make sure he doesn't get himself killed."

I heard gunshots and shouting. When we slipped out of the chamber, we saw slaves and female soldiers hurrying everywhere. The house was a shambles. Chairs and couches were thrown about, broken and splintered; tapestries had been ripped from the walls; jade sculpture and porcelain vases lay broken on the marred floors. Blood was spattered everywhere and thick smoke filled the air.

Outside, beneath the cold winter stars, a battle raged. Thundering booms splintered the air as if the moon had detonated above our heads. I heard many rifle shots and the shouts of men and women. From the deepest shadows came the voice of Dr. Fu Manchu. "I thank you again," he said. "You have given me the key to my destiny. Now I shall rule over all China, and then over every nation east of Suez. In a few short years, I will—"

Lord Mayfield giggled. "I promise you," he said with slurred speech, "we English will dispose of you and your hooligans before those few short years are up." Fu Manchu reached out a long, bony hand toward Mayfield's throat. All was still for a few seconds, and then the Queen's Commissioner uttered a single, drawn-out, rattling gasp. Thus did the Lord Mayfield breathe his last.

He had been a bewildered and misguided old man, officious and hesitant, but he was honest and loyal and ready to serve his beloved queen under any circumstances. He deserved a better end than that, and I have carried a painful burden of guilt for fifty years. His children and grandchildren should know how fine and brave a man he was, because he never received the tribute he had truly earned.

Fu Manchu's face had become a mask of hatred and rage. "Mr. Holmes," he said, "you must have thought me a fool, claiming that the Empress Dowager is plotting her own demise! No, it is *not* Madame Tzu Hsi who is the secret traitor. It is a conspiracy of powers, an alliance of Prince Kung and the Grand Eunuch. Neither could succeed alone. Together they imagine they can reform the dynasty."

"If that is what you wish to believe," Holmes said sadly, "then so be it. I will not quarrel with you."

Fu Manchu was not mollified. "You deserve to die with the others. So be it." Before he could act, however, he was interrupted by a rattle of rifle fire. He muttered something in Chinese, turned, and fled back toward the burning walls of his residence.

"Prince Kung has brought the English," Willard Powers said.

We hurried after Fu Manchu, down the tunnel that led toward the Forbidden City. There was another gigantic explosion, a boiling, storming orange ball of flame and smoke that thundered in the underground passageway. The ceiling fell down around us. We saw Fu Manchu buried in the debris, but Powers, Holmes, and I were unharmed. Our way was blocked and we had to turn back the way we'd come.

We emerged from Fu Manchu's demolished estate to find the battlefield in the hands of the emperor's soldiers. Prince Kung and the British Royal Marines had defeated the doctor's disheartened minions, who surrendered quickly when it was clear that the master himself had finally met his end at last in the violent cataclysm.

We were met by a frightened British diplomat, a few Chinese translators and aides, some Imperial guards, and Prince Kung himself.

"Dr. Fu Manchu is no more," Holmes said. "He chose death rather than be captured."

When the information had been translated, Prince Kung nodded briefly, although his expression did not change. "Our British guests have done us a great service," he said, "one we shall not easily repay. We are in the debt of Mr. Holmes and his fellows, and we will listen to the propositions of the British legation with a patient and open mind."

Thanks to Prince Kung and the influence of the British ambassador, we soon found ourselves with staterooms aboard an English ship bound for London. None of us wished to linger in Peking. We had been torn from our quiet lives, and we longed to return to our families and friends, to our own occupations and interests.

China in the winter is a dull, drab, colorless place, with only the lacquered palaces of the Forbidden City providing hints of life and warmth. Still, we had seen quite enough of the Great Within, of the Outer City, of the entire city of Peking. We wished that the river might be the Thames, that the rolling clouds that threatened snow had passed recently over the English moors and not the immense Mongolian desert. I desperately wanted to see English flowers and hear English birds, to eat English food and listen to the laughter of English children at play.

Perhaps Watson was a little bit right when he wrote of me that I possessed languid and courtly manners, and that I was not truly an adventurous type. I suppose that I am not, yet I have had my fill of adventure, more than most men ever dream of, and I submit that I have accounted well of myself. My wish to return home was not the exhaustion of my spirit, but the natural need of the wanderer to refresh himself among familiar surroundings.

And so we sailed from Tientsin shortly after Christmas, on our way home. When our association began, Holmes was a brash, cocky young fellow. His experiences in China matured him and taught him more than he had learned in all his years of schooling. As the eastern coast of China disappeared astern, Sherlock Holmes had become very much the genius described by Dr. John H. Watson. It had been my privilege to observe and document that transformation.

There is one unusual aspect of the brass box episode that must be recorded, although it did not occur until many years after the events of this memoir. I received a letter from Sherlock Homes in 1908, thirty-three years after the Peking affair and some five years after the most recent appearance of one of Dr. Watson's stories in the popular press. Holmes enclosed a letter he'd received from China. I reproduce here both his note and the other.

> *My dear Musgrave:*
> *I apologize for the long delay in replying to your last letter. I have had a few interesting riddles to engage me but nothing of particular importance, and nothing that my esteemed biographer has seen fit to immortalize in his magazine articles. The only event worth mentioning to you—and indeed, the primary reason for this letter—is the enclosed communication.*
>
> *I received it only today. I trust you will find it as absorbing as I did, and that the terrible implications and consequences will*

not be lost on you. At this moment I am not certain how I shall
respond to it. I find myself in an unfamiliar state of despair.

Yours as ever,
Sherlock Holmes

The letter from China was written in a careful and precise script, oddly angular but not altogether unpleasant. I confess that a shiver of revulsion shook me as I stared at the signature: it was, of course, from Dr. Fu Manchu—the monster was alive! He had been alive all these years. He'd escaped after all, and had used the intervening decades to rebuild his nefarious secret Oriental empire. Here I quote his final message to Sherlock Holmes.

Mr. Holmes:
It has been many years since last we spoke, and in that time I
have learned that I did you a great injustice. I owe you some sort
of recompense, if not apology. It is unusual for me to be in this
position, and I fear that I may be unskilled in the practice of
admitting error.

Not long ago the Empress Dowager passed away under some-
what dubious circumstances. It was revealed after her death that
your reasoning concerning her illicit and treacherous activities
was entirely correct, and my version of events completely mis-
taken. It was indeed Tzu Hsi who instigated the rise of the secret
societies, those which banded together to bring about what you
English called the Boxer Rebellion.

We share in the responsibility for that insurrection, you and
I, for we had the power to avert it and we did nothing. I confess
my blindness and my error. Had I listened to you, I would have
been saved many years of struggle. I have paid for that gross
blunder of my younger self, and I promise you and the world that
such a thing will never happen again.

I am sending to you something to relieve my mind of a sense
of obligation to you. It is the formula for the Elixir of Immortal-
ity, one of the Celestial Snows. I have made great strides in deci-
phering the ancient texts, and I am including all data pertinent to
the ambiguous terminology used by my forebears, even that

which derives from my recent laboratory successes. Only you and I in the whole world share this knowledge. I do not begrudge you this. You are the only person who has ever impressed me with the discipline and integrity of his intellect.

There is but one missing bit of information, the finding of which would make the elixir complete: the ancient texts speak of a particular kind of honey, made by bees from the nectar of the HO KUO *flower. I do not know what is meant by* HO KUO. *The words mean only "pale bird," and none of the commentaries of antiquity shed any further light on this matter. I have begun an elaborate campaign to collect honey made from every sort of flower, those native to China and species that may have been introduced by explorers and traders. I believe this project justifies such an effort. Perhaps, however, you will have better luck than I.*

Dr. Fu Manchu

Six years later, in 1914, Holmes and Watson accepted the challenge that Watson would chronicle in "His Last Bow," Sherlock Holmes's final adventure. In that story, we read the following interesting exchange:

"But you had retired, Holmes. We heard of you as living the life of a hermit among your bees and your books in a small farm upon the South Downs."

"Exactly, Watson. Here is the fruit of my leisured ease, the magnum opus of my latter years!" He picked up the volume from the table and read out the whole title, *Practical Handbook of Bee Culture, with Some Observations upon the Segregation of the Queen.*

This must answer the often-asked question, "Why did Holmes retire at so young an age?" Given the Chinese formula with every unknown quantity deciphered but one, Holmes disappeared to find the missing ingredient. Did he succeed? I have already mentioned that I learned of his death through the university alumni letter, but that notice may have been false and misleading. After all, the world had been notified once before of Sherlock Holmes's certain demise. Dr. Fu Manchu has returned again and again throughout the present century to devil the forces of civilization and order. Perhaps his old adversary—my friend, Sherlock Holmes—is yet alive to shield a sleeping world from the dire threats about which we do not even dream. My old companion may be watching even today, an invisible guardian angel, protecting us as we go blindly through our lives. I prefer to think that this is true, as irrational as it may sound. I prefer to believe in Sherlock Holmes.

GILES LESTRADE, WILHELM GOTTSREICH
SIGISMOND VON ORMSTEIN, BEVIS STAMFORD,
ARTHUR CONAN DOYLE, M.D.,
JAMES MORTIMER, M.D.

"It has always been my habit to hide none of my methods, either from my friend Watson or from anyone who might take an intelligent interest in them."

—"The Reigate Squire"

by C. D. EWING

And the Others . . .

A Pause in the Day's Occupation

One of the casualties of the Great Hurricane of 1907, which did extensive damage to much of London, especially around the older wharves along the inner bend in the Thames, was the entire press run of the September '07 issue of *Hogbine's Illustrated Monthly*. The printing plant, which had been off Lower Thames Street, near the Tower, slid off what turned out to have been an ancient pier, and into the Thames, where it disintegrated and bits and pieces of it made their way to the North Sea.

The magazine struggled on for a few more years before combining with *Pickwick Magazine*, only to cease publication entirely during the paper shortages of World War I. But the September '07 issue, which was reputed to contain a scathing indictment by George Bernard Shaw of all contemporary drama but his own; a memoir called "My Brother-in-Law, the Doctor," by E. W. Hornung; and an article entitled "The Dirigible Balloon—Is Count Zeppelin's Airship Ready for Passengers?" seemed to be forever lost.

And then in July 1952, in one of those wonderful moments of serendipity, the Continental Enquiry and Protective Services Agency Ltd., the British branch of the Continental Detective Agency of the United States, opened its new offices in what had been the Hogbine Building on Fetter Lane, off Fleet Street. The name "Hogbine Building" was still carved into the gray stone slab above the front door, although nobody for a mile in any direction knew who Hogbine had been or what he had done, or why he had needed a building in which to do it. In the process of knocking down a wall to turn two offices into one large file room—a detective agency generates acres of files—a long boarded-up closet was uncovered. In it were a model of the Eiffel Tower; a bound set of photographs showing a rather buxom young woman prancing about in her camisole with the title "In My Lady's Boudoir" stamped in gold-leaf on the cover; a box of printed rejection slips; a series of French postcards showing *La Tour Eiffel* in various stages of construction; a program book for a production of *Lucia* at the Drury Lane; and a complete stitched galley proof for the missing September '07 issue.

One of the articles in the lost issue, the existence of which had been completely forgotten with the passage of time, was the monthly installment of a series called "As They Knew Him" (or, of course, "Her" if the subject was a woman). Among the celebrated subjects over the years had been Charles Dickens, Gustave Doré, Eleanora Duse, W. S. Gilbert & Arthur Sullivan (as a pair, which annoyed them both), James McNeill Whistler, and Pope Leo XIII. Benjamin Disraeli had been the subject the month before, and Queen Victoria herself the month after. The subject for the September '07 issue was the man generally acknowledged to have been the greatest consulting detective of the nineteenth century.

The Continental Agency, which proudly considered itself to be the greatest consulting detective agency of the twentieth century, sent the relevant pages back to its headquarters in New York City's Flatiron Building, where they were framed and hung on the walls of the corridor leading to the general manager's office. There they stayed for nearly a half-century, their significance even more completely forgotten, until by chance, in October of 2001, a young editor at St. Martin's Press happened upon them while waiting in the hallway for a chance to convince "Pop" Gores, who was retiring as general manager after forty-four years with the Continental, that having led an exciting life wasn't enough by itself to create a best-selling memoir—you also had to have some ability to write English sentences, and even paragraphs.

"You might consider using a ghost," Keith Kahla, the St. Martin's editor told Pop. "And what do you know about those magazine pages hanging in the hallway?"

"Speaking of ghosts," Pop enthused, "did I tell you about the time back in Ogallala, Nebraska . . ."

Kahla was eventually able to persuade the Continental's office manager to allow him to take down the pages and photocopy them. After a fair amount of research involving a trip to London and another to Amsterdam—how we suffer for our art—it was possible to establish the history and provenance of the pages. We print them here for the first time in the belief that they are long out of copyright, and that any copyright holders must be long deceased. If we are mistaken in that, and if the rightful heirs of Scotland Yard Assistant

Superintendent Giles Lestrade, Dr. Bevis Stamford, or any of the other con-
tributors to these pages of reminiscences will contact the rights and permis-
sions offices of St. Martin's Press, they will know how to deal with you.

From *Hogbine's Illustrated Monthly* for September 1907:

As They Knew Him

THIS MONTH—SHERLOCK HOLMES

We have a considerable treat for our readers this month; a rare view of one
of Britain's most celebrated sleuths, from some of those who knew him well
during the period that he was England's—nay, the world's—foremost
unofficial detective. Since he has retired to his farm in Sussex and refuses to
give interviews, Mr. Holmes has left the public eye, but he still looms large
in the public imagination. We think our readers will be fascinated, and perhaps enlightened, by these brief memoirs of a man who, thanks to Dr. John
Watson's Boswellian efforts, was as well known in the fin de siècle English-
speaking world as Eleanora Duse, Benjamin Disraeli, Cecil Rhodes, Sitting
Bull, or Messrs. Gilbert and Sullivan.

As usual we will allow our guest writers to speak for themselves, and we
remind our readers that the writers' opinions are their own, unedited (except
for spelling, grammar, and punctuation, where necessary), and we at *Hogbine's Illustrated Monthly* have done nothing to encourage them to agree or
disagree with the known record. And so, stretch your legs before a warming
sea-coal fire and settle down for a good read as, with real pleasure, we begin:

Assistant Superintendent Giles Lestrade, Criminal Investigation Division, Scotland Yard (Retired)

In his own words:

Did I know Sherlock Holmes? What a question! What a joke! The man
was a constant thorn in the side of Scotland Yard, a pest and a nuisance
from the day he set up shop at 221B Baker Street until the day he retired.
And I wouldn't be in the least surprised if he didn't continue to pop up
now and again to bedevil the Yard in cases that the Criminal Investigation
Division could handle perfectly well without his much-vaunted "assistance."

Now don't get me wrong, I actually liked Mr. Holmes, as much as the
insufferable prig would allow himself to be liked. More than many of my

fellows at the Yard, I can tell you that much. Gregson would turn positively red about the ears whenever Holmes's name was mentioned. On the plus side, he did help us with one or two of our more obscure cases. His specialty—his 'forte,' you might say—were the sort of problems that didn't lend themselves to being solved easily by ordinary police work. Oh, we would have solved the cases eventually. But we were bound by routine and regulations, as is necessary in any organized body of men, whereas a freelancer like Holmes went his own way, and often was able to cut straight through to the solution. Then again we of the CID had to find the sort of evidence that would stand up in court. All Holmes had to do was point an accusing finger, intone in that high, squeaky, annoying voice of his, "There's your culprit, Lestrade," and he was done with it, leaving it for us to gather together, if we could, the details that would actually make the case.

It might surprise the reader to know that Holmes did not solve every case he undertook, although you could never tell that from the writings of his amanuensis and companion Dr. Watson. Often, and this might come as an even bigger surprise, after Holmes gave up on a case, we at Scotland Yard, with our plodding, as he would say unimaginative, methods, managed to work our way through to a solution. And when I say he gave up on a case I don't mean to suggest that he threw up his hands and admitted that he was baffled. Oh, no. Not Holmes. It would be more like, "Well, now that I've pointed you in the right direction, Lestrade, I'll be off. Have to consult with the King of Norway on a matter of grave national importance, don't you know."

If you were to ask me, I would say that Holmes's greatest gift was his ability to make pronouncements that *sounded* as if he knew what he was doing, whether he did or whether he didn't. Even when he didn't have the slightest idea in—in a blue moon—as to what had actually transpired in a given case, no more than what we poor coppers did, he was never at a loss for something to say, and it was always something that made it sound like he knew something as we didn't.

Let's take the case that I am going to call "The Case of the Corpulent Plutocrat," when I publish the first volume of my memoirs—*Lestrade of the Yard*, as I plan to call it—in a year or so.

Wadlington-Skitherbiggins (pronounced "Wiggins"), the banker, was found dead in the parlor of his home on Fortinbras Court near the Embankment. A portly man—no, to be honest he had passed portly some time before and was headed toward obese—with mutton-chop whiskers, he was dressed in blue-white and gold motley. He lay in a grotesque heap on the floor and had a sword, of the sort known as a fencing saber, run through his neck from side to side. Some sort of small wooden stock had been fastened about his neck and, in going through the victim's neck, the sword penetrated both sides of that ridiculous-looking contraption. A vile-smelling cheroot cigar sat half-smoked in a stand-alone ashtray by what would have been his side were he still standing. I was assured by his butler that motley was not his usual attire, nor did he normally go about with a wooden stock in place of a cravat, or a sword thrust through his neck.

Just as I was settling down to question the housemaid, Dr. Sempleman, the police surgeon, arrived to examine the body, and Mr. Sherlock Holmes arrived to poke his long nose once more into police business. He began by staring at the body from one side and tapping his nose, and then crossing over to stare from the other side and pulling at his ear. When he had enough of that, he commenced crawling about on the floor and picking up bits of fluff and cat hair and the like and putting them into these small envelopes which he carried about, and which I believe he had made special because I have never seen their like used by anybody else for any purpose whatsoever.

"What do the servants have to say, Lestrade?" he asked upon arising from the floor and dusting off the knees of his trousers.

"Very little, Mr. Holmes," I told him. "They were not here when the murder occurred, having been given the afternoon off by their employer."

Holmes tapped the side of his nose suggestively. "That will bear looking into," he said.

"I am looking into it, Mr. Holmes," I told him. "Indeed, just before you arrived—"

"Notice the lack of blood under the body, Lestrade," Holmes interrupted in that ingratiating way he had.

"It's the very first thing I noticed, Mr. Holmes," I told him.

"The man was not killed here," Holmes said.

"That much is evident, Mr. Holmes."

"The body was moved."

"Do tell, Mr. Holmes."

"The sword through the neck is the mark of the Thuggee, a secret society of pernicious evildoers having its origins in the East."

I took out my notebook and pencil, and wrote down "Thuggee."

"But I believe this to be the work of someone imitating that awful rite," Holmes continued. "The real, genuine Thuggee invariably uses a scimitar."

"Very interesting, Holmes," I told him. "Why do you suppose—"

"I call your attention, Lestrade, to the tantalus on the sideboard," he interrupted, pointing a dramatic finger at the aforementioned object.

"I've already noticed it, Mr. Holmes," I replied politely. "It is a tantalus. It is on the sideboard, where it has always reposed, according to the maid."

"Exactly!" he responded. And then he smiled that infuriating smile, and stalked off to peer at the boot marks in the hallway.

Well now, I ask you, how was I to know whether he was serious or he was just blowing smoke?

About ten minutes later, as I was in the kitchen preparing to arrest the cook, Dr. Sempleman called me back into the parlor. "I'm done here," he told me, shrugging into his overcoat. "Wadlington-Skitherbiggins died of a sudden and massive heart attack. I'll write it up back at the office."

My mouth must have fallen open like a codfish. "Excuse me, Doctor?" I said.

"Certainly," he replied.

"I mean—a heart attack?"

"That's right. Look at all the weight the poor man was carrying around. If people will carry an extra six stone of body fat around, and will not exercise, they stand little chance of reaching their allotted three score and ten years."

"But—the sword through his neck—"

"Oh, that!" He laughed. "It's a conjuring trick." He reached down and pulled the sword out, and then unfastened the small wooden stock. "See? Not a mark on his neck. The sword goes around the stock in some fashion. The lack of blood should have told you that. I would say, judging by his attire, that Wadlington-Skitherbiggins was practicing a conjuring act, perhaps to entertain children, when he fell over."

"But Holmes, that is we thought he'd been moved."

"Look at him," Dr. Sempleman said with a gesture. "Would you like the task of moving him any great distance?"

"Not I," I agreed. "Holmes, do you—" I looked down the hall just in time to see the front door closing behind the consulting detective.

I turned back to the doctor. "I don't suppose the tantalus had anything to do with Wadlington-Skitherbiggins's death?" I inquired.

"The tantalus? Perhaps in the larger sense that drinking contributed to his weight problem. But aside from that, I don't see how."

I shook my head. "Smoke," I said. "I knew it was smoke."

"Perhaps," Dr. Sempleman agreed. "Those cheroot cigars are a terrible strain on the heart."

Wilhelm Gottsreich Sigismond von Ormstein
Grand Duke of Cassel-Fulstein and Hereditary King of Bohemia

In his own words:

Sherlock Holmes? Sherlock Holmes? I cannot say as I have of this gentleman ever heard. Have you of him ever heard, my dear? No, I'm sorry, my wife has of this Sherlock Holmes never heard either. Some sort of British tradesman, is he?

Bevis Stamford, M.D., F.R.C.P.
Resident Physician, Little Sisters of Mercy Hospital
New Providence, Bahamas Islands

In his own words:

Yes, it's true. I'm the "Young Stamford" who first introduced James Watson and Sherlock Holmes. Watson told the story in his screed *A Study in Scarlet,* and he told it well; but he did not get all of the details right. Some facts he altered in the interest of better storytelling, for he did not realize their importance, and some he was not aware of. I will now tell it as it happened, not in the interest of amplifying my own small part in the narrative, but in the service of History. For as Kierkegaard once said—I think it was Kierkegaard—"What is, is, and what was, was, and they are the harbingers of what shall be."*

I worked as a dresser at St. Bartholomew's Hospital, known by all who labor in its precincts as "Barts," when Watson was a young intern there and I was even younger than he. A "dresser" was one who treated and bandaged wounds and surgical incisions, functions that have largely been taken over by nurses, since these competent women have been allowed to take up the occupation of helping the sick and wounded. Thanks to a small bequest from a great-uncle I was subsequently enabled to get my medical degree, and I moved out to the islands to practice medicine someplace where my skills would be more in demand.

On the day in question, when I introduced Mr. Sherlock Holmes to the man who was to become his Boswell, I had seen Holmes off and on around

---

*We cannot find this quote among the translated works of the philosopher Søren Kierkegaard, but perhaps Dr. Stamford has a different edition of his works, or perhaps he was thinking of a different Kierkegaard.—the Editors

the hospital for some six months or so. I had formed the opinion that he was a quite intelligent but unusually cold-blooded individual. He had a total disregard for all human frailty, whether in others or in himself. I had seen him beating corpses in the dissecting room with a stick to see how the human body would bruise after death. Once I noticed that he was sporting quite a shiner: a badly blackened eye, and a puffy and severely lacerated cheek. I chided him about it, commenting that, with his prowess in boxing and single-stick fighting, if he looked like that, the other fellow must be lying comatose in one of our wards.

He laughed and assured me that it was self-inflicted. "I'm keeping a journal," he told me, "recording the healing process. I sketch myself in the mirror every morning and night. I'm no Paget, but I fancy the drawings will do for my purposes."

"And just what are your purposes?" I asked him.

He laughed again. "The advancement of human knowledge, Mr. Stamford," he said. "Just that; the advancement of human knowledge."

The strangest man I ever met? No, I wouldn't say so. That honor belongs to a thin, nervous gentleman named Pilchard who always wore a bowler, indoors and out, and collected fish. Dead fish. He used to carry around a suitcase full of used third-class railway tickets, which he would accumulate from the dustbins outside of government buildings and railway stations. He had some odd habits, but I guess this isn't the place to discuss them.

On the day that I ran into my old friend Watson at the Criterion Bar and we got into the discussion about lodgings, I had left the chemical laboratory at Barts a short time before, and recollected that while there I had a similar discussion with Mr. Sherlock Holmes. He, apparently, had found a suitable suite of rooms in Baker Street, but needed someone to go in with him on the rent. I mentioned this to Watson, and he was eager to meet Holmes and see if they could come to some understanding. I warned him, as best I could, about Holmes's peculiarities, but he was adamant. And besides, I really didn't know anything *against* Holmes, I just felt that he might be a hard man to live with.

We went in the side entrance to Barts, and I left Watson on the staircase landing while I went in to alert Holmes that I had brought someone to speak with him.

"He might be just the man to share lodgings with," I told Holmes.

"Really?" Holmes sounded interested. "What sort of chap is he?"

"He's a medical doctor, served as an army surgeon in Afghanistan. Was wounded by a Jezail bullet at the battle of Maiwand. Seems pretty well recovered. Pleasant companion. No bad habits that I can remember."

Holmes laughed. "That's good enough for me," he said. "Bring him in and I'll give him a chance to discover my bad habits. Who knows, perhaps we'll like each other."

I went to retrieve Watson and brought him back to the laboratory. "Dr. Watson," I said, "Mr. Sherlock Holmes."

Holmes turned and looked Watson over, then grabbed his hand and shook it. "You have been in Afghanistan, I perceive," he said.

"How on earth did you know that?" Watson asked in astonishment.

It was my turn to laugh. But before I could say, "He's pulling your leg; I told him myself," Holmes had gone into a discussion of this supposedly infallible test for hemoglobin that he had just developed. Well, by the time I could get a word in, the moment had passed and it would have been rude of me to play the spoiler.

Sometime later I asked Holmes why he had done it, risking the chance that I would blurt out the damning fact that there was no clever deduction involved. "I don't really know," Holmes told me. "Watson just looked so stolid, so self-assured, so English, that I wanted to see whether I could astonish him. I was counting on you to keep mum, and so you did. And so I did."

I have kept the secret for a quarter of a century now, and am only revealing it because it can certainly no longer do any damage. The opinions that these two old companions have for each other have been tempered by decades of experience—and such experiences they have been! Who can not read the reminiscences of Dr. John Watson without feeling a bit of envy for all those years he shared the lodging at 221B Baker Street?

And yet I wonder whether it would have been different had I not hesitated for those few seconds. If I had said, "Don't believe him, Watson, he's pulling your leg!" might Watson not have responded: "How dare you have me on in such a manner! Good day, Mr. Holmes!" And, perhaps, stalked out of the laboratory never to return?

And thus by the going astray of that one jest, might not the world be a poorer place? On the whole, I'm glad I kept mum.

Arthur Conan Doyle, M.D.
Physician, Writer, Agent

Yes, I came to know Sherlock Holmes fairly well over the years I spent as literary agent for his companion and amanuensis, Dr. John Watson. I liked him well enough, but in truth I must admit that there were times when I wished I'd never met him.

Watson could see nothing but good in Holmes, and professed to be constantly amazed when he pulled this or that deductive rabbit out of his well-known deerstalker. But, if you want my opinion, I always thought that Watson put it on a bit for effect, and to keep Holmes happy. I noted many times how pleased Holmes looked—although he did his best not to show it—when Watson would look at him after a particularly telling deduction and murmur, "Astounding, Holmes, I don't know how you do it!"

But I rather think that Watson did know, at least to a large extent, how Holmes did it. Watson was, after all, a medical man, and from what I could see a particularly competent one. And medical men are, of necessity, trained and practiced in deduction. Perhaps they cannot deduce the existence of a Niagara Falls or the Atlantic Ocean from a drop of water, but I've often seen my old professor, Dr. Joseph Bell of Edinburgh University, deduce the history of a patient as well as his illness from his preliminary examination. I remember the following exchange with a patient Bell presented before our medical class:

"Well, my man, you've served in the Army?" asked Bell.

"Aye, sir," said the patient.

"Not long discharged?"

"No, sir?"

"A highland regiment?"

"Aye, sir."

"A noncommissioned officer"

"Aye, sir."

"Stationed at Barbados?"

"Aye, sir."

Dr. Bell explained his deductions thus: "The man was a respectful man, but he did not remove his hat. They do not in the army, but he would have learned civilian ways had he been long discharged. He has an air of authority, and he is obviously Scottish. As to Barbados, his complaint is elephantiasis, which is West Indian not British, and the Scottish regiments are at present in that particular island."

If this has a certain resemblance to one of Holmes's little displays, as related by Watson, well I cannot account for it; you will have to ask Watson for an explanation.

It has always been my opinion that the popularity of Holmes was based just as much on artist Sidney Paget's heroic portrayal of him as well as on Watson's tales about him. Holmes in person, I must say, was not nearly as pretty as Paget makes him out in his drawings in the *Strand* magazine. He was thinner, gaunter, and his clothing was perpetually in disarray, as he had no time for thinking about his dress except perhaps when he was going in disguise.

I'm sorry, but that's all the time I can spare you right now. I'm working on an historical novel that I'm rather proud of. Yes, I think that if the world remembers me for anything, it will be for my historical novels.

James Mortimer, M.R.C.S.
Medical Officer for Grimpen, Thursley, and High Barrow
Grimpen, Dartmoor, Devonshire

Sherlock Holmes interested me from the first moment I met him, during the strange occurrences that my colleague Dr. Watson chronicled under the name *The Hound of the Baskervilles*. As I told Holmes at the time, I was impressed with the pronounced dolichocephalic shape of his skull which, along with his well-marked supra-orbital development, indicated something rare, if not unique, in the evolutionary line of *Homo sapiens sapiens*. Although whether a throwback or a step ahead, I am not prepared to say. I still covet a cast of his skull and, should he predecease me, the skull itself would be a welcome addition to my small collection.

Since my involvement with the incidents which took place at Baskerville Hall, and Holmes's brilliant resolution of the problem they presented, I have followed his career as related in the writings of Dr. Watson with considerable interest. I have also, when the occasion arose, availed myself of his hospitality in the city, and sat over the occasional glass of wine in his study at 221B Baker Street, discussing the latest advances of science or some new criminal outrage.

I have recently begun an intensive study of the works of the Viennese alienists Sigmund Freud, Carl Jung, and Alfred Adler, particularly Freud's *Drei Abhandlungen zur Sexualtheorie* (Three Essays on the Theory of Sexuality), which have, I believe, given me a deep insight into human behavior. But, while their theories are a good beginning at unraveling this complex subject, and while they may hold true for Vienna, they are but a beginning, and their truths are not universal. England is not Vienna, and the British yeoman is not the Austrian burger.

I will use this space to briefly discuss some of my own insights into human—or more particularly British—behavior, as exemplified by the conduct of Mr. Holmes, and his relationship with Dr. Watson. While Mr.

Holmes is by no means typical, his aberrations lie at one end of a spectrum of behavior that I believe can be seen as particularly British.

(As is the custom in these, as Dr. Freud calls them "psychiatric" analysis, I shall for the remainder of this monograph call Holmes "H" and Watson "W." So remember, when I speak of "H" I mean Sherlock Holmes, and "W" represents Dr. John H. Watson.)

There can be no doubt that the adult behavior of H was heavily influenced by his childhood, and his relationship with his parents. Freud would have it that H's insistence on order—law and order—and his habit of crawling about on his hands and knees looking for "clews" in the dirt and grime of the floor were the result of overly strict toilet training and his mother's withholding of love if he soiled his diapers. When he crawls about on the floor he is metaphorically seeking for the turd that will recapture his mother's love. Freudian psychoanalysis would have it that H never passed out of the Anal Phase of development into the more mature or Genital Phase—which is also shown by his lack of interest in women.

But, as I'm sure you will agree, this is a bit much. To describe H as a coprophilic personality at the same time over-simplifies and misunderstands his behavior. Let us take a deeper look.

Perhaps the answer is to be found in the opinions H has of women, and his relationships with them. What does H say about women? W quotes him: "Love is an emotional thing, and whatever is emotional is opposed to that true, cold reason which I place above all things. I should never marry myself, lest I bias my judgment," H says in *The Sign of Four*. And: "Women are naturally secretive, and they like to do their own secreting," H says in "A Scandal in Bohemia." And again: "The motives of women are so inscrutable," H complains in "The Adventure of the Second Stain."

Does he not protest too much? Do we not have hear the complaints of a man who is in love—deeply in love—with a woman who is unobtainable; who is perhaps too far above his own station for him to hope of wooing her, or perhaps who is already married, or perhaps both? Are there any hints as to whom this lady might be? There are perhaps two: first, H's description of Irene Adler as "The woman," not a phrase indicative of desire, but of great admiration. And what had she done that was so admirable? She had rejected the king of Bohemia to marry a commoner. And second, H's using a revolver to shoot into the wall—surely the sign of great emotion—the initials VR, for his queen, Victoria. And what is the queen, but the strongest mother-figure that can be imagined? And what British boy does not love his mother? I shall say no more.

About the Authors

CARA BLACK ("Cabaret aux Assassins") lives in San Francisco. She and her husband, a bookseller, have a son who wanted her to write about "Sherlock Holmes and the Red-headed League," his favorite. However his mother thought it had been done quite well the first time. Cara Black writes the Anthony award–nominated Aimée Leduc Investigations, set in different arrondissements of Paris, including *Murder in the Marais*, *Murder in Belleville*, and *Murder in the Sentier* (for which she did the cover photograph), and is at work on Aimée's next case. Her Web site address is www.carablack.com.

GERARD DOLE ("The Witch of Greenwich") is a music historian who writes old-fashioned detective stories for his pleasure. He is the author of *The New Adventures of the Chevalier Dupin* and *The Exploits of Harry Dickson, the American Sherlock Holmes*. Dole lives a bohemian life in an artist's studio which was once the garret of Arthur Rimbaud, in Saint-Germain-des-Prés, Paris.

GEORGE ALEC EFFINGER ("The Adventure of the Celestial Snows") is an award-winning, highly regarded science fiction and fantasy writer who, looking for new worlds to conquer, is making the transition to writing in the mystery and crime fields. He has been nominated for the World Science Fiction Convention's Hugo award and for the Science Fiction Writers of America's Nebula awards a total of about a dozen times, and won both the Hugo and the Nebula for the novelette "Schrodinger's Kitten." He has written over twenty novels, including the two crime novels *Felicia* and

Shadow Money, and published six collections of his shorter fiction. Effinger lives in New Orleans, where he spends his time hitting his computer with a stick and complaining about the noise. [Note: George died suddenly in late April 2002. He is missed.]

C. D. EWING ("And the Others") claims to be a direct descendant of Alexandre Dumas the elder, but not the younger. This presents several interesting questions, which can be safely ignored. A graduate of Miskatonic University, with a masters degree in Pre-Human Religion, Mr. Ewing has devoted his life to supporting lost causes, his dog Barnabas, and, sequentially, a number of winsome, waiflike women, who eventually move on to less ephemeral men. His interest in Sherlock Holmes dates back to a chance meeting in a London pub, where he overheard the following dialogue: "I call your attention to what the dog did in the nighttime." "But the dog did nothing in the nighttime." "You are mistaken. Examine your shoe." Ewing sold his first story to a men's magazine called, if he remembers correctly, *Men's Magazine*. It was a well-researched study of nautical commerce in the third century B.C.E., entitled "Assan Mongu and the Slave Girls' War Galley." He then went into the shrubbery, from which he has yet to emerge.

MEL GILDEN ("The Adventure of the Forgotten Umbrella") is the author of many children's books, the latest to appear in hardcover being *The Pumpkins of Time*. In 1999 his first *Cybersurfer* book (written with Ted Pedersen) won the Selezione Bancarellino, a prestigious Italian award for children's fiction. Books for grown-ups include *Surfing Samurai Robots*, and four novels written in the *Star Trek* universe: *The Pet* (written with Pedersen), *Cardassian Imps, Boogeymen,* and *The Starship Trap*. Gilden has also published short stories in many original and reprint anthologies, most recently *Bruce Coville's Book of Alien Visitors* and *The Ultimate Alien*. He spent five years as cohost of Los Angeles radio's science-fiction interview show, *Hour-25*, and was assistant story editor for the DIC production of *The Real Ghostbusters*. He has written cartoons for TV, and has even developed new shows. Among his credits are scripts for *Fraggle Rock, The Defenders of the Earth, James Bond Jr., Phantom: 2040, Flash Gordon,* and *The Mask*. Gilden has been known to teach fiction writing, most recently at the UCLA Extension. He is a member of Science-Fiction and Fantasy Writers of America, The Society of Children's Book Writers and Illustrators, Mystery Writers of America, and PEN. He lives in Los Angeles, California, where the debris meets the sea, and still hopes to be an astronaut when he grows up.

BARBARA HAMBLY ("The Dollmaker of Marigold Walk") is a study in authorial ubiquity. If there's a writing genre around, she has probably written at least one book in it, and been nominated for at least one award in it. "I always wanted to be a writer but everyone kept telling me it was impossible to break into the field or make money," Hambly says. "I've proven them wrong on both counts." And so she has. Her fantasies are dark and richly imagined, and contain more than the usual amount of well-realized romance, but to categorize them any further is impossible since, from *The Ladies of Mandrigyn* and its sequels to *Bride of the Rat God* (now there's a title!), each is brilliantly unique. Her historical mysteries such as *The Quirinal Hill Affair*, which takes place in ancient Rome, and *A Free Man of Color*, set in 1833 New Orleans, are well plotted and show such familiarity with the settings that one would swear that she has a time machine in her basement. Hambly is a past president of the Science Fiction Writers of America, a Locus award winner, and has been nominated many times for the SFWA's Nebula award. She lives in Los Angeles with multiple animals, including a pair of pert Pekingese.

MICHAEL KURLAND ("Years Ago and in a Different Place") is the author of more than thirty books, mostly mysteries and science fiction, but with a smattering of nonfiction, including *How to Solve a Murder: The Forensic Handbook* and *How to Try a Murder: The Handbook for Armchair Lawyers*. His most recent novel is *The Great Game,* third in a series of Professor Moriarty mysteries. The fourth, *The Empress of India,* will be out later this year. His short stories have appeared in many anthologies, including *The Best of Omni II, 100 Malicious Little Mysteries,* and *The Mammoth Book of Locked-Room Mysteries and Impossible Crimes*. He has been nominated twice for the MWA's Edgar award, and once for the American Book Award. Kurland lives in Petaluma, California, with a truly lovely lady and an assortment of dogs and cats. More than you want to know about him can be found at his Web site: www.michaelkurland.com.

GARY LOVISI ("Mycroft's Great Game") has been a Holmes fan and reader for decades. He has written one other pastiche, *The Loss of the British Bark Sophy Anderson,* which was based on a Watson reference in the canon, as well as various Sherlockian articles, including an article on hardcover pas-

368 ABOUT THE AUTHORS

tiches for FIRSTS. His *Sherlock Holmes: The Great Detective in Paperback* bibliography will be out next year. He is the editor of Paperback Parade, the leading publication on collectable paperbacks in the world. As the founder of Gryphon Books he has published many Holmes pastiches by authors such as Frank Thomas, Ralph Vaughan, and others, as well as nonfiction Sherlockiana. You can reach him at his Web site: www.gryphonbooks.com.

RICHARD A. LUPOFF ("The Incident of the Impecunious Cavalier") was introduced to the canon as a small child, when his older brother yielded to parental pressure and dragged him along to a motion picture matinee. The feature film was the 1939 version of *The Hound of the Baskervilles,* with Basil Rathbone and Nigel Bruce as Holmes and Watson. "I was terrified," Lupoff recalls, "but I also fell in love with the characters and their world. And as for my debt to Poe, well, I can only quote Sir Arthur Conan Doyle himself: 'Poe is, to my mind, the supreme short story writer of all time. . . . To him must be ascribed the monstrous progeny of writers on the detection of crime. . . . Each may find some little development of his own but his main art must trace back to those admirable stories of Monsieur Dupin, so wonderful in their masterful force, their reticence, their quick dramatic wit.' In short, while Holmes may have failed to acknowledge his debt to his illustrious predecessor, Holmes's creator did not so fail." Lupoff is too modest to supply us with details of his writing career, but any reference work of science fiction or mystery authors will list his extensive and impressive professional biography. He lives in Berkeley, California, with his lovely wife, Patricia.

MICHAEL MALLORY ("The Riddle of the Young Protester") is author of some seventy short stories, including "Curiosity Kills," which received a Derringer Award from the Short Mystery Fiction Society for Best "Flash" Mystery Story of 1997. His short fiction has appeared everywhere from *Discovery Magazine,* the inflight publication of Hong Kong Airlines, to *Fox Kids Magazine.* His Amelia Watson stories ran in every issue of *Murderous Intent Mystery Magazine* from 1995 to 2000. Twelve of them are collected in the book *The Adventures of the Second Mrs. Watson,* published by Deadly Alibi Press, and one, "The Adventure of the Nefarious Nephew," appears in *The Mammoth Book of Legal Thrillers* (Carroll & Graf). By day Mallory is a freelance entertainment journalist based in Los Angeles, with more than 250 magazine and newspaper articles to his credit. His most recent nonfiction book on American pop culture is *Marvel: The Characters and Their Universe*

(Hugh Lauter Levin Associates). He is also dad to a rambunctious seven-year-old, and in his spare time plays the banjo, very badly.

LINDA ROBERTSON ("Mrs. Hudson Reminisces") is an attorney with the San Francisco–based California Appellate Project, a nonprofit law firm. She is beginning to build a second career as a writer, and has been published in the *San Francisco Chronicle,* and the on-line magazine *Salon,* as well as the *CACJ (California Attorneys for Criminal Justice) Forum.* She is coauthor, along with Michael Kurland, of *The Complete Idiot's Guide to Unsolved Mysteries* but neither of them claims responsibility for the title. She lives in Petaluma, California, with three dogs, two cats, and a writer, and is not sure which of them is the most trouble to care for.

NORMAN SCHREIBER ("Call Me Wiggins") writes that he "chronicles life, liberty and the pursuit of demons in business, the arts, pop culture, travel photography and technology." His writing credits include *American Management Review, Amtrak Express, Camera Arts, Family Circle, Independent Business, Kiplinger's Personal Finance, Ladies' Home Journal, MultiMedia Pro, New Choices, Photo District News, Playboy, Popular Photography, Pulse, Smithsonian, Success, Travel & Leisure,* and *Writer's Digest.* Schreiber was the editor of the trade publication *Magazine Retailer* from its birth in 1996 through its last issue (Winter 2001–2002). His books include *The Ultimate Guide to Independent Record Labels and Artists* and *Your Home Office.* He has contributed material to *Consumer Bible, The Complete Guide to Writing Nonfiction,* and *Digital Deli,* among other publications. He makes his home in New York City and Key Largo, Florida.

PETER TREMAYNE ("A Study in Orange") is best known for his best-selling Sister Fidelma Mysteries, featuring as his sleuth a seventh-century Irish religieuse. Published in seven languages to date, the series is achieving a cult following and there is already an International Sister Fidelma Society based in the USA with an official Web site and magazine. Tremayne, a pseudonym, was born in Coventry, England, of Irish parents and took his degrees in Celtic Studies. His first book was published in 1968, the first of a number of nonfiction works about the Celts under his own name. He published his first Tremayne novel in 1977 and has produced many in the fantasy genre using Celtic myths and legends as background. In 1981 he published *The Return of Raffles,* a pastiche about the "gentleman thief."

This has also led to several Sherlock Holmes short story pastiches. In 1993 came the first appearance of his more enduring creation, Sister Fidelma, and the twelfth novel in the series appears in the UK this year. To date, Tremayne has produced a total of thirty-nine novels and seventy short stories, which have appeared in nearly a score of languages.